7-2012

DATE DUE

LETTER PERFECT

CATHY MARIE HAKE

LETTER PERFECT

BETHANYHOUSE
MINNEAPOLIS, MINNESOTA

Letter Perfect
Copyright © 2006
Cathy Marie Hake

Cover design by Jennifer Parker
Cover photography by Mike Habermann

Scripture quotations are from the King James Version of the Bible.

Published by Bethany House Publishers
11400 Hampshire Avenue South
Bloomington, Minnesota 55438

Bethany House Publishers is a division of
Baker Publishing Group, Grand Rapids, Michigan.

Printed in the United States of America

ISBN-13: 978-0-7642-0284-1   ISBN-10: 0-7642-0284-7

To Tracie Peterson,
a dear friend and a dynamic Christian
whose encouragement and support made this possible.

And Sarah Long,
an editor whose enthusiasm and insights
made all the difference.

To my dear husband, Christopher,
who taught me love is perfect but I don't have to be.

And most of all,
to the Lord—whose mercy and love abound.
To God be the glory!

CATHY MARIE HAKE is a nurse who specializes in teaching Lamaze, breastfeeding, and baby care. She loves reading, scrapbooking, and writing, and is the author or coauthor of more than twenty books. Cathy makes her home in Anaheim, California, with her husband, daughter, and son.

LETTER PERFECT

CHAPTER ONE

Jefferson City, Missouri, 1859

Exactly how much damage can one tiny fish bone do? Ruth Caldwell wondered if she simply ought to swallow the wretched little thing. *Knowing my luck, it'll get stuck and I'll choke to death.*

Just as she decided to lift her napkin and discreetly get rid of the pickery little nuisance, Miss Pettigrew looked at her. Ruth's blood ran cold, and she plastered a smile on her closed lips.

Well, at least my mouth is shut.

The headmistress of Pettigrew Academy graced Ruth with a chilly nod. After her afternoon debacle, Ruth didn't expect any better. A mere slip of the tongue and she'd managed to introduce the new pastor to the Garden Society as "Reverend Mark Clumsy" instead of "Reverend Clark Mumsy." In doing so, she'd embarrassed herself and reflected poorly on the Academy.

Oh, how can I get rid of this bone?

She lifted her napkin. The silver candlesticks teetered precariously, then fell onto Miss Pettigrew's prized snowy Irish linen tablecloth. It wasn't until her plate began to tip and girls started squealing that Ruth realized she hadn't grabbed her napkin—she'd been pulling on the tablecloth!

Whoosh! The artfully spiraled ribbons cascading from the center-piece caught fire, and the squeals turned to screams. Ruth sloshed water from her goblet onto the flames, then followed it by emptying the contents of the nearest teapot. Three other students followed suit with their glasses. Soon the once-beautiful table became a sodden, sooty wreck.

Ruth patted out the last embers. Deep in her heart she knew even if the tea stains came out of Miss Pettigrew's cherished table-cloth, the singed spots relegated it to the ragbag.

"Miss Caldwell, come to my office, if you please." Miss Pettigrew rose, then turned and marched from the dining room.

Ruth knew the "if you please" wasn't a request. Of course it didn't please her to follow the headmistress, but an order was an order. She squared her shoulders and pretended not to see the pity on her classmates' faces.

Once in the hallway, before she turned the corner and entered the office, Ruth slipped the fish bone from her mouth and stuck it in the potted fern.

I'm about to find out exactly how much damage one tiny fish bone can do.

Glancing down, Ruth let out a silent sigh at the sight of her soiled pin-tucked bodice. She quickly brushed off the slivered, fishy-smelling almonds and disposed of them in the fern, too. Unfortunately, her sooty hands left streaks on her best dress. Large wet splotches on it added to the bedraggled effect. The only good thing about her skirts being wet was that they draped lower, hiding her scuffed shoes.

To top the whole disaster off, Ruth felt her hairpins slipping. Miss Pettigrew put great stock in a woman tending her "crown of glory" and wouldn't understand if Ruth's hair came unbound. She glanced about and assured herself that no one was in sight, hiked up her skirts, wiped her hands as best she could on her petticoats, and dropped the skirts back in place. That done, she shoved her hairpins in yet again and marched into the dragon's lair.

"Miss Caldwell," Miss Pettigrew began, "please shut the door."

"Yes, ma'am." As Ruth turned to obey, she couldn't quell a shudder. She'd been through this at other schools. The humiliation of being dismissed ought to be enough to mortify any decent girl, but Ruth felt the crushing guilt of knowing she'd tried her best here and still failed.

I wanted to make Mama proud, and I've botched everything again. She'll welcome me home and act as if nothing went wrong, but she wants me to become a polished woman and marry well. I keep messing up. Would it be so bad for me to stay home and become a spinster?

"Miss Caldwell."

Miss Pettigrew's voice cut through her thoughts. Ruth turned to face her fate.

The headmistress wilted artfully into the seat behind her desk. "I've tried to do my best by you."

"I'm sure you have," Ruth agreed sincerely. Indeed, she'd been here for almost six months—twice as long as she'd lasted anywhere else.

"Everyone deserves a chance, and the Bible instructs us to be longsuffering. However, Ruth, dear, I'm afraid I've suffered long enough."

Ruth stood in respectful silence. At least that way, she figured, she wouldn't open her mouth and make matters worse.

"Pettigrew's Academy for Fine Young Ladies cannot weather the storms you bring. Reputation is all," the headmistress intoned. "Yes, I've tried to impress upon you that reputation is all. Once besmirched, it cannot be recovered. I fear for your reputation, my dear; but even more, I fear for my school and all of the other students. All it takes is for one of you to indulge in hoydenish escapades to make the whole community frown upon the entire institution.

"Dignity. Comportment. Grace. A woman must cultivate these qualities. You, on the other hand, entertain wild, headstrong notions and follow your impulses. This can only lead to ruin."

Ruth fought the impulse to balance on one leg and scratch her calf with the toe of her boot. Miss Pettigrew was warming to her subject, and Ruth figured the woman had a right to a final tirade.

"I forgave you for stealing the cook's best roasting pan since your intention to save those little robin hatchlings showed compassion."

"Two of the three survived," Ruth remembered.

"Yes, but you brought *worms* into the room to feed them." Miss Pettigrew shuddered. "And it was only the beginning of inappropriate things you carried through my doors. While I'm thinking of it . . ." She stood, unlocked a drawer from a cabinet, and withdrew an item. Pinching the suffrage sash between her forefinger and thumb as if the satin might otherwise soil her, Miss Pettigrew extended it toward Ruth. "Here. Take this. I wouldn't have it said I'm a thief."

"Thank you." Ruth accepted her sash. Having slipped out of school that day to participate in the march was transgression enough, but to return wearing the scandalous sash nearly sent Miss Pettigrew into a fit of the vapors. Her reaction would have convinced a stranger that Ruth had stormed into Mr. Buchanan's White House and used the sash to swing from his elegant chandeliers. Miss Pettigrew had promptly confiscated the red satin piece and locked it away, as if doing so would contain the "outrageous" notion that women ought ever be free-thinking enough to vote.

"A young woman of your vivacity and intellect should be an asset to the community." Miss Pettigrew went back to her desk, only this time she sat ramrod straight. The resolve on her pinched face warned Ruth that the softer portion of the exit speech had ended. "In the twenty-seven years I've run my school, I've never seen a young woman I couldn't coax into being finer, better, more polished." She paused significantly, then tacked on, "Until you."

"I've examined my heart and am certain the fault does not lie with me. Why, I am a descendant of King Henry VIII."

Why does she think that's such a fine thing to claim? He was a mean, fat, old man who killed off several wives and wreaked havoc in the church just to satisfy his own needs!

"Each Pettigrew girl develops into a royal swan who glides through life with all of the essential social graces. You, Ruth, paddle mud into the pond and ruffle everyone's feathers."

Which makes me the clumsy, ugly duckling.

"Simply put, you're a misfit."

Ruth's chin jerked up. The abrupt action caused her hairpins to shift. *Misfit.* That description hurt. From the day she arrived, Ruth strove to fit in. She'd tamped down her impulsive nature and assiduously prayed for self-control to make this work—not because she wanted to be *properly finished,* but because she wanted to please her mother.

"The truth is far from flattering, Miss Caldwell, but you cannot deny it."

As if on cue, Ruth's hair broke free and splayed out around her shoulders.

Either unaware or uncaring of the pain her words inflicted, Miss Pettigrew made a disgusted sound, then continued. "For the sake of the others and my school's reputation, I'm sending you home."

St. Louis, Missouri

"Home sweet home," Ruth singsonged under her breath up in her bedchamber. Truly, she belonged here, felt happy here. On the journey home she'd determined to convince Mama to abandon any hope of her marrying at all, let alone well. Within the comforting walls of their home, Ruth knew she would be happy.

She loved her room. The yellow-and-white striped wallpaper gave it a cheerful air, and the deep green counterpane never showed marks from her feet when she'd forget to remove her shoes and sit cross-legged as a heathen on the bed.

Bernadette bustled into the room with a vase full of daisies. "Your mama will wake up in about an hour. I asked Hadley to bring up your trunks. I'll help you unpack them."

"I can do it. I'm sure you're busy."

"Aw, now. I want to hear about everything." Bernadette flashed her an affectionate smile. "Sure as shouting, something happened to bring you back home. You do manage to have a time of it, Ruth. Shameful as it is for me to confess, your stories tickle me."

Heavy footsteps sounded on the stairs. Old Hadley wheezed and grunted his way into the room under the weight of Ruth's smaller trunk. "Where d'you want this?"

"By the wardrobe, please." Ruth fought the temptation to offer him help with her other, heavier trunk. Mr. Hadley might be old, but he had his pride.

"Put it down gently," Bernadette ordered her husband. "No marking up the floor."

"Since when did I ever scratch up your floors?" he grumbled. For all his grouchy tone, he still set down the trunk with care. Shrugging and stretching, he gave Ruth a woeful shake of his head. "They must've made you sew your fingers to the bone at that place. Your trunk wasn't half that full when you left."

"I did considerable sewing," Ruth agreed. She withheld the fact that more often than not, her sewing consisted of mending hems she tore, buttons she popped off, and holes in her stockings that needed darning.

"Humph. Place like that ain't right for you."

"That goes without saying," Bernadette scolded. "She's back here with us, isn't she, old man? Stop your yammering and go get the other trunk."

Ruth waited until Hadley was out of earshot before she indulged her need to giggle. When Bernadette's brows rose in silent inquiry, Ruth whispered, "Miss Pettigrew would swoon if she ever heard a woman tell her husband to stop yammering."

Bernadette grinned. "That's why you're back home. You didn't belong with that pretentious old bat. What does she know about husbands? She never caught herself one."

Hadley chugged back into the room. "Want this by the bureau? Decide quickly, woman. My back's breaking under the load."

"Yes, the bureau," Bernadette helped him set the trunk on end. "You're a strong man, Hadley. Why don't you go swipe a piece of cake to keep your strength up? Just be sure to leave enough for the ladies to enjoy with their tea once the missus wakes up."

"Don't mind if I do." He pinched his wife's cheek. "Nobody makes better pound cake than you."

Ruth marveled at the couple who had helped Mama all her life. Whenever guests came over, Bernadette and Hadley acted like the penultimate servants; when alone with Ruth, they behaved like opinionated, loving relatives. Other than Grandmother and Grandfather, Ruth hadn't seen another husband and wife who actually knew each other well and shared a genuine affection. Most marriages she observed were odd relationships, fraught with polite distance. It made her wonder why the Miss Pettigrews of the world put so much stock in marriage.

Oh, there were the financial issues to be considered. After all, few women could support themselves well by working at an acceptable trade. Men earned more and could own property. But if suffrage passed and women voted to improve their own lot, then marriage would be unnecessary unless a couple truly cared for each other and wished to have children.

Ruth stopped hanging her dresses in the wardrobe and tilted her head toward her mother's bedchamber. "Mama's coughing. When did her cough come back?"

"Truth is, she never got rid of it." Bernadette turned away and put an armful of clothes in the top drawer of the bureau.

"Bernadette! I've been away for six months—don't tell me Mama's been sick that whole time. She's been writing cheerful letters, telling me things are fine."

"Things ain't been fine for a while, child. If you ask me, it's a good thing you've come home."

Ruth dropped the dress she'd just taken out of the trunk and wheeled to run to Mama's room.

The housekeeper flung her arms around Ruth and held her fast. "Now, now. No use you barging in and waking her. She needs her rest. No being tearful or dreary, either. We made an agreement to bear this with courage. Don't you dash in there and shred your mother's dignity."

"I would have come home—"

"Which is what your mother didn't want." Bernadette's hold eased. "She tried to protect you."

Guilt washed over Ruth. "All these months, I could have been here and helped."

"Nothing you could do that we didn't already have in hand." The old housekeeper patted Ruth's cheek. "Your mama loves you and tried hard to make sure you'd be able to go on when she can't be there for you."

"She should have called me home. I would rather have been here."

"If you dare chide her, I'll have Hadley break out the hickory switch, and I'll use it on you myself."

"You've never used a hickory switch in your life."

Bernadette shook her finger at Ruth. "And you've never seen one. It's likely that's why you've been sent back home. If anyone ever bothered to apply the rod of discipline to your backside, you probably wouldn't be so impossible to deal with."

Ruth wrapped her arms around the old woman and squeezed. "I love you, too."

"I'm so glad to have you home," Bernadette whispered to her. "Your mother wouldn't let me send word to you. I'm sure God is tired of hearing me plead for you to be naughty so He could bring you back home where you belong."

Ruth gaped. "You asked God to make me naughty, when I've

been praying so hard to fit in and be good?"

"He's wise, child. I knew I could trust Him to work it all out."

Ruth sighed. "God's going to have to work it out with Mama. She'll be dismayed that I ruined my chances yet again."

Bernadette patted her back. "God already worked that out years ago. He gave you a mother who loves you, regardless. Now let's finish unpacking your things."

"Tell me all about Mama's health."

"No, I promised I wouldn't tell you a thing. You'll just have to wait until she's finished her nap."

———◆———

Leticia sat propped up in bed by a plethora of pillows. *She's the same color as her sheets,* Ruth thought as she entered the room. "Mama!"

Mama muffled a cough, then spread her thin arms wide. "You're home!"

In times past, Ruth would have flown across the room and thrown herself into her mother's arms. This time, she walked sedately, took a seat on the edge of the mattress, and carefully gathered her frail mother in her arms. "Yes, I'm home, and I'm staying here with you now."

Ruth cradled her mother and closed her eyes against the sting of tears. Mama had always been petite, but she'd lost so much weight that every last bone jutted out beneath her nightdress. *I should have been home. . . .*

Ruth opened her eyes and noticed numerous hints about just how fragile her mother had become. Oh, her room still held the cameo-like beauty of apricot and ecru appointments, but the low-backed wire vanity stool had been replaced with a rocking chair. The beautiful beige merino wool shawl draped across the back of it tattled how Mama chilled easily. Beside her lovely silver brush and mirror rested vials, bottles, and tiny paper packages of medicinal powders. A stack of freshly ironed hankies lay on the bedside table. And though Mama loved flowers and always insisted upon having a small arrangement in her room, the chrysanthemums served as a warning to Ruth that her mother had come into the autumn of her life.

This can't be. Please, God, make her well.

"You look even more beautiful than I remembered," Mama said in a raspy whisper that still managed to sound merry.

Ruth cleared her throat. Mama needed her strength. She could indulge in tears some other time, but not now. "It's a marvel Bernadette didn't scream in fright when I walked in the door. She made me change out of my traveling gown and helped me dress my hair." Ruth looked down and tenderly stroked a damp tress from Mama's temple. "You are—"

"—so happy to see you."

Mama never interrupted anyone. Ruth understood then and there that her mother wanted to pretend all was well. What harm would it do? She owed Mama everything. If this was what Mama desired, she'd play along and act as if nothing were amiss.

"Well, well!" Bernadette shouldered through the door with a tea tray. "I told Hadley we ladies were going to have a reunion tea. I'm inviting myself. Ruth's going to have to spin us all of her stories, and I'm feeling selfish enough to hear them at first telling."

"You're always welcome, Bernadette," Leticia said.

"I know." The housekeeper gave them a saucy smile. "That's why I invited myself. You have to promise to eat a whole piece of cake, though. Ruth, don't tell her more than one story if she only eats half."

Ruth propped Mama back against the pillows. "Mama's going to eat two pieces. My stories are bound to keep you both entertained for months."

Please, Mama, tell me you'll still be with us months from now, Ruth inwardly begged as Mama held a tatted-edged hanky to her mouth and coughed.

Bernadette placed a small lap tray across Mama's thighs, served her cake and heavily honeyed tea, and tucked a napkin across her front as if she were a child in need of tending. The actions were lovingly done, but so automatic Ruth realized her mother was almost helpless and had needed extreme assistance for some time now.

Oh, Mama, I would have been here for you....

"So," Bernadette said brightly, "you mentioned robins in one of your letters."

Taking her cue, Ruth forced a laugh. "Oh, did I ruffle a few feathers over that escapade! You see, I found these little hatchlings on the ground. Cook didn't appreciate the fact that I borrowed her favorite roasting pan to serve as a makeshift nest."

"A roasting pan! Imagine!" Bernadette handed Ruth a plate.

"I named them Aria and Soprano because they chirped nonstop." Ruth omitted mentioning Treble. Treble hadn't survived, and the mention of her might upset Mama.

"You are so clever." Leticia took a miniscule sip of tea.

"The headmistress didn't think so when I hired the groundskeeper's son to bring me worms each morning. The poor little birds needed to be fed, so what else was I to do?"

"They weren't just newly hatched, then?"

"Actually, they were. Two of the other girls volunteered to help make sure we fed the tiny babies round the clock. It wasn't long before they were my pets—I mean the birds, not the girls!"

Mama smiled and Bernadette laughed at all the right moments. Ruth resolved she'd spin tales from here to eternity if it made them happy. She could even look back now and see humor in some of the more painful episodes. With the proper perspective, she could slant just about any story into a vignette to entertain Mama.

"Where are those birds now?" Bernadette silently urged Leticia to eat a bite.

"Those little robins are so perky. When I freed them, they nested in the tree just outside my window."

"God smiled on you, just as I prayed He would." Mama finally took a tiny bite of pound cake.

"As for that poor roasting pan—" Ruth shook her head sorrowfully. "No matter how much I scrubbed it, Cook wouldn't use that thing again. I still can't imagine why." She let out a laugh. "I tried to convince her that a bird is a bird. She'd just be putting a bigger, plucked one in it is all."

Mama and Bernadette laughed, and Ruth knew she'd come home.

Only home had changed.

Six months passed. Day by day, Leticia grew weaker, thinner. Only her spirit stayed strong—that, and her faith in the Lord.

Ruth did her best to keep her mother's spirits up. All through the fall season, she filled the room with colorful arrangements of flowers and leaves. During the winter, swags of holiday ribbons and pine decorated the drapery rods. Spring dawned, and the fresh greenery and sprouts everywhere promised life's renewal—all except for Mama.

Dr. Sanborn dropped in frequently. His medical interventions made no difference, but he always made it a point to rest his hand on Mama's shoulder and say a prayer of comfort. One afternoon, after the prayer, he subtly tilted his head toward the door. Ruth followed him from the room.

"She has little time left, Miss Caldwell. We have nothing to offer physically, but her spiritual and emotional welfare are of the utmost import. I'm glad to see you're reading the Bible to her." He paused. "She confided to me that she worries about your future. Any parent would fret over leaving an only child alone. I've remarked on your independence and courage. Let those qualities continue to shine forth. They give her great comfort."

"Yes, Doctor."

Late that night as Ruth sat by the bedside and held her mother's hand, Mama gave her a squeeze. "I've thought things through. I want you to know I've prayed hard about it," Mama said.

"Prayed about what?"

"What is to become of you. I want you to promise me you'll follow my plan."

"You don't need to trouble yourself, Mama. I'll be fine."

"First, I want you to promise me you'll not wear mourning. When God takes me home, I don't want you to wallow in that dreariness."

"Mama—"

"Dear," Mama gave her a brave smile, "we know I'm heaven bound. I don't want to look down from paradise and see you in crow black. I want my daughter to carry on and live life to the fullest."

"What I wear doesn't matter."

"Then you'll humor me." She drew in a shallow breath, paused, and let it out. "I don't want to leave you alone."

"Bernadette and Hadley will be here."

"No. I wrote a letter. It's in my top bureau drawer. Send it by that new Pony Express you read to me about, and then prepare to take a trip by stage."

"Letter? Trip? I don't understand."

"I want you to go to your father."

"Father?" Ruth gawked at her mother. Mama never spoke of the man whom she married. Not even once.

Grandfather never mentioned him either. But on her twelfth birthday, Ruth had gathered her courage and asked about her father. Grandfather made it clear her father was a "rascal, a blackguard, and a miscreant." Grandfather never spoke ill of anyone, so his low opinion of the man who'd wed his daughter let Ruth know her father must be wicked beyond telling.

"When I took sick, I asked Hadley to make inquiries. I was unfair to your father—he never knew I was carrying you when he sent me away. He had personal difficulties, but he's overcome them. Hadley reported he's developed laudable character."

"Regardless of Father's change, your situation is far more important to me. I'm not leaving your side, Mama."

"The time's come for you to meet your father."

"If you truly wish me to meet him, I'll go—but not until after Jesus takes you home."

Mama closed her eyes. Ruth wasn't sure whether it was out of exhaustion, disappointment, or relief. "My place is with you, Mama. Deep in my heart I know it's true. Don't ask me to leave you."

Leticia opened her eyes. Tears shimmered in them. "Stay with him—live there. He's family."

"This is silly, Mama. I'm not going to need to send that letter for ages."

Her mother shook her head sadly, then coughed. "It's my dying wish, Ruth. Please promise me you'll go and live there, no matter what."

My dying wish. Mama wasn't being theatrical; the truth was plain as could be. All of the months of pretense were stripped away in one stark comment. Ruth wanted to bury her face in Mama's lap and weep like a little child. She wanted to fall to her knees and plead with God to intervene with a miraculous recovery. Instead, she covered Mama's hand and nodded. "Because I love you so much, I promise I'll go."

CHAPTER TWO

---

roken P Ranch, Folsom, California.

BJosh McCain, Jr. read the flowing, feminine script on the envelope and flipped it over to see if anything was written on the back. "Odd. No name—just the ranch and no return address?" *A companion for Laney?* The smile that accompanied the thought made the skin on his wind-chapped face stretch and sting.

"Well?" Lester, the postmaster, prodded. "Recognize the writing after all? Good thing you came to town. That came by Pony Express, so I knew it was important. Been sittin' here for more than a week, and I've been itching to know who the mystery writer is."

"So am I." Joshua paced over to a bentwood chair. He lowered himself until the cane seat crackled and moaned beneath his strapping build. He waggled his brows at Lester. "I think maybe I finally got a response to my inquiry about a companion for my sister."

"Imagine!" Lester leaned over the counter. "You gonna read it aloud?"

"No." Joshua stuck a callused thumb under the edge of the beige vellum envelope and swiped along the edge. The lavender wax seal hinted that the sender wasn't just an ordinary woman. She was dainty and classy, too. *Good. She and Laney'll get along well together.*

Joshua wiped his palms down the thighs of his pants to make sure he didn't leave smudges on the note. Laney set store by little details like that, and since she'd want to save the missive, Josh reckoned keeping it clean was the least he could do. He drew out the folded pages. Even though the letter had been stuck in the bottom of the leather Pony Express bag, the paper still felt crisp.

Dear Sir,
 I am sending you Ruth.

Ruth. A Bible name. Old-fashioned. Feminine. My sister's future companion is named Ruth. Maybe she'll have us call her Ruthie. And she's coming! I guess the stipend I offered was generous enough. Good. I want Laney to have someone here as soon as possible. He stopped musing and read on.

She's nineteen.

Younger than I planned, but that's not a bad thing. Nineteen. Old enough to be capable. Young enough to have energy.

She has abundant blond hair, green eyes, and a willowy build. I am certain you'll recognize her the moment she steps from the stage.

Oh, I'll be certain to recognize her. A pretty, slender, green-eyed blonde.

It has been a very difficult decision to send her to you. I reared her to be a godly young woman and worry about unwholesome influences, should you not permit her the freedom to follow the dictates of her heart. I place her entirely in your hands, for she will now be your responsibility. I beg you, please honor her Christian beliefs.

What a dear woman. I'll have to write her a letter of reassurance at once. Knowing she sent Ruth to a home with believers will ease her mind.

Though Ruth's arrival will undoubtedly cause a minor stir, I ask you to do your best to shield her. Surely she deserves your protection. Ruth reads voluminously and has passable skill with a needle. She sings like a nightingale, has a tender heart, and her gregarious nature proves she is your daughter.

Joshua's delight altered to confusion. Daughter? Impossible! At twenty-four he couldn't have a nineteen-year-old! He scowled at the letter while hastily scanning the remainder.

That being said, I must also warn you that at times, your daughter is given to exuberance. Her compassion and creativity have been known to get her into trouble, and she inherited your strong streak of stubbornness. Though her very existence has undoubtedly come as a great shock, one look at her will quell any misgivings you have regarding the veracity of her claim to your name. I'm certain you'll quickly come to see she also inherited your spirited personality.

As I write this, my health is failing. Our daughter has no one but you. I pray you will treat her kindly and that she will adjust well.

It is, I believe, a case of ironic justice that you are now faced with the consequences of your choices. I suffered them during our misbegotten union and tried my best to protect Ruth from your influence. Nonetheless, history repeats itself. You sent me back to my father; I now send your daughter to you. The difference is, you pushed me away in anger. I'm sending Ruth out of desperation. She has no one else to whom she can turn, no place else to go. Our daughter deserves to find happiness, and I pray you'll find joy in her company.

All these years, I have honored our agreement. I have never again spoken your name or crossed your land. Now I must ask this one thing of you—to welcome the child you never knew. It is too late for me to do anything more. Give her the love you withheld from me. Ruth deserves at least that much.

Your dutiful wife,

Leticia

Joshua stood and headed for the door.

"Hey!" Lester shouted. "What did she say?"

"It wasn't a response for a companion." He said nothing more. If Josh had his way, he'd nip this problem in the bud.

He stepped out of the mercantile into the gloomy afternoon and squinted at the low-lying, gray clouds that only served to make the unseasonable April heat even more oppressive. His mood matched the sky. Not that he was a grasping or greedy man, but his family owned the Broken P. Before they arrived, Alan Caldwell just about ran the place into the ground—mostly because he'd been living in the bottom of a whiskey bottle. Just prior to the ranch going under the gavel, the McCains and Caldwell made a gentlemen's agreement. On that handshake, they'd been "partners," and Joshua and his father spent every last dollar they owned and every drop of sweat they could muster to put the ranch back in the black.

Josh needed help finding out where Alan Caldwell's "widow" lived. He'd send a missive informing her of Alan's death so she'd not send Ruth. The one person in town who might know where Leticia Caldwell resided would be the town's only attorney, Rick Maltby.

Josh paused a moment, yanked off his hat, and wiped his brow with a bandana as he devised a plan to handle this situation. Moments later, his spurs jangled on the boardwalk as he started down the street.

———◆———

Ruth reached up and tried to smooth back a springy blond curl. It bounced right back into an undisciplined coil and brought a partner along. She sighed in surrender. Making a good first impression wasn't to be her lot in life.

Ruth didn't want to come to California. She wasn't even sure she wanted to meet her father. *No, that's a lie. I do. I really do.* She jounced along in the stage and worried . . . about what her father would be like and about her own future.

A corkscrew curl breezed across her eyes. Ruth pushed it back into place. That had been the same way Mama touched her for the very last time—to smooth an errant wisp back with her weak hand and bravely smile. The memory knifed through Ruth.

Mama welcomed her home from the academy as if nothing were amiss—either in the report Headmistress Pettigrew sent or with her own health.

Mama declared she'd sent Ruth away to the unceasing string of ladies' academies and finishing schools because she wanted her daughter to be well-educated and prepared adequately for a comfortable life. At least that's what she'd said—but consumption often struck those abiding under the same roof. Mama never once confessed how that fact drove her to protect her daughter. But Bernadette had been more vocal. It had been so like Mama to deny herself the comfort of Ruth's love in an attempt to spare her.

Ruth did her best to make up for it and for her failure to shine at those schools, though. In those last months she'd shown Mama every scrap of devotion she possibly could.

That still didn't take away the guilt of not having been there to comfort Mama throughout the months when she'd been gone. Well, she'd done everything Mama asked—including mailing off that mysterious letter, then boarding the stage and taking this trip. *Following Mama's dying wish is the least I can do.*

She set her hunter green felt hat in her lap and brushed off some of the dust before perching it on her head. The Overland Stage bounced just as she stuck in the hatpin, so the pin scraped painfully across her scalp. She secured the hat in place with a wince. Even the gusting California wind shouldn't dislodge it now.

Keeping the leather shades drawn on the stage windows cut down on the wind-blown dust, but she'd baked in this oven on wheels as long as she could bear. Riding in here ought to convince the worst sinner to repent simply because it felt like a foretaste of how dreadfully miserable it would be to roast for eternity in hell's fire. Finally, she'd rolled up one shade just for the sake of self-preservation.

The stage driver hadn't taken her seriously this morning when she inquired about riding atop with him. Surely that perch had to be cooler and less dusty. As it was, she'd been trapped inside this dreadful conveyance for three weeks. The Widow Andrews had been her companion until early this morning—an arrangement Berna-dette pronounced as satisfactory and proper. There had been other passengers who boarded and exited with boring regularity. None seemed friendly in the least—unless she counted the dandy who tried to smoke his cigar and kept nudging her with his knee. The sharply pointed tip of Widow Andrews's parasol convinced him to alter his ways.

The past few days felt as if they'd lasted a year apiece. Crossing the plains had been dusty and monotonous, but as the stage climbed over the Sierra Nevadas, every last tilt and sway made the stage rebound worse than a storm-tossed ship. By the time they'd stopped last night in Placerville, Ruth took courage in two facts: the worst of the trip was over, and she'd never have to endure such a crossing again. Her new life awaited.

As towns went, Placerville actually looked . . . well, odd. According-ing to the hotel maid, it had originally been called Dry Diggings. Ruth believed her; everywhere she turned, someone had dug. She carefully attended each step for fear of wrenching her ankle in an ill-placed hole in the street. All around the town and hills the land bore pockmarks from prospecting, and she'd even seen a grizzled-looking man pry mortar from the side of a log building as he mut-tered something about gold.

That alone ought to have made her stay in her room for the

night, but hearing the town's name had been changed to something else before Placerville really caught Ruth's attention. For years it had been known as Hangtown. Just a few steps down Main Street, vigilantes used a rope and the center of three oak trees for justice, regardless of the nature of the crime! Convincing Widow Andrews they needed to "stretch their limbs after the arduous journey," she'd wandered up and down Main Street and managed to satisfy her morbid curiosity by looking at the hanging tree.

Her father lived between Placerville and a town called Folsom, on a ranch named the Broken P. A big city called Sacramento lay after Folsom, but Ruth didn't particularly mind the fact that she'd be in a smaller town. She'd already endured living in a big city where society expected pretty manners and silent women. *If Hangtown is rough and Sacramento is cultured, then perhaps—if God is merciful—Folsom will be somewhere in between. That would suit me just fine.*

With that happy thought, Ruth now smiled out the stage window and wished it would go faster. The steep foothills of Placerville had slowly changed to rolling hills. In patches, the area was still heavily wooded; in others, the hills had been cleared and now boasted cattle herds. One of them might be her father's place!

In the distance she occasionally saw a bit of a small town. Hilly and wooded as the land was, she could only see glimpses here and there of civilization. And alone in the stage, she couldn't even share her joy at arriving at her final destination.

She looked down and critically reviewed her appearance. The ivory ruffles at the throat of her traveling gown hung limp. She fluffed them and retied the black silk ribbon that kept her cameo brooch at her throat. Within the privacy of the stage, she had unfastened the large jet buttons of her traveling jacket to make the heat less oppressive. Now she slipped them back into their buttonholes. Sitting in this miserable conveyance had wrinkled the skirt of her ensemble beyond redemption. The last time she'd been this damp and rumpled, she'd slipped out of a vapid poetry reading and gone fishing with the gardener's sons.

She got along well enough with the gardener's young boys, and with Hadley, but other than them, Ruth hadn't ever spent any appreciable time with males ... well, other than Grandfather. Grandfather had been a banker, a gentleman. He and Hadley were both city men.

What kind of man would her father be? Hearing that her father had turned his life around had come as a shock—a pleasant one, but even that knowledge didn't allay Ruth's anxiety over meeting him.

"Oh, Lord, why did you take Mama? I would have managed okay with her in my life. She loved me for who I was. I just wanted to live with her and be plain old Ruth."

In the weeks since Mama went to the hereafter, Ruth had asked God that selfsame question over and over again. He'd been silent.

Mama never seemed to see Ruth's flaws. Even when Ruth's escapades earned her the censure of others, Mama lovingly saw past the problem and gently murmured that everyone spilled, sneezed, or had a slip of the tongue. She could explain away the most egregious mishaps, and in her presence, Ruth didn't mind being tall, clumsy, or so free-thinking.

But Mama went to the bosom of Jesus. Now Ruth knew she'd have to live with everyone expecting her to fit the mold of a lady. Impossible.

Well, they can expect whatever they want, that doesn't mean that's what they'll get. After all, this situation was just as unexpected to her as it would be to them. Still, she couldn't help but wonder what she might find. Who was this man—her father? What kind of life would he offer her?

She grimaced as a collective image of all the finishing schools she'd known came together in one setting. Elegant people dressed in beautiful clothes of rich silks and velvets came to mind, no doubt the latest fashions straight out of *Godey's*. That refined ladies' magazine had graced the parlor table of every feminine reading room she'd ever endured. In fact, one sat beside her even now—a gift from the Widow Andrews.

Ruth picked up the publication and opened it to read: *We know very well that, while some boys are quite content to play at housekeeping with their sisters, others are quite too restless and consider it beneath their dignity. Let the boys have their workshop, then, by all means, as soon as they are old enough or have proved themselves capable of being trusted with mischief-making tools.*

"They could let me have a workshop with mischief-making tools as well," Ruth muttered and flipped several pages. She found a lovely pattern for quilting, a new style of mantilla complete with hood, and an advertisement for Douglas and Sherwood's *celebrated tournure corset*. Closing the pages, Ruth sighed. "I don't want a celebrated corset. I want to go home."

But she had no home. She might never have a home again. It was always possible her father would reject her and send her from his sight. He might believe Ruth to be too unmanageable—too unpredictable. He might have an entirely different family. Ruth had read of men leaving families in the East to hide in the western territories where they began life anew with a new wife. It was also possible her father had done this.

I might have brothers and sisters. The thought was neither alarming nor comforting. It was simply one more possibility in a vast sea of options. Ruth sighed and stared out the window. *I just know I won't meet anyone's expectations. I'm going to be quite disappointing to whomever's there to meet me. Father will remember Mother in her elegance and grace and believe me to be the same. But I won't be anything like her. I'm just plain old Ruth.*

She pictured herself stepping from the stage with wild hair, smudged gloves, and rumpled clothes. Oh, she was going to make a bad first impression on everyone living in California. Much as she'd love to just be herself and not fret over such outward appearances, it wasn't to be. All of her life Mama and teachers had drilled manners and comportment so she would be a woman of consequence.

Unfortunately, the only consequences had been disasters. The moment Ruth went out in public, she invariably stepped into the limelight. Once there, she said or did the wrong thing. Her bold conduct, forthright speech, undisciplined thoughts, and strong sense of justice managed to raise brows. If she failed to conduct herself respectably in the city where she was reared, how would she ever manage to present herself passably in a place where she couldn't begin to know the rules?

But this might be different. Hope began to surge anew. *This is the West. They probably don't follow even half of those elaborate social conventions. This is a chance for me. I could start out new, fresh! Finally, I might fit in.*

Ruth pulled her Bible out of her tapestry valise, seeking comfort and encouragement from one of her favorite passages. The stage jounced so badly, she couldn't follow each line, so she closed God's written word and recited it by memory.

"'Therefore if any man be in Christ, he is a new creature: old things are passed away; behold, all things are become new.'" She smiled. "I'm a new creature and the old things are passed away." But just as quickly as this confidence came, Ruth felt a hint of despair. "At least I hope the old things are in the past."

She tucked away her Bible, then whispered a quick prayer for self-control as they pulled into Folsom.

Built on the side of one of the mountainous foothills, Folsom slanted more than any of the towns back home or in the middle of the flat plains she'd crossed. Clean, bright-looking businesses lined the street, giving it a welcoming air. A flare of excitement rushed through her. She'd finally arrived!

The stage started to slow as it went past a tall, muscular cowboy who stuck a hat atop wavy black hair and shoved a bandana in his rear pocket. It reminded her she ought to tidy up a bit, too.

Ruth made one last desperate attempt to put her hair in order. She dabbed at her forehead to make sure she wouldn't look overheated and tucked the hankie back into her sleeve, then tugged her cuffs in place so she wouldn't look too disheveled.

Time to face her new life.

The stage pulled in and stopped. Joshua didn't pay much attention, just minded his own business and continued up the boardwalk toward Maltby's office. A fire a few years back decimated the town, but they'd rebuilt. Within a year, the buildings and boardwalk looked downright spiffy. He passed the barbershop, the laundry/public bath, and had just reached the door to the jail when the stage driver jumped down.

"Hey, McCain! I've got a delivery fer you!"

Joshua nodded and strode across the rutted dirt street. He expected the customized saddle he'd ordered from Independence to arrive any day, so being called over to pick up the piece quickened Josh's pace. He made his way to the other side of the dusty, persimmon-colored stage as the driver reached up to help someone disembark.

Yards of deep green skirts with fancy swags and the tiniest lace edge of a petticoat peeping from beneath tattled that this was a genuine, high-class lady. Josh smiled—a pretty woman didn't often arrive in town. He wouldn't mind making her acquaintance.

Then Joshua got a sinking feeling. He couldn't be sure, but he thought he heard his name on the driver's lips.

"Here she is. Bound for the Broken P, she said. Lucky thing you was in town today. Miss, this here is Joshua McCain, Junior. He'll git you out to the ranch."

"Thank you ever so much," she murmured.

Joshua stared at her in disbelief and horror. Willowy, blond, and ... oh no. Green-eyed. The moment she turned toward him, the eye color and description weren't even necessary. This woman was the spitting image of her father. Of course her shape was a bit different and her features were finer, but there could be no mistaking the relationship.

A froth of sunny curls spun around her head in whorls too wild to be considered ringlets, and she had a streak of dirt along her right temple. Her wide eyes sparkled with intelligence as she turned toward him. Though she did face him, her gaze wandered, as if she needed to take in every little bit of the town. Her lips quivered—was she fighting laughter or tears? Judging from the fancy buttons, frills, and ribbons, someone had paid far too much for her traveling gown—especially since it looked as if she'd slept in it for half a year, then been dragged through a knothole backward.

She was, without a doubt, the most helpless-looking female he'd ever set eyes on . . . and the most beautiful.

She pinched the sides of her green gown with her gloved hands and dipped a curtsy. "It's a pleasure to make your acquaintance, Mr. McCain."

"Miss Caldwell," he said grimly as he pulled off his hat, "you weren't supposed to come."

CHAPTER THREE

S he gave him a startled look and gasped. Her hand flew up toward her throat, and she blinked at him.

"I'll set her trunks on the boardwalk," the driver said as he deposited a bulging tapestry valise at her feet. "Hope you brought the buckboard. The lady didn't travel light."

"Trunks? She brought *trunks*?"

Miss Caldwell stretched to her full height and tried to look formidable. Seeing as she barely came up to his chin, the attempt failed. Her already-straight shoulders went back a tad more. "I could scarcely come ill-prepared."

Joshua cast a disparaging look up at the huge steamer trunks strapped on the stage, then took another look at her. Yup, she looked antsy as a mustang after a saddle got tossed over his back for the first time. Odd, how a body could stand still, yet give the impression of being ready to jump into motion. Every line of her sang with tension. He owed her the truth, but breaking it to her wasn't going to be an easy proposition.

She hiccupped. The action made her bob unexpectedly, and color flooded her pale cheeks. Her head dipped, and she hastily opened the reticule hanging from her wrist and whipped out a fan. She flicked it open and half-hid her face behind the ivory-and-silk frippery, but it failed to disguise the fact that she'd hiccupped again.

"Excuse me," she murmured.

A shocking thought occurred to Joshua, and he leaned closer to try to catch a whiff. Though he didn't detect any spirits on her, the sweet honeysuckle scent of her perfume might well be a disguise for her vice. After all, blood told—and everyone knew weakness for alcohol was inherited.

"D'ya need another drink?" the stage driver asked.

Another drink? Joshua groaned. He'd dried out her father, and that had been an ordeal. He wasn't about to tackle getting a woman off the bottle.

"Perhaps some lemonade or—*hic*—water," she said in a whispery alto. Each wave of her fan sent her curls dancing.

He nodded, then looked at the driver. "Don't remove her trunks yet."

"Sorry. I'm behind schedule. Gotta move on out."

Josh hoped to just leave her on the stage and send her back, but the destination slate in the stage office window let him know it was going the wrong direction. He scowled, then decided aloud, "Miss Caldwell, I'll take you to Rick Maltby's office. He'll have a pitcher of water." It was the closest place available where they could talk without having an audience. He cupped her elbow and steered her in the right direction. At least she walked with a steady gait. Folks were starting to gather around, and he needed to break the news that her pa had gone to the hereafter before she caught wind of cowboys jawing about it.

They crossed the street to the lawyer's but found the office empty. Most likely Rick hiked off to the Copper Kettle for a bite to eat. Joshua hung his hat on a brass hook and pointed at the closest chair. "Have a seat. I'll get you some water."

He paced to a small oak table alongside one wall and surreptitiously rubbed a few specks of the ever-present dust from the rim before he picked up the pitcher. The water wasn't necessary— the shock of his news would undoubtedly stop that crazy case of hiccups. He turned back around and repeated, "Have a seat."

"If it's all the same to you, sir, I'd rather stand. I've spent the past three weeks sitting in the stage, and the change is welcome." A hiccup jumped between every third or fourth word.

He shrugged. "No skin off my nose." He poured carefully, tilt- ing the pitcher so the sediment in the water wasn't disturbed. The town well was running a bit low, and folks dealt with the grit. Somehow, though, he doubted a lavishly-dressed woman like Miss Caldwell had ever sipped anything but pure water from crystal gob- lets. Oh, well, she'd have to make do. He topped off the glass and headed back toward her.

He'd hoped the lawyer would be here. That not being the case, he'd stall for a moment. Rick would be here soon. Gossip would carry news to Maltby that a strange young woman was waiting in his office.

Clearly, his expectations were in vain. When Maltby didn't hasten back, Joshua accepted he wasn't going to get any help break- ing the sorrowful news. He was just going to have to tough it out.

"Thank—" Miss Caldwell's words halted and her hand froze midair as she reached to accept the glass. Her brows knit, and her gaze narrowed. "I recognize the wax seal on that envelope, Mr. McCain." She locked eyes with him. "It's my mother's, and it's open. What could you be thinking, reading my father's mail?"

Joshua glanced down at the letter protruding from the pocket of his leather vest. It wasn't exactly the way he'd planned to break the news. Joshua put the glass in her hand and curled her fingers around it very deliberately. "Miss Caldwell, I'd not intentionally read a letter sent to someone else."

"Oh." She gave him a smile. "Please forgive me for leaping to conclusions. My father must have given it to you when he sent you to fetch me."

"Miss, your father didn't send me." He grimaced, then took out the envelope and turned it so she could see both sides. "Fact is, my family owns the Broken P. That was written as the address, so it was delivered to us. Alan Caldwell took ill two years ago." He paused meaningfully, hoping that momentary silence would warn her of what he'd say next. "He didn't pull through." When she didn't react, he figured maybe he'd been too roundabout with his technique. "I'm sorry, miss. Your pa's not with us anymore."

He fully expected her hiccups to cease and tears to begin. The hiccups got louder. The woman pressed herself against the wall, and with every jarring hiccup, her left elbow hit the shutters and made them rattle a clattering accompaniment. She tore her gaze away as pain streaked across her pretty features.

"I'm sorry for your loss."

"He sent Mama away." She kept whacking herself as she fluttered the fan in agitation. Anguish darkened her eyes and tainted her whisper. "He's just going through this ruse to get rid of me, isn't he? You said so yourself—out by the stage, you said I wasn't supposed to come."

Joshua took the fan away before she beat herself black and blue with it. "Sip the water, Miss Caldwell."

She looked down and tilted her head to the side. Another hiccup cut short her sigh of despair. In her shock, the poor woman had managed to tip her hand and spill the water down her skirts.

"It's all right," he soothed. He pried the glass from her, set it next to her fan on Maltby's desk, and cupped her shoulders. The way the sweet little thing was shuddering beneath his hands let him know his words were starting to sink in. A strange wave of tenderness and protection washed over him. "Here. You'd better sit down for a spell." It took no effort at all to pivot her slight frame and nudge her into the chair.

She fussed with the wet spot. "I'll have to change before I go out to the ranch. I cannot meet him looking like this."

Joshua slid his tanned hand beneath her soft, pale chin and

tilted her face up to his. He'd never felt less capable in his life. Still, no one else was around, and it fell to him to see her through and get her back to her mama. Her dying mama. That made it all the more urgent. Surely this young woman couldn't know the extent of her mother's condition, else she wouldn't have made this trip. In Alan's memory and honor, he'd take on the responsibility of turning her around and sending her back.

"Miss Caldwell, that little dab of water doesn't matter. What, with the heat like it is, that spot'll dry up in a few minutes. But Alan's gone. . . . I give you my word; he died. No father would ever deny or disown a daughter."

"Yes, he would," she said thickly. She shied away from his touch, so he eased back, then walked to the other side of the small office. A lengthy silence ensued, interrupted by a string of hic-her-heart-off-its-hinges hiccups. "He sent Mama away, and she was pretty and poised; now he doesn't even want to meet me, and I know it's my fault. Please don't feel obligated to put up pretenses."

Joshua stared at her. Clearly, she'd set her heart on finally meeting her father. Instead of accepting the truth, she was cooking up an explanation that might let her earn the right to meet him later ... only there'd never be a later. Pity welled up. She'd said a mouthful. She thought if she were pretty and perfect and poised, she'd earn the right to be a daughter. No girl ought to ever think such a thing. Besides, she *was* pretty and appealing in her very own unique way.

His spurs jangled softly as he closed the distance between them. He lifted her gloved hands and squeezed them. "Miss Caldwell, do you believe the Lord loves you?"

"Yes."

"Did you have to be perfect for Him to care about you?"

"He's everywhere. I guess He couldn't run from me, even if He wanted to." As soon as she'd spoken, she pulled a hand free and clapped it over her mouth. "Oh, I'm sorry. That was a dreadful thing to say. I always say the wrong thing."

Before he could formulate a response to her startling comments, the door opened and Maltby strode in. Joshua cleared his throat and said, "Rick Maltby, let me introduce you to Miss Ruth Caldwell. Miss Caldwell, this is Rick Maltby, attorney-at-law."

To his credit, Rick didn't act surprised in the least. He dipped an urbane bow and murmured, "Pleased to meet you."

Ruth stood, curtsied, grabbed her fan, and sidled back toward the wall once again. "I'm sorry for taking your seat, sir." She managed to jab herself with the fan as she pulled a hankie from her sleeve, then proceeded to hold both fripperies as if armed for war.

Rick dragged a pair of chairs into position across from his desk. "Why don't you both sit here?"

She stared at him and shook her head.

"She isn't convinced Alan's dead," Joshua informed him.

Ten minutes later, Ruth sat by Joshua's side across from Rick's desk. They'd tucked her between themselves, walked her over to the churchyard, and let her see the gravestone. Strangely enough, once she saw it, her hiccups ceased. Her head dipped and her shoulders curled forward. For a moment, Joshua feared she was fixing to swoon; but then she folded her hands together, let out a very unladylike sigh, and had a moment of silent prayer over the grave of the father she never knew.

Now Miss Caldwell clutched her gloves in her lap and stared at the edge of Rick's desk. She'd turned her gloves the wrong way so all of the fingers stood up like a bouquet of rabbit ears. That fact touched Joshua—she tried so hard to behave like a decorous, refined lady, but deep down inside she couldn't seem to keep the silly details straight. But maybe that wasn't a fair assessment. After all, she was in shock.

"I wish I'd never come," she whispered.

"No need to worry," Josh soothed. "I'll send you back to your mother."

Miss Caldwell shook her head. The adamant motion set her curls flying every which way.

Again wondering if she'd not been aware of her mother's ten-uous condition, Josh strove to choose his words carefully. "The letter states your mother's health is fragile."

"Then you'll want to depart immediately," Rick surmised.

"I can't." Her grasp on those bunny ears of gloves became a stranglehold. "Sh-she's passed on."

"I see." Rick mercifully spared her having to explain further.

Eyes shimmering with tears, Miss Caldwell turned to Josh. "I didn't know exactly what was in the letter. I followed her instruc-tions and mailed it. It was her dying wish—"

"Hush," he growled softly as he swiped her hanky and dabbed at her cheek. "What's done is done."

"Mama said that, too." She finally turned loose of those ridic-ulous gloves and claimed the hanky. In mopping her face, the woman turned the smudge by her temple into a streak of mud.

Josh couldn't fathom what to do with the woman. At seventeen, Laney might not be the sharpest knife in the drawer, but she'd exhibit far more poise than this bundle of nerves.

"Perhaps we'd be wise to concentrate on what Miss Caldwell will do now that she's here," Rick said.

The brave way she straightened her shoulders didn't distract Josh from the pained expression on her pretty face. "I'm capable in all domestic matters. Do you gentlemen know of a family in need of a housekeeper or governess?"

"No." They spoke in unison—Rick undoubtedly out of hon-esty, Josh out of the certainty that no family would survive Ruth's so-called assistance.

"It might be crass to discuss money, but I have eighty-three dollars and seventeen cents with me. Could I start a dress shop? I'm able to sew quite well."

The poor girl was scrambling to find a way to support herself. Josh frowned. "That's unnecessary."

"Let me examine the will." Rick opened an oak filing cabinet and pulled out the document. The drawer glided and clicked shut, and the metered *tick tock* of the wall clock's pendulum was the only sound in the room as he silently read the will. Finally he grimaced, glanced up, and gave Joshua a strained look.

"Miss Caldwell, there was a gentlemen's agreement. A few of us were aware of it, but for the sake of your father's dignity, it wasn't written down. Your father's remedy for it was contained in his last will and testament." He picked up the paper and read aloud, "'Since I made other financial arrangements for my wife, Leticia Porter-Caldwell, she is to receive nothing from my estate. As there was no issue from our marriage, I hereby bequeath all of my possessions, both real and personal, as well as my portion of Broken P including lock, stock, and barrel in equal portion to Joshua McCain Senior and Junior.'"

Ruth Caldwell didn't react.

Joshua's blood ran cold as Rick set down the legal document and placed his hand on it, as if to obscure the words. "This will is now invalid since we've established you exist, Miss Caldwell."

Joshua unfolded from his chair and gritted his teeth. He paced as far away from her as he could get, stared out the window, and didn't say a word. He wasn't a man to cuss or drink, but if he were, he'd be doing plenty of both right about now. Instead, he held his tongue and searched his mind for a way to handle this devastating blow. Later on, he and God were going to have to hold a lengthy conversation about this.

"I'm afraid I don't understand," Miss Caldwell said softly.

Joshua wheeled around. "What he's saying, Miss Caldwell, is that you've just inherited a chunk of my family's ranch."

CHAPTER FOUR

⎯⎯⎯►◄⎯⎯⎯

Impossible," Ruth said. She looked from one man to the other. Her gaze kept swinging back to the black-haired cowboy. His hazel eyes commanded attention—the golden centers had glittered with intelligence earlier; now they burned with fury. Pointing out the obvious to him felt ridiculous, but it had to be done. She crumpled her hankie into a ball and said, "In case it escaped your notice, I'm a woman. Women cannot own land."

"They do in California," the attorney informed her.

Confessing her shortcomings ought to be second nature by now, but Ruth still hated to parade her flaws. Nonetheless, she had to admit, "I'm an unmarried woman, not a widow."

"We guessed that." Joshua McCain's dry tone hovered in the room.

The attorney leaned across his desk. "The rest of the nation based property laws on English common law, where a widow is permitted to keep her dowering portion of the marital property or a woman can inherit if a gentleman oversees the funds or property; California constitution took the Spanish heritage of allowing women of single, married, or widowed status to own property in their own right."

Ruth stared at him for a moment before she realized her mouth was hanging wide open. She snapped her jaw shut.

"The will specifically states the marriage was without issue." The attorney's voice sounded more than reasonable, but Ruth picked up on the strained undercurrents as he went on to explain himself. "The property was divided in accordance with that belief. Since the division was predicated on a falsehood, what we need to do is establish your true identity."

"Look at her." Joshua McCain waved a callused hand at her. "She's Alan Caldwell in a dress."

Once again Ruth found herself gaping. She spluttered, "Sir!"

"I mean . . . well, there's no mistaking she's her father's daughter," Joshua stated.

"It remains, I'd be remiss in not tracing the paper work," the attorney persisted.

"Very well." Suddenly beyond weary, Ruth decided to humor the man just to get all of this taken care of. Then she'd go to the hotel, bathe, and sleep for a week. "What do you require?"

"Something official. If you happen to have a birth certificate, that would be the best."

She shook her head. "My birth is recorded in the family Bible beneath Mama and Father's marriage."

Joshua drummed his fingers on the arm of his chair. "Rick, what does this mean?"

"Miss Caldwell has rightful claim to her father's land. Depending on who hears the case, she could inherit his full half of the Broken P."

Ruth felt tension crackle in the room.

"We'll have to put it on a docket and wait till the circuit judge makes his rounds—unless you want to go to Sacramento and have the case heard sooner. Even then you'll have to wait a bit."

Snorting, Joshua rose from his chair. "I'm not racing off to get bad news."

Bad news. That's me. "Excuse me, gentlemen. I don't know that I want to lay claim to any property. It scarcely seems right since Mr. McCain has done all of the work."

Mr. McCain spread his hand wide and rubbed both temples as if he suffered a horrendous headache. "Lady, you don't know how tempting it is to accept that, but it's not what you want or what I want that matters here. It's what your father would have wanted."

"Perhaps, Miss Caldwell, you and Mr. McCain can reach an amicable resolution on your own," the attorney suggested.

Fully aware she was in over her head, Ruth blurted out, "I'd want you to represent me, Mr. Maltby. Surely a woman ought to have a professional advise her in such a matter."

"Now hold on a minute," Joshua protested.

Mr. Maltby lifted a hand. "Wait. I drafted the will. I'm legally obliged to represent the decedent's wishes. If you choose not to iron out the matter among yourselves, you'll need to seek representation from other professionals."

"Like who? You're the only one around," Joshua rumbled. He paced back and forth like prospective grooms did in the parlor before Miss Pettigrew ushered in possible bridal candidates.

"I suppose I'd better—"

"Come with me," Mr. McCain interrupted her. Wrapping his hand around her wrist, he tugged her to her feet. "You can stay at the ranch until we get this ironed out."

Ruth didn't want to go anywhere with him. For once, all of those seemingly silly etiquette lessons came in handy. She blurted out, "I don't think that would be proper."

"It's fine, Miss Caldwell," the attorney assured her. "Josh has a sister and a housekeeper. I recommend you agree to this arrangement for the time being."

So much for etiquette.

"It's settled, then." Josh headed toward the door with her in tow. "You can contact us at the Broken P as soon you find out when the circuit judge is coming."

They stepped outside, and Ruth blinked in the powerful sunlight. "Oh, look! My trunks are over on the boardwalk!"

Josh yanked her back. "Where are you going?"

"My things—"

"Probably weigh a ton. I'm going to have to rent a buggy to haul it all to the ranch."

"Well, then." Ruth glanced up and down the street. "Where is the livery?"

"Other side of the saloon. You stay put here."

Ruth whipped out her fan and opened it. "I'm sure it'll take you a little while to hire a conveyance. Since I'm in town, I'd like to see what's on hand. That mercantile over there looks quite impressive."

"You're not shopping and buying more junk for me to haul around."

She resisted the urge to waft the fan at him. It would probably do him some good. Joshua McCain had a hot temper and needed to cool off. Instead, Ruth forced herself to speak calmly. "It would be foolish for me to buy much. I'm already having things shipped."

The muscles in his jaws twitched. "You've got more stuff on the way?"

"It won't get here for a while, but it made sense. After all, I'll need to set up housekeeping at some point." Feeling her words ought to pacify him, she said, "Why don't you go get a wagon while I explore a little?"

"Lady, the last thing I want is to have to go searching for you. I don't have that kind of time to waste." He heaved a sigh. "Just promise you'll stay on the boardwalk. It won't take me long to hire a rig, and I need to get back home."

"That's a reasonable compromise." She smiled. Mr. McCain could be reasonable, after all.

Half an hour later, Ruth sat in the hired buggy and stared

straight ahead. She couldn't bear to sneak even a furtive peek at Joshua McCain. Somehow, she'd managed to tweak his temper twice now. She didn't want to add to her list of offenses. Bad enough he was certain she'd cheated him out of part of the ranch; but as if that transgression weren't sufficient to put her on his bad side for eternity, she'd stepped amiss once again.

While Joshua went to rent a buggy, Ruth had walked the length of the boardwalk, then crossed the street and headed back toward her trunks. It was the logical thing to do. Joshua McCain would find her and her belongings all ready to go. Halfway down the boardwalk to the stage station, a pleasant-looking woman stepped out of a shop and smiled at her. How was she to know the woman in that plush dress was ... well ...

"Madam Velvet," he muttered under his breath beside her, then shot her a scowl dark enough to wilt the heartiest daisy. He opened his mouth, then shut it. After a prolonged silence, he rasped, "Didn't you ever read about Rahab or Jezebel in the Bible?"

"Yes."

"That ... ah ... *profession* wasn't limited to Bible times." His right spur jingled as he scraped his boot side to side on the floorboard, and he studied her with his glittering eyes. The corners of his mouth tightened, then he rasped, "In case you didn't know, not all women are ladies."

"I didn't realize she was ..." Ruth's voice died out.

Josh's head wagged back and forth. The only thing darker than his black-as-sin hair was his mood. He muttered something unintelligible to himself again.

"Women of easy virtue aren't supposed to—" Ruth groaned.

Heaving a sigh, Josh gripped the reins more tightly. His hands were huge, callused, and capable-looking. "Things are different out here. Back East, women of her ilk stay in the Bowery; here, they pretty much go where they please. The Nugget—that's the local watering hole—has rooms upstairs for them to ..." He cleared his throat. "Has rooms for them."

Awkward as the conversation had been, Ruth appreciated learning such details so she didn't blunder again. Josh looked every bit as uncomfortable as she felt, and for some odd reason, that fact made her like him a little. Nervously drawing whorls on her skirts, Ruth half whispered, "She didn't have paint on her face or nails. Aren't they all—"

"I wouldn't know," he snapped. "I don't avail myself of their company."

"Gratified as I am to be assured of your morals, how am I to recognize such a woman if you cannot?"

"Honey," he drawled, "I didn't say I can't recognize them. I just don't get close enough to study the particulars. No decent woman acknowledges Madame Velvet, let alone speaks to her. You were ready to have her to tea!"

He shook his head once again. Ruth couldn't be sure whether the action depicted utter disbelief or implied she'd proven herself to be impossibly dim-witted. He didn't leave the subject to die an already uncomfortable death. Instead, he accused, "Leave you alone for five minutes, and you're already wading into trouble."

Heat zoomed up her throat clear to her hairline. Ruth flipped open her fan and used it vigorously. She couldn't look at him, let alone respond to his accusation. Other women were blessed with talents like conversing, arranging flowers, and conducting soirees. She'd been cursed with the "talent" of humiliating herself with ill-considered plans. Headmistress Pettigrew labeled it "a predilection for creating a scene." Ruth had the sinking feeling that Joshua McCain and Headmistress Pettigrew were cut of the same cloth. He could shake his head just as condemningly as she had.

Her trunks jostled the vehicle. Josh glanced back to make sure they hadn't lost one. He barely spoke a word the whole rest of the trip, but the sour look on his face let her know she was as welcome as a spider in a teapot.

After an inhospitably silent ride to the Broken P, Ruth looked forward to getting away from Joshua, sponging away the grit, and having a decent cup of tea. As soon as she spied the clapboard house, misgivings assailed her. The fences, barn, and livestock all looked picture-perfect. On the other hand, though sturdily built, the house looked as if it were more for show than hospitality. The tattered plants bracketing the steps of the veranda warned that this place lacked any vitality or warmth.

"I . . . I thought there was a housekeeper."

"There is." Joshua said nothing more. He pulled the reins to stop the buggy, set the brake, and hopped down. To Ruth's surprise, he came to her side and helped her down. The minute her feet hit the ground, he turned loose of her and bellowed, "Hilda! Hilll-dahhh!"

"Hold your horses, cowboy," a rusty voice shouted from inside, "I'm a-comin' as fast as I can."

For a brief moment, Ruth wondered whether Hilda was his sister or the housekeeper. Whoever she was, Ruth already liked her—she bellowed loudly, so she couldn't be too set on proprieties. At the moment, Ruth desperately longed for an ally. The front door shot open. A stout woman with both arms full of laundry barreled through. "Where's the fire?" As soon as she spied Ruth, the laundry tumbled from her arms onto the porch. "Dear me, look at her, will you? Why, the gal looks like Alan Caldwell in a dress."

"She's his daughter, Ruth Caldwell." Josh's voice sounded positively funereal.

"Could be a niece or somethin'," Hilda mused. Then she wagged her head from side to side. "Nope. He was an onliest child. Couldn't have no nieces nor nephews. Well, take her on inside. I'll get these dirty clothes into the boilin' pot and be there soon as I can."

"Where's Laney?"

"The parlor. Diggin' through music. Said she wants to play somethin' different on the piano. I didn't have the heart to tell her everything she plays sounds different than what it's s'posed to." Hilda scooped up the clothes and trundled off.

Ruth remained motionless.

"There's a spare room at the end of the hall. I suppose you can have it for now." Josh lugged a trunk onto his shoulder and grunted loudly. "Come on ahead, and get the door, will you?"

Grabbing her tapestry valise, Ruth muttered under her breath, "Hasn't he ever heard the word *please*?"

"Excuse me?"

Ruth gave him a guilty look. "What?"

"That's what I asked." He started up the porch steps. "You said something, but I couldn't hear it."

"Here." She scampered past him and opened the door.

"Humph." He stomped into the house, through a parlor, and up a flight of stairs.

Uncertain whether to remain downstairs or to follow after him, Ruth balked about the propriety involved in being upstairs in a bedchamber with a man—even for a brief moment for such an innocent cause. She paused as Josh turned down a hallway and out of sight.

"Who are you?" a voice asked from behind her.

"Oh!" Spinning about, Ruth stared at a beautiful girl with cinnamon-colored hair. "You startled me. I'm—"

"You're related to Alan Caldwell!" the young woman crowed gleefully. "You look just like him."

In a dress, Ruth mentally filled in. Since she'd already heard the odd phrase twice, she couldn't banish it from her mind. As she switched her valise to the other hand, Ruth smiled. "I'm Ruth Caldwell. Alan was my father."

"Father!" the girl gasped. She caught her breath and repeated shrilly, "Father!"

Loud boots rang on the porch planks and the door burst open. "What?"

"Father." The girl blushed. "I'm sorry, I was just surprised. Ruth Caldwell, allow me to introduce my father, Joshua McCain, Senior. Father, this is Ruth Caldwell."

"Miss Caldwell." Mr. McCain doffed his hat. "I didn't know Alan had any relatives."

"He didn't, either," Ruth said. "I've been told there's a strong family resemblance."

"Indeed, there is." He gave his daughter a dismissive wave. Ruth noticed his left arm didn't work quite right—it hung a bit askew when he dropped it to his side. "Laney, honey, why don't you go make tea to share with our guest?" Turning back to Ruth, he smiled warmly. "Have a seat and tell me—are you his niece?"

Knowing her answer would elicit a powerful reaction, Ruth chose to remain standing. "Actually, sir, I'm—"

"She's Alan's daughter," Joshua, Jr. called as he trampled down the stairs.

Mr. McCain whistled under his breath, then shook his head. "Something's not right. Alan said he had no children."

"None that he knew of. Mama went back East to live with her parents and—" Ruth tried to phrase the concept acceptably. Especially after riling Josh over the Madame Velvet incident, she felt the need to guard her words. "You know the voyage around South America and back to the East Coast is six months long. I was born just before the ship reached Boston."

"Rick Maltby already knows about her arrival, Dad." Josh's spurs jangled even as he crossed the braided rag rug. "He consulted Alan's will, and there's a huge problem."

"Let's all sit down." Laney brushed between her brother and Ruth. Curling her hand around Ruth's arm, Laney steered her to a settee. Once Ruth sat down, Laney sat right beside her and took hold of her hand. "Don't worry. Daddy's very good at solving problems. So is Josh. They'll take care of you." She looked at her father and brother expectantly. "Won't you?"

They remained standing.

Ruth shifted uncomfortably.

"What's the problem?" McCain asked his son.

It wasn't until Josh shoved his hands into his back pockets that something occurred to Ruth. Odd, how in a moment of such importance, a trifling detail would distract her; but she noticed both men were in their shirtsleeves. Back home, no gentleman ever went out in public without a jacket. But Josh—even under considerable strain and lacking a jacket—displayed admirable restraint and decency.

I thought I was coming to a whole different world—but I'm not. Some of the rules apply, and others don't. How will I figure it out when I failed so miserably back home? He could have jumped on what I said to the attorney— that I might not want to claim any inheritance from my father—but he was honorable. Even now, Josh is trying to be diplomatic with what he says.

Josh cast a quick glance at her, then directed his attention to his father. A small muscle in the side of his cheek twitched. "Maltby reread the will. Our inheritance of Alan's half of the Broken P was predicated on the fact that he had no children."

For the second time, silence crackled in the room.

Laney popped up. "I believe I'll go fetch that tea now."

McCain shifted weight and cleared his throat. "Perhaps Miss Caldwell would like to join you in the kitchen."

"I confess I would like to run off to the kitchen, but that wouldn't be responsible." Ruth felt a catch in her chest and prayed she wouldn't get the hiccups again. "I know I'm complicating matters, but we need to find a way to work things out."

"I don't see a need to work things out immediately." Mr. McCain lowered himself into a large leather armchair and leaned back.

"I invited Miss Caldwell to stay with us for the time being," Josh said as he also took a seat. "She arrived expecting to meet her father, not to get the news that he'd passed away."

"Where do you live?" McCain inquired.

"I was supposed to live with my father." Ruth let out a steadying breath. "It was Mama's last wish."

"Poor dear! You're an orphan!" Laney flounced back down and patted her arm.

"Then that settles the matter." McCain rested his elbows on the arms of his chair and steepled his fingers in front of his chest. He seemed to contemplate matters for a few minutes, then nodded sagely. "Nothing needs to be settled because matters are already put to right. Miss Caldwell shouldn't be alone in the world. She'll live here under our protection, and nothing needs to be done about the Broken P."

"But what shall I do about—"

"Now, now." McCain parted his fingertips and waved his right hand dismissively.

The motion almost called Ruth's attention away from how his left hand dropped into his lap. *He must have worked hard to come up with ways to call attention away from his weakness. I'll have to be mindful he's prideful about it.*

Unaware of her thoughts, Mr. McCain looked Ruth in the eye with a paternalistic smile. "You don't need to worry your pretty little head about anything at all. We'll take care of you."

"Good care," Laney tacked on. "I can tell you all about your papa."

"Oh, I'd love that." Laney couldn't have offered anything more enticing.

Josh seemed to sink back into his chair, and the tic in his cheek stopped. "It's all for the best, Miss Caldwell. You've been through a lot recently."

"You're right. I have." *If I'm prudent, I'll have enough to get by on. I don't want these good people thinking I'll demand much, if anything at all, from the will.* "Because everything is so topsy-turvy, I'd feel better if we could resolve this issue. I can't determine what to do with my life until we straighten out things."

Josh leaned forward and gazed into her eyes. "You don't have to make any decisions right now. None of us can predict what will happen legally, and it'll take a while before the court convenes. Until then, you have a safe place to stay."

"And friends," Laney tacked on.

Ruth glanced down at Laney. Bless her heart, Laney didn't have a selfish or mean bone in her body—but she also didn't have the faintest notion of how angry her brother was about how her presence might alter the interpretation of the will.

Mr. McCain smacked the arm of his chair. "They're right, you know. Giving yourself time to settle in is undoubtedly wise. No use mounting up when you don't know where you'll ride to."

Lord, I want to do the right thing. You gave Solomon wisdom. Could I please have a heap of it now? Oh, I know I'm being impatient, asking for it now, but I don't know what else to do.

"I know!" Laney perked up. "God sent Ruth here for me! Josh advertised for someone to come be my companion. I'm so lonely out here. Until last year, I'd been in a wonderful finishing school, and I'm positively languishing for want of a woman's friendship. See? Ruth arrived. If that isn't an answer to prayer, I don't know what is!"

"I don't believe I've ever been considered an answer to prayer," Ruth said truthfully. *Once they find out what I'm really like, they won't want me around Laney. She's tidy and obedient. I'm anything but.*

"An answer to prayer," McCain repeated. "You know I don't hold with all that, but I think this isn't an accident. Fate sent Miss Caldwell our way, and we're keeping her."

———⊷∘⊷———

Josh hefted Ruth's second trunk up the stairs and over to the vacant bedroom. When Dad drew out the plans for this ranch house, Josh wondered why it had to be so grand. Even with Hilda occupying a bedroom, the place still seemed huge. But by the time Laney came home and Alan grew so ill he needed care, all five bedrooms held occupants.

The only place to put Ruth was in the very bed where her father died. Josh made a mental note to pull Hilda off to the side and tell her to keep silent about that fact. Laney's sensitivity would keep her from saying anything to Ruth, but the finer points of dealing with folks never occurred to Hilda.

He didn't want anyone giving Ruth cause to bolt away. If she left, any number of lonely men would gladly claim her—and the last thing Josh wanted or needed was Ruth's husband nosing in and trying to run the show.

Josh dumped the trunk onto the bare wood floor and winced at the noise it made. The place needed to be fixed up—a rug and maybe a splash of whitewash or something. When Laney came home, she'd made a big to-do about sprucing up her room and making it all girlie. Fancy as Miss Caldwell's clothes looked, Josh suspected she'd insist on twice as much as Laney did.

Can't judge a book by its cover. The old saw flashed through his mind, but he dismissed it. He reckoned he'd seen and heard enough from Miss Ruth Caldwell to warn him that she might be easy on the eye, but she'd likely be just as big a pain in the neck. Well, if he kept his distance and she managed to make Laney cheer up, they could make the arrangement work.

"Excuse me, Mr. McCain."

Josh wheeled around. "Miss Caldwell, it gets confusing since my father and I are Senior and Junior. Call me Josh and him McCain."

"And you must call me Ruth."

"Fine." Well, at least she wasn't standing on formality. He'd wondered if she might be the stuffy type, but so far she'd acted downright friendly. "Did you need something, Ruth?"

"Yes, well . . ." She gave him a forced smile. "I would appreciate your giving me the letter my mother wrote. Since my father isn't with us, I feel it rightfully belongs to me."

"Sure." He pulled the letter out of his shirt pocket and handed it to her. "Here you go."

"Thank you."

The way she bowed her head and pressed the missive to her

bosom tugged at his heart. *Lord have mercy on her.* "You must be tired."

She lifted her head and wrinkled her nose. "Truth be told, Joshua, I'm restless. Being cooped up in that hot old stagecoach nearly drove me to distraction." She let out a small laugh. "I didn't intend that pun."

He grinned. "It was clever, though."

Laney sashayed up and pulled Ruth into the bedchamber. "This dreary old place will be your room. I'll help you unpack. Hilda's brewing tea for us. Josh, tell Daddy that Ruth and I will need to go to town in the next day or so. We simply must do something to this—this—" She swept her hand to encompass the room and shook her head.

"That's not necessary." Ruth pivoted from one side to the other, causing her skirts to swish about her ankles in an unmistakably feminine whisper. "This chamber gets pleasant sunshine and is quite spacious."

"Nonsense!" Laney pattered over to the window. "We need to hang some curtains—eyelet, I think."

"I'm sure whatever curtains used to be on the rod will still serve nicely."

Laney huffed. "Your father loved the sun. He took the curtains out of here."

"This was my father's room?" Ruth's face lit up. "How kind of you, Josh, to think to put me here."

"Your smile looks like your father's," Josh said. The second he voiced that thought, he could see how pleased Ruth was to hear it.

"Only much prettier," Laney tacked on. "Alan looked like a raisin—but the lines were all happy ones that crinkled around his eyes and mouth."

"You cannot possibly imagine how much I'd like to have you share your memories of my father."

"I'll tell you anything you want to know." Laney winced. "As long as you take down that stupid picture of a rooster on a fence over your bed."

Laughter bubbled out of Ruth. It took a moment before she thought to hold a hand up to mute the sound or hide her open mouth. Her mirth pleased Josh. She'd been so somber since he'd met her—this was his first glimpse that she might have a sense of humor. If she did, it would make life a heap easier.

"I knew it!" Laney bobbed her head. "Josh, you'll have to tell Daddy we need to go shopping."

"It's not necessary. Truly, it's not." Ruth tilted her head toward one of the trunks. "I brought my paints. I can replace the picture."

Well, well. Miss Ruth Caldwell might not be such a bother after all. She didn't seem to be very demanding.

"Oh, I love to paint!" Laney grabbed Ruth's hands. "We can spend our mornings painting together!"

That cinched it. Laney hadn't looked this enthusiastic or happy in months. The girls had something in common. Perhaps Laney hit the nail on the head—that God sent Ruth as an answer to prayer. Maybe this was really going to work out.

CHAPTER FIVE

She was going to get him killed. Josh pushed Ruth against the wall and sandwiched her there with his back so if the mare kicked again, he'd take the brunt of it. "Whoa, girl. It's fine. You're fine."

"I'm not fine." Ruth poked him in the ribs. "You're squishing me."

"There's your baby." He kept a soothing stream of words going as he slowly dragged Ruth toward the gate to the foaling stall. He hoped she'd unlatch it and get out. . . . *Only that's hoping for more sense than she has.*

"It's okay, girl." Josh nickered softly, moved slowly, and stayed vigilant. To his relief, he heard the latch on the gate scrape free.

"Got her, Josh," Felipe said.

Josh's relief disappeared an instant later when Ruth kept a handful of his shirt and dragged him backward, too. He reached around and manacled her wrist. A quick, hard squeeze, then he let go. To his relief, she got the message and turned loose of him. Though set free, he didn't move a muscle. The gate shut behind

59

him, and he stayed put. Humming, talking, remaining still, he coaxed Maxie to calm down.

The wobbly-legged foal tried to nurse, but Maxie nosed her away. Josh's heart dropped to his boots. The last thing he needed was for the already high-strung mare to reject her foal because Ruth took a mind to barge in where she didn't belong.

"Hey now. No use getting upset. Everything's fine."

From the corner of his eye he could see the back of Ruth's slim hand and puffy golden yellow sleeve come over the stall.

Slowly, he reached up and tried to shove it back, only she tucked a carrot into his hand and pulled her arm back of her own accord.

Maxie's ears twitched. She'd spied the carrot, and though she'd been given a fine warm bran mash after foaling late last night, that carrot caught her fancy. Now having someone in her foaling stall didn't seem to be so offensive. Josh broke it into pieces and offered a small section in the palm of his hand.

All of a sudden, Maxie turned sociable. She lipped the carrot, backed up a step, and downed the treat. It didn't escape Josh's notice how she'd put herself between him and the foal. That was a good sign. Right about now, he'd gladly accept any scrap of positive news.

He waited until Maxie snorted, then gave her another segment of the carrot. Bite by bite, he regained her cooperation, if not her trust. After giving her the last chunk, Josh figured he'd done about all he could—but Ruth seemingly disagreed. Her hand slipped over the stall again, this time with an apple. Where had she gotten these?

Maxie didn't care where the food came from. She loved apples. The fruit barely landed in Josh's hand before the mare swiped it.

Josh didn't cotton to the notion that a prize-winning brood-mare ate this stuff. What she needed was fresh, green grass. Plenty of water. Oats for a treat. Then again, he didn't dare try to wrestle the horse for the apple or turn to chide Ruth. Calm. Keeping calm and getting Maxie to stay tranquil—those were the most important things.

Smacking her lips, Maxie came back for more. "Greedy mama," Josh said in a low, humored tone.

Ruth's arm slid over the stall again. Dirt streaked the sleeve, but her hand stayed steady as could be as the mare approached and lipped the biggest lump of sugar Josh had ever seen from her palm.

What's next? His stomach growled. *Gravy and biscuits?* He couldn't fathom how Ruth produced all of that food.

But the foal approached Maxie, nudged up close, and started to nurse. Josh held his breath. Maxie allowed it. For having been in a rampaging rage just minutes earlier, the change was nothing short of a miracle. Well, maybe not a miracle, but the result of some hefty bribery. But it worked.

He sidled out of the stall, latched the gate, and turned toward Ruth. A few bits of hay littered her hem—but the skirts fluffed out from a plethora of petticoats and lacked hoops that would have made this whole episode a disaster. Dirt streaked the yellow bodice and sleeves of her city-pretty dress. Her hair straggled out of the pins, springing into touch-me curls all around her face, and the maddening woman had the unmitigated gall to wear an apologetic smile. "Please, let's not argue in front of her. I already upset her once."

"I'd call that belated good sense." Toledo dropped the bale of hay he'd carried over.

Josh shot the ranch hand a quelling look, then grabbed Ruth's arm and led her out of the stable. "You don't belong in here."

"Why not?" She stopped in a banner of early morning sunlight that turned her escapee tresses into spirals of glinting gold.

"Why not?" He couldn't believe she'd challenged his edict. Gritting his teeth, he said, "Because you practically got yourself kicked. Maxie could trample you in an instant. No one goes near a mare and her foal without good cause."

"I was trying to make friends."

"Friends." He caught himself repeating her words as if he'd been kicked in the head. "Miss Caldwell—"

"Ruth," she reminded him with a smile that was altogether too attractive.

He refused to be charmed. "Ruth, you could have gotten yourself maimed or killed. You upset a prized mare so badly, she nearly rejected her foal. I can't have you in there. You'll do irreparable damage if you don't get yourself killed."

"Are you telling me the animals on this farm aren't domesticated enough to be safe?"

"This is a ranch, not a farm."

"Thank you for reminding me of that." The crazy woman continued to smile at him. "But aren't the animals friendly?"

"These aren't pets." He sighed. "They're either work animals or food."

"But we treat them kindly on the Broken P, don't we?"

The pronoun she used struck him; she sure hadn't hesitated to claim what was hers. That whole issue rankled. He snapped, "Of course."

"I wanted to get a basic idea as to where everything was, so that when we discussed my chores, I'd know where to go."

"Chores?" Josh barely choked back his laugh of disbelief. "What do you think you'd be capable of doing?"

"I'm good with birds. Perhaps I could tend the chickens if you show me what to do."

"Chickens aren't kept in the stable."

Her eyes widened and she burst out laughing. When she covered her mouth, Josh noted that her fingers weren't clean. He couldn't help wondering how often Ruth had to wash her hands and face and change her clothes—the woman possessed the singular habit of getting dirty. Laney always looked as if she'd stepped out of her *Godey's Ladies' Book*. He wondered who would rub off on whom. Then again, he didn't. In a way, he wouldn't mind seeing Laney a little less starchy.

He took out his bandana and wiped a smudge from Ruth's cheek. "When you go to town to shop, you'd better buy material for more dresses—ones for ranch living."

"You're so very kind to suggest that, but it's unnecessary." She took the bandana from him and used it to dust off her sleeve—to no avail. "I promised Mama I wouldn't wear mourning."

"I couldn't care less if you don't wear black. Color is fine."

"My gowns are made of material that employs the new color-fast aniline dyes. They all wash and won't fade." She cast a glance back toward the house. "If your concern is about the style, your sister wears full skirts, too."

"Laney wouldn't dream of coming out to the stable."

Ruth's shoulders slumped. "I don't suppose she would. Just spending last evening with her convinced me she's a perfect lady. I may as well confess so you don't have to make the disappointing discovery for yourself: I can't seem to mind all of the rules for young ladies."

"The rules that matter most around here are the ones I set."

"I'll do my best to follow them, but my curiosity is insatiable. I'll go where I'm not supposed to—"

"Thanks for the warning, but I figured that out after that debacle just now."

She compressed her lips, then added, "Whilst I'm confessing, I may as well lay all of my flaws before you, so you're forewarned: I have a tendency to speak my mind when I ought to hold my tongue, and I invent ways to get into trouble."

"Is that so?"

Slowly, she nodded. "One headmistress declared I'd try even Job's patience."

Her apologetic smile and guileless eyes proclaimed she'd told the truth, but an underlying sadness seeped through the words. Josh realized the admission hadn't been easy. Then again, he wished it weren't true. With "recommendations" like that, this young woman would prove to be more of a liability than he wanted around.

"It's plain to see ranching is hard work and there's plenty to get done, Josh. I'm not about to sit on the veranda and watch you and the hands do it all. I want to do my fair share."

"Impossible."

"Josh—"

He loomed over her and growled, "Dad knew what he was doing, and he busted his arm out here. You're liable to kill yourself or get someone else killed when they try to save you. Make no mistake about it, Ruth Caldwell—this is a man's world."

"Surely there are things a woman could do."

"Nope."

The corners of her mouth tightened in exasperation. "Did I catch you at a bad time, or are you always this stubborn?"

"When it comes to safety issues, I'm unyielding."

"Then it makes perfect sense for us to decide how I can pull my weight around here."

She looked entirely too satisfied with herself, and Josh failed to see the logic of her comment. He would tell her so, too.

"By giving me specific chores, I'll be so busy, I won't get into . . . situations." Her rationale made him want to groan; yet she continued on as if he not only understood, but was in complete agreement with her. "With all there is to accomplish, there must be many responsibilities I can shoulder."

"Like what?"

Her eyes sparkled. "Chicken tending, for one thing."

"Chicken tending." *There I go again, repeating her words. But only a city gal would even concoct such a term.* "I suppose we could arrange some of that." *And only that. Nothing more. If it salves your pride, then I'll grant you that one chore.*

"What else?" she pursued eagerly.

"More than anything, Laney needs your attention. When Mom passed away, Dad sent her back East to a finishing school. He brought her home just over a year ago, and she's been lonely. I know she's looking forward to painting with you."

"Oh. Was I being obtuse? When you suggested buying fabric, I assumed you meant my clothing might be unsuitable. If your sister enjoys sewing, I'd be happy to play along with your plan."

"I hold no doubt that you'll need more dresses." *Yesterday you spilled water all over yourself, and today you've gotten dirt everywhere. It's a wonder you only brought two trunks.*

"What about your sister?"

"My sister could probably use a new one or two, herself." He nodded at that brilliant plan. It would keep them together and Ruth out of his way.

While he was at it, he might as well toss a few other projects her way to add time and distance. "Laney mentioned curtains for your room. She spent a lot of time and attention on her own bed-chamber and is rightly proud of the results. I don't doubt for a moment that stitching curtains and painting your walls would give her considerable satisfaction."

Ruth perked up. "You'll allow us to paint the walls?"

"Sure. Why not?"

"It'll be messy."

"Life is chaotic, Ruth." He gestured in an arc. "Look around us. Felipe is mucking out the stable. The pigs are wallowing in mud. Even Hilda's good cooking makes for a jumble in the kitchen. I don't expect much ever gets done without the effort causing a mess. Stuff can be tidied up afterward—but the results are what matters."

"Oh, I like your way of thinking!"

"You'd best scamper along back into the house and freshen up. Dad plans to go to town after breakfast, and he doesn't cotton to waiting on anyone."

"I suppose I could meet the animals later today."

Stubbornly folding his arms across his chest, Josh glowered at her. "You'll stay away from the beasts unless someone is with you."

"Yes, well, that seems like a reasonable request."

"It wasn't a request; it was an order. Regardless of the finer points of who owns what, this place has to turn a profit. Dad sees to the business matters; I'm in charge of the working end of things. Any mistake is costly, and you're going to have to face the fact that you're wholly ignorant and must rely on us to make decisions."

"I'm good at sums. I could help your father with the books and free him up to see to other matters."

Josh shook his head. "Ruth, Dad busted his left arm right after we struck up the partnership with your father. I'm sure you noticed it's not quite right. He can't lift heavy loads or do most of the physical labor. Handling the books and business end of the ranch lets him keep his pride. I want your word that you won't horn in on him."

Her expression softened, and compassion deepened the green of her remarkable eyes. "I know what it's like to want to protect a parent. You just tell me what I need to do, and I'll work with you in every way possible."

"For now, go back to the house. Dad won't want to wait to leave after breakfast, so you'd best uh . . ." He glanced meaningfully at her dress. "Spruce up a little."

"I'll do that." She pivoted around, then wheeled right back. Her skirts billowed and swept around his ankles. "And Josh? I'm sorry about the mare. Her new baby is darling. I didn't know she'd be so protective. I won't make that mistake again."

"Good." He watched as she grabbed fistfuls of her bright skirts, lifted them, and ran like a deer toward the house—straight through a mud puddle.

"Lord, help me. That woman's an accident waiting to happen."

***

"Thank you, Toledo." Laney smiled at the hand as he tipped his hat to them, then sauntered off. She patted her hoopskirts into submission and beamed at Ruth. "I told you we'd both fit back here."

Ruth surveyed the back of the buckboard and giggled. "Just barely."

"We're ladies." Laney leaned forward and whispered, "Besides, the hoops are far cooler whilst we walk about town. Furthermore, they force the riffraff to keep decent distance from us. I'll teach you all those tricks."

"It's already growing warm, isn't it?"

Laney popped open a parasol. Instead of being cloth, it boasted a beautifully painted papery canopy. "Here. I brought one for you, too. Josh went to San Francisco and toted back several of these for me. A Chinese woman painted them. Aren't they positively charming?"

"Lovely. And it's so kind of you to share."

"We're practically sisters now. Of course we'll share things." Laney twirled her parasol until the decoration on it reached just the right spot. "I brought Hilda's list along, so you and I can spend time in the mercantile. Daddy hates to shop. He'll likely wander off and pick us up. It's perfectly safe."

"I'm sure he wouldn't leave you if he felt any danger existed."

"That's right," McCain said as he swaggered up and climbed into the front of the buckboard. He used his left arm as a counterbalance and managed the feat with surprising grace. "Laney's welfare is uppermost in my mind. You, too, Ruth. Now that you're under my roof, you're part of the family."

"You've all been most welcoming. I'm unaccustomed to having men around. I'll beg your forgiveness because I'm sure I'll probably charge ahead at times."

"You didn't grow up with a man as the head of your home," McCain declared as he picked up the reins. "But now that you're under my roof and authority, the natural order of things will assert itself."

Ruth thought about what he'd said and couldn't convince

herself that Mr. McCain had spoken the truth. Simply put, self-control and self-determination were her problems, just as they always had been. Having men around merely complicated the matter because McCain assumed she'd acquiesce to him, and when it came to Josh—well, she couldn't begin to decide what he thought.

Lacking any appreciable exposure to men, Ruth couldn't figure out where she stood with Josh. Yesterday he'd been the personification of kindness when he told her of her father's passing. Even in his anger over the ranch's ownership, he'd thought to provide for her. Then, too, he'd waded through all of the awkwardness regarding Madame Velvet—surely that counted as a point in his favor. Mad as he'd been to discover her in Maxie's stall, Josh still put himself in jeopardy for Ruth's sake. But beneath all of that, she knew he'd probably summed up his whole stance the moment they met when he said she shouldn't have come.

I promised Mama I'd come and live here, no matter what. I was foolish to pledge that to her. Father's not here, but I'm still honor bound to remain in California. Not that there's anywhere else for me to stay. I'll have to make the best of this.

The ride into Folsom rated as far more comfortable than the stuffy stage. Fresh air, good company, and lighter clothing made for a pleasant journey. Best of all, Laney told her stories about her father. Mr. McCain originally warned, "Laney, you'll make Ruth sad if you say things about the daddy she never knew."

"Oh, please—I'd be delighted to know anything you could tell me."

"Well, then," McCain drawled, "there was the time Alan decided he was goin' eyeball to eyeball with the orneriest colt on the Broken P. We all worried he'd get stomped to death. All that worry was in vain. Alan moseyed into the corral wearin' his holster. I thought for sure he was drawin' a pistol, but he pulled out the fattest carrot you ever did see. . . ."

Ruth listened avidly, and in no time at all, Mr. McCain was parking the rig in a field across from the Pony Express office. Three other buckboards lined up there as well, but it made sense. Main Street rode the swell of a hill. Anyone leaving a conveyance in front of most businesses would come out to find it rolling away.

Squiring a girl on either side of him, Mr. McCain headed toward the boardwalk. "I'll leave you gals in the mercantile. Business needs tending, and I can't see me shuffling around the dry goods while you dither over fripperies. Stay put, and I'll collect you when I'm done."

"Yes, Daddy." Laney went up on tiptoe and pressed a kiss on his cheek.

Four rather steep wooden steps led from the field up to the level of the boardwalk. McCain dropped back a step and kept hold of the girls' arms to help them balance. Even then, there wasn't quite enough space up on the boardwalk. Ruth hesitated a moment to allow Laney to move ahead so there would be sufficient room for their hoopskirts. Mr. McCain momentarily released her.

Several cowboys stood on the corner. They murmured greetings and shuffled for a better look at Laney. The next thing Ruth knew, someone bumped her. She lost her footing and tumbled off the boardwalk and straight into the street.

CHAPTER SIX

Now who would this be, fallin' into my arms?" A young red-headed man caught and righted her just before she toppled in front of a wagon rolling by.

"I'm sorry. How clumsy of me. Thank you."

"Ruth!" Laney leaned forward and looked down at her. "Are you okay?"

"I'm thinkin' she's far more than just okay, Elaine McCain," the man said as he continued to keep a grip on Ruth. He grinned at her. "The lass is fair as the day is long."

"O'Sullivan." Mr. McCain nodded. "Thanks for saving our Ruth. Ruth, are you all right?"

"Yes, thanks to this gentleman."

"Galen O'Sullivan at your service." The young man swept off his hat and gave a courtly bow—one that would earn even Miss Pettigrew's approval.

"We're much obliged." Mr. McCain extended his hand to Ruth. From the front of the street, it was one huge step up onto the boardwalk. Ruth reached for his hand.

"Permit me." Galen cinched his hands about her waist and

71

lifted her as if she weighed as little as Laney.

"Thank you both." Ruth wished she'd brought her fan. Hot as her face felt, it probably looked red as a barn. No one formally introduced her to Mr. O'Sullivan, and she couldn't decide whether to introduce herself or stay silent. Just yesterday she'd introduced herself to Madame Velvet. Perhaps it was best for her to hold her tongue.

"You must be more careful," McCain said gently. "Things here are rough."

Ruth didn't want to argue with him, but someone had bumped her. Then again, if she weren't so awkward, she would have kept her balance.

"All's well that ends well," Laney chirped. "We'll be fine, Daddy. You take all the time you need. Ruthie and I will enjoy ourselves."

He chuckled. "I know when I've been dismissed. Just as well. I have men I need to see." He opened the door to the mercantile, allowed them inside, and then sauntered off.

"There's nothing worse than Daddy shuffling from one boot to the other when I shop," Laney confided. "He has to be the most impatient man God ever made."

"You're blessed to have a father," Ruth said.

"I am. And he spoils me rotten. Come on. Let's go look at the fabric first. You need curtains, a counterpane, and new dresses."

"Actually, I wanted to ask you if you'd mind helping me make a quilt like the one you have on your bed. I thought it would be fun to make it out of feed sacks. Hilda has a stack in the mud-room."

"Sure, we can do that." Laney sashayed toward the fabric.

Ruth admired her smooth glide. Try as she might to move with such grace, Ruth always felt her skirts swayed back and forth like a church bell. Exerting pressure on the sides of her hoops, she managed to compress them sufficiently to walk down the aisle between two rows of sundry items and joined Laney.

"Good day, ladies." A lanky storekeeper slipped from behind

the counter. "How can I help you?"

Laney pulled a piece of paper from her sleeve. "Hello, Lester. Hilda wrote down a list. Could you please fill it while we look around? Thank you ever so much."

"I'd be delighted to." He accepted the list, then ran his hand over a nearby bolt. "If you're looking for material, I got a shipment from Lowell—came in through San Francisco since the last time you were in town."

"You always carry a wonderful selection," Laney praised.

Ruth watched as Laney visited a few minutes with the storekeeper. She chatted effortlessly, and the man hung on her every word. Just like the cowboys on the corner, he was smitten. Back at school, all of the pretty manners seemed so frivolous; but watching Laney effortlessly employ them, they were natural and charming. With her feminine ways, petite frame, and sweet words, Laney had probably won the heart of every man for miles around.

I could live to be one hundred and never show a fraction of her poise. When I get to heaven, I'm going to ask God why measles are catching and manners aren't.

Studying Hilda's list, Lester ambled off. Laney surveyed the bolts and let out a small sigh. "I'm so tired of wearing the same old thing."

"Josh said we could get material for you."

"I know." Laney trailed her fingertips along a length of brilliant magenta cloth. "But I'll end up doing the same as I always do. I'll settle for something brown or cream or gold or green instead of one of the new, vibrant colors that are so stylish. Anything else looks hideous with my hair."

"I think your hair looks like cinnamon and spice all mixed together." After the words left her mouth, Ruth felt gauche. "I mean, the color is beautiful. Rich."

"It's ugly. Watch." Laney held the magenta up to her throat.

"I think the color of that fabric is hideous." Once she realized she'd spoken her thought aloud, Ruth glanced to see if Lester overheard her. To her relief, he seemed too preoccupied to have been eavesdropping. She dropped her volume and used a term Miss Pettigrew used as one of her worst adjectives. "It's garish."

"I suppose it might be." Laney dropped it. "But for once in my life, I'd love to wear pink."

"Why don't you?"

"Mama said a redhead oughtn't ever wear pink."

A derisive male snort from directly behind them made Ruth jump. The man who caught her when she fell from the boardwalk folded his arms akimbo. "You know my ma, Laney. Redder hair you'll ne'er see, but she wears pink, and I think she's beautiful in it."

"Your mother would look beautiful in a burlap sack." Laney grabbed Ruth's hand. "Ruth, this is Galen O'Sullivan. Galen, this is Ruth Caldwell. She's living with us at the Broken P."

"Thank you for your assistance earlier," Ruth said.

"The pleasure 'twas all mine, I assure you." He grinned at her. "Would you be kin to the dearly departed Alan Caldwell?"

"Yes. He was my father." Odd, how that one word never felt right. How could she call a man her father when she'd never seen him or heard his voice?

Galen nodded. "I remember Alan havin' a heart for the Lord those last years. You can be sure he's walkin' the streets of gold even as we speak."

"It's kind of you to say so."

Laney squeezed Ruth's hand. "How is your father, Galen?"

Ruth wondered whether that squeeze had been a supportive gesture or a warning that Galen's father was in failing health.

"Ma sent me to fetch red flannel. She's wantin' to apply an onion poultice to his chest."

"I'm sorry he's ill." Ruth remembered all of the treatments she'd tried in vain to help Mama.

"We have plenty of onions in our garden," Laney said. "I'll be sure to bring some by." Her eyes sparkled as she turned back to

Ruth. "The O'Sullivans are our nearest neighbors. Their place is one of the Pony Express exchange stations!"

"How exciting! I read all about the Pony Express when I was back East." Ruth couldn't contain her enthusiasm. "It sounds like a very dangerous and exciting undertaking."

"I suppose you could say that. For sure there are plenty of troubles."

"Do you ride for the Pony Express?" Ruth asked.

Galen laughed. "Not me, lassie. The riders have to weigh less than one hundred twenty-five pounds. I was born weighin' more than that—at least to hear my ma tell of it. No, I help with the horses—good, fast horses with the ability to run for at least ten miles straight. That's where we come in at the station. It's all a matter of having a horse ready at the right time." Galen shrugged. "Fine horses, they are. I'd best not dally. With Da under the weather, I've plenty to see to."

"Here, then. Take the red flannel." Ruth let go of Laney's hand and reached for the bolt.

"Thanks." He accepted it and gave Laney a stern look. "I'll be expectin' to see you in a grand new dress at church soon—a pink one. Else I'll have your daddy send you to bed without supper." With that, he walked over to the counter.

Laney let out a dainty sigh and gave Ruth a helpless look. She stooped, ostensibly to inspect some of the material on the lower shelf. Ruth ducked down beside her.

"He's so wonderful, but he treats me as if I'm his little sister. I declare, Ruth, I make a fool of myself every time Galen O'Sullivan comes around!"

"Nonsense. You were gracious to offer him onions."

"I can't believe I did that. His mother has the best garden in the whole township!"

"That doesn't mean she planted a lot of onions."

"I'm sure she did. I've eaten her stew." Laney's mouth turned downward. "The woman grows everything in abundance—carrots, onions, potatoes, tomatoes, beans—just everything!"

"I noticed the garden back at the ranch." Ruth couldn't honestly tack on any words of praise. The patch rated as one of the most sorrowful things she'd seen in a long time. "Perhaps we could ask Mrs. O'Sullivan for some suggestions."

"We could!" Laney perked up, then blushed and added in a hasty whisper, "Don't think I'm searching for an excuse just to go gawk at Galen. His mother is wonderful. I love to spend time with her."

Ruth leaned closer and whispered back, "Even if it were just so you could catch a glimpse of Galen, I'd help you concoct an excuse. Isn't that what friends are for?"

Laney brightened considerably. "If I don't go alone, it's not improper for me to see him."

Knees cramping, Ruth rose. "That will work out beautifully."

"What will?" Lester came over and looked at the selection of fabric.

Ruth hastily pulled out a bolt of crisp, pale pink dimity. "This. Won't Laney be beautiful in this? We need to add lace and maybe a white bodice to it."

"Not white," Laney moaned. "I look dead in white. Eggshell or candlelight—but even then, I don't believe it's a good color."

"Miss Elaine, you'd look fetching in any color." Lester bobbed his head as if to agree with himself. "Yes, you would."

"What about Ruth?" Laney deflected his attention quite smoothly.

He took the pink from Ruth and cocked his head to the side. "What about that new lavender right beside you, Miss Elaine? The two of you would look like—" he searched for a moment—"like a pair of sweet peas next to one another in the pink and lavender."

Laney would definitely look dainty as a little sweet pea, but I'll look more like a spill of wisteria.

"I adore wisteria!"

It wasn't until Laney's exclamation that Ruth realized she'd spoken aloud. Ruth muffled a groan.

"Here. We'll need a dress length of the lavender." Laney handed Lester the bolt. "Ruth, you'll need riding clothes. Something dark. Green? Blue? Oh, look at this handsome paisley!"

"It wouldn't show the dirt." Ruth figured that was about the best thing she could summon to say about the homely brown print.

"It needs to be livened up. Lester, we'll want to match this with some grosgrain ribbon. We could bring out the golden yellow and rust, don't you think, Ruth?"

Ruth wrinkled her nose. "I can't see going to a lot of fuss over a riding skirt. I'd rather just do something plain."

"Trust me. I saw a print in *Godey's* that would be ideal. In fact, Lester, I want some of that material, too. Ruth and I will have matching riding skirts! Won't that be fun?"

Laney's enthusiasm proved contagious. "We could do that. We'll reverse the ribbon, though. One will be gold on top, and the other will be rust."

"You'll be able to tell 'em apart then." Lester added that bolt to the stack in his arms.

As he walked off, Ruth glanced down, then murmured, "The length alone would tell us which is whose. If we ever switched them, you'd be tripping everywhere, and I'd have to walk on my knees to keep my ankles from showing."

"What a sight we'd be!" Laney turned back to the fabric. "I need a new Sunday-best dress. My cream-and-brown brocade is far too hot for summer. What do you think of the taffeta?"

"The water-stained green is gorgeous. So is the ombré blue stripe."

"You take the green. It's Josh's favorite color, you know." Laney draped a swath across Ruth. "Oh, it brings out your remarkable eyes! I'll take the stripe."

"You and your brother are very close, aren't you?"

"Yes. God blessed me with a wonderful big brother. When Mama took sick, Josh helped me care for her." Laney blinked back tears. "Then he sent me little packages almost every week while I was at school. In fact, he knew it took forever for mail to get through, so he sent some before I even left to make sure I'd have something soon after I arrived!"

"How thoughtful!" Ruth filed those facts away. Mama always said you could tell a lot about a man by how he treated his mother and sisters. Under the circumstances, she needed to assess him. *I've probably seen him at his worst. Any man learning he might lose a portion of his ranch would have just cause to be in a bad temper.*

Laney continued to hold the fabric up to Ruth. "Yes, this green is just made for you!"

"It is pretty." *And if green is Josh's favorite color, I suppose wearing it to please him wouldn't be a bad idea.* In fact, the notion of making Laney's big, strong brother happy suddenly seemed like a fine notion. Nodding her head, Ruth said, "I'll take it."

"Wonderful!" Laney shoved the bolt into Ruth's hands and turned to the linen and lace. "What color engageantes shall we make to go with it?"

The whole notion of making lacy false undersleeves struck Ruth as preposterous. "I thought things were simpler in the West."

"Ladies are ladies, no matter where they abide." Laney frowned a moment. "Let's wait to decide what color, because your fabric choices for everyday dresses might influence your decision."

"We already decided on the lavender dimity."

"You need more everyday dresses," Laney chirped.

"This is gracious plenty."

Laney shook her head. "No, no. Josh specifically told me that you're to have four everyday dresses, and we only have the one for you so far."

"Four! Why would your brother—"

"He said I'm to have a few, too," Laney said absently as she surveyed the bolts. "Among the books and magazines you brought, I noticed you had a copy of *Les Modes Parisienne.*"

"I did?" Ruth shrugged. "Bernadette must have slipped it in there. I wouldn't have."

"I'm glad! We'll be able to copy the patterns. I'd like to make something especially fashionable for the state fair in the fall."

"The state fair? You'll go?"

"Of course we'll go. I'll ask Josh to take us. Actually, Hilda will make him. She won second place last year for the best tub of lard. This muslin here went out of style years ago." Laney skipped a segment of bolts, then clapped her hands. "Can't you imagine a mantlette of this?"

Ruth couldn't reconcile a discussion that combined a tub of lard with the latest fashions. For once in her life, she was speechless.

Yards of eyelet, cotton, ribbon, and lace, a gallon of whitewash, and brown-paper-wrapped packages for Hilda filled the back of the buckboard. Laney settled herself on one of the packages, smoothed her hoops over many of the others, and smiled down at Ruth. "There's plenty of room."

Back home, when Bernadette said hoops could cover a multitude of sins, she meant an extra slice of cake or a few lemon drops. Ruth determined to write Bernadette a letter and expound on just how much her hoops managed to hide today.

One of the local men had lifted Laney into the buckboard. He rubbed his hands together. "You ready, Miss Caldwell?"

"Um..." She positioned her hands to keep control of her skirts. "Yes. Thank you."

Though she didn't manage as gracefully as Laney had, Ruth consoled herself with the knowledge that she hadn't flipped her skirts up over her head.

"Back East, the men weren't nearly as strong or handsome as they are here," Laney declared.

A picture of broad-shouldered, suntanned Josh flashed in Ruth's mind. "Strong and handsome. Yes." As soon as she spoke, she wondered *What's come over me?*

"I don't care how strong or handsome they are." McCain leveled a stern gaze at his daughter. "You're too young to be thinking about that yet."

Laney dipped her head and made no reply.

Ruth suspected this wasn't the first time they'd had this discussion. At seventeen, Laney wasn't particularly young for some courting. An abundance of women were married by her age. From the way things had gone in town, Ruth could see Laney wouldn't suffer any lack of swains at her doorstep once her father allowed her some latitude.

Maybe he's being stern because he's embarrassed that he couldn't lift us up. Ruth waited until Mr. McCain started the buckboard into motion, then said, "If your father and brother are any example, I'd have to say Western men are extremely intelligent and kind."

"We've got plenty of men out here. Not half as many women," McCain said gruffly. "No use in either of you girls being swept off your feet when you're still wet behind the ears."

"You forgot," Laney said, "to mention that they're overprotective."

The next morning Josh saw Toledo standing at the stable door, peering at something. Wondering what it was, he strode out of the stable and ran straight into Ruth. "What're you doing here?" he barked as he grabbed her arms to keep from knocking her over.

"Laney and I are going to take a ride."

"I specifically ordered you not to come to the stable alone."

"I didn't." Ruth stood her ground and told that lie without blinking.

Toledo silently slipped off. Josh frowned, both at the hand's behavior and Ruth's lie. "No one's with you."

"Your sister will be with me in just a moment."

"Where is she?"

"She paused a moment."

"Paused?" When Ruth's cheeks went red, Josh felt like a dolt for not immediately understanding her meaning. He tugged on the basket hanging from her arm. "What do you have in here?"

"Onions."

"You're not feeding my livestock onions!"

"Of course I won't. These are intended for Mr. O'Sullivan."

He folded his arms akimbo. "After yesterday, you can't blame a man for wondering. You brought half a pantry into my stable with you."

Ruth smiled at his assertion. "Come, now. It was only a carrot, an apple, and a little sugar."

"I've never once fed a lump of sugar that size to a horse." He cast a glance at the onions and let out a gusty sigh. "Do you usually haul around fruits and vegetables to meet animals and people?"

"Flowers are nice, too." She didn't bat an eye at his tongue-in-cheek question. "Laney and I met Galen O'Sullivan in town yesterday. His father is ailing, so Laney promised them onions."

"I need to see Galen. I'll take the onions."

"Oh, no! Really, we want to go."

She sounded entirely too enthusiastic. Josh's eyes narrowed. "Why?"

"After reading all about them, I want to see the Pony Express horses. Then, too, I ought to meet our neighbor."

Our neighbor? Yesterday it wasn't a slip of the tongue when she called this our ranch. She's changed her mind from not necessarily wanting the land to being dead set on claiming a share of the Broken P.

Oblivious to his dark thoughts, Ruth went on. "Laney sang Mrs. O'Sullivan's praises."

"Kelly O'Sullivan's a good woman." Josh thought for a moment. "I'll take you and Laney over, but I can't afford to wait for you to visit all morning. How well do you ride?"

"In a lady's saddle—"

Josh closed his eyes in horror. She used a sidesaddle? They

didn't even have one anywhere on the Broken P.

"—I'm an absolute disaster. In a western saddle, I'm quite adept—if I do say so myself."

"Sidesaddles are deathtraps out here. We don't have any."

"Oh, good!" Ruth's face lit up. "Miss Pettigrew and Mrs. Raventhal—they were the headmistresses at the last two schools I attended—both insisted upon sidesaddles. They're terribly old-fashioned and miserable."

"The headmistresses or the saddles?"

Ruth burst out laughing. "Both!"

He filed away the implication that she'd been a pupil at more than one of those fancy schools. Tempted to inquire about the details, he squelched his questions. Doing so would go against the "Code of the West." Folks left behind their failures, shortcomings, and history when they crossed the Mississippi. Everyone deserved a fresh chance—a tacit understanding men out here extended to one another. After her admission yesterday that she'd not succeeded at being society's darling, Josh figured he owed her the same opportunity. That determination didn't cancel his curiosity, though. Ruth rated as the most enigmatic woman he'd ever met.

He decided to see if she'd chatter and reveal more about herself if given the opportunity. "So you attended more than one school?"

"Several." She wrinkled her nose. "Actually, now that I think about it, the headmistresses were worse than the saddles. I survived them, but they were all certain they wouldn't survive keeping me around. In case you haven't noticed, I tend more toward disastrous than decorous."

"Hmm." He couldn't come up with a polite way of agreeing with her assessment.

Shrugging, she said, "I can't honestly say I regret slipping away from a vapid poetry recitation to go fishing. Fishing is far more interesting. Then, too, I'd be lying to say I'd ever remember any of those moves with the fan to convey a message. I'd likely rest it against the wrong cheek and signal no when I meant yes. If God meant for a woman to talk with a fan, He would have created her with one attached to the wrist and not given her a mouth." She let out a little laugh. "And plainly, my mouth is with me wherever I go; the same cannot be said of my fan."

He chuckled and didn't voice the opinion that a fan might have been an improvement on a select few women he knew. Josh admired Ruth for coming away from what had probably been unhappy situations with a sense of humor. In all fairness, some of the affectations drilled into young girls rated as ludicrous. He had to agree that fishing rated far above poetry recitation, too.

"When Laney returned home, half the stuff she learned at that fancy finishing school was nonsense. She's still kept some odd notions, but Dad and I let her have 'em."

"Your sister is delightful."

"Yeah, she is." Maybe Ruth wasn't quite as bumbling as she thought. Perhaps the places she went were ridiculously outdated in their expectations. "Laney's school put the gals in buggies instead of sticking them in sidesaddles."

"Sidesaddle?" Laney echoed as she walked up. "Those are dreadfully old-fashioned. The pictures look so romantic, though."

"There's nothing romantic about falling off and nursing a crop of bruises," Ruth said.

"Oh my!" Laney gave her a startled look. "Are you able to ride in a regular saddle, or shall we take the buckboard?"

"I can ride." Ruth looked down and scuffed the toe of her shoe in the dirt. "And I've fired a pistol, too. Just don't ask about my aim."

Staring at her in disbelief, Josh rasped, "You own a gun?"

She looked up at him. "I couldn't very well travel across the nation without some form of protection."

"Where is it?"

"Up in my room. The housekeeper's husband bought a muff pistol for me. It's really quite pretty."

"Is it loaded?"

"It wouldn't do me any good if it weren't." Ruth shrugged. "Then again, I'm not sure it would have done me any good, anyway. I never did manage to shoot a single one of the jars Hadley lined up for me to hit."

Josh decided then and there he'd gain possession of that little pistol before she hurt herself or someone else.

"I'm far better with a knife," Ruth said. "I don't mean to sound boastful, but I can hit just about anything with my knife."

Yeah, just about anything except what she'd aim at. This woman is a menace.

"Really?" Laney's voice carried wonderment.

"Hadley taught me when I was about nine. He was our handyman and said every woman ought to have a trick or two up her sleeve to defend herself. Mama believed staying in good company was protection enough, but with my penchant for finding trouble, Hadley decided it just made sense for me to carry a little something."

"Let me get this right." Josh glowered at Ruth. "You've carried a knife?"

"But you've never had to use it." Laney patted Ruth's arm.

Ruth blushed.

"Whom did you hit?" Josh gave her an accusing look.

"Not who," Ruth hedged. "What." She hitched her shoulder as if the whole matter were inconsequential. When Josh gave her a stern look, she grudgingly provided, "A hat."

"And just who," he demanded, "was wearing the hat at that time?"

"The mayor." Ruth's chin tilted in defiance. "But he had no business skulking in the bushes when we were playing croquet. Mrs. Spandler about had kittens over the incident, and I couldn't convince her that I knew precisely where the knife would land. All she could do was imagine my committing murder while attending her school."

That accounted for her dismissal from one place. So far, she'd named three headmistresses. Given this recent revelation, Josh didn't doubt for a single moment that the count would continue to rise. Wondering what else she'd done and fearing what more she might do, Josh demanded, "Do you always carry a knife with you?"

Ruth nodded.

He stuck out his hand in a silent command.

She passed the basket of onions to Laney. Slipping the fingers of her right hand up her left sleeve, Ruth didn't even look down. A second later, she produced a four-inch ivory piece. "It's spring-loaded. Be careful not to press the button."

He took the knife and hit the button. A three-and-one-half-inch blade swung out and clicked into place.

"Wow." Laney gawked at Ruth. "All I put up my sleeve is a hanky or a fan."

"You don't need this anymore."

"That's for me to decide." Ruth swiped back the knife, snapped the blade closed, and slipped it up her sleeve. "The West is reputed to be quite wild. I'm better able to take care of myself with this in my possession."

You're every bit as wild as the West. While that thought flashed through his mind, Josh watched as Ruth smoothed her skirts.

If that quintessentially feminine action weren't enough, she turned to Laney and gently rearranged the shawl to drape over her shoulder. "There. We can't let you catch a chill. Oh, you look so very lovely. Have I told you how reassuring it is not to have to take a calling card? I was seeing to so many details before I left home, I failed to pack many."

Josh looked at Ruth, doting on Laney and fussing. Given half a chance, perhaps she'd calm down and settle in. She'd figure out she didn't need that puny knife or have to do a man's work. *Time and a little patience—that's what she needs.*

She'd grown up without a father or brother to shield her. And she was beautiful enough to turn just about any man's head. Those realities suddenly took on a whole different significance. Josh figured he shouldn't be insulted that she wanted to safeguard herself. She didn't know any better. With time, she'd learn to trust him. Until then, if a little bitty knife gave her a sense of safety, he wouldn't kick. "You go ahead and carry that knife as long as you think you need to, Ruthie."

"I will."

"But I get the gun."

"It's too small for you. It would practically fall out of your holster."

"I don't plan to carry it. I just don't want you to."

"Then it's perfectly fine up in my bedchamber." Ruth's face lit up as she looked at Laney. "Maybe we could talk Galen into teaching us how to shoot it!"

Josh gritted, "Over my dead body."

CHAPTER SEVEN

"All ready, my love." Galen gave the mare an affectionate pat on the withers. He took up the reins, led the snappy little mustang out to the fence, and tied her there. She tossed her head and whinnied as if eager to get to her job.

"Expecting an exchange, I see," Josh called out as he rode up, flanked by a young woman on either side.

"The rider's due anywhere from ten minutes to a half hour from now."

"You don't know the precise time?" Laney asked.

"Horses can't tell time, lass." Galen reached up to help Laney dismount. "Did you listen to me and buy something pink yesternoon?"

"I did."

He turned to assist Miss Caldwell down, but he was too late; Josh beat him to it. *A shame, that.* Galen rather enjoyed the odd way they'd met yesterday when she fell from the boardwalk. He made a mental note to be sure to help her mount up again when she took her leave. "And you, Miss Caldwell—did you find anything that suited you?"

"The only fabric Laney didn't suggest I needed was the red flannel you bought." Ruth smiled at him. "I think she's of the opinion that as long as she keeps me sewing, I'll stay here."

"Then we'll have to be sure Lester stocks plenty of material at the mercantile."

"I brought onions for your daddy." Laney touched his arm. "How's he feeling?"

"He was still asleep when I left the house. Run on up and find out for yourself. I'm sure Ma would love to see you."

Ruth lagged back. "Will it be too taxing for your parents to have guests?"

"Nay, not a-tall." Galen shook his head. "You're new here, but you'll find out fast that the door's always open at the O'Sullivans'. Da and Ma love folks droppin' in. 'Tis a blessing to have the company of friends."

Laney tugged on his sleeve. "You'll call us out when the rider comes, won't you?"

"No need. You'll hear the hooves a-flyin'. Ma likes to give the riders a bit to eat or drink. Mayhap you could bring that out this time."

"How exciting!" Laney turned loose of him, grabbed Ruth's hand, and headed for the house.

When they were out of earshot, Josh murmured, "Laney's got it bad for you."

"She'll get o'er it." His friend gave him a dark look. "I'm not a man to play a woman false. I can't pretend to feel that way for her. I know she's seventeen, but she's still a wee lassie to me, Josh."

"Don't you break her heart."

"Half of the attraction is Ma. Laney misses her mama, so when she comes here, the warmth fills her up. 'Tis understandable that she wants to gather it all in and be a part of it. In time, she'll see she can have all of the attention she craves from Ma without having to be shackled to me."

"She wouldn't consider it being shackled."

"I would." Galen squinted at the horizon and said nothing more. Six months and ... three days. He calculated it in that moment. That's how long it had been since Melinda ran off with the butcher from Sacramento and left him with a hole the size of Texas in his heart. Last he'd heard, they were expecting their first child. That news jolted him into finally letting go and realizing he had to move on with life.

"The girl's a beaut, isn't she?"

"Huh?" Galen jolted out of his thoughts.

"She's a beaut."

"Miss Caldwell?"

Josh chortled. "She is, too, but I was talking about this sweet little pony. I always had a fondness for her."

"Of the ones you sold me, she's my favorite, too." Galen gently caressed her nose. "Big heart and smart as can be."

"I promised you first pick of the next ones, and I have three horses about ready to sell. When you get a chance, come on over and take a look."

"I'll do that."

"Don't take too long. I have Eddie Lufe breathing down my neck about them."

Galen winced. "Time's pressing these days. When Da has another good day, I'll have a wee bit more freedom to come and go."

"What did Doc say?"

"Nothing good." The ground beneath Galen's boots stayed solid, but in his heart, it moved. Da always said the Lord should be a man's foundation, and Galen believed that to be true, but knowing his father's days were numbered still sent quakes through him.

Josh squeezed his shoulder. "I'm more sorry than I can say. When you need help, you holler."

"Ma and I have it under control. School ends in a few weeks. The boys'll be home during the daytime to pitch in."

"That Colin"—Josh grinned as he mentioned Galen's oldest

little brother—"I saw him riding off to school. He couldn't sit taller in the saddle. He's so proud to have a horse of his own to ride."

Galen chuckled. "That, he is. If I buy a pair of horses from you, Dale and Sean are going to pester me to let them ride alone instead of share a mount."

"I'm due to get my new saddle from Independence any day now." Josh cast a glance at the saddle on his gelding. "This one still has plenty of life in it. You're welcome to it."

"Buying the horses'll be a stretch already."

"I'm not selling it—" Josh stopped short, then grinned. "Yes, I am. You're going to have almonds and walnuts this fall. I want the very first pound of each."

"You can have them, regardless."

"And you can have the saddle, regardless." Josh stared him in the eye.

"We're getting by, Josh. We don't need charity."

"I know you don't need charity." Josh squinted over at the house, then looked back at him. "I'm offering my friendship and help. Your little brothers are going to have to do some growing up fast. Let's make it as painless as possible."

The knowledge that his brothers would be fatherless weighed heavily on Galen. He'd be the man of the house and have to provide a good example. Knowing Josh wanted to help bear the burden— well, that counted as a gift from the Almighty. "God blessed my family the day you moved into the Broken P."

"I think you got that backward." Josh let out a hefty sigh. "Hilda's good at cooking, cleaning, and such, but when it comes to Laney, she's no help at all. Dad and I are glad that Laney can run over here and talk to your mom."

"You have Ruth to help with that now."

"I'm not so sure she'll be much help. I gather she's good at getting herself into fixes. So far, she's proving my theory."

"Mayhap that streak of independence is what she needs to manage out here."

A wry smile kicked up the corner of Josh's lips. "I prayed last Sunday for more patience, and God sent Ruth here. What do you make of that?"

"You're a brave man to pray for such a thing." They both laughed.

Hooves beat in the distance. Galen turned to his left and watched as the Pony Express rider approached. Even if his speed didn't announce his identity, the customary outfit proclaimed it for him. The combination of a broad-brimmed hat, yellow bandana, red shirt, leather vest, and blue jeans was distinctive. "Looks like Sam Hamilton."

Laney twittered in the background, and soon the flurried sound of petticoats joined the thrumming hoofbeats. Laney and Ruth dashed across the yard and arrived at the fence just as the rider skidded to a halt.

"I'll get the mail," Galen said as Sam Hamilton dismounted.

"Obliged." Hamilton leaned over the fence. "Ah, ladies, that looks great!" He took a big wedge of pie from Laney and downed it in four huge bites.

While he ate, Galen sweet-talked the lathered pony as he yanked off the large, square leather *mochilla*. The mail in the four corner pouches barely shifted as Galen tossed the carrier onto the fresh mare. Long, customized slits allowed the saddlehorn and cantle to serve as anchors when the blanket-like leather carrier draped over the saddle.

Eager to work, the mare pranced in place. Galen untied her. "Ready to go."

The rider accepted the glass Ruth held out. He emptied it in a few quick gulps, passed it back, and mounted up. "Thanks!" With that, he was gone.

"Wasn't that exciting?" Laney looked up at Galen all bright-eyed.

"Absolutely," Ruth agreed. "I read all about the Central Overland California and Pike's Peak Express, but words on a page didn't do that justice."

Laney's smile melted into a look of utter confusion. "The Overland is the stage company."

"Overland Stage is what brought Ruth," Josh said, "but Central Overland California and Pike's Peak Express is the formal name for the Pony Express."

"Oh. I see." Laney's smile returned. "Galen, you were so quick changing out the mail."

Ruth twisted the empty cup she held and agreed, "You were. I'm surprised at a few things, though. It never occurred to me that the rider would sit on that whole mail pouch thing."

Galen shrugged. "His weight holds the mochilla in place and protects it. The four corner pouches distribute the weight so the horse carries it easily."

"But the horse..." Ruth cast a dubious look at the mustang. "I read that they were using the best-blooded horses money could buy. Back East, they have magnificent Morgans."

Galen chuckled and picked up the mustang's reins. "No horse is sturdier or hardier for California terrain than these mustangs. They're smart and tough. Whoever bought the horses paid attention to the task at hand and made a wise decision."

"I'm sorry." Ruth winced. "I didn't mean to insult your stock."

"No offense taken. You were merely thinkin' aloud and asking a reasonable question. Now, if you ladies will excuse me, I need to give this baby a cooldown."

The lasses went back into the house and Galen began to walk the beast around the yard.

Josh took a few paces along with them. "I led the girls to believe I rode over to let you know about the horses and to make sure Ruth wouldn't kill herself by falling off her mount."

"So why did you really come?"

Josh grimaced. "I can't swear to it, but I have an odd feeling that Toledo is following Ruth. I've caught him watching her the past two days."

"She's comely. Lively too. Such a lass is bound to catch any man's attention."

His friend shook his head. "I can't explain it. Something doesn't feel right. Do you mind if they stay awhile?"

"Ma always wanted a daughter. Whenever Laney drops by, Ma's the happiest woman in three counties. I'm sure she'll be thrilled with Ruth, too. Hold no worries about it, Josh. They're more than welcome to brighten Ma's days."

"Okay. Thanks."

"I'll keep a look out for anything strange."

"I'd appreciate that."

Trying to lighten the mood, Galen said, "Ruth looked capable in the saddle."

"She had to be." Josh finally chuckled. "God knew I didn't have the patience to teach a woman to ride."

After Josh left, Galen finished cooling down the Pony Express mount, then took it into the stable. Motes danced on the golden streams of light, turning the wooden structure into a haven. Galen loved the stable. A pleasant breeze blew through the doorway, helping cool the horse as Galen removed his saddle and tack.

Nostrils still flared and skin hot, the horse showed how hard he'd run to perform his duty. He pushed toward the trough.

"None of that for you, yet." Galen pushed him into a stall. "Drink too soon, and you'll founder. Here. This'll suit you better." He scooped water into an empty tin can and poured it over the horse's head and neck, then repeated the kindness and included its legs. "Feels fine, doesn't it? Cools you off."

The horse stood still and relished the attention. "You're a fine beast, you are. We'll cool you down, and later I'll be sure you have a treat. You'd like that, wouldn't you?"

"Do you always talk to animals?"

Galen turned around and looked at Ruth. "That, I do. To my

way of reckonin', Adam named them all. Why name something if you're not planning to talk to it again?"

She smiled. "You have a point. Your mother wanted to ask you something. Shall I lead the horse to water so he can have a drink?"

"Nay, lass. He'll sicken if he drinks too soon." Satisfied the horse was cooling down sufficiently, Galen led him to a stall and latched him in.

Ruth fell into step with him as he headed toward the house. "You're right about your mother."

"Hmm?" He shot her a questioning look.

"She's beautiful in pink."

Galen nodded. "Aye. She's a fine woman, and I don't mind sayin' so. 'Tisn't my doin', so it's not pride speaking. God gave her a heart for others, and that shines through."

He stomped his boots clean before entering the cabin. "Sam Hamilton just came through. All four pouches on the mochilla felt full. I'm thinkin' this Pony Express idea pleases folks even more than the organizers anticipated."

"The stage took just over three weeks to get here," Ruth said from beside him. "If the news is important, that is a long time compared to ten days."

"I always said bad news can wait and good news only gets better." Ma walked from Da's bedside and over to the stove, where she stirred something in a pot. "Galen, I was hopin' Josh was still here. Your da and I have been talkin' about takin' on another horse."

"Is that so?" Galen walked to the bedside and pulled up a chair. He leaned forward and rested his forearms on his thighs. "Truth be told, Da, Josh just offered us first pick of the three horses he's ready to sell."

Laney sidled over and handed Galen a tin cup of water. The tin felt cool to the touch, prompting thirst Galen hadn't realized he felt until now; but he lifted Da's head. "Here. Have a sip."

"Mmm. Thanks."

Laney didn't move. In fact, she rested her hand on his shoulder.

"You ought to get two of the three ponies. Really, you should. I heard Daddy and Josh talking, and the mustangs are the best ones yet. The other one—well, Josh calls him a headache on hooves."

Da looked at Galen. "Could be we'd go for two. You take a gander at them and use your best judgment."

"Laney," Ma called, "would you be a dear and fetch me some butter from the springhouse?"

"Sure. How much would you like?"

"One block. Warm as the days are growin', I don't dare keep extra in the house."

Laney's skirts whispered her departure, and Galen threw his mother a grateful look. She winked back at him.

Heat crept up Galen's neck when he caught Ruth's wide eyes. She'd seen the exchange. "I suppose I'll have to beg your discretion, Ruth Caldwell. Your friend Laney is a sweet lass, but that's all she is—a wee lassie."

Da let out a rusty laugh, then coughed. Galen lifted his head and shoulders and offered him another sip of water. "Ach, son, a bald head on a man can be excused, but a bald tongue—that's another matter."

"Da, I can't have anyone—most of all, Laney—thinking I return her fancy."

"It's a shame you don't." As soon as she spoke the words, Ruth clapped her hand over her mouth.

"The less fuss we all make of it, the better." Ma took a mixing bowl from a shelf and set it on the table. "There's not a lass alive who didn't set her cap for the wrong lad at some point in her tender years. Given time, our Laney'll meet the lad the good Lord intends for her. We all know 'tis the truth. In the meantime, we'll temper honesty with Christian love."

Galen looked to Ruth for some response. She slowly lowered her hand and moistened her lips. "I don't imagine I'd be much of a friend if I encouraged Laney to pursue eventual heartbreak."

"That's the truth of it." Ma briskly rubbed her hands together.

"Now, Galen, you get on back to your chores. I'm going to talk Laney and Ruth into staying the day. You just might find a nice treat on the table come dinnertime."

"Sure, Ma." Galen gave his father one last sip of water and rose. To his surprise, Ruth slipped to the other side of the bed.

"Mr. O'Sullivan, while your son's here, why don't we have him lift you into the rocking chair? By lunch, he'll be back and can tuck you in for another rest, but I'm sure you'd enjoy being able to sit by the window for a while."

"I'm strong enough to make it on my own."

Ma shook her spoon at Da. "The only way I'll let you up, old man, is if you promise not to boss me around in my kitchen."

"Kelly-mine," Da said as he shifted in the bed, "you must think I'm a fool if you believe I'd tamper with perfection."

"He's right, Ma. You're the best cook I know."

"You're the best cook I know, too," Laney said as she reentered the cabin. "Are we going to use the butter to bake something?"

"Aye." Ma smiled.

Ruth crossed the room, took the butter from Laney, and set it on the table. "But I'm sure we'll need eggs. I don't know where anything is. Why don't you take me out to the coop, and we'll gather eggs for Mrs. O'Sullivan?"

"I'd appreciate that." Ma handed her the egg basket.

Galen waited until they left, then hovered as his father threw back the quilt and hobbled to the rocking chair. Ma dragged it over to the window and tied back the drapery so Da could see as much as possible. Galen left the house as his mother tucked a lap blanket around his father. It hurt to watch them care for one another, knowing that whatever time they had would soon be over.

He headed back to the stable. There, he silently curried the horse. The repetitive action helped calm him. Afterward, he watered the pony and set him out to pasture.

Plenty of work needed doing, but he stood by the fence and looked at the property. Until two months ago, it had taken both him and Da to get all the chores done. As Da began to weaken, Galen started getting up earlier and going to bed later. He'd also taken to awakening his brother Colin in the morning to help with more chores before he left for school. With summer coming, he'd be able to rely on all three of his brothers for more help—*But, Lord, what will I do when the school year begins again? We can't afford to hire a hand.*

Galen knew he'd need a lot more help by then. He'd have to keep the boys out of school when it came harvesting time—something that troubled him no end. But he couldn't harvest the corn and do the haying alone.

There was also the orchard. Ma hadn't been able to decide what she wanted most, so Da gave her a little of everything. Their orchard boasted a variety of trees. Each corner of the lot held a half dozen nut trees—almonds in the east and west, pecans in the south, and walnuts in the north. A stripe of fruit trees drew a line between the nuts—apples on one side, orange on another, pears on a third, and sweet cherries on the last. In the middle of the plot, Mama grew her precious garden.

With all that food, a milk cow, and the chicken coop, Galen knew they'd be able to barter for staples. His family wouldn't go hungry. The money for the Pony Express would pay the mortgage. With God's blessing on the crops and careful stewardship, he'd be able to provide for his family. Still, responsibility weighed heavily on his shoulders.

Galen turned to get back to work, but halted. There in the distance, a man sat on his horse. Due to the sun's glare, Galen couldn't identify who it was. From the direction he faced, the figure wasn't looking at the stable, the fields, or the garden. He was staring directly at the clothesline, where Laney and Ruth were beating a rug.

CHAPTER EIGHT

"What do you think?" Ruth leaned back so Laney could look at the paint she'd just mixed.

"We can paint a flower here and there, then add more red to get a medium pink. After sprinkling more flowers around with it, we can add more red and have a rosy hue."

"This is so much fun!" Ruth straightened up and looked about her room. She and Laney had whitewashed the walls the day before. Ruth wore the same dress today. Careful as she'd been, she still got whitewash on the right sleeve and hem yesterday. As long as she might repeat that clumsiness, she figured to just make the damage worse instead of sacrificing another gown.

Josh was right about how work creates a mess, but most of it can be cleaned up. Well, everything but me. He's remarkably astute to have figured I need more dresses.

"I'm afraid we'll decide you need more pale pink after we've already darkened the mix," Laney confessed.

"Do you think Hilda has some empty jars? We could just pour each one half-full and not have to worry."

Several hours later, Ruth glanced across the wall and nodded.

99

"This is turning out far better than I dared imagine. You're so talented, Laney!"

"I love flowers. I can't grow them—my gardens always wither away—but I adore painting or arranging them." Laney dabbed a little more paint on the wall to form one last petal. "Of all the things God created, I love flowers most. What about you?"

Ruth thought for a moment. "Clouds. When I was a little girl, Mama and I used to sit on the seat in the garden and watch the clouds drift by." The bittersweet memory washed over her. Ruth struggled to keep her voice light. "We'd decide what the clouds looked like."

"Clouds look like clouds."

"Only if you don't pay attention." Ruth scooted to a new section and started to paint another rose. "When you use your imagination, the shapes suddenly look like things. I'd see a puppy's head or a boot." The memories welled up. "Mama never pointed because it's so rude, but she broke the rule when we played the cloud game. She'd point toward a formation and show me a sailing ship or a lamb."

"That sounds like a fun thing to do. Maybe we could teach that game to Mr. O'Sullivan so when he sits by his window, he can keep his mind busy. I used to sit with your daddy. He'd bask like a kitten in the sun by the window and read from the Bible to me."

"Did he have a favorite passage?"

"The Psalms—all of the Psalms." Laney closed one eye and dabbed a tiny speck more paint on a petal. "He knew lots of them by heart."

Heavy footsteps sounded on the stairs. *It can't be Josh. If it were, his spurs would be making that I-mean-business jangle.*

"I wonder what Hilda's doing up here at this time of day," Laney said.

Ruth surveyed the beautiful wall and called out, "Hilda, come see what we've gotten done!"

The housekeeper appeared in the doorway. "I'll be—" Her eyes widened, then narrowed. "Is that what I think it is?"

"A garland of roses," Laney said. "We still need to mix some green for leaves and st—"

"Those," Hilda interrupted, "are my muffin tins!"

"Isn't it clever?" Laney hadn't turned around, so she couldn't see the housekeeper's stern expression. "They make wonderful palettes."

"They aren't for paint; they're meant for food."

Ruth swallowed hard. "It's my fault. It was my idea. I'm sorry. We'll wash them out a dozen times before returning them to the kitchen."

"Hilda really doesn't mind. Do you, Hilda?"

The housekeeper stared at Laney, then heaved a theatrical sigh. "I'll just make cornbread instead of muffins today. But you girls stay outta my kitchen from now on. I have enough to do around here without having to chase down my dishes and clean up your messes."

"I'm happy to help around the house, Hilda." Ruth slowly set aside the muffin tin.

"No, no. I need this job. The minute Mr. McCain sees you doing my work, he'll show me the door."

"Daddy wouldn't do that!"

Hilda gave Laney an exasperated look. "Child, your father dotes on you, so you don't see the forest for the trees. The man pinches pennies till they weep." She straightened her apron. "Not that being thrifty is a sin. The Good Book tells us to be good stewards of what the Lord gives us. Some folks just take to the notion with more zeal than others."

Ruth didn't want to argue with Hilda, but she'd found Mr. McCain to be generous and kind. She'd blundered in the past by voicing unwanted opinions, so instead she offered, "At most of the schools I attended, the headmistresses insisted upon our avoiding the kitchen and laundry. They said if we learned the social graces and feminine wiles, we'd marry wealthy men and never need to do a thing for ourselves."

"That's right," Laney chimed in.

Ruth shook her head. "All of that seems like utter nonsense to me. Just because a man is rich and can afford servants doesn't mean he'd be a good husband. The reverse of that is also true: just because a man doesn't have deep pockets wouldn't mean he'd be a bad mate."

Hilda huffed. "You're talking in circles."

"Laney and I could assist you. In fact, I think we ought to." Ruth beamed at her. "We'll tell Mr. McCain that you're being diligent to prepare us for the day when we marry."

"That's right," Laney agreed.

Hilda looked dubious. "Elaine Louise McCain, your papa doesn't want to think about your marryin' up and leaving him. Burying your mama—that hit him hard. Real hard. He don't wanna turn loose of you."

"I know," Laney said quietly.

Hilda waddled off muttering about marriage and muffin tins.

Ruth kept painting, but her heart wasn't in it. *Lord, why do I always do the wrong thing? I should have found Hilda and asked her permission. After the way the cook didn't want the roasting pan back at school, I should have known Hilda would be upset. I wanted to make a fresh start here, and I'm already messing up.*

"Mama used to say Hilda crawled out of the wrong side of the bed every other day," Laney whispered.

"I didn't realize she'd been with your family. I just pictured her as having taken care of my father when he was alone here."

Laney's brow puckered as she put the finishing strokes on another flower. "When we came along, there were a few sad-looking saddle tramps in the bunkhouse and your father in the little house. Daddy sent me away to school the next day, but I always got the impression your father was a loner."

"That's so sad."

"Oh, things changed. That last year of his life, when I came home, your father was pleasant as could be. I used to play draughts with him. As I said, he'd read to me from the Bible."

"Thank you for keeping him company. I'm sure it comforted him."

"He would have liked you." Laney continued to paint as she mused aloud, "He had the same spark for life that you do. I'll bet he could have looked at the clouds and imagined all sorts of pictures in them."

"I've never had a friend say a sweeter thing to me."

"Speaking of sweet things, isn't Galen the most wonderful man you've ever met?"

"No!" After blurting out that response, Ruth scrambled to soften her answer. "Josh and your father are nice, too. And Josh is bigger and more handsome than Galen." *Oh, dear. What made me say that?* Ruth hastened on to cover for that silly slip of the tongue. "I've been in the academy. I haven't met many men. For that matter, you haven't either, have you?" She didn't wait for Laney to respond, but kept chattering, "Your father is right. We shouldn't settle for the first man who sweeps us off our feet."

"Galen hasn't tried to sweep me off my feet."

"I didn't necessarily agree with many of the rules they drilled into us at school, but I do think there is wisdom in not pursuing a man."

"I'm not pursuing Galen." Laney waved her paintbrush in the air. "I'm simply making myself available so he can make the first move."

"What's the difference?"

Tilting her head at a jaunty angle, Laney wore a satisfied smile. "I've been very discreet. Why, when the girl he was sweet on up and ran off with a butcher from Sacramento, a woman who pursued a man would have been on Galen's doorstep with a pie in hand the very next day. I did no such thing." She dabbed her brush in paint, then gave Ruth an inquiring look. "Besides, what do you know about chasing and catching a man? Have you had scores of suitors?"

"Mercy, no!" Ruth recoiled. "I'm not even sure I want to marry."

"You're playing with me, right?" Laney's laughter died out. "You're not teasing—you're serious!"

Nodding her head, Ruth asserted, "Yes, I'm serious. Men wed because they want namesakes and someone to manage their home. Women accept proposals because of social expectations or because they can't financially support themselves. Very few marriages turn out to be the love bond that all of the romantics idealize."

"You're cynical. I'm not, because Mama and Daddy positively adored one another. Trusted each other, too. A man's going to have to earn your trust before you'll ever give him your heart—I can see that."

"I'm not going to hold my breath until that day comes." Ruth managed to tilt the muffin tin and slop dark pink onto her left sleeve. *Whitewash on the right, pink on the left.* "Oh, I can't believe how clumsy I am. I'm a disaster."

"You are not!" Laney dabbed a little of the paint off Ruth's sleeve with her brush and proceeded to use it to paint a flower. "Waste not, want not. Besides, we'll keep that dress as your work dress. A little paint won't matter, and this beautiful garland will last a lot longer than any old dress would, anyway."

"You make this sound economical."

"Economical? That was you asking Josh for barn paint. I wouldn't have dreamed of mixing that ugly old red with the whitewash, but look at the results!"

Ruth looked from the painted garland to the multicolored muffin tin and back. "I guess all of those art lessons we endured at school finally amounted to something."

"It'll look much better when we add the leaves and stems." Laney paused, then added, "You don't have to worry about being economical. Hilda's just being grumpy. Daddy's always taken very good care of us."

"I'm sure he has."

"And as for the difference—with Galen, I mean—well, isn't a man supposed to notice?"

Ruth wrinkled her nose. "Laney, if I didn't know the difference between your not pursuing him and just being available, how would he? From what I gather, men tend to be obtuse about the finer points like that."

"So far, he has been. It vexes me no end. I wish I were clever. I'd be able to say something witty to capture his attention."

"Who says you're not clever?"

"Everybody." Laney's chin began to quiver.

"Well, how do you like that? I'm left out again, because I'm not part of 'everybody.'"

Tears filled Laney's eyes. "See? That's what I mean. I'd never think of anything that smart to say."

"I wasn't trying to be smart, Laney. I was being honest. I never fit in. Everyone else at the schools and back home thought alike and acted so refined. I stuck out like a sore thumb. The last headmistress actually called me a misfit, and she was right."

"What a dreadful thing for her to say!" Laney sniffled. "But I think you fit in here just fine. Me? I'm never going to manage. My headmistress told me as a decoration for a rich man's home and arm, I would be a grand success—but her canary was smarter."

"That's an outrage!" Ruth wrapped her arms around Laney. "And she was wrong. I know it."

Laney shook her head. "It's true. I'm good at all the proper conduct and social things, and I never gave my teachers a moment of grief. They told me it was good enough, but it's not." She sucked in a deep breath, then whispered, "The shameful truth is, I can barely read."

Her admission stunned Ruth. Ruth squeezed tighter.

"I told you I'm stupid," Laney wailed.

"Nonsense!" Ruth declared briskly. "You just had the wrong teacher. If you can learn brushstrokes to paint, you can learn letters to read and write."

"I don't think so."

"I know so." Ruth winked at Laney. "I'm sinfully stubborn, and I'm going to teach you to read."

Laney bit her lip and looked away.

"Don't you give up." Ruth shook her. "I'm not going to."

"I don't want Daddy to find out. Josh knows, and he helps me. Daddy—well, he's the only one who thinks I'm perfect. I don't want to disappoint him."

"We already said we'd paint each morning. Part of that time, when we're alone, we can use the tablet to paint words. I'll keep your secret, Laney. You needn't be ashamed around me. If anything, I envy you. You can learn to read. I don't think I'll ever learn how to keep my mouth shut and behave."

"I like you just the way you are." Laney pulled away.

Ruth groaned. "I don't think you will once I confess that, when I hugged you, I got paint from my sleeve all over your shoulder."

Ruth scoured the muffin tins once more for good measure. Not a speck of paint remained on them, but she didn't want to take a chance that she might have missed a spot. Hilda was outside, taking linens off the clothesline. By the time she returned, Ruth wanted to have the tins rinsed, dried, and able to pass the housekeeper's inspection.

Laney rummaged around in the hutch.

"What are you doing?"

Laney stood on tiptoe and reached for the top shelf. "I found my mother's vase. Let's go for a walk and find flowers. Just think of how beautiful your room will be with flowers painted on the walls and a real bouquet on the bedside table."

"I have plenty of flowers, thanks to your help. Let's put the bouquet in your room."

Laney clutched the crystal vase to her chest. "Are you sure?"

"Of course I am." Ruth turned her attention back to the suds so she wouldn't start to cry. Seeing how Laney treasured her mama's vase struck a chord. Ruth remembered doing the exact same thing after Mama went to be with the Lord and she helped Bernadette pack up all of the things in Mama's room.

"You've scrubbed that tin so hard, it's a wonder you haven't worn holes in it. Let's go!"

"I'll be done in a minute." Plunging the pan into the rinse bucket, Ruth said, "I've seen flowers growing all over the place. Did you seed them, or are they wild flowers?"

"Wild flowers." Laney grabbed a dishtowel and dried one tin as Ruth saw to the other. "I wasn't home for the first two years, and the last year I was too busy to bother. Mrs. O'Sullivan's garden always makes me think I ought to plant some, but I haven't gotten around to it."

"It won't be hard at all to gather a huge bouquet. Let's get enough that we can put some on the supper table and also give Hilda an arrangement for her room."

Laney tugged the muffin tin from her. "While I put these away, you get buckets or baskets for us."

Ruth vehemently shook her head from side to side. "I already earned Hilda's wrath for swiping the muffin tins. I'm not about to dash off with her buckets or baskets."

Laney smiled as she looked out the window. "Here she comes. I'll handle it." Laney ran to the door and opened it just in time for the housekeeper to bustle in with an overflowing wicker basket.

"Ruth and I can fold the linens, Hilda. Why don't you go ahead and brew us all some tea? Oh—better still, why don't you relax awhile. Ruth and I can make supper. Mrs. O'Sullivan taught us how to make stew."

Horror twisted the housekeeper's face. "Oh no. No one's

standing in front of that stove but me. I've tasted your cooking, Elaine Louise. Like to thought I'd die from indigestion all three times. You couldn't follow a recipe if your life depended on it. You girls go on and get out of my kitchen."

"Are you sure?" Laney plucked a pillowslip from the laundry basket, snapped it in the air, and began to fold it.

"Positive." Hilda snatched back the linen. "Can't you girls find something else to do?"

"We did discuss taking a walk and picking flowers," Ruth said.

"Now there's a dandy idea. Out you go."

"Please don't put Mama's vase away. I want to use it for the flowers."

The sour puckers in Hilda's face relaxed into a true smile. "Now there was a fine woman. She always kept that vase full of posies, sitting smack-dab in the middle of the parlor table. Used to be a game she played—she'd see him comin' up the walk with flowers for her, and she'd dash in and yank out whatever she'd arranged that day from her flower garden. I took to keeping a big old jelly jar in the kitchen so's she could hide 'em in plain sight. After all that hurrying and scurrying, she'd smooth her skirts and straighten her hair. Met him at the front door, looking like a page straight outta *Godey's Ladies' Book*." Hilda set down the laundry basket. "Yup. She was quite a woman."

"I'd forgotten about that." Laney pressed her hand over her heart. "It was so romantic!"

Ruth plastered a smile on her face, though her heart ached. *Mama loved flowers. I kept her room full of them, and she appreciated them so. If only things had been different and father cherished her and brought her bouquets. . . .*

Laney tugged on her sleeve. "Ruth, stop gathering wool and come on."

Ruth jolted out of her thoughts and stared at the bucket in Laney's other hand. "I'll carry that."

They wandered outside and soon stopped at a clump of daisy-faced asters. After gathering a generous supply of them, Laney pointed off in the distance. "Oh, poppies! I love those. Come on. We'll get enough to make bouquets for everywhere!"

"I recognize the lupine, wild lilac, and sage," Ruth said a short time later. "But what are these?"

"Your father called them baby blue eyes. I'm not sure that's really the name or if he made it up, but I liked how it sounded."

Ruth blinked in surprise. "My father talked about flowers?"

A winsome smile crossed Laney's face. "I used to pick flowers for his room. Since he was stuck in bed, I liked to brighten his room."

"Oh, Laney." Ruth embraced her. "Thank you for doing that for him."

"It was fun. Once, when I took a bunch of buckwheat into his room, a butterfly came through the window and landed on the arrangement. Alan was delighted. You're like him that way—you appreciate the little things."

"It's strange to think we are alike at all since I never met him." Ruth looked off in the distance. McCain waved at them. He started striding their way, and Laney skipped toward him. Ruth carried the bucket and lagged behind.

"So you girls are gathering flowers. What a charming sight." He smiled at them. "I recall seeing some wild roses the other day."

Laney perked up even more. "Where?"

McCain shook his head. "No, no. It's too far for you to walk. Tell you what—I'll dig up a bush or two and transplant them by the house. That way, you can enjoy them all of the time."

"That's wonderful!" Laney went up on tiptoe and kissed his cheek. She then told Ruth, "California wild roses are simply beautiful. They have five petals, and they're exactly the same shade of pink we used for the palest flowers in your room."

"I peeked in your room, Ruth. You girls did a magnificent job of decorating the walls." McCain reached over and took the flower bucket from her. "I'll carry this back to the house." As they drew closer to the house, McCain cleared his throat. "Laney, honey, I wanted to speak with you about something."

Feeling the need to lend them privacy, Ruth murmured, "If you two will excuse me . . ."

"But, Ruth, you don't need to—"

"Laney," McCain interjected, "let's take these flowers into the kitchen. I'm sure Ruth will meet you there in a few minutes, and the two of you will have fun arranging them."

Laney blushed and nodded.

Thankful to make an escape, Ruth headed toward the necessary. Back home, Bernadette ordered Hadley to build a spacious outhouse so it could accommodate a woman's voluminous skirts. Bless him, for Hadley even whitewashed the inside. Ruth felt certain the outhouse on the Broken P had to have been built years ago. After fighting with her skirts and petticoats to get through the narrow door, there wasn't enough room to turn around. As a result, Ruth had learned to gather all of her voluminous clothing, open the door, and step in backward.

"So much for being graceful," she muttered, filling her left hand with layers of cloth. Since the door tended to be stubborn, she gave it a no-nonsense jerk. The door made an odd sound, and Ruth let out a yelp as it fell toward her. Tripping over her own feet, she landed flat on her back with the door on top of her. Ruth lay there and moaned, "How am I ever going to explain this?"

———⊰•⊱———

Josh smacked his hat against his thigh and shook his head. "Dumb animal." Then he headed around the far end of the hedge to see if he could flush the calf out. The cow stood just on the other side of the mud bog, bawling for her baby.

Toledo roped the calf, tied the lariat around his saddle horn, and started to pull, but the calf slipped free and made twice as much noise as he sank up to his knees.

Josh threw the ranch hand a frustrated look. Toledo was one of their best hands, but Josh assigned the man to work alongside him today just to be sure he wasn't lurking around the house and watching Ruth. He dismounted and tried to ignore the way the mud sucked at his boots. Using his own rope as well as Toledo's to gain purchase of the calf, he muttered, "C'mon, you stupid hunk of veal. This'll teach you not to leave your mama's side."

When he remounted, only one boot came along. Josh looked down at the other and groaned. He'd yank it free and wear it, but the mud inside would make an already bad day worse. Last night's storm left bogs like this and loosened the footings on some of the fence posts. Between reinforcing the fence and pulling calves free, Josh hadn't caught his breath all day.

They hauled the calf free, gave him back to his anxious mama, and carried on. Toledo didn't say much. Most hands tended to be on the taciturn side, but they were downright talkative compared to Toledo. The only one Toledo ever unbent enough with to speak more than one sentence at a time was Dad. Then again, he did a fair day's work for a fair day's wage and didn't stir up any trouble. Josh couldn't fault him for being quiet. *If he troubles Ruth, though, I'll cut him loose.*

Come midday, Josh decided he'd worked his way close enough to home that he'd stop in for lunch. One of Hilda's good meals might just turn his day around. He'd no more than set foot onto the back patio steps when Hilda filled the doorway.

"I got a good look at you through the window. If you think you're comin' into my nice clean kitchen, you've got another think a'comin', cowboy."

"I'll scrape off my boots." He trudged up the next two steps.

"You'd have to shuck outta every stitch you're wearing. What've you been doing? Wallowing in the mud with the hogs?"

"I'll go sluice off at the pump. How about having Laney bring me a plate?"

"She's busy."

Josh stared at the housekeeper. "Doing what?"

"Helping Ruth."

Something in Hilda's tone made the hair stand up on the nape of his neck. "I repeat, doing what?"

"Can't say for certain. Ruth asked where you keep a hammer and nails."

"She can't use a fan without beating herself black and blue. What business does she have with a hammer?" Josh ignored his growling belly and headed for the barn.

Bang. Bang. Bang. Three awkwardly spaced sounds made him change direction. He made it past the cottonwood, stopped dead, and stared in disbelief. "What," he asked in the mildest voice he could manage, "are the two of you doing to the outhouse?"

CHAPTER NINE

"We're fixing it. Furthermore, we can hear you just fine, so you don't have to roar at us," Laney said as she continued to brace the door with one hand while prissily holding her skirts up with the other.

Ruth rivaled an apple for color. She didn't say anything—probably because she held several nails between her teeth as if she were a giant, human pincushion. Halfway up the handle of the hammer, she held a stranglehold—which accounted, no doubt, for the fact that the nail she'd been driving barely pierced the door. It would have taken her all day to finish this simple task.

"The outhouse doesn't need fixing."

"That's what you think! Why, the door fell on poor Ruth."

Josh didn't bother to ask just how Ruth managed to tear down a sound door. Some things defied explanation. After witnessing her ability to rile a mare, cover herself in paint, and trip on her hem, Josh knew for certain he'd been right: Ruth Caldwell was an accident going somewhere to happen. *Lord, I just don't understand why you sent her to my doorstep.*

"Here." He pulled the hammer from her and stuck out his left hand. "Nails."

One by one, she took them from her mouth, fastidiously wiped them on her sleeve, then laid them in his palm. With the last one, she declared, "We cut new hinges from a scrap of leather. The old ones must have rotted through."

Josh stared at the leather piece she'd tacked up. *It can't be.* He looked down at the other one she held out. *It is. Of all the leather around here, why did they take the piece I was fixin' to use for a wallet?*

"I'm sure these will work," Ruth's smile didn't disguise the embarrassment in her voice. "They're sturdy."

"Yes. Sturdy." Josh couldn't bellow at them; they'd tried their best to remedy the situation. Instead, he ordered, "Move, Ruth. I'll get this taken care of."

Josh thought about mentioning she'd have more driving force if she held the hammer properly, then dismissed that foolish notion. The last thing he wanted was for Ruth to take a mind to using his tools. Sure as God made little green apples, Ruth would maim or murder something or someone if he did.

Bam. He sank the first nail with a single, well-placed blow. *Bam.* The second followed suit.

"Wow." Ruth kept her gaze trained on his hand. "I thought I was supposed to hold the hammer in the middle so the handle would counterbalance the heavy metal thing on the end. You use your forearm as the counterbalance, and keep your wrist straight so it acts like a fulcrum."

Counterbalances and fulcrums? "Where did you learn about physics?"

Ruth shrugged. "I didn't get to finish the book. When Miss Pettigrew found out I checked *Modern Physics* out of the library, she took it back and brought me something more suitable." She cocked her head to the side. "Which reminds me—is there a library in town?"

"No," Josh and Laney said in unison.

"Oh, that's terrible!"

Josh tried to redirect the conversation. "What did Miss Pettigrew make you read?"

"Something about happy homemaking." Ruth's expression made it clear the book failed at making her happy. "She specifically wanted me to read all of the instructions for making suitable seating assignments for formal suppers with multiple distinguished guests, but it bored me to distraction."

"Oh, I can help you with that." Laney finally let go of her skirts and patted Ruth's arm. "As long as you know the rules, you can manage just about anything."

"See? I told you, you're smart." Ruth beamed at his sister. "I never did manage to get any of those details straight, and you know all about that stuff."

Laney looked stunned, then an uncertain smile lit her face. "I do know all about that."

Josh had watched Laney struggle through her primers. In their younger years, Mama spent hours drilling Laney so she could toe the mark at school and recite her spelling words and poems. Josh helped her as much as he could, but his poor little sister considered herself dumb as a fencepost.

Ruth—bless her awkward ways—just made Laney feel smart. Josh held up the next nail and drove it home. He'd gladly sacrifice his wallet leather and hang a new privy door every day of the week if this was the result.

———

"I've been thinking," Ruth said as she sat down to the breakfast table.

"That's enough to make my hair stand on end." Josh scooted past Laney's seat and took his own.

Ruth laughed at his temerity, then continued on as if he hadn't interrupted her. "About the chickens. We don't have very many.

Maybe we ought to get more and expand the coop."

"Did Hilda put you up to this?" McCain frowned at her.

"No." Ruth put her napkin in her lap. "So Hilda agrees with me?"

"She's always scrounging around for more eggs," Josh said.

"So what's the problem? Are they expensive?"

Mr. McCain gave Ruth a strange look. She didn't know how to interpret it.

"They're cheap as they come," Josh answered.

Ruth giggled, and everyone looked at her. "Cheap?" She smiled at Josh. "I thought you were being clever with that pun."

"I didn't intend it, but I can see how that caught your funny bone. Anyway, it's not a matter of money; it's a matter of time. We'd have to add on to the coop, and other matters are more pressing."

"I could build it!"

"You," Josh said repressively, "don't know how to hold a hammer."

"You showed me. I could do it."

"And I'd help," Laney tacked on.

"Absolutely not!" Josh planted both elbows on the table, rested his chin on his clasped hands, and glowered. "I've never heard a more harebrained scheme in my life."

"We could do it," Ruth declared.

"Just thinking about it gives me indigestion," Josh shot back. Even though he'd made that proclamation, he proceeded to pick up his fork and shovel in his eggs and hash browns with stunning speed.

"We men will get around to it sooner or later," McCain said. "You gals shouldn't trouble yourselves over those kinds of things. Didn't I just buy a bunch of material for you?"

"Yes, Daddy." Laney took a bite of her eggs.

"I feel quite awkward about that, Mr. McCain. Truly, I need to repay you—"

"Nonsense, Ruth." He crooked a brow. "The Broken P can certainly afford to grace her pretty ladies with elegant dresses."

"Well, they've been stitching every afternoon," Hilda said as she came through the kitchen door holding the coffeepot. "I can't for the life of me figure out why dresses have to be so big, though. That silly stylebook of Laney's has them using fourteen yards for one dress!"

"It's fashionable," Laney said. "You don't want us to look dowdy."

"Dowdy? I'd call that style ridiculously impractical," Hilda accused. "It's gotten to the point you can't get through a doorway without pushing in on your hoops."

"You look charming, honey. You go ahead and make your dresses as big around as your little heart desires." Mr. McCain smiled at Laney. "I think you look pretty as a picture."

"I wanted to have my new dress done by Sunday, but I'm nowhere near finishing it." Laney let out a little sigh. "Galen said he wanted to see me in pink."

"Knowing Galen, he'll be too busy keeping track of his brothers in the churchyard to bother noticing what color you're wearing." Josh sopped up egg yolk with his biscuit. "Besides, if that dress really is half as full as Hilda says it is, you'll take a month of Sundays before you finish hemming it."

"If I start on one side, and you start on the other," Ruth offered, "we could get it done."

"But what about your dress?" Laney shook her head. "You need to finish it, too."

"Don't be such a goose," Ruth teased. "No one here has seen my Sunday dress. They wouldn't know if it's first-time new or something I've worn for years."

"I seriously doubt," Josh said in a wry tone, "that you've kept any of your dresses for years."

Ruth wrinkled her nose. "I'm afraid you're right. I'm forever spoiling them by spilling something or tearing them. I even saved aside some fabric on this new dress to use for repairs—just in case."

"That was very practical of you," McCain praised.

Ruth smiled at him. "You've so very kind. I can't thank all of you enough. I know my being here was . . . problematic, but you've been so gracious."

"Nothing's been settled yet," Josh said as he pushed away from the table.

"Well, I know God sent you here to be my friend." Laney patted Ruth's hand. "I haven't been this happy since I came home from finishing school. I've been dreadfully lonely."

"Regardless of what happens, Laney, we'll still be friends. Josh, how are we to settle the matter?"

His father cleared his throat. "Has Mr. Maltby taken any steps?"

Josh folded his arms across his chest. "He told me he'd put it on the docket. It's not considered an urgent matter, so we'll have to bide our time."

Ruth shifted in her chair, and it creaked slightly, giving away her discomfort. Josh's eyes narrowed, and she shrugged guiltily. "Patience isn't one of my virtues. Maybe what I ought to do is arrange for an attorney to look into expediting the matter."

"Now, now." McCain patted the table as if he were soothing a cranky baby. "No use rushing headlong into anything. You're a young woman, and it's not right for you to be on your lonesome. Whether or not you receive any inheritance doesn't matter—you still belong here, in this house with us. Since that's not going to change, we can sit tight and wait until the circuit judge assigns a court date for the matter."

"I appreciate your hospitality, but—"

"The subject is closed." Josh headed toward the door.

Laney giggled. "Ruth, let it go. My brother's just glad I'm not driving him to distraction asking what color floss to use on my samplers, now that you're here."

Ruth leaned toward Laney and whispered, "If he gave me his opinion, I'd choose the exact opposite. For the past two days, he hasn't even managed to match his shirt to his britches."

"He never does," Laney said.

"I heard both of you," Josh said.

Ruth groaned and Laney laughed.

"Who cares what I wear?" Josh gave them a bland look. "I'm with horses and cattle all day, and not a one of them complains."

"Men are hopeless," Laney said. "Daddy's no better."

"Your father's shirt and pants are both blue."

"Only," Laney said, "because I set that out for him last night. He's going to town today, and I wanted him to look handsome."

"It's a bunch of nonsense if you ask me. The man's clean and covered." Hilda scowled. "All those silly fashion ideas are made up just to occupy the minds of city folk who have nothing better to do. Around here, we work for a livin' and dress accordingly."

"I do feel useless," Ruth said. "I'm sure there's something I could do."

"You're helping Laney with her new dress." McCain wolfed down his last bite and rose. "Neither of you girls is meant to labor around here. You're ladies, and your job is to bring warmth and joy to our home. So far, you're doing admirably. There's no need to change matters when they're working so well."

He left, and Ruth stared at her plate in confusion. By not doing anything, she'd done the right thing. *But there has to be more to life than painting and sewing and socializing, Lord. It wasn't enough for me at school. I don't think it'll keep me happy for long here, either. What am I to do?*

The ponies strung along behind Josh, and he kept them at a lively trot—partly because he didn't have a lot of time, mostly because one of them was a headstrong troublemaker who'd find a way to veer off course if given any leeway. *Sort of like Ruth.*

Josh yanked his hat down lower on his brow. Ruth wasn't going to be easy to keep corralled. He resented her for being there; but that wasn't really fair. His sense of honor led him to say that Alan's will should be settled according to Alan's wishes.

Regardless of who inherited what from Alan, someone had to tend to the day-in-and-day-out running of the Broken P. Josh didn't mind shouldering that responsibility. He loved the land. The gritty work demanded a lot, but he enjoyed the challenge. The stallion tried to pull sideways, and Josh yanked him back in line. A wry smile twisted his lips. *Well, most days I like it. I'll be happier when I sell off this bent-for-trouble pony.*

He'd been dead-level honest when he told Galen about the knothead, but Galen still wanted to see all three. Anyone else would have come to the Broken P to examine and buy horses. But with Mr. O'Sullivan sick and Galen taking up all the slack, Josh figured he could go to his friend instead.

Smoke curled from the stovepipe in a thin, lazy ribbon. Windows and doors lay wide open. Though his house on the Broken P looked far grander, Josh couldn't help longing for the simple, comfortable welcome invariably given at the O'Sullivans'. Kelly O'Sullivan made her house a home by loving the Lord and all He sent her way. *As Mama did when she was with us.* Josh tugged on the lead rope when the knothead got willful.

Laney tried to liven up their lives and make the house special with some of the things they taught her at that fancy school back East. Josh knew the motive behind her efforts—but they all seemed so stiff and contrived. As for Ruth, she'd livened things up considerably with her table discussions ... even if they often presented crazy notions such as her building a chicken coop. Left alone, Laney had been bored to tears. Josh suspected when left alone back East, Ruth probably started everyone praying for boredom's return.

Hilda shooed the girls away, and Dad's stance was that they were to be pretty, not practical. Wound up in the day-to-day, nitty-gritty demands of ranching, Josh couldn't very well teach Ruth and his sister the things they ought to know. Both needed a woman's touch to coax them into understanding what a home should be. *At least Laney and Ruth can come here to see how Kelly O'Sullivan does it.*

"Hey!" he shouted.

"In the barn!" Galen called back.

Mrs. O'Sullivan came to the door and wiped her hands on the hem of her apron. "What a fine spring day it is that brings you here, Joshua McCain."

"Yes, ma'am."

"And isn't that a first-rate string of ponies you have there!"

"If I'm being truthful, ma'am, I'd say two of the three are prizes."

She laughed. "When you and my son are done, drop in for lunch."

"I'd be a liar if I said I hadn't been hoping for an invitation." Her laughter followed him as he led the horses toward the barn. Galen strode out and opened the gate to a corral, so Josh led the string right in.

Galen entered the corral and shut the gate. "Oh, will you get a look at these beauties?"

"Looks aren't everything." Josh dismounted and started to untie the closest horse while his friend worked the last free. "This first one, I'm warning you, is a headache on hooves. I only brought him because you asked me to. But if you choose him, I'm going to fight you."

"Spirited, eh?"

"Stupid and stubborn. There's a world of difference. You could handle him, but your brothers—" Josh shook his head. "He'll dump them off and run."

"He has exquisite conformation."

"You'd find something good to say about the horses ridden in Revelation's apocalypse."

"They are God's creatures," Galen teased. He slapped the nearest mustang on the haunch and watched her trot to the trough.

121

The other horses joined her, then separated and milled about.

Josh kept his mouth shut and let Galen study the animals.

Singing under his breath, Galen approached the brown-and-white mustang. With sure, steady hands, he examined the horse, then grinned at Josh. "Oh, now this one's a sweetheart, isn't she?"

"Yup. Other mustang's temperament is just as agreeable."

"Is that so?" Galen moved to the black-and-white. After a few minutes, he nodded. "Aye, you're a grand little gelding, aren't you? Strong and hardy."

"They'll serve you well."

"But the stallion..." Galen grinned. "He's givin' you fits, is he?"

"I've been tempted to cut him or haul him off to the glue factory." Josh scowled at the animal.

"Now, don't you be blamin' him. 'Tisn't his fault." Galen pasted on a cocky smile and headed for that last animal. "You prayed for patience. Mayhap God wanted to teach you a lesson with this one."

Josh snorted. "Don't go blaming God; the fault lies squarely on Eddie Lufe's shoulders. Gelding that horse would probably solve the problem, but Lufe specified he wanted a stallion."

Singing again, Galen ran his hands over the stallion. At first, the stallion shied away, but Galen's talent won him over.

"Son," Mrs. O'Sullivan called from about ten feet away. "Would—"

The stallion jolted. Instantaneously Josh and Galen grabbed his halter and jerked to keep him from rearing. It took both of them to control him. He continued to paw the earth and toss his head.

Josh gritted, "You had a look-see, Galen, but you're not getting this horse."

"No, I'm not."

"I didn't mean to startle the poor pony," Mrs. O'Sullivan half-whispered.

"This one's daft, Ma. Josh thought to geld him, but Eddie Lufe's wanting a stallion."

"Well, now, Eddie Lufe's a powerful moose of a man. I'm not sayin' he's cruel, because he's not; but the man tends to be firm with his beasts. It'll be a good match, I'm sure."

"Did you need something, Ma?"

"Aye. Your da heard the horses, and he'd love to see what you buy. If I walk him out to the porch, could you bring the new ponies up to him?"

Galen glanced at a fencepost shadow, and Josh understood he was determining the time. "You have a relay due in?"

"Aye."

"You get the horse ready. I'll go help your dad onto the porch."

"I can take care of Cullen."

Josh rested his hands on his hips. "Mrs. O'Sullivan, you're the one who said it's a fine spring day. With it being so nice, I reckon I could bring your husband down the steps, into the sunshine."

"Make it a picnic, Ma." Galen climbed over the corral fence and went into the stable.

Cullen O'Sullivan passed judgment on the two mustangs and agreed the stallion ought to go to Eddie Lufe. Josh hadn't brought the stallion over to the ailing man—he didn't want to chance a problem, but it was good to see how the ponies allowed him to lead them right up to Mr. O'Sullivan's chair and tolerated his touch.

When Galen helped his father back into the house, Josh reached over and stilled Mrs. O'Sullivan as she started to pick up from lunch. He said in a quiet tone, "I plan to help out around here."

She looked up at him. "Galen's doin' a fine job."

"You all are. But that's not to say there isn't plenty to do. Galen's my friend, and I aim to help him—but you'll make it easier if you accept my offers. Same as when the girls come over. I want you to put them to work. They want you to—we discussed it last night."

"Josh—"

He held up his hand to silence her. "Hilda won't let them lift a hand around the house. She holds the crazy notion that Dad'll let her go if he thinks the girls can handle matters. That being the case, you can put them to chores so they help out and learn how to organize themselves. Both have fancy training, but when it comes to practicalities, they're lost. I don't think either of them could cook a complete meal."

"I've taught them to make stew. They both can make a decent pot now."

Josh grinned. "Great! Don't hesitate to rope 'em into pitching in and helping out. Consider it training for the day they become wives."

"I'm happy to do things with them. You know that."

"They're happy to do things with you and for you."

"They come as guests, Josh. I'm not about to ruin every visit by expecting them to do my labors."

"You'll be giving them the opportunity to learn valuable skills. Surely you can see how important it is for them to be able to do all of those sorts of things. They need a woman's guidance and wisdom. I can't think of a finer Christian woman to teach them."

"If I listened to your cockeyed plan, I'll be getting far more from those lasses than a guest should ever give."

He chuckled. "I've worried more than once you'd consider them to be pests, not guests. Remember what the Good Book says in Acts: 'It is more blessed to give than to receive.'"

"I heard your asking price on those mustangs." She gave him a meaningful look. "You're ranch is already giving and my family's receiving plenty."

Josh scoffed. "I know the Pony Express paid up to two hundred dollars for some of their horses, but you and I both know that's absurd—especially for common little mustangs. I got 'em for a song and used spare time to saddle break 'em. Broken P's making a profit."

"God bless you, Josh. You know my boys are longing for horses of their own."

"They'll put 'em to good use."

He heard hooves flying and turned. Galen came out of the house and ran to the relay pony. Mrs. O'Sullivan grabbed the sandwich, hitched up her skirts, and ran, too.

"Trouble!" the rider shouted from seventy yards away. "Trouble!"

CHAPTER TEN

"It was bound to happen," Mr. McCain said as he poured gravy over his plate.

"But an entire Pony Express station?" Laney took a dab of mashed potatoes and set down the bowl.

"Paiutes ain't friendly." McCain shook his fork at his son. "I told you this'd happen."

Josh nodded. "I didn't expect them to act so quickly or fiercely."

"Where is—I mean was—Williams Station?" Ruth pushed the butter beans around on her plate.

"Oh, my word!" Laney's eyes grew huge. "You barely got here, Ruth! The Indians could have attacked the stagecoach."

"But they didn't." Ruth lifted her chin. "We'll have to pray for the men who continue to serve the Pony Express."

"Prayin' isn't going to amount to a hill of beans' worth of difference," McCain muttered. "You've got thousands of heathens roamin' around out there, eager to make trouble."

"Are you referring to the attack on Fort Defiance?" Ruth asked.

"That too. Them Navajos up and went after a United States fort end of last month. Today, they mounted an attack against the Pony."

"I thought you said the Paiutes attacked Williams Station," Laney said quietly.

"They did," Josh said in support.

McCain heaved a sigh. "Mark my words, this is just the start of it, and the Pony Express business is going to have an uphill fight on their hands. They cross the land of dozens of bands of Indians, and the redskins won't put up with it for long."

"The Pony Express isn't going to buckle under from one incident," Josh said. "Once the natives see that the stations and riders are peaceful, matters ought to cool down—at least that's the general wisdom."

"That sounds right," Ruth said. "It's not reasonable to expect them to understand our motives. Some things take time."

"Any business suffers losses, and the Pony Express is a dangerous one." Josh cut more of his meat. "I'm sure they anticipated some of this, but the loss of life is a travesty."

"Why d'you think they advertised for orphans to be their riders?" McCain took a huge bite of pot roast.

"I read that most of the riders aren't orphans," Ruth said. "But even if they were, it would still be a shame."

"We don't have the particulars yet," Josh said. "Could be the station employees snuck off. Just because the station was attacked doesn't mean the people are dead."

"Hope they are." McCain shoveled more food into his mouth. "Indians torture their captives."

Laney gasped and went pale.

Josh and Ruth exchanged a glance. Ruth hurriedly said, "Since we don't know the details, suppositions won't do us any good or change matters. Josh, you rode off with three ponies. I noticed when you came back, you didn't have any."

He took her lead beautifully and plunged right in on the

changed subject. "Yup. Time came to sell 'em. O'Sullivans bought the mare and the gelding."

"Oh, I'm so glad!" A little color returned to Laney's cheeks. "I told Galen they were wonderful."

"He didn't need to be told. He assessed them for himself. The man's got a good eye for horseflesh and handles the animals well." Josh nodded. "They took to him straight off."

"What about that stallion?" McCain took a gulp of coffee.

"Sold it to Eddie Lufe. He's tickled pink to have him, but I'm happier to be rid of the stupid beast. I've never seen a horse more bent on causing trouble. I said so to Lufe, and the crazy man just laughed. He can't say I didn't warn him."

Ruth listened to the conversation and appreciated that Josh hadn't tried to deceive a buyer by misrepresenting the horse. *Just as he said my father's will should be settled according to what he would have wanted instead of trying to keep everything for himself. He's such an honorable man.*

"Ruth, please pass the gravy," McCain asked.

"Here. Would you like more mashed potatoes, too?"

"Nah." He paused. "Yeah. Yeah, I would."

Ruth sent the gravy and potatoes to Josh so he could hand them to his father. "How many horses and cattle do you sell each year?"

"It varies," Josh said.

"No need for you to fret over those details, girl." Mr. McCain plopped a mound of mashed potatoes onto his plate and grabbed the gravy boat. "Plenty enough to keep you and my Laney as the best-dressed gals around."

"I'm not worried about my wardrobe."

"What are you worried about?" Laney tilted her head to the side, her brow furrowed. "Tell us. I'm sure Daddy and Josh can help."

"It's all this talk about Indians. Poor girl's scared half out of her wits," McCain declared. "Well, Ruth, you needn't worry any-more. You're safe here. You'll never have to face crossing the continent again, so you can calm down and enjoy your meal."

"You've hardly eaten a bite," Laney said.

"Only because I've spoken so much. I'm very interested in what's going on in the world, and the conversation engaged me fully." Ruth picked up her fork. "Hilda is a wonderful cook. I've enjoyed every meal I've eaten at this table."

"It didn't occur to me to offer you the newspaper," Josh said. "Mom and Laney never bothered with it."

"Women aren't interested in men's affairs," McCain said. "Though the *Sacramento Bee* does have an article or two that might amuse you, Ruth."

Ruth felt obliged to respond. She swallowed thickly and gathered her courage. "Back home, I read the paper to Mama. We enjoyed conversing about the articles."

"I look at the advertisements sometimes," Laney said. She gave Ruth a longing look. "If you're used to reading articles aloud, I'd listen."

"You girls might enjoy that." Josh nodded.

McCain shook his finger at them. "Before you go any further, promise me you're not going to try to talk me into buying a bunch of those ridiculous patent medicines and nonsense in those advertisements."

"I know better," Ruth said. "They don't work." The huge collection of bottles and medicinal powders on Mama's dresser hadn't improved her health one iota.

Laney perked up. "See? We won't ask for anything silly. Will we, Ruth?"

Laney's hopeful look banished Ruth's sorrow. A thought pinged through Ruth's mind. "Laney and I would love to have the newspaper when you're done with it." She shot Laney a conspiratorial smile. She'd be able to read all of the stories to stay well-informed, but she also decided Laney might do well to use headlines or advertisements to learn to read better. Silently congratulating herself, Ruth lifted a bite to her mouth.

God is providing all that I need.

She didn't even mind that some of the bite fell off of her fork. After all, it landed back on her plate.

"Now let's look at the *Bee* and see what words you already recognize." Ruth spread the newspaper out on the bed.

Laney stared at it from across the room as if it were a whole knot of snakes.

"Laney, remember how you helped me get gravy out of my bodice last night?"

"Yes. It came out completely, didn't it?"

"Of course it did. You knew exactly what to do. I would have used hot water and set in the stain, though. If you weren't such a dear friend, I would have been embarrassed to ask you for help."

"You're going to tell me I shouldn't be embarrassed to have you teach me to read now."

"See how smart you are? You figured that out right away."

"It's not going to work." Tears filled Laney's eyes.

"Now how do you like that?" Ruth asked the room. "Here I thought Laney and I were friends and we trusted one another. And I thought she believed in God."

"God has nothing to do with this."

"That's where you're wrong. We're supposed to commit our undertakings to the Lord, and as long as they are in His will, He blesses them."

Laney looked stunned.

Ruth pounced on the opening. "See? That's why this is going to work. Now you march right over here, and we're going to kneel by this bed and ask our heavenly Father for His blessing." Ruth slipped off the bed and knelt there.

Laney's steps lagged, but she came over and slowly lowered herself. Resting her elbows on the mattress, she asked, "Do you really believe this, or are you just pretending so I'll get my hopes up?"

Ruth clasped Laney's hand in hers. "Psalm thirty-seven says, 'Delight thyself also in the Lord; and he shall give thee the desires of thine heart. Commit thy way unto the Lord; trust also in him; and he shall bring it to pass.' We're going to commit this to Him and trust Him with it. If you truly want to read, Laney, I'm sure He will bless your efforts."

"I never thought of it that way." Laney bowed her head. "Lord, I want to read. You know how much I want to read. I never thought to ask you to help me, but I'm asking you now. Please help Ruth to teach me. In Jesus' precious name, amen."

"Amen," Ruth chimed in. As she rose, she directed, "Go get a pencil."

"I want to read, not write," Laney said.

"You are going to read. I'm going to have you circle all of the words you know on the newspaper."

An hour later, Ruth took the pencil from Laney. "That was great. Now we need to go ahead and paint for a while so when your father asks, you can honestly tell him you and I painted this morning."

Ruth folded the newspaper and slipped it into her bureau. Later that night, she took it back out. Laney's self-confidence needed a boost. She'd been able to read scattered words on two pages—far more than Ruth had anticipated. Carefully reviewing those words, Ruth took out the pencil and started to construct sentences. Much later, she put away her work and blew out the lamp. Tomorrow, Laney would read a whole story, one full page with nothing more than the words she already knew.

"Josh, could I please come into the barn?"

Josh slung the saddle on his horse and gave Ruth a stern look. "Why?"

"I need to get the hammer."

"You didn't tear off the outhouse door again, did you?"

"No."

"Then what do you need a hammer for? Dad already said you're not to add on to the coop."

"I just want to hang a few pictures in my room."

He headed her way. "How heavy are they?"

"Oh, they're light. Why?"

"I need to figure out what nails to use."

She shook her head. "Thank you, but I don't need nails."

"What are you going to use?"

"Sewing needles." She stated that fact as if it made all the sense in the world.

"Why would you use a needle when we have nails?"

"Sewing needles are amazingly strong. They support a lot of weight, and they don't leave big holes in the wall." She smiled. "Some of the girls at one of the schools showed me that. It's always worked like a charm."

"You could barely hit a nail with the hammer. How do you expect to hit a skinny little needle?"

"I'll hold it in place with my comb."

Josh tilted his head back and stared at the rafters. *This woman is going to drive me daft.*

"If you'd rather I not use your tools, I could try to use the heel of my boots. I'm sure I could make do."

"You'd use a needle, comb, and boot to hang a picture." He looked her in the eye. "Ruth, doesn't that strike you as rather . . . eccentric?"

"I'm trying to be practical." She hitched her shoulder in a casual, it's-really-nothing air. "I'm using what's on hand to get the job done."

Envisioning her bashing her heel through the plaster wall, he decided she wasn't about to do the task. "How many pictures?"

"Three. Laney painted one of them. It's a wonderful miniature of a cottage."

"Laney's good with a paintbrush. She did that landscape over the piano."

"I didn't know she painted that! It's exquisite."

Josh nodded. "Wish she was as good at playing the piano as she was at the painting over it. All that money Dad spent for her lessons, and Sis couldn't pound out a tune if her life depended on it."

"I've heard her sing. She has a beautiful voice."

"Yeah. If she spends a little time at the piano, she can pick out a tune; but give her some of that sheet music, and she slaughters the song in ways that would make the composer rip it to shreds."

Ruth's brow furrowed.

Josh felt guilty for his disloyalty. "But as you said, her voice is real nice."

Ruth cast a glance around, then leaned forward. "Josh, I know Laney struggles with reading."

He jolted. Ashamed as she felt about her illiteracy, Laney never revealed that shortcoming to anyone.

"Doesn't it occur to you, if she can't decipher words, it's probably equally difficult for her to read music? Following the notes' placement on the staff would not be unlike reading."

"Never thought of it that way. Makes sense, though." He locked eyes with Ruth. "You know Laney's feelings would be crushed if you let her know you found out—about her reading."

"Laney told me."

Ruth's revelation nearly knocked him clean out of his boots.

"I know it's a secret, so don't worry. I'll be worthy of her trust."

"That's good of you."

Earth grated beneath boots in the distance. Ruth reached up to shove one of her ever-escaping curls back into a pin and raised her voice, "So may I please have a hammer?"

"I'll take care of it for you later." There. That would keep her from knocking holes in the wall.

"Something broke?" Toledo asked.

"My heart." Ruth turned toward him. "Josh doesn't believe I can hang a few little pictures."

Toledo didn't even pause. He kept walking on by and shook his head.

"Don't you think I could do it?" Ruth called after him.

The hand turned, gave her an all-encompassing look, and snorted.

Josh appreciated the wealth of meaning behind that wordless response. Toledo's silence didn't keep him from having registered an opinion. Looking at Ruth, Josh said, "The sign over the gate reads *Broken P,* not *Bedlam.*"

"Are you implying he'd be insane to agree with me, or that he'd be insane to go against your dictates?"

"I told you from the start, you'd have to submit to my decisions on this ranch. I don't appreciate your trying to beguile my hands into disagreeing with me."

She blinked in shock. "I attempted no such thing!"

Josh realized she really hadn't intended to use her beauty and womanly charms to get her way. *Ruth really doesn't see herself as desirable. But I'm not about to let that turn my head.* "Go on back to the house where you belong, Ruth. I don't have time to argue with you."

"I'm not arguing. I just came to ask for a hammer."

"Well, you're not getting one. I told you I'd take care of hanging the pictures later on."

"What ever gave you the impression that I'm helpless?"

"You might not be helpless, but you're definitely inept. I don't want you pounding holes into the walls."

"I'd do no such thing!"

"You're right. You won't. You'll wait until I can get to the task."

"Shall I start a list for you? The chicken coop, the pictures . . ."

"Ruth—"

"Don't you say my name in that tone of voice. This isn't a school where you can send me back home if I vex you. Until we get my father's will settled, you're stuck with me and I'm stuck with you."

"So far, I've done my level best to deal with the situation," he gritted. *Irritating woman. I've sweat and bled and put every penny I had into this ranch, and she's done nothing but show up—*

Ruth's eyes narrowed. "Diplomatic words like 'situation' don't hide your true feelings, Joshua McCain. You said it more clearly back at the attorney's office when you blurted out that I'm taking half of your ranch."

"That has yet to be legally confirmed."

"You're right. Waiting isn't easy for either of us. Supposing I don't get a single inch of land, you'll be free of me; but if I do inherit a portion of the Broken P, even if I don't decide to stay here, we'll still have to deal with each other."

"You'll stay here, regardless."

Ruth glowered at him. "I exasperate you, and life has taught me such reactions result in a parting of the ways."

He stared at her. Part of Josh wanted to reassure Ruth that he hadn't been ready to pitch her out; the other part of him actually wanted to shake some sense into the silly woman. If only she were biddable and meek, this whole ridiculous conversation wouldn't be necessary. "Your name sure doesn't fit you. How about if you try saying what your biblical namesake said—you know, 'Withersoever thou goest, I will go....'"

She bristled. "Ruth said that to her mother-in-law, not to a man she barely knew."

She had a point, but Josh didn't want to concede it.

"I'm not some china doll on a shelf, Joshua McCain. I have a mind and I use it; God gave me hands, and I aim to keep them busy. Don't think for a single moment that I'll just turn into a mealy-mouthed girl who agrees with you at every turn."

"You don't have to agree. You do have to abide by my decisions, though. It's a fact you'll have to live with, like it or not."

"I'll defer to your decisions regarding the ranch. That's only right. I admit total ignorance about those matters."

Well, that was a step in the right direction.

"But," she went on, "that doesn't mean you get the last word on anything else."

Josh smirked. "I doubt you let anyone else get the last word on anything."

"Well, far be it from me to disagree with you on the rare occasion that you're right!" She turned and flounced off.

Josh tightened the cinch strap on his saddle. *Lord, when I prayed for patience, I didn't expect you to test me with the likes of that woman.*

The mare swatted him in the face with a wicked twitch of her tail, and Josh straightened up. "You women always stick together, don't you?"

"Huh?" Toledo gave him a questioning look.

"Adam had it easy until Eve came along. Since then, we've all been doomed."

———————

Doomed. That about encapsulated it all. Josh stood in the open doorway to Ruth's bedchamber and clutched the hammer in his fist. He needn't have brought it; she'd managed to hang the pictures, just as she'd said she could.

And they looked good. No, they looked great. The whole room did. Since her room was on the opposite side of the staircase, he hadn't had cause to pass by and see what she and Laney had done.

They'd done plenty. What had been a very spartan room now looked fresh and feminine. Airy curtains fluttered in the window. Who would have ever guessed the walls would look so good after getting a coat of whitewash? That, and a bunch of painted flowers that formed a rope-sort-of-thing about waist-high all around the room. The bed still needed a counterpane, but an elaborately embroidered pillowslip let him know Ruth would be equal to the task of sewing a beautiful one.

"What're you up to?" Hilda asked as she trudged by with an armful of folded clothes.

Josh frowned. "Why doesn't Ruth have a rug in her room yet?"

"I'm sure she'll get round to it. Laney and her—they've been diggin' through all my empty flour sacks, deciding on what to use to make a quilt and rag rug. 'Course, they plan to finish those fancy Sunday-best dresses first."

"So she has plenty to keep her busy?"

Hilda's face scrunched into a weathered web of wrinkles. "Don't know that some folks are ever too busy. Ruth strikes me as someone who's always gotta stick a few more irons in the fire."

And then she fans the flames. Josh didn't voice that opinion.

Studying him, Hilda asked, "What're you doin' here, anyhow?"

"I was going to hang some pictures."

"Ah. No need. Ruth got the job done already."

"With her boot?"

"Nope." Hilda shrugged. "I offered her my smallest skillet, but she ended up usin' her hairbrush."

Josh turned and walked off. He couldn't believe she'd used a hairbrush as a hammer. *Why didn't I see that coming? She already used the comb to hold the stupid needle.*

As he headed down the stairs, his dad rounded the corner. "Josh."

"Yeah, Dad?"

"I talked with Toledo. We have some spare lumber, so he's going to add a little to the coop."

Josh nodded an acknowledgment.

"I reckon it'll only cost us a few yards of chicken wire, but it'll keep Hilda from nagging me. That woman's sour as a pickle. If she weren't such a good cook, I'd replace her."

"She doesn't have anyone, Dad. She'd have no place to go."

"Well, neither does Ruth, but you don't see her stirrin' up trouble."

Josh let out a mirthless laugh. Compared to Ruth, Hilda was an absolute dream.

Chapter Eleven

Laney dropped her sewing bag onto the O'Sullivans' table and gave Mrs. O'Sullivan a hug. "It's so kind of you to invite us over."

"You're always welcome, and well you know it."

Ruth stood off to the side and held the bulging flour sack. She didn't know where to set it because breakfast dishes still covered the table. She'd stand here all day and be happy, though. Anything to be away from Josh. Things back at the Broken P were strained. Oh, they were civil to one another; courteous. If he acted any more polite, he'd have to become a diplomat instead of a rancher. At breakfast each morning, he'd inquire if she needed his help with anything and asked what she and Laney had planned.

Laney believed her brother was being thoughtful.

Ruth knew better. He was trying his hardest to keep her in line.

"Ah, Ruth, now don't you be standin' there, carryin' that heavy thing," Mrs. O'Sullivan said. "Plop it down by the window and give us a hug. You'll have to pardon the mess about here, but I've gotten a slow start on the day."

Setting down the bag, Ruth wondered, "Where's your husband?"

Mrs. O'Sullivan grinned. "Out in the stable. Galen built him a throne of hay, and I covered it with a quilt. He's having one of his better days, so we figured on his enjoyin' a change of scenery."

"Praise the Lord for those good days." Ruth gave the older woman a jubilant hug.

"Indeed, I do." Mrs. O'Sullivan patted Ruth's back. "And I thank Him for all the years my dear Cullen and I have had together. I've been blessed."

"Daddy doesn't feel that way," Laney said quietly. "He says God cheated him when He took Mama. In fact, Daddy leaves the room when we talk about her."

Mrs. O'Sullivan let loose of Ruth and shook her head sadly. "Your father doesn't walk with the Lord, Laney. He can't find solace and consolation because of that sad fact."

Ruth turned to Laney. "Your father didn't attend church on Sunday, but I didn't think much of it. I thought maybe he was under the weather a little. He's such a good, decent man, I just assumed he was a Christian."

Laney's head dipped and her voice went soft with hurt. "Josh and I keep praying for him. He's so bitter at God for taking Mama."

"I'll pray for him, too. It's dreadful to lose someone you love." Ruth felt tears well up. "I keep telling myself that Mama's not sick anymore, and we'll meet again in heaven. Even in my sorrow, I have that consolation. Your father doesn't have that comfort to cling to."

"Cullen and I—we know we're walking through the valley of the shadow of death." Mrs. O'Sullivan started to clear the table. "The day'll come when the precious Lord calls him home, and I'll have to walk the rest of the way on my own. I'll not pretend 'tis an easy journey. What I know is, I'll not be livin' with regrets on what I wish I would have said or done. My husband and I live each day together as a gift, and I'm thankful for what we have."

Ruth's hand fisted around the silverware she'd begun to gather as guilt washed over her. *I regret so much. I should have been with Mama all those months.*

"Another thing," Mrs. O'Sullivan said. "It pleases me and Cullen to have you lasses come pay us visits. My man says 'tis like havin' two sunbeams in the cabin. If you can, I'd ask you to help make glad the time he has left. The good Lord above never blessed us with daughters, and having chatter fill the house ... Well, I'm not sure who's happier about that, Cullen or me. If 'tis hard for you, then I'll understand; but if you come, I'll entertain no pity."

"I'll do my best," Laney promised.

Ruth slowly unknotted her grip and dropped the silverware into the sink. "I remember when callers would sit at Mama's bedside. They'd *tsk* and *tut* and sigh. I understand why you don't want that in your home."

"Isn't this just like a prayer meeting?" Mrs. O'Sullivan slid her skillet into the sudsy water. "It puts me in mind of the second chapter of Philippians: 'If there be therefore any consolation in Christ, if any comfort of love, if any fellowship of the Spirit, if any bowels and mercies, fulfill ye my joy, that ye be likeminded, having the same love, being of one accord, of one mind.' See? We'll find joy and consolation together by being of one mind."

"I'm not very good at remembering Bible verses," Laney said.

"Neither am I," Ruth confessed. "We could work on that together. Mrs. O'Sullivan, we'll get the dishes done."

"I won't turn away your offer. I need to make some bread, then I'll scrub the table and we'll start to sewing."

Laney pushed up her sleeves. "Just wait till you see what we're making! I want to keep it a secret from Daddy and Josh, but Ruth and I want to stitch matching riding skirts."

"The both of you'll look so grand together! You'll have to leave the skirts here to work on so you can keep it as a surprise."

Laney cast a wistful look at the door. "Will Galen notice what we're doing?"

"My son has more on his mind than what the neighbor lasses are sewing."

Ruth pretended to concentrate on the plate she was scrubbing. Laney let out a hopeless little sigh.

Searching for a way to change the topic, Ruth blurted out, "After I finish the dishes, why don't I strip your bed?" Suddenly that sounded far too personal, so she stammered, "When we got Mama up, we'd put fresh sheets on the bed. She liked how crisp they felt."

"I'd been plannin' on doin' just that." Mrs. O'Sullivan started wiping down the table with a damp rag. "Fact is, I have the washpot boilin' out back."

"It's a warm day. The sheets ought to dry quickly." Laney rinsed a plate and wiped it with her dishtowel.

"Laney and I can have things washed before you know it—hung out, too. That ought to help balance the time you'll be spending with us," Ruth interjected.

"Well, 'tis blessed I am. The rain from the other day watered my garden. God's smiling on His earth. Smiling on His children, too. I have one less job to do since the good Lord watered the land for me and you lasses are offering to ease my burdens all the more."

"We wanted to ask you about gardening," Laney said. "The garden on the Broken P is . . ." She looked at Ruth for an adjective.

"Abysmal."

"I never learned to garden, and Hilda says she's too busy to bother with canning when we can trade a steer for plenty of what we need. She says everyone else preserves too many tomatoes, squash, and beans, so why should she put herself out?"

"We're all different. Me?" Mrs. O'Sullivan let out a merry laugh. "I love my time in the garden. There's a special feelin', bein' on my knees under God's great sky. 'Tis like He and I have a partnership, coaxin' bounty from the soil."

"The fair's supposed to be in Sacramento this year. You ought to enter some of your fruit and vegetables."

"We'll see. Mayhap you lasses ought to make something and enter it. 'Twould be a worthy endeavor."

Putting a dry plate atop the stack on the shelf, Laney giggled. "I tried to make grape jelly last year. It was a disaster."

"What's so funny about that?" Ruth stopped scrubbing the skillet.

"I tried to hide my failure by dumping the results in with the hogs. You've never seen a funnier sight than pink hogs with purple splotches. Josh and Toledo were sure they'd contracted a terrible affliction until I confessed the wretched batch hadn't gelled."

"You probably needed only to cook it down more," Mrs. O'Sullivan suggested. "Still, purple and pink go well together." She offered the girls a brilliant smile. Ruth had learned quickly that the older woman was rarely condemning.

"That sounds like something I would have done." Ruth laughed, then shook her head. "Poor Josh. He's so diligent, I can just see him worrying over the animals."

"There's a fact if e'er I heard one," Mrs. O'Sullivan said. "'Tis the truth that Josh is diligent. Not just in his work, but in his walk with the Lord."

"I don't think I've done a single useful thing since I came here," Ruth said.

"I can show you lasses how to make jelly. We can spend some days doing cooking." Mrs. O'Sullivan set flour, salt, and a pitcher of water on her table. "You need to know how to do these things."

"I'm able to cook a few things, but my baking is horrid." Ruth finished scouring the skillet and rinsed it for Laney. "My cookies could chip teeth, and my bread—well, I don't know what's wrong with it. The few times I tried, the dough rose just fine outside the oven, and I punched it down, but once the loaf went into the oven, it shrank into a brick."

"Mine too." Laney blushed. "Josh calls them 'runt loaves.'"

Ruth burst out laughing, then stopped abruptly. She didn't want Laney to feel bad—but Mrs. O'Sullivan tilted back her head and let out a hearty laugh. Relief flooded Ruth. She'd been the subject of titters and unkind sniggers more often than she cared to admit; but this was simple, honest mirth. Laney laughed along— and that made it all right.

"Mercy me," Mrs. O'Sullivan said after she caught her breath, "we can't have you lasses making bricks and runt loaves. The Good Book says bread is the staff of life—you'll end up widows soon as you're brides if you serve your grooms that kind of food!"

"Maybe we ought to bake instead of sew today so I can learn all of that." Laney's voice softened. "Ruth's not sure she ever wants to marry, but I'd like to marry soon."

"Marriage is like bread." Mrs. O'Sullivan walked over to a crock and pinched out a wad of starter to make her loaf. "You can have the right ingredients, but if you don't work it right and give it time, it falls flat. Starter, it's like the soul of the bread. You lasses need to be sure your men have hearts for the Almighty so as your days and family multiply, your spirit grows along with it. Starter has to be refreshed—if you don't, nothing else you try will make the difference."

Ruth and Laney watched as she went back to the table and put the starter into a huge, brown earthenware bowl. She tossed in several cups of flour and some water. "Man and woman blend together to become one, but something's still missing."

She added salt and stirred. "Love. If you rush to the altar, you can mistake infatuation for love." She stirred more, then dumped the dough onto the floured tabletop and started to knead it. "Life'll push you around, punch you down. Without spiritual leavening, you can't rise up again. Without love, life loses its flavor. Many couples have respect and honor, but I pity them for the lack of love."

"If a bride loves the groom, won't that season the marriage?" Laney watched as Mrs. O'Sullivan continued to knead the dough.

"It didn't work for Leah in the Bible," Ruth said.

"That's right. It didn't, and she was miserable. You lasses give God time to bring the right man to you. I'm not hurrying my bread into the oven. It has to have time to rest and grow. Same goes for love—you need time to court and go through some ups and downs."

Ruth leaned against the pump. "That's a lot of wisdom, but I'm afraid if I ever meet a man who captures my interest, I'll want to hurry things along. If he discovers how clumsy and opinionated I am, he'll be long gone."

"Ruth Caldwell," Mrs. O'Sullivan shook her head. "God made you just as you are. For sure He wants to bring you around to perfection, but He knows your heart. He's got a man in mind for you, and it'll be a happy match."

"I'm afraid it'll take a saint, not a mere man, to put up with me."

Mrs. O'Sullivan divided the dough and dumped it into greased loaf pans. "I'll cover these and set them aside. While we're busy with other things, they'll rise up. Life's that way, too. Oftentimes, when we're busy doing one thing, God's working out of our sight. Don't doubt that He's there and in charge, just because you can't see the effects straightaway."

Setting the *Sacramento Bee* aside on the parlor table, Josh said, "Things got far worse than I expected. They say the Pony Express has lost sixteen men, seven stations, and one hundred fifty horses."

Laney looked up from her sewing. "That's dreadful."

Josh nodded. Whenever they got a newspaper, he'd come to the parlor after supper and read every last article. Those that would be of interest to Laney, he'd often read aloud to her. After all, since she'd do needlework, her hands were full and no one would wonder why he was reading to her. Other articles he'd sum up in a few sentences for her benefit, then discuss them with Dad. That way, she wouldn't be left out of the conversation—if the topic held any appeal to her.

"Dreadful," Laney repeated herself.

"What are they going to do about it?" Ruth added, "Mrs. O'Sullivan said the riders haven't come through in three days."

"They've temporarily suspended the service."

"Temporarily?" McCain rested his head against the back of the winged chair and settled in for a rousing conversation. "Bet you that it's not so temporary. Can't be. William Russell went off half-cocked when he cooked up the plan for that business. If I were Majors or Waddell, I'd have dissolved our partnership the minute I learned we'd only have sixty stinkin' days to set up the whole system. It was done for before the very first run."

"Why did they have only sixty days?" Laney wondered.

"Mr. Russell promised Senator Gwin he could have the business up and running by spring," Ruth told her. "He was hoping that, by doing so, Russell, Majors, and Waddell would get a government subsidy. From what I understand, they had to scramble to put everything together in time for the first run."

Josh couldn't believe his ears. Admittedly, the whole nation seemed swept up with the bold notion of the Pony Express, but few women bothered to keep track of the business details of such a venture. Ruth discussed the Russell, Majors, and Waddell partnership and their motives as a matter of course. *She has to be the brightest woman I've ever met. Most women simper and stick to small talk. Ruth jumps straight in. It's refreshing.*

"That Russell's a wily man, if you ask me." McCain absently rubbed his arm. His tone suggested approval.

"Wily?" Josh chuckled. "Dad, you just said if you were in business with Russell, you would have broken the partnership. Why are you admiring him now?"

"Man had a good reason for the time he chose. Spring and summer deliveries would be easiest. The riders could plan on fair weather and long days. He could rope unthinking investors into the Central Overland California and Pike's Peak Express and bail out before the truth dawned on folks."

Josh knew his father was pausing because he wanted someone to prod him into revealing his opinion. He obliged. "What truth is that?"

"Once winter came, even if the riders and stations hadn't had trouble with the Indians, the weather would close 'em down."

"The weather might well slow them down," Ruth said, "but since the Pony is adding relay stations every five to fifteen miles, don't you think fresh horses will help the delivery go through?"

"Not with the Indians stealing the ponies and killing the station keepers," Dad replied. As always, his tone carried great certainty.

"It's a staggering blow," Josh said as he settled in for a rousing debate. He enjoyed these sessions with his father. Drumming his fingers on the arm of his chair, he said, "I'm not sure I agree that these attacks can be considered the end of the Pony Express."

"The whole plan's nothing more than a folly, son. The romance of such an idea is sure to draw investors, and it's bound to dupe enough people to make the originators a pretty penny. Men will look at the Pony's grand success and clamor to invest before they consider all of the eventualities. It never fails to astonish me how imprudent and irrational people can be."

"The founders already own a highly successful freighting company," Ruth pointed out. "Certainly they've already taken your points into consideration."

"It's true freight still comes through in the winter. A single, light rider on a well-known path would have to be faster." Josh shifted slightly in his chair. "Regardless of who may eventually own the company, I can't imagine their giving up. Californians already rely on the Express."

"No reason we ought to," Dad said. "The state can take care of itself. We grow and raise whatever we need—crops of every kind and herds enough to keep a man's plate heaping forever and a day. We got shipping, too."

"We're part of the Union, though. I'm sure you agree that communication is vitally important. Waiting for mail to be carried across the Isthmus of Panama is uncertain and takes too long."

"Shipping takes up to six months," Laney said.

Josh winked at her. She tried hard to participate the best she could, and he was always proud when she remembered something and added in a comment.

"The Overland Stage takes a solid three weeks," Ruth chimed in. "Supposing something crucially important happened, that's still a huge lapse of time before the news comes through. The Pony is a significant improvement."

McCain gave Laney and Ruth a paternal smile. "But the assumption that anything there has a real impact on us is faulty. California is doing splendidly on her own. If communication is the issue, Josh, the telegraph is growing, and there are plans to expand it even further."

"But that's just California. Again, I point out that we are part of the Union."

"Something we might well regret," his father said in a ponderous tone.

"You can't mean that." Ruth looked shocked.

"I do." He heaved a deep sigh. "If anything, I'd rather we not have much to do with the other coast."

"Daddy, we're part of the United States," Laney said. "I remember your cheering when California became a state. How can you want to ignore the nation now?"

"Because the country's flinging itself head on into war. It'll be ugly, and no good can come of it." McCain banged his right fist on the arm of his chair. "California doesn't have anything to gain from the war, but we sure can lose a lot of men and money."

Josh winced. "With the Republican Convention nominating Abraham Lincoln as their presidential candidate last week in

Chicago, I have to admit that the chance that we'll see war is far greater. He's been clear in his speeches regarding slavery. The South won't abide by his opinions or leadership if he's elected."

"Democrats are split." Dad shook his head. "They can't come up with a candidate to please both North and South." He paused and said gravely, "It's going to be a bitter election, and those feelings will carry over."

"What about John Bell of the Constitutional Union party?" Ruth wasn't even pretending to be absorbed in her needlework. She'd told Josh that she had a brain and used it. It hadn't been a false boast. *But she also told me she has a mouth, and there are times I wish she'd muzzle it.* Unaware of his thoughts, she went on, "From what I've read, John Bell wants to preserve the Union and keep the Constitution, both as they are."

Josh snorted. "He owns a bunch of slaves. It's clear where he stands on the issues."

"The problem," McCain said, "is that Bell's idea might sound nice, but the Union and Constitution can't both be kept as is. Times changed—for some people but not for others. The North changed to an industrial-based economy; the South is firmly agricultural. The economic differences between the North and South are so extreme, they're already like two completely different countries."

"So you don't think reasonable men can somehow work out a compromise?" Ruth leaned forward, intent on the answer.

"No, they won't," Dad said. "This has been brewing for a while, and no one's come up with anything satisfactory. It's bound to boil over soon. As far as I'm concerned, Oregon and California ought to stay out of the fray and let them settle their own differences on the other side of the continent."

"Population density in the North will tilt the election." Josh thought for a moment. "It might have taken the Republicans three ballots before they settled on Lincoln, but he'll win unless the Democrats dig up someone who can make both North and South happy . . . and I don't think there's a man alive who can do that."

"There isn't." His father folded his arms across his chest. "Plain and simple, war's coming."

"If there's a war," Laney's voice shook, "you'd still stay home, wouldn't you, Josh?"

"Of course he would." McCain looked from Laney to Josh. "Family comes first."

Josh cleared his throat. "I'd have to pray about it, Laney. I know I'm needed here—"

"And here's exactly where you'll stay," his father interrupted in a harsh tone. "You can't leave a cripple to run the ranch. What kind of man would turn his back on his kin and roam off to fight for something that isn't any of his business?"

Dad rarely acknowledged his infirmity. In fact, he did all he could to be as independent and helpful as possible. Once, though Josh would never reveal it, he'd seen his father in front of a mirror, practicing gestures and movements to make his left arm look as normal as possible. That injury hurt more than Dad's arm; it cut his pride.

Josh stretched out his legs. His spurs jangled softly, and he took care not to hit Hilda's just-polished wood floor with them. If he did, war of a different kind would start right away. "No use in borrowing tomorrow's troubles. We're doing well and none of us knows what lies ahead. I'll pray for wisdom and pray for our nation."

Swiftly rising to his feet, Dad snapped, "Prayer doesn't make any difference. If it did, your mother would still be alive. I put up with you and Laney and Ruth asking a blessing on the food because it's a family tradition, but that's all it is. Don't waste my time or your breath talking to God about anything important. He doesn't listen. He doesn't care." He strode from the room, then the front door slammed.

"Oh, dear." Laney drew in an unsteady breath, then turned to Ruth. "I'm sorry you had to see that."

"Your father's words weren't a surprise," Ruth said. "Mrs. O'Sullivan mentioned that he's not walking with God. Why would he pretend otherwise, just because I'm here?"

"Dad went to church, but he never showed or spoke of his beliefs. When Mom passed on, he turned his back on God." The admission tore at Josh. "Laney and I keep him in our prayers, hoping he'll finally come around."

Unconsciously knotting her stitching up in her fist, Ruth nodded. "When Mama grew so frail, I thought about bargaining with God—only I didn't have anything to offer. Desperation does strange things to a person. Your father's been good to me, and I know you love him. I'll be praying for him, too."

"Thanks." The strain on Ruth's face made him ask, "Your mother . . . she was a believer, wasn't she?"

"Yes." A faint smile flickered across Ruth's features. "Mama loved the Lord with all her heart."

"Isn't it sweet to imagine our mamas together in heaven?" Laney asked.

Ruth nodded, but her expression turned somber once again.

Josh wondered if fresh grief was the only reason Ruth looked so strained. *Of course it isn't. As if her sorrow isn't burden enough, I've been surly with her. She's gotta feel like she's walking on eggshells whenever I'm around.*

"If you're finished with the paper, do you mind if I take it to my room?" Ruth tried to smooth out the wrinkles in the piecework she'd crumpled minutes before.

"Sure. Feel free." He cleared his throat. "You sound as if you've been doing some reading on the upcoming election."

"I have."

Laney perked up. "You'll never guess what Ruth has, Josh!"

"Oh?" He gave Ruth a questioning look.

Ruth gave Laney a baffled glance, and Laney made a slash-like gesture from her shoulder to the opposite hip.

She raised her chin a notch. "Oh, that. I have a red sash I wore when I participated in a suffragette march."

Josh sat and stared at her.

"I can see I've shocked you." She squared her shoulders. "Well, any worthwhile cause is bound to raise brows."

"Causes, worthwhile or not, elicit reactions." He gave her a level stare.

"Am I to infer you feel suffrage isn't a worthwhile cause?"

Josh waited a moment before responding. "Can't say I ever gave it any consideration."

"Neither did I," Laney said. "Even if I could, I don't know whom I'd vote for. I'd end up asking Daddy and Josh what they thought."

Whoa. Josh steeled himself. One wrong word, and Laney would feel stupid. On the other hand, he could offend Ruth seven ways to Sunday if he came down on another side of the fence.

Ruth turned to Laney and patted her hand. "There's nothing wrong with that. The Bible tells us to seek wise counsel. Plenty of women out there don't have brothers or fathers. They have to rely on newspapers, speeches, and those whom they respect. Either way, God gave women sound minds. After gathering information, why shouldn't a woman also have a voice?"

"I'm not agreeing or disagreeing." Josh rubbed his chin. "My mother was a highly intelligent woman. Mrs. O'Sullivan's sharp as they come, and Hilda—you couldn't find a harder worker. They all deserve respect and could voice a sound opinion. When I stop to think of them, allowing women to vote makes sense. But don't you think men are more affected by the government?"

Ruth finally gave up on her stitchery. She shoved it off to the side. "Not in the least! Just think about it: When the government repealed the Missouri Compromise with the Kansas-Nebraska Act six years ago, it wasn't just men who settled the land—they took their wives and daughters along. If a war does occur between the North and the South, men will be fighting it—but that means women will have to keep the homesteads going. Wives and mothers will lose their husbands and sons and have to carry on alone."

"Your points are well made, but the foundation is an emotional one. There are times in life when decisions are made because facts demand action, not feeling."

Ruth's brows rose. "I wouldn't disagree with that; what I question is your supposition that a woman would be an emotional voter and a man would be a logical one. Not a solitary woman attended the Democratic Convention, where several members walked out in a huff and made it so a candidate couldn't be nominated."

"Did that really happen?" Laney's eyes grew huge.

"Yes," Josh clipped. "Ruth, I told you, until you just brought it up, I hadn't given any consideration to suffrage. Many other matters demand my attention."

"Well, Toledo's seeing to the chicken coop, and I managed to hang the pictures, so the list of things waiting for your attention is shrinking." She gave him a cat-that-swallowed-the-canary smile. "We'll just have to add suffrage to your list."

"Fine." He returned her smile. "It'll be down there after my directing the hands, riding the fence, pulling late-spring calves, breaking horses, keeping an eye on the water level, and a few hundred other details."

"In no way did I mean to imply that you don't work hard. It's plain to see you do. If you think it's easy for me to sit around and be useless in this partnership, you can guess again. I've asked you to assign me chores."

"We don't need your help." As soon as he stated that stark fact, Josh regretted it. Her eyes darkened with pain, and he quickly sought to soften his words. "What I'd ask you to do is help the O'Sullivans. Part of life out here is helping our neighbors, and they'll be needing more of our assistance. You and Laney can go over to help Mrs. O'Sullivan with the house and her garden. I'd really appreciate that, and I'm sure she would, too."

"Laney and I already determined to do that." Ruth rose and stuffed her sewing into a basket. Part of it popped out when she flipped down the lid, and the needle trailed by the thread. "If you don't mind, I believe I'll retire and read the newspaper. Laney, I'll see you in the morning."

"Good night, Ruth. Sweet dreams." Laney watched as Ruth left the parlor, then she turned to Josh. "How could you?"

"What?"

"You made her feel stupid and useless. For your information, I need her even if you don't."

"I'm sure she's good company for you, sis."

"She's more than that." Laney glanced around to be sure they were alone, then whispered hotly, "Ruth is spending her mornings teaching me to read."

CHAPTER TWELVE

W e don't need your help...."

Josh's words echoed in Ruth's mind as she angrily reached for her right ankle-top boot. He treated his sister kindly and sang Kelly O'Sullivan's praises, so it wasn't that he disliked women.

It's me. The elastic gusset on the side of the boot stretched as she yanked the fashionable spool heel. Ruth didn't have the patience to lace or button her boots. Elastic required no fuss—not only in donning and removing the footwear, but also in polishing, which she rarely remembered to do. Ruth scowled as she pitched her boot toward the armoire. It landed with a satisfying thump. *Actually, maybe it's not me Josh's reacting to—maybe he's angry at the situation. I suppose he has good cause. If a judge finds favor in my claim, I'll receive a portion of what he's expected to get.*

She yanked off her other boot and sent it sailing across the room, where it landed close to the other one. "It's not my fault if he was counting his chickens before they hatched," she muttered to herself. She twisted to lie on her tummy, propped her chin in her hands, and blew a stream of air upward to move a few wild curls that flopped down toward her eyes.

"The answers are always in the Bible." Her mother's gentle words streamed through Ruth's mind. She wiggled a little farther, grabbed her Bible from the bedside table, and clutched it to her bosom. "Lord, I don't know what to do. I came here to start a new life, and all I'm doing is a whole lot of nothing. Surely you must have a purpose for me. Can't you show me the way?"

Someone tapped on her door. "Ruth?"

Lifting her head, she gave serious thought to ignoring Josh.

The tap grew louder. "Ruth?"

Suspecting if she didn't answer, he'd bang on the door and bellow her name as loudly as he'd called for Hilda on the day he brought her here, Ruth huffed, "What?"

"I don't want to talk to you through the door."

She set aside her Bible, walked to the door, and opened it as she observed, "You've been doing a fair job of it."

"We need to talk."

Her hand tightened around the ornate brass doorknob. He leaned to the side and propped his tall form against the doorframe, as if he could wait all night long for her to yield to his invitation. She, on the other hand, curled her stocking-covered toes under and rued the two inches she'd lost by taking off her boots.

He tilted his head toward the stairs and cajoled, "Come back down to the parlor."

A small, tense laugh bubbled out of her.

"What's so funny?"

"I was thinking of a rhyme." His brows rose in silent inquiry, so she quoted the first line of the Mary Howitt poem, "'"Will you walk into my parlor?" said the Spider to the Fly....'"

Josh let out a short bark of a laugh. "Rest assured, I'm not going to pounce and murder you."

She shifted, then stopped.

"What's wrong?"

"I took off my shoes."

"So what?" His arm snaked out and his hand hooked around her elbow. Drawing her into the hallway, he said, "We're going down to hold a conversation, not a cotillion."

"Then I suppose one of the two of us ought to be pleased. I tend to put my foot in my mouth whenever I speak, so not having a shoe on will make it less awkward for me. If it were a cotillion—well, with my lack of grace, you'd be far safer with me unshod."

His mouth twitched.

Ruth heaved a sigh. "Yes, I know. Unshod makes me sound like a horse. But ladies aren't supposed to mention specific garments."

"Back to the rules, huh?"

"I'd hoped I could abandon most of them, seeing as the West is reputed to be untamed." She started down the stairs. "So far, the only things that have changed are Hilda uses less silver at each place setting and I didn't need a calling card when we visited the O'Sullivans."

"That's all?"

"For me, it is. It's far different for men. Many of you go about in your shirtsleeves and gloveless in public. Regardless of the normal dictates, men seem to wear whichever hat suits their fancy. Men address women to whom they've not been introduced, and they bellow to one another instead of closing the distance and speaking in moderate tones. I could dither on and on, but I'm sure you understand what I mean."

"All of those differences reflect simple practicality."

"I suppose they do." Ruth wrinkled her nose. "But if practicality is valued, why don't you allow me to pitch in and help? I'm strong and can put my hands to a task."

"Toledo will finish expanding the chicken coop by tomorrow. You can take over gathering eggs and feeding the chickens."

"That's a start. What about—"

He held up a hand to silence her, then cast a quick look over his shoulder. In a bare whisper, he ordered, "Wait till we're in the parlor. I don't want Dad to overhear this."

Ruth bobbed her head. Josh led her into the parlor, seated her on the settee, then proceeded to take the spot immediately beside her. *Well, there's another difference. Back home, a man didn't share a woman's settee unless they were courting. Josh is far more likely to kick me out than kiss me.*

"Ruth, Laney needs your help," he said a muted tone. "She tells me you're working with her, teaching her to read. Don't you think that's far more important than mucking a stall or pitching hay?"

"I'm doing that because she's my friend and I care about her. There's a vast difference between assisting a friend and doing real work."

"I disagree. When you go visit Kelly O'Sullivan, you delve in and take over whatever chore she's doing. Galen's even told me so."

"That's just assisting a friend."

"It's a matter of perspective. Those tasks are her work, and I know she appreciates how you and Laney help shoulder her burdens. With Cullen's health as tenuous as it is, when you and Laney help with tasks, Kelly's load is lightened. Part of ranching is helping neighbors. I think you underestimated the importance of my asking you to lend a hand over at the O'Sullivans'."

"Josh, you don't understand. Laney and I have a delightful time over there. If anything, Mrs. O'Sullivan has taken us under her wing. Just a breath ago, you praised practicality—well, the embarrassing fact is, Laney and I don't have the vaguest notion about how to do the practical, everyday things most women do. Mrs. O'Sullivan is teaching us, and the value of what she's sharing with us cannot be imagined."

Josh grinned. "I'm glad she's teaching you those things. But, Ruth, don't you see? If you value her lessons, why shouldn't Laney and I find great worth in your teaching her to read?"

"But it's such a simple thing."

Josh shook his head. "What you've done for her is nothing short of astonishing. Never once, in all of her years of schooling, did anyone call her clever or tell her she would succeed. You build her up and boost her confidence. Whatever you need to work with her—just let me know, and I'll obtain it. She actually believes you're going to have her reading."

"As well she should. Josh, she can read. Truly, she can. Maybe not complicated treatises, but Laney can sound out words."

Josh broke into an enormous smile. "See? To my way of reckoning, between the lessons you're giving her and the help you're extending to the O'Sullivans, you are pulling your weight around the Broken P. I want you to stop searching for a backbreaking chore and recognize the value of what you are doing."

"It's precious little."

"I disagree."

"Josh?"

"Yeah?"

"It's a good thing your father does the books for the ranch. Your idea of accounting doesn't add up."

"What doesn't add up?" McCain rapped out from the parlor entryway.

"Ruth and I were discussing her desire to help around here."

McCain snorted. "Girl, this is a man's world. Laney understands how it is—you don't see her wanting to rope calves. After a hard day's work, a man wants to come home to a warm welcome and a cool drink."

Ruth flashed Josh a look.

He reached over and squeezed her hand. "I've told Ruth that pitching in at the O'Sullivans' is important."

"Of course it is." McCain sauntered over to his customary chair, but he didn't sit down. "Laney and you represent the Broken P when you go out. Relations with neighbors are important. They just bought two of our mustangs, and twice a year, they buy half a steer. One hand washes the other."

"See?" Josh gave her an I-told-you-so look.

McCain's brows furrowed. "Is this about money? Do you need me to buy you something?"

"No. Oh, not at all." Ruth shook her head. "You've already been remarkably generous. Laney and I haven't finished sewing up all the material you bought for us."

McCain finally eased into the chair. "If you need something, you only have to ask."

"I appreciate the offer; it's most kind of you. But I do have funds available to me." Ruth felt confident the eighty dollars she'd brought with her would see her through quite adequately until her mother's estate settled.

"The Broken P accounts are all paid up," McCain said slowly. "Our credit is good, but we run a lean operation. You should know that."

Ruth looked from father to son. "I'm sure with all of the hard work you men put into this ranch, you've been good stewards of what the Lord entrusted to you."

"It's not the Bible that's keeping the profit line. Brains, sweat, and blood are what it takes." McCain drummed the fingers of his right hand on the arm of the chair. "Was there anything else you wanted to know about the finances?"

"Dad, you came in on the tail end of the conversation. Ruth's concern was that she contributed, not that there would be any hitches in the bookkeeping."

"Humpf."

Ruth figured she was better off to keep silent. Clearly Josh was right when he said his father's pride stung that he couldn't labor about the place and he needed to feel good about managing the finances. Unable to concoct anything diplomatic, she decided to escape to her room. "Well, then, I think I'll retire."

She took three steps, then jerked back. "Ouch!"

"What's wrong?" Josh asked.

Spying a needle on the carpet, Ruth stooped to pick it up. "I just found that needle I was missing."

"Are you okay?" Josh reached to take the needle from her.

"Of course I am. Thank you." She stuck the needle through

her sleeve. "Good night, gentlemen."

As she mounted the stairs, Ruth overheard McCain tell his son, "I've never known a woman so bent on hurting herself. Did you know the first day we went to town, she fell off the boardwalk and about got herself killed?"

Unwilling to eavesdrop and hear more about her flaws, Ruth trudged upstairs.

"I've been thinking," Ruth said as she wandered back and forth in the parlor.

Josh eyed her with trepidation. Couldn't she ever just sit down and be placid? After stepping on the needle last night, she ought to hold a tad more caution.

"I noticed a sad lack of something vital around here." Ruth's skirts swished as she turned back around.

Go peek in the mirror, Ruth. You're vital. Look at you—you can't even stand still, Josh thought.

"What are we missing?" Laney continued to crochet a lacy edging around a pillowslip.

"Nothing," Josh said repressively. "We've gotten along just fine. I can't think of a thing we lack."

Pulling to a halt, Ruth gave him an icy look. *No wonder she got kicked out of ladies' academies. The girl doesn't have a scrap of charm or womanly wiles.*

"I'm sure once you hear my plan, you'll agree it's something I should set to at once." Ruth started toward the far side of the parlor once again. She stopped at the shelf and gestured toward it. "Josh, how many of these books have you read?"

He smothered a smile. She'd distracted herself. "All of them. You're welcome to borrow whatever you'd like, Ruth."

She studied the spines of the dozen or so books, then gave him a woebegone look. "You don't have one on physics."

"Do you need a physician?" McCain gave Ruth a guarded look.

Her cheeks flushed to the same color as the stagecoach she'd ridden in on. "I appreciate your concern, but I assure you, I'm in the pink of health, sir. I was referring to the subject of the science of modern physics."

"Humph." Dad levered himself out of his chair. "It'd be a waste of space. Boring, useless information. *Farmer's Almanac, Animal Husbandry*—those have a place on a ranch. No use wasting time with fancy numbers that don't change the water table or the head count of the livestock." He sauntered over to the humidor and took out a cigar.

"Oh, Daddy," Laney sighed. "Those smell so awful."

He rolled the cigar between his hands. "You never complained about Alan's smoking."

"His cigarettes didn't stink even half as much as your cigars. Why don't you roll yourself a cigarette like you used to make for him?"

"They don't last long enough to give me thinking time." He stooped over and kissed Laney's brow. "I'll go outside with it."

"Thank you, Daddy."

After he left, Ruth turned back toward the books. "I disagree with your father. There must be several practical applications for physics on a ranch."

Josh nodded. He agreed, but he also wanted to let her ramble on. As long as she stayed distracted, she wouldn't try to pitch whatever harebrained scheme she'd planned to spring on him.

"Knowledge is never wasted," Ruth continued.

"Ruth's read a lot." Laney tied a knot and clipped the fragile crochet thread. "She's quite clever, Josh."

"You're clever, too," Ruth said. "Look at what a thing of beauty you've made. Wouldn't you like a book of different patterns to crochet and stitch?"

"Why, yes."

"That's a nice idea, Ruth." Grinning, Josh rested his ankle on the opposite knee. Ruth never stopped thinking, but her mind wandered. Her conversation resembled a spray of buckshot—and in this instance, he'd encourage that flaw because he didn't want to have to dissuade her from whatever else she'd set her mind to. "The next time someone goes to town, we could get a book for Laney."

Laney's jaw dropped. "You're doing this so I'll read!"

"You were my inspiration," Ruth declared as she headed back to the settee. Her skirts billowed out with a complete lack of control as she half-flopped down. Belatedly smoothing them into a modicum of order, she smiled at Laney. "Truly, Laney, watching you made all my thoughts fall into line."

Doubting her thoughts were ever half that orderly, Josh still admired Ruth's concept. Ruth's practical way of coaxing Laney to read pleased him, so Josh figured, at least this once, her never-ceasing habit of hatching up plans had proven to be beneficial. "I'm sure you and Ruth could share a book."

Ruth beamed at him. "Exactly! That's what books are for—sharing."

Josh nodded.

"I'm so glad you see it my way." Ruth hopped up again. "I've already started a list of my favorite books." She pulled two sheets of crumpled paper from her sleeve.

Is there anything more she could possibly pull from her sleeves? A hanky or a fan is normal—but a knife and sheets of paper? This woman never ceases to amaze me.

Ruth messed with the papers, trying to smooth them out. "You can tell me what your favorites are, so I can add them."

Josh chuckled. "I appreciate your enthusiasm, Ruth, but it'll be a while before Laney might want to tackle them, and I'm sure many won't be to her liking. We hold vastly different interests."

"But we want to have a wide assortment. Having a good selection is essential to success." Ruth slipped the papers into his hands.

"Josh's books are too hard. I'm sure yours will be, too," Laney whispered.

"We're going to have a variety," Ruth reassured her. "My list includes many of the more basic books I enjoyed as I started to read, not just more recent selections."

Josh glanced down at the first sheet of paper and nearly choked. Four columns snaked down the page in itty-bitty print. Ink blots marred several of the words. When he flipped it over to see if the second sheet was equally crammed, Josh discovered the back of that first sheet also bore top-to-bottom columns. "You must have two hundred books listed here."

"Three hundred twenty-three," Ruth provided. "I know it's just a start—"

"A start!" He stared at her. "Variety is one thing, excess is another."

"That list is far from excessive. If you bother to look, you'll notice some of the books are important references, such as a dictionary."

"A dictionary!" He'd praised her last night for working with Laney and told her he'd get the materials she required to do the job, but he hadn't thought she'd take matters to such an extreme. "Ruth—"

"Don't worry. The dictionary and the books with dots beside them are ones I still own. Books are like old friends to me. Bernadette—she was our housekeeper back home—and I packed them. They'll arrive by boat through Sacramento."

Josh studied the list with a mixture of surprise and dismay. She'd included everything from Hans Christian Andersen's fairy-tales to Hawthorne and Thoreau. *Jane Eyre* was scribed beside *Robinson Crusoe*. The assortment rated as nothing less than astonishing, but much of it would be far beyond Laney's abilities for a long while yet. How could he talk sense into Ruth without crushing his sister?

Why didn't she come to me privately? The answer flitted through his mind immediately. *Because she's Ruth. Ruth told me of her tendency to speak when she ought to hold her tongue.*

Beaming at him, Ruth gushed, "As you can see, my books will provide a nice, albeit small, foundation. I'm open to any additions or suggestions."

"I've never thought of books as being like friends," Laney marveled softly. "I considered them to be ... well ... enemies."

"Oh, but you'll never be lonely or bored again when you love books!" Ruth moved beside Laney and patted her shoulder. She was always in motion, so it strained Josh's imagination to picture her sitting quietly, reading. "The minute I take a book from the shelf and open it, I can travel anywhere, become a different person, and experience so much! You will, too."

"Truly?"

The hope in Laney's eyes made Josh relent. "I tell you what— I'll either knock together a bookshelf or see about buying one in town."

"Oh, thank you!" Ruth clasped her hands together in front of her bosom. "I appreciate your support, and I'll count on you to let me know what else I need to order."

Staring back down at her list, Josh muttered, "This looks like plenty to me."

"Dickens' *A Tale of Two Cities* came out last year. I haven't read it, have you?"

"Can't say as I have."

"Then we'll have to add that title to the list. I enjoyed his *Oliver Twist* more than *David Copperfield,* but both stories were entertaining. It won't do to fill the shelves entirely with books we've both read. Part of the fun is discovering new authors."

"I tell you what: Let me get the shelf, then once your books arrive and you've had an opportunity to enjoy them again, we can add a book or two each time we go to town." Pleased with the tactful way he'd reined in her enthusiasm, Josh handed back the list.

Face puckered in confusion, Ruth accepted the pages.

"Do you want me to whitewash the shelf to match your room?"

"My room?!"

"Where else would you put it?"

"Why, in the library, of course! What did you think I was talking about?"

"What library?" Laney took the words right out of his mouth. She and he both looked to Ruth for an explanation.

"The lending library I'm going to start for the town."

"Back up a minute here." Josh snatched back the list. He immediately rolled up the pages, stuffed them in his shirt pocket so she couldn't reclaim them, and folded his arms across his chest.

"Surely you didn't think I wanted to buy all of those books only to hoard them to myself. That would be horrendously selfish of me."

Hadn't she heard what Dad just said about the Broken P? Three years of hard work pulled it out of the red and into the black. Almost every penny got poured back into the place—building this house, buying better breeding stock. The only extravagance had been Laney's two years at finishing school—and that rated as a necessity because it was one of their mother's wishes for Laney.

"If there isn't a storefront available—"

"There's not going to be a library." He gave Ruth a stern look.

"Oh, don't react so, Josh. As I was going to say, if there's no storefront, we can just hire someone to build to our specifications. That might be best."

Laney got to her feet. "You're really serious about this."

"It's always nice to have dreams and aspirations," Josh said, "but they can't always be realized into being. Even if they are, it takes a lot to make them happen." *A lot of money we can't spare.*

"You underestimate me, Josh. I can do this. I prayed last night, and everything just fell into place. Hard work doesn't bother me. When I started thinking about it, I realized there are undoubtedly other adults who would like to participate in reading lessons. I could go in twice a week."

"There's no other way for me to say it, so I'm going to come right on out and put it on the line."

"Please do."

"No library. Do you understand me? It's not going to happen. No one can take time away to escort you to and from town a couple times a week, and that's just the start of the problems."

"I even thought of having an upstairs where I could live."

"Ruth, no!" Distraught, Laney grabbed Ruth's sleeve. "You belong here."

"Maybe I don't. A lot depends on what the courts decide about my father's will."

"I don't care about that old will," Laney declared. "Alan was your daddy. You deserve to stay here, regardless of whether or not you end up inheriting a single inch of the property. Isn't that right, Josh?"

Wishing Laney hadn't put him on the spot like that, Josh unfolded his arms, then promptly crammed his hands in his pockets. "Ruth is welcome to live here. As for this library or anything else—it's premature to make any decisions."

"Not necessarily," Ruth said. "There's nothing wrong with my putting my plan into motion and—"

"And you'd be counting your chickens before they hatch," he cut in. Josh strode out of the parlor, to the front door, and resisted the temptation to bang it shut.

"What was that about?" McCain asked as he puffed on his cigar.

"Ruth." That one word summed up the problem in total.

"Oh?"

"I may as well fill you in on her latest scheme."

"She's not talking about organizing a suffragette march in town, is she?"

"No."

Dad chuckled. "Then whatever it is, it can't be half as hard to squelch. The gal has an iron will and an overabundance of energy."

"She's taken a mind to start up a town library." Josh watched his father's reaction.

"I trust you convinced her it's preposterous?" Dad blew out a cloud of smoke. "I just told her the ranch is on a tight budget. There's no way we could begin to fund such a thing."

"She asked for my suggestions on what books to acquire and gave me a list of three hundred twenty-three she—"

Dad choked, then coughed. "Three hundred!"

Josh nodded. "And twenty-three. During the conversation, she thought of another to add on. Given a day or so, we could easily see her list triple in size."

"We've got to put an end to this."

"Considering it's Ruth we're dealing with, that's easier said than done."

Rolling up his sleeves, Galen walked toward the stable. The air carried a decided nip, but he'd work up some heat in no time as he mucked out the stalls.

"Wait up!" Colin hastened out of the house.

Galen paused. He'd wanted to let his brother sleep in today. He'd stayed up late last night reading the Bible to Da. Colin's cocky smile made Galen decide to hold his tongue. His brother was doing his best to show maturity and responsibility—both qualities he'd sorely need, and soon. Might as well let him do it as quickly as he could.

He waited until Colin drew up, then gave him a brotherly slap on the shoulder and nodded his approval. "Bet we can get plenty done before breakfast."

"Yep." Colin started to roll up his sleeves. Half an hour later, Colin leaned on his shovel. "Galen?"

"Huh?"

"The Pony's not coming through. Hasn't for days now."

"No, it hasn't. Service is temporarily interrupted."

"That's what I hear, but I'm wondering if those are just fancy words for their saying that the company is quitting."

"I doubt it. They invested too much to give up."

"I guess you have a point. What if they do, though? What happens to the horses?"

"They're property of the Central Overland California and Pike's Peak Express. Russell, Majors, and Waddell would decide what to do with them." Galen looked at Colin. Since all three of his little brothers now had a horse of their own to ride, the questions took him by surprise. Sure, if the three of them had all still been sharing one horse, it would make sense. "What's with all the questions?"

"So do they still pay for us to maintain the mounts, even when the delivery's not coming through?"

"I can't honestly answer that. Hasn't come time for them to settle the monthly account. By all rights, they should. Horses still have to be fed, watered, mucked after, and babied."

Colin nodded. "That's what I thought, too." He worked another couple of minutes, then stopped. "I don't know how money is, but I was thinking it would be good to have the money from the Express saved to pay Doc."

"We'll make do, regardless." Galen set aside his shovel and moved toward his brother. "Our heavenly Father will provide and take care of us."

Colin's chin lifted. "Is that your way of telling me I'm not going to have a father here much longer?"

Galen slowly settled his hand on his brother's shoulder. He stared him in the eye and let out a sigh. "Aye, Colin. That's exactly what we're facing."

"I feared 'twas so." Colin's eyes filled up.

Galen pulled him into a hug and held him tightly. His frame was still that of a skinny youth—his thin shoulders not yet ready to bear the burdens that lay ahead. Resting his temple against

Colin's unruly russet mop, Galen allowed himself the luxury of tears. After a while, he roughly patted Colin's shuddering back. "There's no shame in loving, and I'll have you remember Jesus himself wept when Lazarus died. 'Tis a mark of the respect we hold for Da, but this sadness—I'm thinking it's best if we keep it between ourselves. We need to be strong for Ma."

"And Dale and Sean," Colin said as he wiped his face.

Galen nodded. "You and I—we'll have to be the men in the family and stand as sound examples for Dale and Sean. You'll be shedding your youth and becoming a man before your time."

"When do you reckon the boys ought be told?"

"Ma and Da and I discussed it the other day. They're of the opinion that the boys'll ask questions when they're good and ready for the truth. Until then, we'll not tell them the facts—but we'll not lie, either."

"So you were waiting for me to ask?" Colin's eyes narrowed in anger.

"Nay, Colin. You and I—we may have years between us, but we've never let that make a difference. I've not kept secrets from you. I owed you this knowledge, but finding the right time to impart it—well, that's been hard."

"You've been working two men's jobs." Colin straightened his shoulders. "But no more. I'll step up."

"I knew you would." It wasn't hard to sound confident. Galen knew Colin had a strong streak of determination in his constitution. "Now let's finish up here. I'm getting hungry."

"I'm hungry, too," Dale said from the barn door. "Ma's put the biscuits in the oven, so she's telling me I'm slow this morning."

"Then you'd best get to milking." Galen winked at Colin, then called after Dale, "and no giving the cats a squirt or two. I spied a couple of mice this morning, so I want the tabbies hungry."

"All right," Dale called back. A minute later, he stuck his head around the edge of the stall. "Galen, how didja know—about the cats?"

Galen grinned. "Ah, Dale. Once upon a time, milkin' was my chore. The cats surely liked me a lot back then."

"Oh." Dale and Colin both started to laugh.

Their laughter warmed Galen's heart. After breakfast, as he sent his brothers off to school, he overheard Dale telling Sean all about it. All three of them left toward town, each on his own horse, with a few schoolbooks buckled tight in a leather book strap and fastened to the saddle along with a lunch bucket.

Just as he'd promised, Josh had given the O'Sullivans his old saddle, and Da told Colin to use his, but that had still left them one short. Galen didn't know where the third saddle came from. A couple days after he bought the pair of mustangs, he'd been out in the fields. When he came back in, that other saddle was sitting in the middle of the barn floor.

He had a sneaking suspicion Josh had plenty to do with it. If Josh wanted to play the game that way, fine. Come harvesttime, sacks of nuts and bushels of fruit would mysteriously show up on the McCain porch.

These past days had been odd. Galen hadn't realized how he'd planned his days to fit around the Pony relays. Each morning, he'd plot out what to do and where to be in accordance with when a rider might be through. Today, he didn't need to conform to that. He hadn't for a little while, and it left him strangely adrift. It wasn't as if he didn't have plenty to fill his hours, because he did. It was just that he'd been timing his days by that event.

Now that Da wasn't doing so well, Galen also planned his days around whether the gals were coming over from the Broken P. If they came, he knew Ma would have help or that she could send Ruth to fetch him. Bless her gentle and wise heart, on the rare occasions when she needed his help, Ma never sent Laney to summon him. At breakfast, Ma mentioned that the lasses were going to help her in the garden today. Keeping that in mind, Galen planned to do chores that would keep him close to the house.

In another week, when the boys were out of school, this

wouldn't be a consideration. Even if Ma needed to leave the house for a while, either Sean or Dale would be around. Da would love havin' his youngest sons nearby the whole day long. Their silliness never failed to delight him. Until the Lord took Da home, Galen wanted him to be showered with every joy possible.

It wasn't long before Ruth and Laney rode up. He helped them dismount and casually looked about to be sure Toledo hadn't shadowed them. "I'll put your horses out to pasture. Day's going to be hot, so we'll pamper them a wee bit."

"That's so thoughtful of you," Laney gushed.

"Thank you, Galen." Ruth stepped closer. "I brought something over you might want to read." She handed him a slip of paper. "I copied it down because I didn't think you'd want your dad to read it in the newspaper. It's about the Pony Express."

"Okay." He tucked the paper in his pocket and led the horses toward the barn so he could unsaddle them. The paper nearly burned a hole in his pocket, but he tended the horses first. Once they contentedly cropped grass in the pasture, he sat under a cottonwood and leaned against the trunk.

What he'd taken as one slip of paper turned out to be two. Ruth's penmanship made him grin. For all of her fancy schooling, he'd expected her to use all the pretty flourishes and elegant sweeps. Instead, her script was far worse than his own, and that was saying plenty.

June 6, 1860 William Finney, writing from Carson City

She'd placed that at the top of the page, and Galen perked up. William Finney was the pony agent in San Francisco. The fact that he'd gone to Carson City underscored the gravity of what had already transpired.

Will the people of Sacramento help the Pony in its difficulty?

Galen's pulse picked up. Surely, this meant something was bound to happen. Sacramento was proud as could be about being the last Pony stop. From there, everything was dispersed via the Post Office. Sacramentans wouldn't want to lose the prestige.

Finney's approaching them for assistance rated as nothing short of brilliant.

We have conferred some benefits, asked but little, and perhaps the people will assist. Can anything be done in your city toward paying expenses to furnish arms and provisions for the twenty-five men to go through with me to Salt Lake to take and bring on the Express?

I will be responsible for the return of the arms, will have transportation of my own, and can get men here. What is wanted is $1,000 for the pay of the men, $500 for provisions, and twenty-five Sharp's rifles and as many dragoon pistols. I will guarantee to keep the Pony alive a while longer.

Galen whistled under his breath. Finney was asking for a lot. Then again, the stakes were high—the Pony Express hung in the balance. The United States Cavalry couldn't be expected to escort the riders or camp out at all of the stations, so private individuals would have to venture out and make a show of force.

His father owned a shotgun, but they needed it for hunting. As for pistols—the O'Sullivans wouldn't have one in the house. Da said they were for killing men, and he'd not have one on his hip or in his house. No, their family wouldn't be donating a weapon.

But what about money? Grimacing, Galen knew they didn't have any to spare—especially after having bought two horses. Colin was right on the mark, supposing whatever the Pony paid for them to run the relay needed to be held in reserve for medical expenses. Especially after Finney's comment that he'd only keep the business open *a while longer,* every last cent counted.

The parson and Da both said God always provided. Well, right about now, this looked like a mighty big opportunity for Him to come through.

"Galen!"

He popped to his feet and hastened around the corner of the stable. "Yeah, Ma?"

"The lasses and I are headin' toward the garden."

He nodded and glanced toward the house meaningfully, then shot her a big smile.

Ma grinned back. "God blessed me the day you were born," she called to him.

He chuckled. "Ma, you got it turned around. He blessed me when He planted me in this family."

"Well, think of it however you may. Long as you're talkin' o' plantin', I might as well warn you, I'm getting a hankering for flowers about the porch. Next time you go to town, I'll be wantin' some flower seeds."

He said nothing about the fact that Ma hadn't cultivated her customary spring flower garden. She'd been too busy, and whatever had reseeded itself from last year was all that grew at the present.

Laney smoothed her skirts and asked, "Isn't it a little late in the season to be planting summer flowers?"

"It's never too late for beauty." Ma curled her hands around the handles of the wheelbarrow.

Ruth let out a squawk and nudged her away. "It's my turn!"

Galen shook his head. Ruth. She had a way of asserting herself that was downright entertaining. In fact, she was the only woman he'd ever met who matched Ma for sheer gumption and spirit.

Ruth had been a subtle ally in keeping Laney's infatuation reined in, a delightful visitor for Da, and managed to keep Ma's mind diverted onto pleasant things in the midst of the looming sorrow. *God provides....* The phrase echoed in his mind. *Aye, God provided when He sent Ruth Caldwell here.*

CHAPTER THIRTEEN

The smooth wooden handles felt good in her hands. Ruth gripped them and pushed the wheelbarrow along the path toward an enormous square of trees. The flour and sugar sacks in the bed didn't begin to muffle the rattle of the hoes. All in all, it made for a merry racket.

If ever there was a day she wanted to be away from the Broken P, surely this was it. Tension crackled at the breakfast table, and Josh had started in on listing any number of ridiculous reasons why she shouldn't establish a library. His father was equally opinionated. *They have no right to dictate what I do.* Difficult as it had been, Ruth tried to remain silent—but she'd hit her limit.

If Toledo hadn't come to retrieve those meddlesome men and take them to the barn, I would have told them it's none of their affair how I spend the inheritance I receive from Mama. Why, I even thought to name the library after her. I still will, too. They're not going to stop me.

"Oh, now, will you look there." Kelly O'Sullivan stooped and picked a poppy. Tucking it in her hair, she said, "Nothing raises a woman's spirits like flowers. I didn't manage to plant any this year, but God's good to strew my path with them."

"Ruth and I could ride to town tomorrow and get flower seeds," Laney offered.

And I could buy some books. I do have eighty dollars to start with.

Completely unaware Ruth was hatching that plot, Laney said longingly, "I'd love to plant flowers at home. Daddy found a pair of wild rose bushes he dug up and planted out back, but there's nothing else. We have that big new house and it looks so stark. Don't you think so, too, Ruth?"

"Uh, yes." Ruth decided she'd better pay more attention to the conversation.

"In Sacramento, just before Mama passed on, she bought a beautiful camellia. They were the rage. I'd adore having one on either side of the steps leading to our front veranda."

"Lester has a catalog from the New England Seed Company on his store counter. Despite their name, they happen to be located nearby. We could ask him to order a pair of potted camellias." Ruth laughed. "I don't know how to take them out of the pot and put them in the ground, but Mrs. O'Sullivan would tell us, wouldn't you?"

"Sure and enough, I would. Flowers do have a way of perking up a place. It's as if a rainbow touches the earth whenever you look at a patch of flowers."

"I love the way you speak," Ruth said. She smiled at Mrs. O'Sullivan. "Not just your accent, though it's lilty and fun, but you choose wonderful words."

"I agree," Laney said. "'A rainbow touches the earth' is such a picturesque way to describe it."

"Now aren't the both of you kind as can be?"

Ruth let out a relieved sigh. "I'm so glad you took what I said in the right way. I truly intended it as a compliment, but back at school, I'm sure someone would have misconstrued my meaning."

"I'm a firm believer in plain talking." Mrs. O'Sullivan reached around and retied her apron strings as she spoke. "Folks who have to shade their meanings or look for the same in others vex me.

Speaking from the heart and taking things at face value makes it easy to get along."

"It's just that I don't think before I open my mouth. I'm sure I wouldn't have hurt feelings if I'd thought before I spoke."

"Ruth, you'd never say something mean," Laney said. "Anyone who doesn't know that can't see past the nose on their face."

Mrs. O'Sullivan nodded. "You'll find Westerners speak frankly. The bluntness cuts to the core of the matter, and folks appreciate you're not wasting their time by beatin' 'round the bush. Don't e'er fear speakin' amiss with me, lass. I'll nab ye if I feel the need, but I've yet to see a need."

The hoes rattled sharply as Ruth turned into the garden. "I'll take it in the loving spirit in which it would be given."

Mrs. O'Sullivan nodded. "A honest heart is a happy one. Oh, look. God's been sproutin' my garden whilst my back was turned."

"You have a lot of cabbage and lettuce." Ruth settled the wheelbarrow on the soft earth.

"More cabbage than lettuce," Mrs. O'Sullivan said. "'Tis a more useful vegetable. It stores longer, and I can use it in several recipes."

Laney wrinkled her nose. "Hilda loves sauerkraut."

"Aye, you can make the cabbage into sauerkraut."

Ruth winked at Laney and whispered, "Sauerkraut is dreadful. It makes me feel like a liar to bow my head and listen to grace when I'm not in the least bit thankful to eat it!"

"'Tisn't my favorite dish, I confess, but I'm always grateful for it. Time was, back home, when the potatoes got blight. We had precious little to eat. I put up every last scrap I could from our garden and we prayed to the dear Lord to stretch it to last."

Laney exclaimed, "Galen must have been just a little boy!"

"He was." Mrs. O'Sullivan let out a sigh. "We had two other sons after him, but they were too frail. Cholera took them ere we came to America."

"I'm so sorry!" Laney threw her arms around Mrs. O'Sullivan in an ardent embrace.

Looking at the woman in awe, Ruth couldn't fathom her strength. *She's buried two sons and will soon lose her husband, yet she faces each day with joy. When I'm around others, I can set aside my grief, but when I'm alone, it nearly chokes me. How does she keep her serenity and joy?*

"I'm a blessed woman, I am. God let me keep my Galen and gave me three more sons to replace the two I sent back to Him." Mrs. O'Sullivan patted Laney, then reached over and cupped Ruth's cheek. "Your own grief is raw, Ruth Caldwell. Don't be hard on yourself. Lean on God's strength and mercy."

"'The Lord gave, and the Lord hath taken away; blessed be the name of the Lord.'" Ruth murmured hesitantly.

"Ach, yes. That's from the first chapter of Job. Now there was a man who lost everything. What did he do? He clung to his faith. When God grants us the love of a mate, a child, or a friend, 'tis a blessing. We have no right to tell Him how long to allow us the enjoyment of that blessing, so if He takes that loved one back to His bosom, we're to thank Him for the time He granted us."

Tears filled Ruth's eyes. "But I miss Mama so much!"

"Of course you do." Mrs. O'Sullivan enveloped her in an embrace and cupped Ruth's head to her shoulder. "And you'll weep, just as Our Savior did when He heard of His friend Lazarus's passing. We weep for our own loss. There's no shame in that."

"But you're s-so h-h-happy."

"Time and grace soften the loss. For now with my Cullen, I'm cherishing every day we share. Once he hears the Lord's voice and follows Him home, I'll weep an ocean. In those days, you lasses will come comfort me with the certainty that my dear Cullen awaits me in paradise and will allow me the solace of talking about my sweet memories."

"Of course we will," Laney pledged.

Ruth squeezed Mrs. Sullivan but didn't say a word. *You'll have those memories because you stayed by his side. I left Mama and went off to those dumb schools when I should have been by her side, helping and loving her.*

"It's a good thing we brought our hats. Sunny as it is today, we'd suffer terribly otherwise." Laney retied her bonnet's ribbons into a jaunty bow.

Taking her cue to set to work, Ruth turned loose of Mrs. O'Sullivan. "I know I'm supposed to cover up so I won't get burned or baked by the sun. Lily white skin is fashionable, but I like the warmth of the sun on my face."

"You'll put on your hat, lass." Mrs. O'Sullivan covered her own bright hair with a sunbonnet. "The only things ripening in my garden are the fruits and vegetables. The both o' you are sweet as plums; I'll not have you turnin' into prunes!"

"I think plums are the one and only thing you don't grow," Laney said as she took up a hoe.

"Why is that?" Ruth wondered.

"You can't have everything in the world. My Cullen, he planted me more'n I ever dreamed to own. The trick in life is to be satisfied with whate'er you have and whate'er your lot is."

"Paul said that in the Bible, too." Laney started to work.

"That, he did." Mrs. O'Sullivan went to the next row over. "I reckon if he could be content in a prison cell, certain as can be, I can find happiness in my home and garden."

Ruth picked up the last hoe and set to work.

By midday, they'd accomplished a great deal. Cabbage, lettuce, and carrots filled the flour sacks. The women stacked them in the wheelbarrow, and Laney declared, "It's my turn to push now!"

Ruth held the hoes. "Okay. Then let's go."

Mrs. O'Sullivan set her hands on her hips. "But what am I to carry?"

"You can carry your head high, because you're a daughter of the King," Laney said.

"Listen to her. She's right." Ruth set out walking. "I wish I were more like you, Laney. You have a talent for saying something that's fitting. I'd call it a silver tongue, but that makes you sound glib, and you're not."

"'Words aptly spoken are like apples of gold,'" Mrs. O'Sullivan quoted.

Laney shoved the wheelbarrow over a rut. "I don't want a golden apple in my mouth, because I know whatever we're going to have for lunch will be far tastier!"

"'Tis a humble meal we'll be having—corned beef on this mornin's leftover biscuits and coleslaw." Mrs. O'Sullivan added a little jig between her steps. "Why, ye'd be thinkin' I'm Irish or somethin'!"

"To look at me, you'd think I'm a dirt clod." Ruth stared at her skirt. "We all worked in the garden, but the two of you are still nearly spotless. Once you dust off your hems and wash your hands, you'll be fine. Anyone spying me would think I wallowed with the hogs!"

"Dirt washes," Laney said.

Mrs. O'Sullivan shook her head. "Lass, that riding skirt you've been workin' on is all done, save the button at the waist. You can change and stop fretting."

"Laney and I wanted to wear them on the same day."

"And you still can. Just not today."

"You can switch into something else once we get home. No one will see you, so we can be alike tomorrow." Laney set down the wheelbarrow by the house.

As plans went, it all sounded good. Ruth dusted most of the dirt from her shirtwaist and changed into the brown paisley. Catching her reflection in a mirror as she came out from behind the screen, she groaned. The sunbonnet had slipped to and fro a little, and as a result her hairpins all worked loose. Ringlets sprang from her in wild profusion.

Mr. O'Sullivan let out a rusty chuckle from the bed. "Oh, lass. You look like you suffered a terrible fright!"

"Cullen O'Sullivan!" his wife chided.

"He told the unvarnished truth." Ruth started stabbing the pins back in. They escaped as quickly as she tried to anchor them.

"Here. Let me help." Laney stood on tiptoe and gathered Ruth's hair. A twist here and a pin there, and in a matter of a few moments, she'd arranged the disorderly mass into something quite passable.

"Thank you." Ruth gave her a hug.

"You lasses take this bag back home now. I'm sure Hilda can use some fresh vegetables." Mrs. O'Sullivan set a bulging flour sack on the table. "Laney, I rolled your riding skirt up tight as can be and put it in this second bag. That way, no one'll see it till you and Ruth traipse downstairs, matching like a chipper pair of wee sparrows."

For once, Ruth lagged behind as they returned to the Broken P. *Lord, I know I'm supposed to have a humble spirit. I'm bad about that. You know I am. I don't want to have Josh boss me around and ruin the library. It's such a special notion. I'm sure you put it in my mind. Your Word says to honor my father and mother—well, I didn't really know my father, but Mama . . . a library is such a perfect tribute to her.*

"Ruth?"

"Yes, Laney?"

"Did you see that paper at Galen's house?"

"I didn't pay much attention. Why?"

Laney turned in her saddle. Her eyes were wide and earnest. "There's a novel that costs only a dime. I was thinking if it is only that much, it must be small and not so hard to read. What do you think?"

"I think since you spotted the article and read it that well, we ought to buy the book for you at once." Ruth smiled broadly. "In fact, to celebrate, we're going to order it and have it come by Pony Express so it'll get here right away."

"That's too expensive!"

"Ha! I'm so proud of you, I could shout. You deserve that book, and I'll do whatever I need to in order for you to have it as quickly as possible. You can't turn me down, Laney. It's rude to refuse a gift."

"Every once in a while, someone's given me a book, but I never appreciated them because I felt like a liar for saying I was thankful when I didn't want it. It was embarrassing not to be able to read. This is the first time I'll get a book and actually enjoy it."

Ruth laughed.

"What's so funny?"

"I'm laughing with joy for your accomplishment, but I'm also thinking that we asked God to help you learn to read, even though you disliked it."

"God has been faithful, hasn't He?"

"Absolutely. And I'm thankful to Him for that . . . but here we are, taking home cabbage." Ruth scrunched her face into a displeased pucker. "I'm not going to pray that Hilda makes sauerkraut, because it would take more than a miracle to make me enjoy a single mouthful."

Giggles spilled out of Laney. "Oh, Ruth, I'm so glad you're here. I haven't been this happy in a long, long time. I always wanted a sister, and having you here is like a dream come true."

"I wished I had a sister, too."

"Won't it be fun to wear our matching riding skirts tomorrow? At school, there was a pair of sisters whose clothes sometimes matched. I thought they were darling."

"You'd look darling in a burlap bag," Ruth said as they reached the stable. Felipe started unsaddling the horses as they headed back toward the house.

Ruth fought the urge to drag her feet. Doing so wouldn't change things. She'd still have to sit across the supper table from Josh, knowing full well from the thunderous expression on his face and terse responses that he was still angry about her planning the library.

I'm in California. I can buy land and hire someone to build on it. I can handle money for myself. It'll be months before my books arrive, and I don't know when Mama's estate will finish settling. Until then, I can start planning. Just making the list of books brought back so many memories of Mama reading to me or our sharing a book and discussing it together. I'd hoped Josh would be pleased. Working on the project together would have been a lot of fun. I didn't realize how much I wanted his help. I need a man's viewpoint, and Josh is a man's man—he works harder than anyone I've ever met; yet as Mrs. O'Sullivan said, he walks close to the Lord. He's intelligent and very well read, too. She sighed. *But if he wants to turn his back on the library, I'll do it on my own.*

"Oh, fiddlesticks!"

Ruth snapped out of her thoughts and looked around. "What's the matter?"

Laney tilted her head toward the house. "Daddy's talking to Josh and Toledo on the veranda."

"He's smoking. I thought you wanted him to take his cigars outside."

Laney pouted, "But everyone will see your skirt."

Ruth shrugged. "So what? No one will know about yours until tomorrow."

"What've you girls got there?" McCain called to them.

"Vegetables," Ruth called back.

Josh curled his hands around the railing and leaned forward. Pasting on a ferocious look, he focused on Ruth. "You're not planning to go feed one of my broodmares, are you?"

Ruth skipped ahead. "Do we have another new baby?"

"Any day now." He straightened up and shook his finger at them. "But you stay out of the stable. I'll take you out to see the foal when it's safe."

McCain squinted at the burlap sack, then directed his attention to Laney. "If there's cabbage in there, when you take it in to Hilda, you tell her I want coleslaw."

"Yes, Daddy."

As they opened the back door to the kitchen, Laney whispered, "He hates sauerkraut, too."

The girls went into the house, and Josh turned to Toledo. "Tell me more."

"Not much more to say. Butterfield Stage and the railroad are both nosing around. Railroad wants to cross the Sierras. Depends on who's jawin' as to whether Butterfield wants to go east-west or north-south."

"Pony Express runs straight through the O'Sullivans' and cuts a swath through our land. I'd expect the railroad to do the same," Josh said.

Dad leaned forward. "And if they did?"

"I'd have to think on it."

"I wouldn't." Dad sat back. He took a long draw off his cigar, then let out a steady stream of smoke. "Best thing that could happen to us. Land value goes up, and we'd have it easy getting the cattle to market."

"We'd lose cattle. Train would hit 'em. Either that, or it'll be the end of free-ranging."

"It'd take miles of fences," Toledo drawled.

"A lot of money and man-hours, too."

Dad puffed again. "The money the railroad will pay would more than cover those costs."

Toledo shrugged. "Just thought you'd wanna know what I heard."

"Appreciate it," Josh said.

As the hand sauntered off, Josh said, "Dad, you're making no sense. In one conversation, you think the Pony Express is a folly. Now you support a transcontinental railroad. You wanted California to stay out of the North-South fray, but a railroad would inevitably force our state to become involved."

"There's a difference between ideals and practicality."

"Well, at this point, it's just talk. Plenty of schemes fall by the wayside." Josh stood.

"Mark my words, son. It's more than just talk. This isn't the first time I've heard something."

"Even if it pans out, there have to be a hundred different routes. There's no reason to believe the Broken P lies directly in line with the path they choose."

"And if it is?" Dad pressed.

"If it comes up, we'll talk it over."

"Times come when a decision has to be made. If I'm present, I'll agree."

Josh jerked his thumb toward the house. "Ruth might own half. If so, you can't sign anything without her agreement."

"She complicates things." Dad scowled.

"Hey, Josh!" Felipe hollered from the pasture. "I think we'd best get Bayside into the stable."

"Yeah?" Dad stubbed out his cigar and walked alongside Josh. "That mare's going to put off a fine foal."

"This birthing better go smoother than her last." Josh grimaced. "She throws a good foal, but she throws a fit having it."

Felipe handed Josh a rope. "She won't let me near her."

"I put her in the birthing stall two days ago when she started waxing. I wanted her used to her surroundings. Why's she out?"

Dad cleared his throat. "I let her out. She needed to have fresh grass."

Saying anything more with Felipe present would be a mistake, so Josh clamped his jaw shut, fashioned a rope halter, and approached the mare. It took considerable sweet talking, but she allowed him to draw near and lead her into the stall.

The next morning, Josh stretched to ease his tired muscles. It had been a long night—but a worthwhile one. Bayside nosed and licked her pretty, wobbly-legged foal.

"How'd the little one end up with a blaze and stockings?" Dad wondered aloud. "I thought Copper sired him."

"No, Barry did." He reached over, picked up a stone-cold biscuit and popped it into his mouth.

"You can't be hungry still." Dad slanted him a look. "Ruth brought out enough food for an army."

"She did." Josh grinned. Never before had someone knocked on the barn door, but Ruth did just that two hours earlier. He'd grabbed the heavily-laden breakfast tray, then shut the door with a terse, "Thanks."

Dad jerked his chin toward the foal. "That gal was itching to come take a peek."

"She has atrocious timing."

"So I noticed," Dad said wryly. "At least Laney knows better than to gallop out here."

"I'll probably bring the girls out after supper tonight. For now, I'll carry the tray back to the house and make the mash for our new mama."

"Go on ahead." Dad leaned against a post. "I'll stick around and enjoy the sight."

"Fine." Josh toted the tray back toward the house. All around him, life teemed. Birds sang, cows lowed, and horses in the paddock frolicked. When Dad first showed him the ranch, Josh felt sure they'd never whip it into this shape. Mornings like this made every drop of sweat more than worth it. Well, almost. If Ruth's claim prevailed, it would be a terrible blow.

The kitchen door opened. The woman he'd been thinking about poked out her head. "Josh, have you seen your sister?"

"No." He shouldered past her and set the tray on the drain board.

"I've looked everywhere, but I can't find her."

"The door on the springhouse sometimes sticks. Could be she's trapped."

Ruth shook her head. "I checked there. I even thought maybe she decided to go to the Fishers' with Hilda."

"Probably did. Ada Fisher had her baby last week." He checked to be sure the stove was still hot so he could heat the bran mash for the mare. "Laney's been eager to pay them a visit."

"She couldn't have gone there. The pretty little gowns we've stitched for the baby are still upstairs."

Lifting his palms in a who-knows gesture, Josh headed back out. "She'll turn up. Laney's a homebody."

"That's why I'm worried!" The closing door muffled whatever else Ruth had to say.

Josh hadn't meant to be rude, but he'd be back in the kitchen in a few minutes. Most likely she would show up during his absence. He strode toward the far side of the stable.

Originally, the building had been a combination bunkhouse/barn. As the ranch grew, a new bunkhouse went up and the vacated side became a tack room, the feed storage area, and the place where they garaged the buckboard.

Josh pushed the door wide open. The place tended to be dark. Stepping inside, he grabbed a tin bucket and headed toward the feed. Suddenly he dropped the pail. It rolled away, making racket as he rushed ahead. "Laney!"

CHAPTER FOURTEEN

"Laney! Sis?" Josh knelt beside her and slowly turned her onto her back, then pressed his fingers to the side of her neck. Rapid, thready pulses beneath his fingers told him she was alive, but she hadn't roused one bit.

"Sis?" He winced at the big lump on her temple. When he barely grazed it, her arms curled up and she turned her head away in reaction.

At least she can move. That's a good sign. Josh slid his arms beneath her and lifted. Pitching his voice to carry, but not to alarm, he called, "Dad."

McCain opened the door from the stable and tromped in. "Yeah?" He stopped in his tracks and rasped, "Laney!"

"I'm taking her to the house. Go get Doc." Josh rushed toward the house and bellowed, "Hildahhh! Get the door!"

Ruth opened the door and gasped.

Striding by, he ordered, "Get Hilda."

Ruth sprinted up the stairs alongside him. "Hilda's still at the Fishers'. What happened?"

"I don't know."

"Let me turn down her bed." Ruth dashed ahead of him and yanked back the bedclothes. By the time he'd placed his sister on the mattress, Ruth turned back around from the washstand and placed a damp cloth over the bump on Laney's head. "This'll help with the swelling."

"How is she?" McCain rasped as he leaned over the footboard.

"I don't know. You need to go fetch Doc."

"I sent Felipe." Dad's hand shook as he reached over and jostled Laney's leg. "Honey, wake up."

"You men need to step outside for a moment." Ruth pulled Laney's nightdress from the bureau. Once she realized he'd spotted the garment, she went beet red and shoved it behind herself. "Josh, your father's whiter than the sheets. Take him downstairs and give him a strong cup of coffee with two spoons of sugar."

"I'm not going anywhere till she rouses."

"Neither am I," Dad said. He rounded the end of the bed and sat on the edge of the mattress.

"Then make yourselves useful. Take off her shoes." Ruth stuffed the gown into a wad at the head of the bed and loosened the buttons at the throat of Laney's shirtwaist and the waist of her riding skirt.

"Your clothes match," Dad mumbled as his gaze went from Laney to Ruth and back.

"Pretend you didn't notice," Ruth commanded. "Laney wanted to see your reaction." She lifted the compress, turned it over, and put it back in place. "Josh, take one of her hankies and dip the edge in Hilda's ammonia."

"Ammonia will burn her! The skin's broken."

"It's not to clean the wound; it's to help bring her to consciousness. A good whiff works wonders." As she spoke, Ruth started to gently locate and remove Laney's hairpins.

She acted as if she knew what she was doing, so Josh followed her instructions and hastened back with the handkerchief. He'd soaked half of the dinky, embroidered linen square, and it stank. "Here."

Ammonia dripped all over. Ruth hastily snatched the compress, cupped it around the hanky, and waved it beneath Laney's nose.

Her reaction was immediate. Laney threw back her head and started to cough. Ruth showed no mercy whatsoever—she held the cloth under Laney's nose again. "Laney, honey, wake up. Open your eyes."

Josh reached over and was about to snatch it from Ruth's hand when Laney's eyes fluttered open. Ruth set aside the ammonia and captured Laney's hand as she reached up to touch her head.

"Ohhh," Laney moaned. "My head."

"She's all right!" Dad's voice held undiluted relief.

"If you men will please leave us for a few moments?" Ruth's firm tone left no doubt that the question was a politely worded command. "Josh, help yourself to some coffee, too."

"Bossy thing, isn't she?" Dad grumbled as he and Josh went down to the kitchen.

"She's taking better care of Laney than we could." Josh stared out the window, toward the stable. "I'm trying to figure out what happened."

Toledo rapped on the open back door. "Felipe's fetching Doc. How's the girl?"

"Ruth revived her."

Toledo nodded. "Need anything?"

"I was going to make the mare a warm bran mash."

"Consider it done." Toledo sauntered off.

Josh poured two cups of coffee, then watched as his father walked to the hutch, pulled out a bottle, and did something Josh had seen him do only once before: He drank whiskey straight from the bottle. Memories of his mother's death washed over him. Josh cleared his throat and rasped, "Laney's going to be okay, Dad."

"My baby girl." Dad took another good swig. "I almost lost her."

Josh pried the bottle from his father and shoved the coffee into his hands. "No use making a big deal out of this. Laney probably tripped. She'll be embarrassed if we fuss over her." He corked the whiskey and put the bottle away.

"Josh?"

He headed to the stairs. Ruth stood on the landing. "Did you need anything?"

"Could you please bring me a dark blanket and some clothespins?"

"What for?"

"Light bothers Laney. Her eyelet curtains don't block the sun well enough."

A few scant minutes later, Josh finished clipping the blanket in place over the window. Ruth had changed Laney into her nightdress and loosely braided her hair. Once he'd completed his task, Ruth pulled him out of the room.

"Ruth, thanks for helping Laney. I—"

"Josh," she interrupted, "something's dreadfully wrong."

"Doc should be here soon."

"You already told me that." Ruth shook her head. Tears filled her eyes and worry tainted her voice. "Josh, someone *hit* Laney."

"What!"

"She has another bump on her head. I discovered it when I did her hair. It's in the back, up high. If she had fallen, she wouldn't have two."

"Did she say who did it?"

"She told me something hit her. I thought she meant the bump on her temple. I'm sure she has a concussion. She's too woozy to answer questions."

The front door opened. Josh glanced down, expecting the doctor. Instead, Hilda tromped in. She looked up at him and demanded, "What's goin' on? Felipe and Doc are ridin' this way."

"Laney hit her head." Josh shot Ruth a look. Under his breath, he said, "I want everyone to think it was an accident until I can go out and inspect the stable." He raised his voice slightly. "She's got a nasty headache. Maybe you could brew her some tea, Hilda."

"Willow bark and mint—that's what she needs." The housekeeper bustled to the kitchen.

Ruth stared at him and gave him the slightest nod. She'd proven her reliability by keeping Laney's illiteracy a secret. Josh could see by the resolve in her eyes that she'd help him protect his sister. "I'll go sit with Laney," she murmured.

He hoped maybe Laney might tell him something, but when he followed Ruth back to his sister's bedside, Laney let out a tiny whimper.

"There, there," Ruth said in the barest whisper. She took the damp compress off Laney's brow, turned it over, and replaced it. "Rest. I'm right here."

Laney looked too miserable to pester. Doc came, examined Laney, and left a few packets of medicinal powders at the bedside before he departed. While Dad showed him out, Josh stood in the doorway of Laney's room.

Ruth had pulled up a chair and sat facing the headboard. Holding Laney's hand, she soothed, "You go ahead and slumber awhile. I'll sit here with you."

Odd, impulsive Ruth—she'd irritated him, vexed him, turned his world inside out; but Josh stood there and felt something give way. Her love for the Lord and her dedication to Laney were unmistakable. Over and over, she'd displayed a servant's heart by offering to pitch in around the Broken P, in the hours she spent teaching Laney to read, and the days she went to the O'Sullivans' to help out. Even her crazy notion to start a library was because she wanted to share books and her love of reading.

Lord, when I asked you to send a companion for Laney, I didn't count on someone like Ruth. She's one of a kind, Father, but now I see how special she is. The only thing bigger than her wild plans is her heart—and what a heart she has. I've been sore over losing part of the ranch, when all along, you were showing

*me a woman whose value is far above earthly riches. Thank you, Lord, for
bringing Ruth here.*

He let out a fake cough. When Ruth turned his way, Josh said,
"I'm going to go check things out."

Ruth continued to hold Laney's hand; but with her other hand,
she patted herself then pointed toward Laney as she silently
mouthed, "I'll stay here."

He nodded and mouthed, "Thanks."

He'd thought to take Dad out with him to nose around the
stable, but Dad was helping himself to another belt of whiskey. On
rare occasions, Dad drank—but from the level of the amber liquid
in the bottle, Josh knew Dad had been imbibing since Ruth called
down to him. Hilda squawked and yanked the bottle from Dad.
"Drink more of this, and you'll have a worse headache than Laney."

"A concussion." Dad sat down and gave Josh a pained look.
"She has a concussion."

"Yeah, Dad, she does. But she woke up and knows who she is.
She'll recover."

Josh went out to the stable alone, for Dad wasn't in any condition to help. The door still stood wide open. Dissatisfied with
the dank interior, Josh lit a lantern and looked around. As he
approached the spot where he'd discovered his sister, Toledo walked
through the door that led to the mare.

"Ate it all." He turned the bucket upside down.

"Good."

Toledo whistled under his breath. "Lotta blood on the floor
there. Didn't know it was serious."

"Concussion."

"Doesn't add up."

Josh stared at the hand. "What doesn't add up?"

"Laney falling. Ruth, I'd believe—but not Laney."

Silence hung heavily in the air. Josh couldn't be sure what to
think. He decided to string Toledo along and watch what happened.
"I don't believe it, either."

Setting aside the pail, Toledo squinted at the area. "Find anything?"

"Just got here. Laney was lying right there."

"You found her?"

Josh nodded.

"Feet over yonder or toward the door?"

"The door." Josh pictured the scene again in his mind.

"Nothing there to trip on." Toledo wandered to the area and hunkered down. "No sign of something being tied across to trip her." He straightened up.

"No one would anticipate her being in here, anyway."

"Yeah, they would." Toledo jerked his thumb toward the chicken feed.

The minute Josh looked at the bag stuffed in the corner, air hissed out of his lungs. A yard-long, narrow scrap of lumber lay there. As he and Toledo walked toward it, light from the lantern highlighted a few strands of reddish-brown hair clinging to the board.

———◆———

"Have a nice time in town?" Galen lifted his mother down from the buckboard.

"Aye, we did." She smiled at him. "We fared right nicely, if I do say so, myself."

Colin hopped down and boasted, "Got six dollars for all of Ma's vegetables!"

"That's better than 'nice,' Ma." Galen smiled at her. "You outdid yourself."

"I've had extra help in the garden. Ruth and Laney made a difference."

"They haven't been here for two weeks," Colin refuted.

"Ach! Son, 'tisn't just the reaper who takes credit for the harvest." Ma shook her finger at Colin. "The plowsman, the sower, the one who tends by weeding and watering—they all played a part in bringing bounty to bear."

"Sean and Dale would be glad to hear that." Galen grinned. "After lunch, I sent them off to the garden to do some more weeding."

"I'm glad of it. The only thing growing faster than the weeds are those little brothers of yours. I just let out the hem in Dale's trousers." Ma's warm tone made it clear she wasn't complaining.

"Did you hear any word in town about how Laney's doing?"

Colin burst out laughing and poked him in the ribs. "I thought you weren't sweet on her."

"I'm not." Galen leveled his brother with a harsh look. "It's neighborly concern I'm showing, nothing more. I'd be asking the same thing if 'twere any other person who got hurt."

"We dropped by the Broken P to deliver their mail," Ma said. She knew just when to cut in. "Hilda let me go upstairs to visit a few minutes. The bruise is nigh unto gone, and Laney claims her headache's disappeared along with it. Ruth's hovering o'er her."

Galen grinned. "Ruth's probably ordering everyone around and minding Laney like a mama bear with a wee cub."

"Just so." Ma laughed.

"Da's sleeping. He said to be sure to tell you the stew you left for lunch was the best you've e'er made."

"He always says that," Colin said to Galen as Mama bustled into the house.

"Aye, and he means it." Galen slapped his brother on the back. "Not a day passes that they don't show their appreciation to one another. I'm thinking one of these days, when I get married, I'll do the selfsame thing. A wee bit o' praise goes a long way toward makin' a woman feel valued."

"When Melinda ran off with that butcher, you stopped talkin' on e'er taking a bride. Have you taken a fancy to someone?"

"I've not made my mind up yet. A man oughtn't rush into matters—I learned that sad lesson already." Galen hooked his thumbs into his suspenders. "The only filly I'm troubling myself o'er at the moment is Sorcha."

Colin started. "What's wrong with her?"

"Come to the stable. She's your mare. You need to be the one treating her."

Colin stood taller and lengthened his stride. The slight swagger to his step left Galen smothering a grin. He usually saw to the horses when they ailed, but part of his plan for the summer was to teach Colin more and let him stretch toward manhood. Aye, he was a tad younger than Galen thought would work; but with Da's condition as it was, Colin was already maturing before his time.

Lord, grant me wisdom.

"It's not something bad, is it?" Colin worried aloud.

"If it were dreadful, I'd already be with her." They entered the stable and went to Sorcha's stall. "Walk her a few steps and tell me which leg you think's ailing."

Colin led the mustang to the end of the stable and back. "It's her right foreleg."

"Aye. Now, gentle-like, run your hand down it and back like this." Galen demonstrated on Sorcha's left foreleg. "Tell me where she's tender."

Face puckered with concern and concentration, Colin followed his example. "It's down low. Here, on the inside by her knee. Easy, girl. She flinched, Galen!"

"That, she did. It's a splint. She's the age where the ligament turns to bone there."

"What do I do to treat it?"

Galen noticed how his brother assumed responsibility. He rose and patted Sorcha. "Time does most of the work. She needs to be on soft ground. We'll put her in the pasture and rest her for the next month."

"A whole month!"

"Aye. She'll serve you well for many a year if you sacrifice this time. I know you relish the freedom of owning a mount, but with that ownership comes the duty to do right by her. We'll all share our horses. Until late, we did well enough at that. There's no reason we can't do so again."

"A month," Colin repeated.

"Aye, and e'en after a month, you'll need to take care not to ask her to jump or do heavy work for a while."

Colin cast a glance over at the Pony Express horses' stalls.

"We'll not be borrowing horses from the Express. It's not honorable to use company property for private use. Now go on and lead Sorcha out to the pasture. I didn't give her much water this morning so she'd head toward the creek. The shade and soft grass there'll suit her fine."

While his brother did as he bade, Galen hefted the handles to the wheelbarrow. He'd mucked the stalls and saved the manure for Ma's almond trees. Each tree needed about thirty pounds around it. Though Ma was willing to do the chore, Galen didn't want her to. He could haul twice as much in a trip, and Ma was already too busy.

Arriving at the east edge of the garden, he spotted his two youngest brothers off to the side.

"En guarde!" Dale shouted, brandishing a carrot.

"En guarde!" Sean attacked with a carrot of his own.

They fenced for a few minutes before Sean's carrot met Dale's chest. "Touché!"

"I'm dying!" Dale dropped his carrot, clutched his chest, and slumped to the earth.

"You might not be dyin' boy-oh," Galen said in a slight growl, "but your backside surely will be burning if I don't see a great big pile o' weeds about here someplace."

Scrambling to his feet, Dale stammered, "We did do some weeding. Didn't we, Sean?"

Sean's red head bobbed vigorously.

"That may well be, but I sent you little men out here to work, not to play. There's a world of difference between some weeding and a lot of weeding."

"Okay, Galen."

As they set to work, he headed toward the almond trees. Sean shouted, "Galen, that stinks so bad, I'll bet Sacramento can smell it!"

"Yeah," Dale agreed. "Can't you wait and spread it later?"

"Nope. A man does what needs to be done, when it needs to be done. 'Tis a lesson the both of you ought take to heart."

Two more trips, and he'd gotten the almonds fertilized. "Is that the last one?"

"Aye, Dale, 'tis. But now they're all needin' to be watered. Ten buckets apiece."

"Ten!"

"Aye. Irrigating them now keeps the manure from burning the roots."

"But there are six trees." Dale's little sun-kissed face wrinkled as he concentrated.

"Six times ten is sixty," Sean calculated. "Sixty buckets of water!"

"Right you are. I'll be sending Colin to help you. The three of you are to take two trees apiece." He pressed his finger to his mouth. "Sean, don't answer. Dale, you are to water two trees. Each requires ten buckets. How many are you going to have to haul?"

"Aw, Galen. School's over."

"But you're going to stay sharp o'er the summer by recalling these things. Here." He squatted down and wrote in the dirt. "You have ten buckets plus ten buckets."

"Twenty!"

"That's right, lad. And no skimping. We need all of the almonds the tree can produce."

"To pay for Da's medicine?" Sean peeked over Dale's head and gave Galen a wary look.

"Aye. Our garden and orchard are important for the family. You boys have jobs to do. There's more than enough work here for us, and I don't want to have to catch you shirking again."

Walking away, Galen's steps felt as heavy as his heart. *Sean's a sharp-witted boy. He's figuring out the truth. I hoped he'd have a month or so more of blissful innocence, Lord. Truly, I did.*

"Galen?"

He froze.

Sean ran up. "Could you leave the wheelbarrow? I reckon we can use it to carry the buckets. It'll make the chore easier."

"Sure. And that's good thinking on your part. You're a clever lad." He left the garden and went over to the corn. With free-range cattlemen around, Galen and his father had needed to fence in their property. He stood on a fence slat, shaded his eyes, and made sure the enclosure was secure. Satisfied, Galen took a look at the corn and calculated when he'd harvest the field.

Ma, Da, and he had planted two cornfields so they'd ripen in succession. After having suffered through the potato famine, Ma and Da refused to rely on any single crop. As a result, a diversity of crops filled other plots: peas, oats, and barley covered the land.

"You're lookin' right pleased with all you spy," Ma said from behind him.

"The crops are doing well—God be praised."

"Aye, He gets the credit. Your da and I appreciate all the hard work you're doing, too."

"You needn't thank me, Ma." He walked to the fence and gave her a peck on the cheek. "I wasn't so young before we came here that I forget what hunger is or does. Whene'er I take a moment to witness this bounty, it fills my heart. When do you think we ought to plant the beans?"

"I bought seeds in town today." She smiled. "I thought to have the boys plant them by the corn this week. Dale and Sean are old enough to do it on their own, but giving Colin the task of overseeing them will make him feel important."

"I had him put Sorcha to pasture for the next month. She's

developed splints. It'll do him good to stay busy so he doesn't fret o'er having to stay home."

"He does like to wander, doesn't he?"

"Be that as it may, we need him home." Galen bent and picked a weed. "On days when he can't stand to stay put, I'll take him off to the far boundary of our land. We'll drag back some downed limbs for firewood."

"I don't want him chopping or sawing down trees yet, Galen-mine. He's still too young for that."

Galen nodded. *Much as I hate to ask, it'll be a task I need to have Josh help me with.*

"You asked me to tell you if I heard anything more about the railroad."

"Aye. Josh told me some folks are making grand plans." He raised his brows in silent inquiry.

"Lester mentioned it."

Half laughing, Galen said, "Then every soul in the township knows about it. Ever notice how he's either the first to know something and passes it to everyone who walks in the store, or he's the very last one to catch wind of something?"

Ma smiled and nodded.

"If 'tis true that they'll follow the Pony route, I'm going to fight a bit. I won't have them laying track right past our front door."

"No used borrowin' trouble that isn't here yet." Ma sighed. "Speaking of trouble . . . I ought to warn you: Laney and Ruth will be coming in a few days. Laney was pouting that you haven't noticed she sewed a pink dress. She says you asked her to make one."

"I did?" Galen watched a crow. "I can't say as I recall that."

"You have to mind offhanded comments, son. That lass has her heart set on you, and those wee slips o' the tongue can be miscon-strued."

He nodded. "Ma? What do you think of Ruth?"

"As a person, or as someone who might mean more to you?"

"What's the difference?"

"There's a world of difference. If you asked me about her in generalities, I'd say she's a fine girl. If you're thinkin' on wooing the lass, I'd say she needs to untie a few knots in her soul. The grief she holds is fresh—so fresh that she cannot bear to speak much of it. Until she comes to peace with God's decisions, she can't very well be heart-whole."

"I see."

"Nay, son, you don't. There's another complication."

He scowled. "Laney?"

"Aye. Ruth's her friend. She's a loyal lass, and I fear you'd put your heart on the line only to have her turn you down because she loves Laney too much to wound her."

"God wouldn't put a fondness in my heart for Ruth if He didn't plan to work things out."

"Don't be too certain of that. I don't mean to prod a sore spot, but you thought the same of Melinda. Colossians exhorts us to set our affection on things above, not on things on the earth. You need to pray for the Lord to guide your steps instead of planning them out and asking Him to bless them."

"Ma!" Sean shouted.

"What?"

The little boy ran around the corner and came into sight. "I stopped in the house to fetch another pail so we could water the trees. Da—" His voice broke.

CHAPTER FIFTEEN

What do you have there?" Josh asked.

Ruth casually set the dime novel atop a few other books and pushed them across the counter toward Lester. "I appreciate your ordering those camellias. Laney and I can hardly wait to plant them in the front by the steps."

"I'll send them out to the Broken P as soon as they arrive."

"Thank you."

Josh drummed his fingers on the countertop. "I asked what you're buying, Ruth."

Turning to him, she said, "You'll be pleased to know I found the Dickens book, *A Tale of Two Cities,* that neither of us has read."

"Good. Perhaps we can read it to Laney." He clamped his jaw shut, realizing too late he'd spoken without thinking.

"Why not let Laney read it for herself?" Lester asked as he started to total up Ruth's purchases.

"Oh, I wouldn't think of it!" Ruth glanced at Josh. In no way would she ever betray Laney's secret, yet she couldn't lie, either. Choosing her words carefully, she asked, "You know we're still worried about her. Laney couldn't possibly read that just now, could she?"

"That was dumb of me." Lester pushed too hard on his pencil and broke the lead. "Does her head still ache from that concussion? I've missed seeing her at church."

"Ruth's been very protective." Josh smiled at her. "But she has Laney's welfare at heart. You'll let her attend this Sunday, won't you?"

"Most likely so."

Josh reached across the counter and spread out the books.

Crack! Ruth's closed fan hit the back of his hand. She piled the books up again and gave him a coy smile. "You weren't really snooping, were you, Joshua McCain?"

"I've invited you to read whatever books we already possess on the Broken P. Don't you plan to extend the same courtesy with yours?"

"She just offered the biggest one to you, Josh," Lester said as he took a knife to his pencil and started to shave a new point.

"Yes, I did." *Whew. Lester rescued me on that one!*

"Indeed, but it's always nice to anticipate what lies ahead." Josh gave Ruth an I-dare-you smile and lifted the books, one-by-one, to identify the titles.

She'd hoped he wouldn't see the dime novel. That hope dashed, Ruth brazened it out. "The first one is a ladies' novel, Josh. Surely it wouldn't suit your taste."

"*Malaseka, The Indian Wife of the White Hunter,* by Mrs. Ann Stevens," he read aloud. "I might be interested, Ruth. I enjoy hunting on occasion."

The sparkle in his eyes taunted her. Josh wasn't ever mean, though. This was more of a boyish cockiness. After worrying about Laney the past two weeks, the change felt fun. Eager for him to put down that little novel, she lifted the next book and popped it into his hand. "This might be to your liking, too. You do tie knots, don't you?"

"I tie knots, but I haven't tied the knot." He chuckled as he set down the volume of *Knotted and Crocheted Laces.*

"Miss Caldwell said it's special for Laney."

"Laney's handwork is beautiful. Since embroidery is hard on her eyes right now, I thought she would enjoy trying new crochet patterns."

Lester kept shaving at the pencil tip. "Kelly O'Sullivan and her youngest boys were in yesterday. She looked at that book, herself."

Josh thumbed through the volume, then shut the cover. His eyes no longer sparked with mischief. Sincerity filled his voice. "That was thoughtful of you, Ruth. Much as my sister loves handwork, it'll give her plenty of projects to keep her busy."

Feeling foolish for having made a big deal about his simple curiosity about the books, Ruth flashed him a smile. "We could take it over to Galen's and share it with his mom. After all, books are for sharing."

Things had shifted dramatically between them as they'd forged an alliance over Laney's well-being, and Ruth felt a longing to make it spread to other matters. She'd discovered many facets to Josh, and most intrigued her.

I've never had a man for a friend. But that's what Josh has become. He's always busy, but there's a quietness in his soul that I admire. I've been silly about the dime novel. She fingered a thin sheaf of papers on the counter.

"Would you mind looking through the sheet music I selected? There's no use in my buying something Laney already owns."

He leafed through and set aside a few sheets. "Hilda loves Stephen Foster's music. We have probably everything he's composed. I'd take it as a personal favor if you wouldn't get the 'Ocean Telegraph March.' When the undersea line was completed two years ago, everyone played that tune until I grew heartily sick of it."

Ruth burst out laughing.

"What's so funny?" Lester wondered aloud.

"I was going to buy it because I thought everyone else liked that piece. Every last girl at school played that song *ad nauseum.* I loathe it!" Ruth scooped up the sheets they'd rejected and dashed over to place them back on the display shelf. When she returned, Josh was handing Lester money.

"I beg your pardon, but those were my purchases."

"I'm reading Dickens first, and Laney's getting the crochet book." Josh threaded Ruth's arm through his. "Now we're going to have lunch at the Copper Kettle while Lester fills the rest of my order."

"Honestly, Josh—"

"You have to be hungry by now. Breakfast was hours ago."

Pulling away, she insisted, "I need to get back to Laney."

"You haven't left her side since she got hurt. There's nothing wrong with your taking a little break."

Ruth shook her head in protest. *If I'd stayed home with Mama...*

"Hilda's with Laney, Ruth. You and I both know Hilda would scold anyone to death before they ever reached my sister. Laney is perfectly safe."

"Hey—before you folks leave, mail came in." Lester waved a few envelopes in the air. "One's for Miss Caldwell."

"Thanks, Lester. Why don't you put them inside one of the books? We'll be sure to pull them out once we get home." Josh steered her out the door and down the boardwalk.

Ruth reached up her right sleeve.

He dipped his head and asked quietly, "Why are you fishing for your knife?"

"My knife is up my left sleeve," she whispered. "I didn't want to carry a reticule, so I put my money up my right sleeve. Since you bought the books, I'll slip you funds for lunch."

Ire darkened his features. "You'll do no such thing!"

"I meant you no offense. Oh, this is so awkward. If we're partners, Josh, it's only right that—"

"Stop right there. First off, I refuse to have a woman pay for my meals. Second, you said a mouthful when you said, '*If we're* partners.' We might not be." He tugged her out of the way as someone else walked by, then kept hold and started for the diner again.

"Waiting doesn't come easily, you know. I'm very impatient. Until matters are cleared up, I can't very well just sponge off of you!"

In a low tone, he said, "Ruth, save your money. If things don't turn out the way you're hoping regarding the ranch, you'll still be welcome to stay with us, but you'll want to have a little nest egg."

She pivoted toward him. "Now I understand."

He didn't look as if he was gloating. "Good."

"No. I understand that you don't understand!"

"Suppose you explain it to me." He opened the door to the diner.

Ruth battled her crinoline as she made her way through the entrance and shuffled to the side toward the nearest table. For it being midday, the place hardly held any patrons. Josh seated her, then took the chair opposite her. Ruth fussed with her skirts, then gave him a disgruntled look. "You have no idea how much I envy men for their right to wear britches."

He scowled. "You're not going to run about in those disgusting bloomers."

She sighed. "I promised Mama I wouldn't. Truly, they seem like a wonderful concept. They cover everything quite decently and would be far less troublesome."

"I've seen a woman in them once. It made for quite a scene. She looked as if she was wearing only half a dress and her unmentionables were showing."

"Nonsense! It was the same as wearing a well-styled shirtwaist and fancy trousers."

"None of the men present thought so. You'd shame yourself and my family if you tried such a stunt."

"Well, it's nothing you need fear since I made my promise to

Mama." She braced herself with a deep breath. "Speaking of Mama—"

"Hello, Josh." A young girl swished over. "What would you folks like to order today?"

"Hi, Myrtle. Who's cooking today—your aunt or your dad?"

Myrtle dipped her head and muffled a giggle. "Aunt Ethel."

"Sandwiches for us today, then." Josh nodded. "Yes. And pie."

"Ham or chicken salad?"

Josh looked to Ruth.

"Chicken salad, please."

"Me too. And make it apple pie."

"All right." Myrtle scurried off.

Josh pretended to scoot his chair in as he leaned forward. "Always ask who's cooking here. Ethel burns everything."

"Thanks for the warning," Ruth whispered back.

He straightened up. "So what was it you think I don't understand?"

Plenty. Ruth tamped down that response. Taking the napkin off the table, she slid it into her lap and said, "I've figured out why you're upset about my starting a library."

"That subject is closed."

"No, it isn't." She leaned forward and hissed, "You thought I was counting on money from the ranch. I'm not."

"You're not making any sense, Ruth." He gave her a patient look. "I'm sure you haven't had to do any budgeting, so eighty dollars seems like a lot of money. It won't begin to cover the expenses involved in buying the land, let alone erecting the building or filling it with books."

"I'm not foolish enough to formulate a plan on the unstable foundation as to whether I'll inherit anything from my father."

"Then, as I said, the subject is—"

"Still going to become a reality." She glanced down at the hem of her left sleeve and wondered how she'd managed to get the lacy edging soiled. "Let me explain."

Josh folded his arms on the tabletop. "Go ahead."

"Thank you." Pleased that he was being so reasonable, Ruth pitched her voice as low as she could. "I know it's crass to discuss finances, but as that matter seems to be at the heart of your concern, I'll address it."

"I voiced other concerns as well."

"Yes, well, first things first. Josh, the eighty dollars I have with me was just my traveling fund. Once Mama's estate is closed, the attorney will send me my inheritance. Though I don't expect it to be extravagant, it should be enough to keep me comfortable if I'm prudent. I thought it would be sweet to use a portion of Mama's bequest to build a library in memory of her love of reading."

Josh sat in silence and studied her.

Ruth fought the urge to wiggle in her seat. She lost the battle. After fidgeting, she sighed. "I'm sorry. I shouldn't have said anything. I know it's not ladylike to discuss financial issues."

"If anything, I'm sorry you didn't say anything sooner."

Her head shot up.

"When you told me at Rick Maltby's office that you had eighty dollars, I assumed that your mother had sacrificed and scrimped to send you to those fancy academies."

"Oh."

"Dad and I sank every last penny we owned into the Broken P. Sending Laney away to school was a necessity, but it meant we barely scraped by. When Hilda says dad's a skinflint, it's because she remembers how tight things were that first year."

Ruth chewed on her lower lip for a moment. "Perhaps when I hear from Mama's attorney, I should plan to invest in the Broken P. It would only be right. . . ."

"No." His harsh word made others turn to look at them.

Knowing all too well how embarrassing it was to create a public scene and feeling guilty that she bore the responsibility for bringing up such a touchy subject, Ruth immediately straightened her shoulders and declared in a loud voice. "Yes, Josh. Laney ought to be allowed to attend church this Sunday. You're being too protective."

Myrtle appeared with their plates. "Sorry the bread's a little . . . well done. Josh, Ruth's right. You know how much Laney adores babies, and Ada Fisher is due to bring her new one to worship this week."

"Okay, Laney can go." His glare about bored a hole through Ruth. "But that other thing—forget about it."

"Surly as you are, Josh, I marvel you don't suffer from indigestion."

"Who says I don't?"

"I can take care of that." Ruth cut the burned edge off her bread and slipped the singed crust onto his plate. "There. Everyone knows a little charcoal is the cure."

Myrtle slapped her hand over her mouth, but her laughter filled the Copper Kettle as she dashed back into the kitchen.

Unable to read Josh's reaction, Ruth blurted out, "Burnt offerings are biblical, you know."

"They're for atonement," Josh shot back.

"Well, if you're going to be that way . . ." She reached over and took back half of the crispy crust. Josh's face twisted with confusion, so she lifted a portion and said, "I'm not completely sorry, Josh. Only halfway. You wouldn't want me to lie, would you?"

His lips twitched, then he gave in and chuckled. For the rest of lunch, he seemed to be in a good mood.

Lester waved at them as they passed his storefront. "Everything's in your wagon."

"Thanks, Lester." Josh lifted Ruth into the buckboard and climbed up himself.

"Isn't your father coming home with us?"

"He said he still had business to conduct. He might go on to Sacramento for a few days."

"But he didn't have a valise."

"That's never stopped him before."

As they rode home, Josh cast a glance at Ruth. "You calling me protective of Laney is the supreme example of the pot calling the kettle black."

"I have good reason." Ruth gave him an exasperated look. "And staying in town to eat made absolutely no sense to me whatsoever. Hilda's sandwiches and pie are thrice as good, and I could have been keeping watch over Laney."

"Ruth, you needed to get away. You've been with her night and day for two weeks."

"Two weeks is nothing. With Mama—" She caught herself and turned away. Josh shouldn't see her cry. No one ought to.

Josh's warm hand skimmed back and forth between her shoulder blades. "Did you spend a long time caring for your mother?"

"Not much," she said tightly. "Nowhere near as much as I should have. I was away at that dumb academy when I ought to—" She took a choppy breath and shook her head. "I was only there for her last six months."

Wrapping his arm around her, Josh drew her close to his side. One quick tug, and he'd untied the bonnet and flicked it into the buckboard's bed. A shiver ran through her as he toyed with her wild curls.

"Mom sent Laney away the last couple of weeks. Even before then, she'd asked several of her friends to take Laney off for little trips or visits. If your mother was anything like ours, she wanted to protect you, Ruth."

Ruth fought the urge to weep into his shoulder. What Josh said made sense, but it didn't give her peace. Still, she'd never had a man care about her feelings or comfort her like this. How could it be that his hold made her stronger and weaker at the same time?

They rode along in silence. His rough fingers kept smoothing out a coil of her hair, then releasing it and letting it spring back. Over and over again, he repeated that simple contact. "You can't undo the past, Ruth. I get the impression that you blame yourself for not being with your mother. You were being an obedient daughter to do her bidding. It was her right to decide who she wanted to know about her illness."

"But I would have cared for her," Ruth whispered thickly.

"And you did. Six months is a long while, and I don't doubt that you were with her constantly. She did her best to equip you for a good life when she'd be gone. I'll bet that was why she sent you to those schools. When push came to shove, though, your mama kept you close to her side."

"But I failed her. Every school sent me back in disgrace. I didn't fit in."

"God doesn't make any two people alike, Ruthie. Just because you didn't fit into their idea of a 'perfect lady' doesn't mean you aren't a daughter of the King."

"I bet He's tired of me being a wild, rebellious child, too." She pushed away from Josh and sat up.

Josh slid his hand under her chin and turned her to face him. His hazel eyes radiated warmth, not the judgment she expected. "God made you special in your own right. It occurs to me that you were true to Him when you didn't let them squish you into a mold that didn't fit."

When he withdrew his touch, she missed the contact. Ruth tried to gather her wits. "Laney—"

"You know I love my sister, Ruth. But my sister has a docile temperament. She's a lamb and you're a lioness. God created both."

"He made a lot more lambs than lions."

Josh chuckled, and Ruth knotted her hands in her lap. *I'm making an utter fool of myself. I'm not going to say another word. No, maybe I should. I could change the subject to something safe.* She moistened her lips. "It's taking forever to get back home." Just as soon as she'd spoken, she tacked on, "It's no reflection on your companionship, Josh. I'm just nervous about Laney."

"No offense taken. I feel much the same way."

She sighed. "I can't for the life of me imagine anyone trying to harm her. I've been praying for the Lord to keep a score of angels about her."

"Me too."

"Those poor angels. They're having to contend with Hilda today." Ruth clapped her hand over her mouth. "Oh, I don't believe I said that. It's dreadful, the way I blurt things out like that."

Josh started laughing. "Hilda's been difficult, hasn't she?"

"Difficult?" Ruth compressed her lips and started to fan herself.

"Oh, I get it. This is one of those times where you're falling back on manners. It's the old if-you-can't-say-something-nice situation, eh?"

"Are all summers in California this warm?"

"Ruth?"

"Yes, Josh?"

"Do me a favor and stop carrying a fan. You're going to put out your eye with it one of these days."

Thoroughly disgruntled, Ruth closed the ivory-and-silk frippery with a snap. "I wish your father was going back home with us."

He shot her an impish grin. "He would have told you to put away the fan, too. You're dangerous with the silly thing."

"Well, if I don't carry it, I'll just start toting around my muff pistol."

"I told you that fan was dangerous. It just wafted your brains clear out of your head."

———

"That trip to town took forever," Laney complained as Ruth entered her room.

"Tell me about it," Ruth muttered.

"Well, I'll go on down and get busy." Hilda pried herself out of the rocking chair and trundled to the door. "Elaine Louise, if you dare try to get out of that bed, I'm going to come back up here and sit on you!"

"I'll make sure she behaves," Ruth said.

"I've heard some tall promises in my day, but that one..." Hilda snorted and left.

"I don't think she's forgiven me for bumping into the clothesline yet." Ruth shed her crinoline and plopped down next to Laney.

"I'm sure she has." Laney grinned. "But it's going to take a while before she forgives you for sneezing over the sauerkraut at supper night before last."

"I didn't do that on purpose, Laney. Truly I didn't."

"Don't tell Daddy or Josh. They both considered that to be a brilliant tactical move."

Ruth couldn't contain her laughter. Then spying the books Josh had purchased, she held one aloft before Laney. "Look here! I never imagined it possible, but Lester had that dime novel we were going to order!"

"For true?"

"The proof's right here." She pressed the book into Laney's hands. "I peeked at it already—and it's going to be a wonderful adventure."

"I never thought of a book as an adventure."

"Well, they are. We're going to share it. I'll read one page, and you'll read the next."

"I don't know if I can. I won't be able to read very fast."

"This isn't a race, Laney. It's a book. What's wrong with relishing the story instead of rushing through it?" Ruth scooted back against the headboard.

Laney wiggled next to her. "I'm in trouble already. I can't even pronounce the first word in the title."

Ruth drummed her fingers on the paper cover. "I've been trying to decide how to say it, too. It's an Indian name, so it probably doesn't follow normal rules. Why don't we just decide on something, and since we agree, it'll work."

"Okay."

"*Malaseka, The Indian Wife of the White Hunter.*" Ruth shivered.

"Doesn't the title just give you a thrill?"

"Wait a minute," Laney whispered.

"What's wrong?"

"My door's open. Daddy might hear me bumbling to read."

"That's not a problem. He's on his way to Sacramento. Here. The first page is on your side."

Laney started out very slowly and tentatively. Her finger trailed across the page beneath each word as she sounded it out. When she finished the first page, Ruth congratulated her, then read her page aloud at a slow pace so Laney could follow along. They continued to take turns.

"Hey."

Ruth and Laney both jumped.

Josh stood in the doorway. "It's suppertime, and you didn't answer when Hilda called. That must be a good book."

"It's wonderful, Josh!" Laney started to stuff her arms into the sleeves of her robe. "We lost all track of time."

"I heard you reading, Laney Lou. I'm so proud of you."

"Thank you, but it's all because of Ruth."

"No, it's not." Ruth smiled. "We dedicated your reading to the Lord. He's blessing your efforts."

"From what I heard, He's showering His blessing on your efforts." Josh jerked his head toward the stairs. "Come on, Ruth."

"I'll be there in a minute." Ruth remained on the bed. She couldn't very well stand and call Josh's attention to the fact that her skirts all draped around her ankles while the crinoline formed a collapsed beehive on the far side of the bed. They'd just discussed what an abysmal misfit she was when it came to ladylike comportment; the last thing she wanted to do was provide another example for him.

"I'm such a dolt!" Laney pushed her brother. "Josh, you go on downstairs."

"The only way I'm letting you go downstairs is if I'm with you."

"Now you're the one who's being a dolt." Laney poked at his arm.

"Supper's getting stone cold!" Hilda hollered.

"Talk about being trapped between a rock and a hard place..." Josh muttered. He crooked his forefinger at Ruth and called down, "We'll be there in just a minute."

"Josh—"

"Laney, tell Ruth not to make a liar out of me. Even with your help, it'll take five minutes for her to"—he waved his hand toward her skirts—"tend to things."

Ruth muffled a moan. Of course he noticed.

Laney made a shooing motion with her hands. "Go on. She'll break her neck if she tries to go downstairs in her current state."

"I get no appreciation around here!" Hilda yelled.

"Far be it from me to get her any more upset with me than she already is." Ruth flung herself out of the bed, grabbed handfuls of her skirts and traipsed to the door. "So help me, Josh, if you dare say one thing, I'll take it as cause to abandon all of the expensive education I received. Then you'll wish you'd tangled with Hilda."

Suave as could be, he braced her elbow and led her and Laney to the top of the stairs. "Shall we, ladies?"

Yards of material dragged behind her. Head held high, Ruth whispered to Laney, "No matter what, Hilda's going to be upset. Your brother is making me get my new dress all dirty."

"Did Hilda say a word to you at all the time you came down in your—I mean to say, without your shoes?"

"When did you do that?" Laney demanded.

"Never you mind. Laney, your brother talks too much."

"In this case," Laney asserted, "he hasn't talked enough."

"I'm going to take supper off the table—"

"Hilda, we're right here," Laney said. "And supper smells marvelous."

"No thanks to you youngsters. No appreciation. I tell you—

Well, lo and behold! Ruth finally got some common sense and gave up on those ridiculous hoops."

"She made the sacrifice only because we all knew you'd make such a fine meal." Josh seated Ruth and had to seesaw the chair in and out three times before it didn't catch on her voluminous gown. In a wry tone, he added, "Ruth didn't want to hold us up."

"I'm ever so glad you're finally letting me out of my room." Laney took her seat.

Hilda shook her finger at Laney. "Right after you eat, you're going right back up to your bed."

"I'll ask the blessing." Josh bowed his head.

"Be sure to tell God to rope in that father of yours," Hilda ordered. "Seein' as how he's not here at the table, and the Good Book says where two or three are gathered and all that, you might as well hit the Lord with important matters instead of reminding Him you're grateful for 'taters and gravy."

CHAPTER SIXTEEN

I've been thinking," Ruth said as she set down her silverware.

Not again. Josh plunked his empty coffee cup on the table. *How can I get Ruth to stop concocting wild plans before an implementation turns into an execution?*

"Tomorrow Laney and I will spend the day in the parlor."

Laney's expression lit with delight. "What a wonderful idea! I'm so sick of my room, I could weep."

"If you do well," Ruth patted Laney's arm, "then you ought to be able to attend church on Sunday. Supposing that goes well, we could go to visit the O'Sullivans on Monday."

"I don't know if I'll have time to take you there." Josh pushed away from the table. "I don't want you girls going off on your own."

"You're worried, Josh. I understand." Ruth touched her sleeve. "But remember how I have a knife?"

Josh looked over his shoulder to make certain Hilda wouldn't overhear them. "That little pig sticker wouldn't begin to protect the two of you. Your grand plans for a library are going to have to sit by the wayside until we figure out who hit Laney. Until I'm

convinced you'll both be safe, you're not going trotting off anywhere."

"You're the one who pointed out how we need to help over
there," Laney wheedled.

"Whoever struck you is obviously not right in the head. He's
just as likely to try to strike Ruth. Anytime you girls step foot
outside this house, you are not to be alone. Is that understood?"

"We'll work something out," Ruth said as her chair slid across
the floor. She gave him a we'll-talk-later look while resting her hand
on Laney's shoulder. "Let's go back upstairs. We can read a bit more
before you go to sleep."

"I'll help you ladies up the stairs."

Ruth looked down at herself, then back at him. "If you were
any gentleman whatsoever, you'd walk out the door."

"And if I weren't a gentleman?" he teased.

"You'd wear the dress and tackle the stairs, yourself!" Ruth
looked just as surprised at her response as Laney did. The two of
them flushed brightly and broke out laughing.

Josh shoved his hands into his pockets, puckered up, and
started whistling as he headed toward the door.

Three hours later, Josh came back into the house. He'd tried to
catch up on more chores since he'd lost half the day by taking Ruth
to town. The ranch hands were a good bunch—reliable and moti-
vated by decent pay. They'd accomplished their usual duties without him present. Nevertheless, Josh monitored everything and paid
one last visit to the stables to see how the mares and their new
foals looked.

Light shone out of the parlor. Someone hit a note twice, then
struck another one a few times. Ruth was talking to herself as she
hit the next note.

He stood in the parlor entrance and watched her. She sat at the piano, her skirts now billowing out thanks to the hoops she'd donned ... but the hoops circled behind her perfectly. *She's managed to wedge the piano stool beneath her gown.*

Josh backed up several steps and cleared his throat loudly.

"Oh!" A flurry of activity ensued.

His boots made a lot of racket as he half-stomped back to the parlor and found Ruth struggling to subdue her skirts in the middle of the room. Standing in the aperture, he waved at the piano. "Don't stop playing on my behalf."

"I wasn't playing."

"You weren't?"

"Not exactly." She gestured toward the piano. "I was preparing a surprise for Laney."

"What kind of surprise?" He walked toward the instrument. His eyes narrowed as he viewed the keys. "You wrote on the ivories?"

"Only lightly, with a pencil. It rubs off. See?" She scrambled over and rubbed the pad of her forefinger on Middle C. The mark on it disappeared. "Laney has a hard time figuring out where the notes are on the keys compared to where they appear on the staff. It doesn't make a whole lot of sense that the alphabet begins with the letter A, but music revolves around C."

"I never thought of it that way." He smiled at her. "Ruth, you'll never know how grateful I am for you. Eavesdropping is supposed to be rude, but I listened to her reading aloud today. I stood there for a good five minutes, and Laney was reading—really reading."

"Of course she was. She's been working so hard, Josh. God's blessing her effort."

"You can take a little credit, too, Ruth. No one else ever made it so she could understand—and believe me, Mom tried. I tried. The teachers tried, too."

"You all sowed the seeds. I've just watered them so she flowered."

"You discount the importance of your patience and caring. You know, Ruth, you're quite remarkable. All of those fancy schools were so busy trying to string girls onto a cord as if they were all similar pearls, they never realized the fire-bright diamond you are."

"Joshua!" She blinked at him in shock.

He grinned. Finishing schools taught women to lower their lashes and simper something about flattery, but Ruth couldn't hide her shock. *The men back East must be blind idiots not to have appreciated her.* "Truth is truth." Folding his arms across his chest, he nodded to emphasize his point. "Your mother was right to send you here. In the right setting, you shine."

The sweetest smile he'd ever seen lit her face. "That was the nicest thing anyone has ever said to me. Mama must be looking down from heaven and glowing at your words."

Only Ruth. Only Ruth would receive a compliment and turn it around to belong to someone else. She looked so genuinely happy, he refused to ruin the moment by trying to get her to understand his praise. "Laney pictures our mothers having tea together in heaven, you know."

"From what I've heard of your mother, they'd be good friends. If there's going to be a banquet table in paradise, I don't see why there can't be a tea table, too."

Josh drummed a few bass chords on the piano. "Mom didn't have any more musical talent than Laney. I hope there's a tea table, because she'd be terrible on a harp."

Ruth giggled, but when her laughter died out, her smile faded.

He probably wasn't supposed to notice how her skirts shifted a little this way and that. Ruth never managed to hold still for very long. "What are you nervous about, Ruthie?"

Her eyes widened. "How did you know I'm nervous?"

He shrugged.

Her hair started sliding, and she automatically reached up and shoved in the pins. "Well, since we're talking about mothers..." She sucked in a quick breath and said in a rush, "I already broached the subject at lunch, so I suppose it's not completely unexpected."

No, you are not going to invest in the ranch.

"You were right."

Well, well. You can say that anytime.

"About me. And budgets. I really haven't ever had to do any practical budgeting. Mrs. Tudbert made us work on pretend household budgets regarding servants, entertaining, and such."

Tudbert? How many schools does that make now? Four?

Ruth kept talking, "That was a while ago, and she listed all of the expenses—we just had to assign them to the proper category and do the sums to total them. I thought maybe you could help me estimate the cost of setting up the library."

"We could do that."

"I know you're busy. You've started working before you come to breakfast, and after supper, you go back out and do more. I've never seen a harder-working man, Josh. Just tell me what time is best for you."

"It's not wise to do anything until you know how much you can afford to commit to the project."

"We picked up mail. Remember? I received a letter from Mama's attorney." Her shoulders lifted and fell with the deep breath she took and expelled. "At lunch, you felt I should have said something sooner about my finances. Well, I now have a general idea as to what my inheritance will be."

He nodded toward the settee. Ruth took the cue and had a seat. Josh sat down in his customary winged chair.

"Before I left home, I asked the attorney to keep whatever was invested in stocks and bonds to remain as my grandfather had seen fit. At the time, he estimated approximately twenty percent of the estate was either in cash or the house and property. I felt..." She sighed.

"You felt..." Josh prodded.

"I felt that if he sent me the proceeds from the sale of the property and the belongings I didn't have shipped, along with whatever cash that was in the bank, it would be gracious plenty to see me through a few years."

"Ruthie, I told you in town that you don't have to fret about having a home. You're welcome to stay here."

"I appreciate that, Josh. Truly I do."

If she wrings her hands much more, they'll be raw.

"Mama sent me to exclusive schools. Considering that we lived modestly and had only two servants, I always imagined we were comfortably situated."

"Honey, if you can't fund the library, that's okay. We can make it a town project. You don't need to scrimp on your living expenses so you can budget for—"

"Twelve thousand dollars," she blurted out.

"Twelve thousand," he repeated, sure he hadn't heard correctly.

"Yes." She tried to cram in another hairpin and wound up having the bun skid downward and off to one side as she added, "That's how much the attorney is sending."

Josh sat there, unmoving. A man could make a decent living at three hundred dollars a year. Highly skilled men might make twice that. Housing and food were included for ranch hands, so they averaged one hundred forty dollars a year; Dad and he talked it over and felt keeping a stable crew was worth paying a bit more, so the Broken P paid hands one hundred eighty dollars. *Twelve thousand—and that was only one fifth of her inheritance. Twelve thousand times five . . . she's wealthy beyond belief!*

Josh strove to keep his tone even. "You were prudent to keep your investments as they were. As for the um . . . sum that is to arrive, you'll need to consider several issues in budgeting that."

"Half of it is tithe. That would make it ten percent of the inheritance. I'm hoping maybe now the congregation will be able to hire a full-time pastor instead of using a circuit rider."

"We'd certainly be able to afford it."

"I'd really love to commission a pair of stained glass windows, too. It wouldn't be part of the tithe, of course. You see, I'd like to do one in honor of each of my parents—but I wouldn't tell anyone that's what they're for. I'd just know deep in my heart."

"That's mighty sweet, Ruthie." He still couldn't quite comprehend the sum she'd mentioned.

"The one for Mama would be based on that verse in the Bible that talks about the Son of Man coming back in the clouds of heaven. Mama and I loved to look at clouds."

Josh nodded. "Laney told me about the game you and your mother played, finding pictures in cloud formations."

A bittersweet smile sketched across her features. "Yes. It's been harder to decide on one for my father. You and Laney have been so kind to tell me about him, and I think I found a fitting verse. Tell me what you think of Psalm 104:14: 'He causeth the grass to grow for the cattle, and herb for the service of man: that he may bring forth food out of the earth.'"

"The farmers and the cattlemen in the area would both appreciate their work being represented."

"I hoped so. Does anyone in Folsom do stained glass, or will we need to commission someone in Sacramento?"

We. She's cooked up yet another scheme, and I'm agreeing to be part of it. "Sacramento is a beehive of activity. I'm sure there are a couple of places that would be glad to be given such a contract."

She started fidgeting again.

"What else, Ruth?"

"Oh, I couldn't keep a secret from you if I tried. How is it you always know when something's on my mind?"

Josh's heartbeat quickened. "I just do. So what is it?"

"I'm not good at being discreet. I'm trying to find a delicate way of saying it."

"Ruth, you don't have to pussyfoot around with me. I'm a simple man. We're friends. You can speak freely."

She smiled. "We really are friends, aren't we? That's such a twist. I've never had a lot of friends, but now I have you and Laney. If I didn't have one red cent, I'd still feel rich as Midas."

Josh sank more deeply into the chair. She'd gone off on a tangent, and pleasant as it was, he needed to get her back on track. "So what was it you were trying to say?"

Ruth's expression turned sober. "Laney told me your mama and daddy lost several babies."

Josh nodded. He was more than a little surprised they'd discussed that fact. After Laney was born, there'd been two more little girls—neither lived to be two, and three little babies that sickened and passed on in a matter of months. All of their graves were grouped together by Mom's in the Sacramento graveyard. Whenever Josh went to Sacramento, he always took care to visit them and place flowers by the stones. *I hope Dad remembers to do that while he's there.*

Unaware of his thoughts, Ruth continued on. "Mrs. O'Sullivan lost two sons, too. I thought it would be precious to have a third window done of Jesus with seven little children all about Him."

He studied her in silence.

She sighed. "I told you the subject wasn't very discreet."

"I'm not offended. Ruthie, sometimes you concoct plans that make my hair stand on end; but this time, you've come up with one that touches me deeply. I'm sure many in the congregation will find solace in such a window."

"Thank you, Josh." She stayed still all of three breaths before turning to the side and grabbing a sheet of paper from the cherry-wood end table. "I already made a list of items I expect we'll need for the library."

"Before you do that, Ruth, you need to make decisions about your inheritance." He stood and went to the desk. "I'll get some paper, and we can outline the considerations."

"I'd appreciate that."

He opened the top desk drawer and found a pencil among a few receipts and scraps of paper. Taking the key, he reached for the locked drawer. "There's got to be some paper here somewhere." A moment later, he sat on the settee by Ruth.

She twisted to face him and fleetingly touched his hand. "First off, I want to say that it's ludicrous for me to ever receive an inch of the ranch. You and your father deserve it. Daddy would understand if I said I wouldn't pursue a claim."

Josh tapped the pencil on the tablet. "I can't say I don't appreciate that—I do. But let's set that aside for now."

"You haven't read the mail yet, have you?"

"No. Why?"

"Because I received a letter from that kind Mr. Maltby in town. It informed me of a court date. The circuit judge is due here, so Mr. Maltby set the hearing for the third week in July. I presume you and your father also received notification. I could ask Mr. Maltby to assist me in relinquishing any claim on the Broken P."

"Ruth, you're reacting to stunning news and may not have considered all of the ramifications. It wouldn't be honorable of me to accept your offer—generous as it is—without allowing you time to mull over exactly what you want."

She gave him an exasperated look. "For the life of me, I can't imagine how you do it."

"Do what?"

"Manage to be honorable and stubborn all at the same time!"

Josh leaned toward her. "I could say precisely the same thing about you."

She started laughing, and he joined in. Tilting her head to the side, she asked, "What am I going to do with you?"

You're going to marry me someday. The thought ran through his mind, and he stayed still for a moment, allowing the notion to sink in. *Yes, I've grown fond of Ruth—very fond—but I hadn't realized just how deeply I feel until now. Yes, though. It's right. I'm going to make you my wife someday. If I declare myself now, you'll always wonder if it's because of the money, but it's not. I'd marry you if you were a penniless beggar.*

"Oh no." Ruth laughed. "I shouldn't have asked what I was going to do with you. You're probably trying to come up with a polite way of running for your life."

Josh chuckled at how she thought he was trying to get away when he was thinking just the opposite. "For now, Ruth, you're going to work with me on a budget. I assume you will want to open a bank account and keep a portion of your assets readily available."

"That's a good idea. I thought maybe I should open an account at Lester's mercantile so I won't have to carry money into town." She fiddled with her sleeve. "Could I just give him one hundred dollars and have him deduct my purchases from that, then he'll let me know when the funds are running low?"

Josh rubbed the back of his neck as he tried to find the right words to use. "You can't do that, Ruth. It's far too much money. A man who makes three hundred dollars a year can provide well for his family. If you want to open an account, fifty dollars is plenty, maybe even too much at that."

"Oh, okay. Do you know how much Hilda earns?"

"I can't say as I do. I can look it up. Why?"

"I'm probably going to be the death of that poor woman. You know I accidentally pulled down the clothesline when my horse bolted."

"Yes. I'm glad you were all right."

"That's nice of you to say, but poor Hilda's fresh laundry got muddy."

"I still can't figure out how you got a burr under that saddle."

"There's no explaining why these things happen to me, Josh. They just do. I'd hoped when I came out here that I'd become more graceful. The sad fact of the matter is, I've never come close to getting into half as many fixes and predicaments as I do here on the Broken P. Since I cause Hilda so much hardship and I'm thinking of remaining here, I'd like to double her salary."

"Before you do anything that rash, let's see what Dad's paying her." Josh crossed the parlor, removed the ledger from the drawer, and opened it. After flipping the pages, he stopped on one.

Odd. I told Dad the O'Sullivans bought those two mustangs for eighteen dollars apiece. He must have misunderstood. He has them down as nine apiece for a total of eighteen. But one line lower, he showed the stallion Eddie Lufe bought for twenty as twelve. *This isn't right.*

The opposite page showed accounts paid. The names of all the hands were there with a notation that each received his monthly pay of twelve dollars. *Twelve times twelve is one hundred forty-four. Dad and I agreed the yearly wage was supposed to be one eighty. The men should have been getting an additional three bucks a month!*

Sick inside, Josh looked farther down the page. *Hilda's earning seven and a half dollars a month.* Flipping backward, he looked at the accounts for previous months. Those showed the hands each earning fifteen dollars a month and Hilda earning thirteen. *Something's wrong. Very, very wrong.* He closed the book.

"Did you find what she's earning?"

Josh placed the ledger into the drawer, shut it, and gripped the edge of the desk. *He's my father. There's got to be an explanation for this.*

Ruth stood beside him and gently placed her hand on his arm. "I'm sorry. It was rude of me to ask you what your financial arrangements are with Hilda. You don't have to say a word, Josh. It's just that I was trying to make up for the extra work I put her through."

"You don't need to apologize, Ruth. We're discussing financial issues, and the topics can be touchy. It occurs to me that neither of us has prayed about this, and that should come first. Let's agree on praying and not discussing any of this with anyone but God. In a few days, you and I can talk again."

"I don't mind if Laney and your father know."

"No. Just you and me." From her wide eyes, he knew he'd spoken too swiftly, too forcefully. Josh leaned against the desk and feigned nonchalance. "It'll be a while until the funds arrive. There's no hurry. Let's agree to pray for wisdom and discernment."

"That's a good idea. Josh? I do want to keep a little fund for frivolous expenses. Today, I sent a letter by stage to Bernadette. I wish the Pony Express was working again. It would be much faster."

"From what I hear, it'll be running again soon."

Ruth nodded. "I'm glad. Anyway, Bernadette was our house-keeper back home. I asked her to send dime novels to Laney and me by Pony so we won't have to wait for them."

"Pony charges by weight, Ruth. It's five bucks per half-ounce."

She laughed. "I know. It'll be outrageously expensive, but it's worth every penny to listen to your sister read."

He forced a smile.

"Well, I guess I'll turn in for the night. Thank you for praying and helping me with this. I know I can trust you."

Don't trust anyone else, Ruth. "Sweet dreams." Josh waited until she went upstairs and gave her a little time to change and settle into bed. Ever since someone hit Laney, Ruth had been sleeping in his sister's room. For all of her claims of being clumsy, Ruth managed to move very silently and gracefully so she never woke his sister.

Finally sure Ruth must be asleep, Josh faced the desk with mounting dread. The desk had been Alan Caldwell's. Alan had shown him the trick latch that opened what appeared to be the base of the drawer section. Josh felt along the wood, tripped the latch, and slowly withdrew another ledger from the cavity.

The cover matched the other book in appearance, but the sums in it were far different. Page after page, proof of Dad's deceit mounted.

But why did the book in the drawer under-record the fee for the horses when wages were recorded at a lower-than-agreed upon rate? The other months, that book showed the men and Hilda earned more. But those other months showed irregularities. The feed store bill was a dollar higher than it should have been. Josh pored over the books, trying to make sense of it.

The book in the drawer—he accidentally wrote the real wages in it instead of the ones we agreed upon. The books look alike and Dad got careless. He's been skimming money from every source. Josh shook his head. *But why? Why would Dad do this?*

"So you're not sleepy, either."

Josh wheeled around.

Ruth stood in the doorway, bundled in a velvet robe that matched her green, green eyes. "I came down to make some warm milk." Her smile faded as she spotted the two books on the desk. "Oh, Josh. No."

CHAPTER SEVENTEEN

———✦———

"Come to sleep, Kelly-mine." Da patted the mattress beside himself.

Galen hugged his mother. "I'm thinking Da's in the right of it. We could all use a wee bit o' sleep."

"More 'n a wee bit. Last night the both of you hovered o'er me all the night long." Da's voice grew gruff, "Made a big deal outta nothing."

"Now, then, don't you be giving me a hard time, Cullen O'Sullivan." Ma shook her finger at Da. "If you'd ask for a wee bit o' help, you wouldn't have scared us all half out of our skin. Deciding to take a nap on the floor—'twasn't the best notion you ever took."

"You'll forgive me, Kelly-mine. I know you will." Da smiled at her. "Aye, and I'll be telling you and Galen that asking you to marry me was one of the best notions I e'er had. She's too big-hearted to carry a grudge."

"You're not fair, Cullen. Sayin' such a thing takes the wind right out of my sails." Ma pulled back the quilt on her side of the bed.

Galen started up the ladder to the loft he shared with his little brothers. "God rest on your pillow," he said.

"Aye, and may the dear Lord tuck the covers clear up to your chin," Da said back.

Galen stood by the bed he shared with Colin and frowned. He always slept on the side nearest the ladder, but tonight Colin lay in that spot. Planning to nudge his brother into rolling over, Galen bent over.

Colin's eyes popped open. He whispered, "You stayed up last night. I'll keep watch tonight."

"I doubt there's need, Colin. Da's fair-to-middlin' tonight."

"Well, I'll still be here at our parents' beck and call. You're too tired to be much good to them."

Rather than argue, Galen crawled over Colin and got beneath the covers.

"Why," Colin whispered, "is Ma saying Da was taking a nap on the floor? 'Tis a lie, flat out."

"Da's pride got dented. In his weakness, he fell."

"I know that."

"So Ma's catering to Da's feelings, teasing him about a nap." Galen yanked the pillow out from beneath his brother's head and traded so he had his own. He didn't lay his head down right away. Instead, he looked at Colin and murmured, "For now, 'tis far better she make light of it than weep. The days of weeping will come soon enough."

"You, me, or Ma—one of us should be with Da from now on."

Galen heard the catch in Colin's voice. He reached over and ruffled his brother's hair. "Best it be Ma at night, else Da will waken and think he's still havin' a nightmare."

Colin let out a tense laugh.

"Eh, you boys," Ma called from below, "you're supposed to be closin' your eyes and your mouths."

Galen winked at Colin. "Ma, I do my best, but you can't expect that of Colin. E'en with his eyes shut tight and sleep claimin' him, his mouth hangs wide open and he snores worse than a bear."

Da's chortle drifted up to them. "The boy takes after me, he does."

"Sleep now," Galen whispered. "You'll never receive a finer compliment than that, boy-oh."

⟫⊷≪

Saturday passed with all the normal chores, and Ma filled the big tub with steaming water. "You boys all scrub up. Sean, be mindful to wash behind your ears this time. I nigh unto perished when I spied all the dirt you left there last Sunday."

"It spoiled her worship, it did." Colin grinned.

Galen noticed the ornery glint in his eye and waited for whatever was to follow.

"It did?" Sean's earnest little face scrunched in dismay as he peeled out of his shirt.

"Aye, to be certain it did." Colin leaned forward and poked Sean in the middle of his scrawny chest. "Ma couldn't help thinkin' on all the 'taters she could have planted in that dirt instead of paying heed to the circuit rider's fine sermon."

Sean's mouth dropped open, then he collapsed into a fit of giggles.

Galen lifted another bucket of water onto the stove. "Do we know who's fillin' the pulpit tomorrow?"

"Can't say as I recall." Ma set to ironing a shirt. "Folks all do well enough, taking turns; but I still wish our flock had a single shepherd."

"While you're a-wishin'," Dale said, peeling off his sock, "why don't you pray for God to give the flock hymnals? It's fearfully hard for me not to laugh when Mr. Lufe makes up his own words since he can't recollect the real ones to the songs."

A few minutes later, Galen plucked his shirt off the ironing board.

"Put that back. I'm getting to it," Ma ordered.

Galen shook his head. "Do your Sunday dress, Ma. I'm staying home with Da this week."

"Now why would you be thinkin' that?" she demanded.

"Because," he smirked and leaned close to her. "I'm avoiding temptation."

"Since when did you find temptation in a pew?"

"Ever since Eddie Lufe decided he liked to sit directly behind me. Dale's not the only one who wants to laugh."

"You're a bad boy, you are, Galen O'Sullivan." Ma snatched his shirt from him. "And you're going to church tomorrow because of it."

Indeed, the next morning, Galen rounded up his brothers, let Ma walk down the line of them to do a quick inspection, then led them to Sunday service. Time was, they would have all gone as a family in the buckboard. He missed sitting in a knot of arms and legs with his brothers in the bed as his parents conversed up on the bench.

"Galen? Is it sinful for me to be proud, riding to church on my very own horse?"

"Why don't you think on being thankful instead of proud, Sean? Getting a horse is an honor. After all, it marks you as being a little man instead of a mere boy—but being a man holds responsibilities. Be thankful God provided for you and ask Him to make you worthy."

Dale sat before Galen in the saddle. He blew out a noisy sigh.

Colin matched that sigh. He turned to Dale. "Responsibilities can wear on a body. Galen says I have to rest my mare. Sorcha's looking a mite better, but it rankles to be without her for a time."

"Nevertheless, you're doing the right thing." Galen squeezed Dale's arm. "As are you, Dale. By loaning your horse to a brother, you're showing Christian charity. 'Tis a rare man who can give in silence. Most want credit, but then they're doing the act for man's approval. You—well, you haven't breathed a word. I'm thinking our heavenly Father must be pleased with you."

Dale's shoulders straightened and his head came up. He didn't say a word, but Galen gave him another squeeze. *Lord, they're all in need of guidance. I don't know that I'm up to the task. I'm asking for wisdom because 'tis plain to see that mantle will soon fall to me.*

They pulled to a halt beneath a huge, leafy sycamore tree. After hitching the beasts to the tree, Galen sent his brothers into the sanctuary. Josh had just drawn up. Galen figured he'd help Ruth down, so he sauntered over. "Top o' the mornin' to you."

"Galen! How's your father?"

"He and Ma are worshiping together at home today. I thank you for asking, Laney."

As he answered, Josh reached up and helped Ruth down. It would be rude not to help Laney, so Galen obliged. "Ma told me you're feeling better yourself."

"I am. We're trying to talk my brother into letting us come visit tomorrow."

Josh scowled. "I won't be coerced, Elaine Louise."

Ruth took Laney by the arm. "Come on. We'll go inside."

Josh waited until they were out of sight. "Ruth's been so good to Laney."

"That I can believe."

"She's a fine woman, Galen. I don't think anyone except her mother ever bothered to appreciate her."

Something about Josh's tone gave Galen pause. He didn't respond.

"I'm worried about Ruth and Laney." Josh lowered his voice, "Laney didn't fall, Galen. Someone hit her on the head."

"Are you sure?"

"Yes. She had a lump on the back of her head and another on the temple. Had she fallen, she wouldn't have gotten both. Anyone evil enough to strike a woman is just as apt to hurt another. I'm not letting them leave the Broken P unless I'm with them."

"Can't blame you. I'd feel the same way." Galen rubbed the

back of his knuckles across his chin a few times. "Any idea who did it?"

"Not a one." Josh's jaw clenched, and he looked away.

"You might fool someone else with that lie, but not me. I know you too well."

Josh scuffed the toe of his boot in the dirt. "It wasn't a lie. I've got trouble of a different kind."

Galen chuckled. "Oh, so Ruth's giving you fits, is she?"

"That's not it," Josh snapped.

"Calm down. Earlier, the way you spoke of her, you sounded like a man at the end of his rope."

"Things have changed."

Something about the tone of his friend's voice troubled Galen. He forced a chuckle. "Don't tell me you're regarding the lass as dear to your heart." *Please . . . tell me you don't.*

"I do."

No, Lord. No. I've prayed that you'd heal Ruth from her grief and bring her to me.

"It's taken me by surprise, but I confess, Ruth's won my heart. But until other matters are settled, I can't very well ask her to marry me."

"Don't you think that's awful fast? A proper courtship would let you get to know her better."

"We practically trip over one another every day. I've seen her vexed, I've seen her joyful. When it comes to Ruth, I never have to guess where she stands on an issue—she's as easy to read as all the books she loves."

"So you aim to propose?"

"I fully intend to." Josh cast a glance toward the church. "There's never been a woman for me, Galen. Not a one ever struck my fancy. Ruth—she's the one. She's been worth waiting for. She barged in and stole my heart."

"Does she return the sentiment?"

"Neither of us has declared our feelings, but I sense something between us. She trusts me with her personal business and shares her innermost thoughts."

"I see." Galen slowly unknotted his hands.

"It might be premature, but I'd like you to stand up with me as the best man."

"She's a fine young woman, Josh." Galen extended his hand. "You honor me with that request."

Josh shook hands, but as they released the grip, he cleared his throat. "That was the good news. Galen, I have a problem."

The bell started pealing, calling them to worship.

"Ruth and Laney's safety?"

"Something else." Josh heaved a sigh as the bell pealed again. "I'll lay my burden on the altar. It's not right of me to trouble you when your father's doing so poorly."

"The Holy Bible exhorts us to bear one another's burdens. You and the lasses have been considerable help. There's nothing I'd like more than to share the weight you're carryin'."

A smile sketched across Josh's strained features, but it didn't last more than a fleeting second. "Maybe after church."

Galen nodded. *It's best I release my hopes and dreams and shed the sadness I feel. I'm happy for Josh and miserable for myself. Ma warned me not to think on Ruth as being the one I'd wed.* "We both have things to lay at Jesus' feet today. I'm supposing we'd best head inside."

"Eddie Lufe's doing the sermon today."

"Well, now. He does a fine job when he does the preaching."

"He does." A sly smile crooked Josh's mouth. "His nerves always get the better of him before he stands in the pulpit, so he doesn't sing on the Sundays when he preaches."

Galen slapped him on the back. "Ach, you're a good friend. You remind me to count my blessings." Galen slipped into the pew with his brothers. He watched as Josh walked up the aisle and slipped in next to Ruth. She turned her face up to his. Tenderness shone in her countenance, and at that moment, Galen knew it was only a matter of time before he'd stand at the altar as best man and watch the woman he loved pledge her heart to Josh.

———◆———

"They arrived safe as can be," Galen reported to Josh at the fence the next morning.

"I figured they'd made it when I couldn't hear the jelly jars rattling anymore."

Galen chortled. "That Hilda—when she said she'd come along to help with canning, she didn't spare a thing. Colin's grousing about unloading the buckboard, and Ma's in a dither on account of their bringing two fifty-pound bags of sugar."

"After Hilda had me load a dozen flats of canning jars into the buckboard, I wondered aloud if one hundred pounds would be sufficient." He pushed back the brim of his hat and ran his sleeve across his forehead. "If I held any doubts whether she could protect the girls, they evaporated then and there."

"Singed your ears to a crisp, did she?"

Josh raised his brows and whistled.

Galen chuckled. "The women need days like this to get together. Ma said neither of the lasses has ever canned a single thing and Laney's only made jelly once."

"Don't remind me of that disaster." Josh grimaced. "I worried for a solid hour that the hogs had contracted a new disease. The purple splotches turned out to be from Laney trying to hide her failure by feeding it to the hogs. They didn't eat the jelly; they wallowed in it!"

"How did you ever figure it out?"

"I went into the house to read up on hogs in the *Animal Husbandry Guide*. When Laney heard I was concerned, she confessed. She's never been able to keep a secret from me."

"Josh, you mentioned a problem before worship yesterday. Are you wantin' to talk it through now that we're alone?"

"How's your dad?"

"No better, no worse. But that's not what we're discussing. I'd be a mighty poor friend and an even worse brother in Christ if all I ever thought about was my own life. You've come up alongside me and are sharing the yoke to pull me through, Josh. 'Tis right and good that I do likewise for you. Are you still worried about Toledo watching Ruth?"

"Either he's getting better about sneaking around to do it, or he's eased off."

Galen folded his arms across his chest. "I've been prayin' for her safety."

"So have I." Josh shook his head. "I've never known a woman to be so accident prone." He didn't inform Galen about how Ruth managed to trip over a tree root on her way to the stable that very morning. If he hadn't been by her side, she would have fallen flat on her face.

"Suppose you tell me what's weighin' so heavily on your heart." Galen looked at him steadily.

"Your dad is a good man." Josh steeled himself, then let out a slow, long breath. "Mine isn't. Galen, he's keeping two sets of books on the ranch."

Galen's features pulled tight. "That doesn't bode well."

"He's recording less than the true sum we receive for cattle and horses and more than we pay the hands and pay for goods. Lower recorded profit and higher expenses end up showing the ranch isn't doing nearly as well as it truly is."

"You're not one to make a snap judgment. I take it you've seen both sets and studied them carefully?"

Josh nodded.

"Do you have any notion as to why he's doing it or where the funds are going?"

"Not a one. But if it were above board, he wouldn't resort to this. I'd gladly support investing if he were interested. If he wanted to set up a dowry for Laney, old-fashioned as it is, I'd be the first to want to establish an account in her name." He gritted his teeth and blew out a long, slow breath. "No, it's a betrayal. I can't manufacture any honest reason for him to have done this."

"How long has it been going on? Since Ruth arrived?"

"Much longer. Over two years. From the time he took over bookkeeping."

"The Broken P was run to the ground and nigh unto goin' under the gavel. The first years of pulling a place back are inevitably lean. Any profit a-tall was laudable. I hope you're not faulting yourself for not figuring it out sooner."

"I do hold myself partly to blame. The laborer is worthy of his hire. I stand by that biblical principle. The hands were to be earning three bucks more a month than they have."

"How were you to know? You trusted your father."

"I can't anymore." The wind shifted direction. Instead of smelling cattle, the sweet, fruity fragrance from Kelly's garden drifted by. "I'm praying for wisdom. Part of me wants to confront my father the minute he gets back from Sacramento; the other cautions me to measure my steps."

"In asking the Lord for guidance, you can't insist that He answers you at once."

"I've already determined that once this is resolved, I'm paying those men the back pay they deserve and make sure they receive fifteen a month."

"If that's the case, then as long as you keep an eye on matters to be sure you and Laney aren't cheated, you can bide your time. It'll be hard for you not to let on that you know he's been up to no good, but a bit of time might well let you determine where the missing funds have gone. I'm thinking you ought to have Rick Maltby out to the ranch so he can take a look at the books. The sheriff, too."

"Since the girls and Hilda are with your mom today, I could just ride into town with the books."

"There's a grand idea. You need a few people knowin' the truth. That way, if your father disposes of the book with the accurate figures in it, you'll still have witnesses. Until then, you're the only one who's seen the proof."

Josh crammed his hands in his rear pockets. "Ruth's seen them."

"Has she, now?"

"She came into the parlor after I'd discovered the second ledger. They were both on the desk. I couldn't lie to her, Galen. Then, too, I felt an obligation to tell Ruth because part of the ranch might well be hers."

"I saw Ruth at church Sunday and at my house this mornin'." Galen's brow furrowed. "To look at the lass, you'd ne'er guess the least little thing is amiss."

"She didn't want Laney to find out. We decided to shield Laney as best we could."

"Your sister will ne'er grow up if you don't allow her to."

"Recovering from the concussion is enough." Josh lifted his chin. "Besides, Laney won't be able to sit across from Dad without bursting into tears if she knows."

"I suppose she'll end up knowing when matters have to be settled." Leaning on the fencepost, Galen asked, "Tell me, how can I help you? You already have my prayers."

"I covet those prayers. If you and your mom don't mind, I'd like the girls over here as much as possible."

"They're always more than welcome." Grinning widely, Galen added, "Dale and Sean are scared half out of their skins of Hilda. She took one look at the both of them and said she wanted a bucket apiece of beans from them straight away. Folks probably think the express rider came hours early from the dust cloud those brothers of mine made, speeding to the task."

"After tangling with Hilda this morning," Josh shrugged, "I can't say as I blame them."

"With the girls here, you might be able to get to the bottom of who hurt Laney."

"The women are my biggest concern. The matter of Dad embezzling is bad—but I'd gladly walk away penniless and have Ruth and Laney safe than own a dozen ranches and let either of them be harmed."

"Our farm should be safe enough. With so many of us around, no one's bound to get near either one of them without being spotted. Ma and Hilda—they'd be more likely to wield a skillet or a rolling pin as to let someone touch a hair on their heads."

"I'm relying on that fact. While I'm in town, is there anything you need?"

Galen thought a moment. "Not a thing. Not unless you bring lumber, nails, and five braw men to build on to the house to hold all the wax, jars, sugar, and such that Hilda hauled over this morn."

"If I'm right about Hilda and your mom, they'll have every last jar full in a matter of days."

"'Tis a distinct possibility. The garden's bountiful."

"I'll pick up more jars. It'll give me an excuse to be in town."

"God go with you."

"Thanks, Galen. I need Him to."

CHAPTER EIGHTEEN

Y ou look like somethin' the cat dragged in," Hilda declared as she eyed Ruth's damp hair and limp dress.

Ruth shoved a plethora of curls from her damp forehead and climbed into the buckboard.. "I don't doubt that for a second."

Laney sat in the bed of the buckboard and smoothed her rumpled pink dress. "This frock is never going to be the same." Leaning toward the edge, she added to Kelly O'Sullivan, "And I'm not sad one bit. I made a pink dress because your son is so bossy, but I look atrocious in it."

"I've never seen you look atrocious," Galen said as he sauntered up. "Until now. Oh, you lasses are quite a sight!"

"Galen!" his mother huffed.

"He's right." Ruth couldn't keep from smiling. "Laney and I will keep these as our work dresses. It won't matter if they get stained or need patching. With your garden and orchard, we'll have plenty to do to keep up with what God grows."

"'Tis good for you to help, but I don't expect you to work each and every time you show up," Mrs. O'Sullivan said.

"Nonsense." Laney folded her hands in her lap as if she were at a garden party. "It wasn't work. It was fun. I've never put up tomatoes or beans before."

"Many hands make work light, you know." Hilda took up the reins.

"It was nice of you to come, Hilda. I enjoyed swappin' recipes with you." Mrs. O'Sullivan motioned to her boys. Sean and Dale scrambled up, one holding a flat of canned tomatoes and the other a flat of beans. "You'll want to be havin' these. More'll come home once the jars cool enough to be touched."

"We've got plenty." Hilda pursed her lips, then said, "But I've come up with a hankerin' for cherries. Your trees putting out yet?"

"We'll be pickin' them tomorrow," Galen answered.

"You got any spare clean canvas?"

"I suppose we do," Mrs. O'Sullivan said slowly. "Why?"

"I'm bringin' the girls back tomorrow and the next day, too. I've got lemons. We'll use 'em along with the sugar. Cherry fruit leathers'd taste mighty fine in the winter. Them young boys'll do good at keepin' the birds from pecking at the canvas once we spread the fruit puree on it."

Colin turned to his mother. "Oh, you made raspberry leathers a few years back. Remember how good they tasted?"

"It's blackberry and raspberry season now. Just like it is cherries. They all come ripe the same time." Hilda scooted from side to side to settle herself more comfortably on the buckboard bench. "Cherries tomorrow. If your boys find brambles, we can go a-berryin' the next day."

"I know where some are!" Sean shouted.

"We'll have to be sure to make pies and tarts to send home with you. You don't want your boss mad at you for letting chores pass you by," Mrs. O'Sullivan said.

"The mister is outta town. Josh won't care a lick if I sear a steak for his supper. Timing is right; might as well help one another out."

As they rode home, Hilda turned halfway around on the seat.

"Your dresses are ruined. Don't be expecting me to launder them just so you can go add berry stains to the mess."

"Of course we don't." Laney gave a dainty shrug. "It won't matter a whit to me. I'm just sitting here, trying to figure out how to talk you into making raspberry syrup."

"All depends on how many raspberries get picked. Syrup's nice for a short while, but it don't store none too good. Blackberries, raspberries, cherries—tasty little things, but they gotta be dried up. They won't gel, so can't make jellies or preserves."

"Back home, Bernadette added grapes or quince to berries and made preserves," Ruth remembered. "The taste was wonderful."

"Crabapples work, too." Hilda sniffed. "But McCain won't be happy if I spend grocery money on any of those fruits. They're not in season."

"If they're not in season," Laney wondered, "how could you get any?"

"South America has seasons upside down to ours," Ruth explained. "Our winter is their summer. Our spring is their autumn. They ought to have crabapples and grapes aplenty now."

"Yeah, but I'd have to pay dearly for them." Hilda turned around and didn't say another word.

Once they reached home, Hilda stopped the buckboard by the back of the house. A couple of the hands came over and helped the women down. Hilda told one, "Just unhitch the horses. We'll be using the wagon for the next few days. No use draggin' it in and out. You—haul those beans and tomatoes into the pantry for me. I've got supper to see to."

Josh came out of the house, took one look at his sister, and turned to Ruth. "That's not my sister. Where did you leave Laney?"

Ruth burst out laughing.

"That bump on the head knocked some sense into her," Hilda grumbled. "Finally made her see she's not your daddy's little china doll. Don't you dare try to fancify her again, Joshua. I'll double starch your Sunday shirts if you do."

"Well . . ." he drawled and paused. "Instead of everyone dressing for supper, why don't we just eat in the kitchen?"

"Oh, could we?" Laney grabbed Hilda's hand. "Remember when you used to let Josh and me have supper with you when we were little?"

"Long as you don't mind my talkin' business to Josh whilst we eat."

Half an hour later, they sat around the table. Josh reached over and took Ruth's hand in his. She gave him a startled look. "When Mom was alive, we always joined hands at the table for prayer. Dad put an end to that practice when she passed on, but I'd like us to do it again."

His fingers and palm were callused and rough against hers, but it felt good. *I could sit at the table all night and just let him hold my hand. He makes me feel warm and safe, like I belong here.* Ruth smiled at him and took Hilda's hand.

"Almighty, bountiful Father, we thank you for all of the blessings in our lives. Most of all, we thank you for one another and the unity we feel as your children. Bless this meal, and bless Hilda's dear hands that prepared it. Help us, Lord, to serve you in all we do. Amen."

They didn't pass around the platter and bowls—Hilda had already served the supper on their plates. Hilda started cutting her steak and said, "I warned you that I'm talking business, so here goes—I need someone to go to town and get me a bunch of stuff."

"What do you need?" Josh asked.

"More jars—eighteen flats oughta do. A dozen lemons and another ladle."

Ruth added, "Grapes, crabapples, and quince." When the housekeeper's jaw dropped, Ruth said, "It was rude of me to interrupt. I'm sorry. I just wanted to remind you of what we talked over on the way home."

Hilda's gape turned into a grin. "I appreciate your reminding me. Yes. I need all of those. And canvas. Fifteen—" She looked at how Ruth's chin lifted. "No, twenty yards of cheap canvas."

"Whoa. I'm going to need to write this down." Josh scooped a bite into his mouth, left the table, and returned with a pencil and sheet of paper.

Ruth listened the whole time to the way his spurs sang as he walked.

As he sat down, Josh said, "Now go over that again."

Laney recited everything back to him.

Ruth gawked at her. "How did you do that?"

"I'm a good listener."

"Always was," Hilda said. "Your mama used to read poems and such to you, and you'd rattle it right back word for word. The very next day, you'd go off to school and have the teacher praising you ten ways to tomorrow for givin' a beautiful recitation. Josh, your dad's gonna throw a hissy fit over my wanting all this stuff, and I'm not done yet."

"I'll deal with Dad."

Ruth didn't dare look at Josh. He'd had an edge to his voice she hoped no one else picked up on. The past week or so he'd been acting different. It wasn't just the discovery of his father's perfidy. She couldn't decide what had happened, but he was ... different.

"As long as your dad's gone, I reckon I ought to go with the girls over to the O'Sullivans. Kelly's bearing up well, but I suspect she's not sleeping much at night. Her husband's needing a lot of care. We'll pitch in and do a lot of canning, make jelly, and some fruit leathers—"

"Fruit leathers!" Josh perked up.

Ruth laughed. "You're as bad as Galen's little brothers. They got excited about them, too."

"Those boys are growin' like weeds. Saw 'em yesterday at church. If I didn't know better, I'd swear on a stack of Bibles the littlest grew an inch overnight." Hilda propped her elbows on the table. "It'd be too hard on Cullen's pride for us to buy his children clothes, but I figure he'd be a happy man if we got his missus a pretty store-bought dress."

"What a wonderful idea!" Ruth took a sip of milk. "You and she are about the same size. Whoever goes to town needs to know what to buy."

"Excellent point." Josh bent over the list. "What do you recommend, Hilda?"

"Nothing with a print. When she has to dye it black so she can wear it for mourning, if it's got a print, the dye'll look splotchy."

"How about another apron for her?"

"Good idea, Ruth. Put that down, Josh." Hilda slathered butter on a slice of bread. "Kelly and me—we're of an age that we don't trouble to cinch ourselves in tight. Tell whoever gets the dress to make it roomy around the middle."

Laney perked up. "A matching hair ribbon and hair pins."

"Other thing is, we're gonna be over there at midday. I'm not about to eat them outta house and home."

Josh hitched a shoulder. "Why don't you take over a roast? Whatever they don't eat for supper can be used for sandwiches the next day."

"Now you're talkin', cowboy!" Hilda slapped the table.

At the end of supper, Ruth looked at Laney. "You're exhausted."

"After you tuck her in, would you meet me in the parlor?" Josh gazed at her intently. "I want to discuss something with you."

"I don't need to be tucked in. I can take care of myself." Laney rose. "You two go on ahead."

Ruth allowed Josh to escort her to the parlor. After seating her on the settee, he sat beside her—just as a man ought to do when he was courting. But he wasn't. She tamped down the urge to giggle.

Josh took her hand in his. "I want to ask something important of you."

She gave no response.

"Ruth, I want you to pursue your right to inherit the Broken P. You and I get along exceptionally well. I think we'll make good partners. If you win your case, you and I could essentially band together and outvote anything Dad might want to do. By your having ownership, we could decide to hire a bookkeeper or have you take over that responsibility."

"I think I'd enjoy that. I wouldn't want it to interfere with starting the library, though." She wrinkled her nose. "But, Josh, I still feel it's wrong for me to claim any of the property."

"Laney and I need your help, Ruth. So does Hilda. She's only earning seven-fifty a month."

"That's . . ." She did the math in her head. "Only a quarter a day? Unconscionable!"

"I agree. I'll go to town tomorrow. I left the books with Rick Maltby. He's copying each entry for the past two years. I'm going to tell him we're keeping the appointment next month in Sacramento, and I'm not going to challenge your right. That way, Dad will either have to capitulate or fight you alone."

"I don't want to come between you and your father."

"Ruth, you're not. When you first arrived, I was admittedly upset that the will would be contested. However, I'm positive Alan wouldn't ever accept how Dad's been embezzling. All along I said it wasn't what either of us wanted; it's what your father would have wanted. I knew your father, Ruth."

She slid her hand over his. "I know you did, Josh. I never met him, but from all you've said, I would have loved him."

"He would have adored you, Ruth." Josh cupped her cheek. "Sure as I sit here with you, I know he would have cherished the strong, witty, loving woman you are."

Ruth closed her eyes to keep from crying. The tenderness of his words overwhelmed her. "Thank you, Josh."

He withdrew his touch, and she felt bereft.

"I meant what I said, Ruth. I don't want you to feel as if I'm pulling on your heartstrings to manipulate you."

"You wouldn't do that, Josh. You're too honorable. It's because I know you to be so truthful that your words carry weight with me."

He smiled. "Thanks, Ruthie."

They sat in silence for a moment, then he broke it. "Your father would want you to inherit your half rather than allow my father to use his position to cheat the hands, Hilda, and my sister. If it were just me, I'd not take action. I don't need much to be happy. I'm asking you to step forward—for all of them."

"When you go to town, would you please buy Hilda a new dress and apron, too?"

"Yes, Ruth—but will you please answer my question? Are you going to follow through on the claim?"

"For you and Laney, I'd do anything."

———※———

Five days later Hilda pulled the buckboard to a stop outside the back door again. "Laney Louise, don't you dare so much as sneeze until you hand down those pies."

"Yes, Hilda." Laney laughed. "I'm such a mess, it wouldn't matter if I got anything more on my dress."

"I don't care about your dress," Hilda declared. "I care about the pies!"

Ruth tried her best to sit still. The bed of the buckboard held canning jars full of vegetables and jelly, two crates of lettuce, carrots, and cabbage, three pies, a half dozen tarts each of raspberry and cherry, and a pitcher of fruit syrup.

Josh stepped out onto the porch and gave her a strained look. A second later, his father shouldered past him. Ruth's heart fell.

"Girls! Welcome home." McCain drew closer. "Come on down from there."

"Hilda won't let me move till she gets the pies," Laney said as she passed them to the housekeeper. "Welcome home to you!" She glanced down and bit her lip before admitting, "I'm afraid I'm a terrible mess, Daddy."

Her father took a closer look and lowered his voice. "We have a caller. You girls need to scoot upstairs and freshen up."

Holding up her hands for inspection, Ruth said, "I'm afraid we're so stained by the berries, we'll be red-handed for days to come."

"Do your best, and be quick about it," McCain ordered.

Josh rounded the buckboard. "Here, Ruth, let me lift you out. I'll help Hilda unload all of this. I'm sure the O'Sullivans appreciate the help you ladies have given them this week. You've done the Broken P proud."

"Thank you, Josh." She allowed him to cup her waist and lift her out of the wagon and down.

He didn't let go. Instead, his warm, strong hands tugged her a little closer. He dipped his head and murmured, "We've got trouble."

CHAPTER NINETEEN

Your attorney is inside. Dad's figured out you have money coming."

Ruth turned her face to Josh and smiled as she said, "I appreciate your help."

Fifteen minutes later, the mantel clock struck six. Laney and Ruth descended the stairs, freshly scrubbed, hair smoothed into order, and in nice dresses. McCain stood at the foot of the stairs and invited in a jovial tone, "Come into my parlor."

Said the spider to the fly. Ruth couldn't keep from thinking how apt the poem was. She edged in front of Laney so she and Josh could have a second before his father came into the room. Josh met her and slid his arm about her waist. Ruth leaned as close as her hoops would allow.

"Ruth, do you know Daryl Farnsworth of the law firm Farnsworth, Tabbard, and Farnsworth?"

"I don't believe I've had the pleasure. I know his father, though."

"Miss Caldwell." Mr. Farnsworth sketched a polite bow.

"And this is my daughter, Elaine," McCain said. Even before

the attorney could give Laney a sociable greeting, McCain declared, "We're all like family. We keep no secrets, Farnsworth. Why don't we all sit down and let the man tell Ruth why he's traveled all this way."

Farnsworth's brow creased. "Miss Caldwell?"

Ruth turned to Josh. "Mama taught me people ought not discuss finances openly. Perhaps just you could remain in the room. I'd appreciate your guidance."

"Oh, I understand. Excuse me." Laney slipped out of the room.

McCain came to stand on Ruth's other side. "There. I'm sure you feel better now that we'll be in private."

Mr. Farnsworth stretched to his full height. "I believe Miss Caldwell expressed her wishes. She, I, and Mr. McCain—"

"Josh, go on and get outta here," McCain ordered.

Ruth gasped at his audacity.

Josh immediately turned to her. His movement set her off balance, and she teetered.

"She's faint," Farnsworth declared.

Josh pulled her closer still. She'd been ready to deny any faintness. Never once had she been in the slightest bit swoony. Well, not until Josh held her so tight. Ruth closed her eyes and dared to rest her head on his chest.

"McCain, does your daughter have any smelling salts?" Farnsworth hinted as he gently touched Ruth's shoulder. "Let's lie her down."

Josh's father growled as he stomped out of the parlor.

"She'll be okay if we can sit her down," Josh declared. "Come, Ruth."

She shuffled along beside him for a few steps and sank onto the settee. Josh sat on part of her skirts and kept her head cupped to his shoulder.

Farnsworth stood behind the settee, bent forward, and whispered, "Miss Caldwell, you have every right to privacy. Shall we meet in town tomorrow?"

Ruth let out a shaky breath. "It's not right for Josh to be caught in the middle. We may as well lay things out in the open."

"You don't have to," Josh said softly.

"Here." McCain rushed into the room. "A burning feather's supposed to work."

Ruth pushed away from Josh. "Thank you, but I'm much improved."

"She's delicate," McCain said to the attorney as he set a feather from one of Laney's hats off to the side. "Perhaps we men should handle the business. You can be assured we'll take good care of our little Ruth."

"I traveled across the nation to conduct this business with Miss Caldwell personally. I must insist that she be included in all conversations."

"Fine." McCain took his usual seat. "Ruthie, dear, you just sit back and listen. I'll handle things for you."

"My father assured me Miss Caldwell is quite competent to take care of all her personal business matters."

"Of course I am." Ruth felt her hairpins slipping. "I'm sure you must have prepared a written report for me."

"Indeed." The attorney withdrew a sizable packet of papers from a case she hadn't noticed until now. "This portfolio outlines your current investments. They're sensibly diversified, as per your grandfather's instructions. Before you traveled here, I understand you asked my father to keep the investments in place as they were."

"I did." Ruth accepted the papers.

"You'll be pleased to know that the Hadleys have received their portion of the inheritance and purchased a lovely cottage."

"That is wonderful news. Thank you."

"I was asked to deliver this to you." He pulled a glittering item from his vest pocket. "I believe it belonged to your grandmother."

"Oh! Grandmother's brooch." She cradled the diamond-studded gold piece in her hands. "I remember her wearing this.

When Haley's comet came through in 1835, Grandfather commissioned this star for her."

"It's a beautiful keepsake," Josh said.

"As for the remaining portion of the estate . . ." Mr. Farnsworth paused.

"Would those be the items Ruth mentioned are being shipped through Sacramento?" Josh asked.

"There were things I couldn't bear to part with." Ruth fished her fan out of her sleeve and fluttered it twice before hitting her chin.

Josh reached over and swiped it from her. "I'll make sure those are freighted here." His hand dwarfed the fan, but he held the ivory-and-silk piece with surprising dexterity.

Easing back into his chair, Farnsworth stated, "Actually, the housekeeper and her husband felt six months was far too long for Miss Caldwell to wait for her goods. Instead of shipping them around the Horn, they requested my leave to hire the Overland Freight to fill two of their wagons in order to expedite their arrival. I wouldn't be surprised for them to reach here any day now."

"How nice," Ruth said.

Swishing her fan toward her a few times, Josh asked, "Are we done, then? I'm sure Ruth would like to be given time to—"

"Surely the girl must have some funds to provide for her immediate financial needs, doesn't she?" McCain prodded.

Ruth couldn't lie. She let out a little sigh. "Naturally I do."

Farnsworth asked, "Miss Caldwell, would you like to go rest? I can return tomorrow, or we can meet in town if you'd rather."

"Can't you see this is a strain on her?" McCain scowled. "Drawing the matter out is far too hard on the woman. Just say what you came to and be done with it!"

"What would you like to do, Ruth?" Josh asked.

She thought for a moment. McCain had proven to be remarkably tenacious. She might delay allowing him full knowledge of the scope of her inheritance, but not for long. As a woman of independent means and a sound mind, she could do whatever she wished; but Proverbs frequently exhorted to "seek wise counsel." *Josh is honorable and kind. I can rely on him. Unless I'm impossibly rude, I won't get rid of his father. Even then, if I do, I'm pitting father against son. I cannot do that.*

Looking from Josh to Farnsworth and back, she said, "Let's see this through to the conclusion."

"As you wish," Farnsworth said. "Transporting funds turned out to be a bit of a challenge. Free banking has made the notes issued by some institutions unstable, if not downright worthless. Since eastern and western banks don't hold reciprocal agreements, double golden eagles are the prudent choice. Unfortunately, they are heavy in any bulk."

"Bulk," McCain repeated under his breath.

"I took the liberty of purchasing some excellent diamonds from the new Henry Morse cutting factory in Boston. Diamonds are easy to carry and conceal. Their value only stands to appreciate. The portfolio has a second section in the back which contains the certificates for these." Farnsworth withdrew a small black velvet pouch from his case.

Ruth accepted the diamonds and held them in her lap along with the brooch.

"Don't you want to look at them, girl?" McCain rasped.

"That would be unforgivably rude of me. Please, Mr. Farnsworth, continue."

"I alluded to double eagles." He cleared his throat. "My valise is in the hallway. It's a specially made piece with a reinforced false bottom. The valise contains slightly more than fifteen pounds of double eagles."

"Fifteen pounds." McCain tried to cover his choking sound with a gruff cough.

"Of course you won't want to keep them here at home, Ruth," Josh said. "I'll take you to town tomorrow, and you can keep them in the bank."

"How kind of you, Joshua."

"In fact," Josh said, "Mr. Farnsworth, if you'd be willing to stay to supper and spend the night, we could both accompany Ruth tomorrow."

"I'd be delighted. Thank you."

Josh rested his arm across the back of the settee and toyed with the little tendrils across her nape.

Such a tiny gesture, but Ruth felt all shivery inside. No man had ever been this close to her or this familiar. Was he putting on a show to trick his father into believing they held an affinity for one another, or was this just an absentminded action? She cast him a quick glance.

Josh winked at her. "Farnsworth, am I mistaken, or do double eagles weigh just shy of an ounce apiece?"

"You're correct, sir."

"Sixteen ounces in a pound," McCain said.

"Yes, I know," Ruth said. "But you were kind to remind me."

"And you have fifteen pounds in your valise. . . ." Josh's voice trailed off.

"Slightly more," Farnsworth said. "Fifteen pounds was just over four thousand, eight hundred dollars. In the interest of keeping her financial figures round, I added in a few more so she'd have a small nest egg of five thousand dollars to start her new life out here in California."

"I don't like that kind of money lying around." Josh rose. "There's a secret compartment in the desk—"

"No!" McCain barked.

"I don't understand why you'd be opposed." Farnsworth gave McCain a quizzical look.

"I just returned from Sacramento. I . . . I bought Christmas gifts for Josh and Laney. And you, too, Ruth. They're in there, and I don't want to ruin the surprise."

"Christmas is half a year away." Ruth looked at McCain with owl-eyed innocence.

"I don't get to Sacramento that often." A calculating smile lit his face. "But I suppose I'll need to take you there—actually, on to San Francisco so you can convert the diamonds back into real money."

"I'd discourage you from doing so," Farnsworth said. "As I mentioned, the diamonds will only appreciate in value. You can liquidate them as necessary, but since you have sufficient funds for the time being..." He shrugged.

"We're so pleased for you, Ruth." McCain came over and kissed her cheek.

Ruth fought the urge to wipe away the contact.

"Everything's worked out so well," McCain continued on. "I was concerned for your future, but I now see it was needless worry. You're quite the heiress." He turned and walked toward the door. "Everything's worked out beautifully. I'll go on into town with you tomorrow and see Rick Maltby."

"Whyever would you do that?" Ruth wondered.

McCain turned toward her. "Surely, since you've discovered your good fortune, you'll not want to bother claiming any portion of the ranch."

"Are you suggesting my client renounce her birthright?" Farnsworth shook his head. "No. Absolutely not. Miss Caldwell, I must advise you against such a hasty and imprudent decision."

"Ruth's not a selfish woman. I'm sure she understands she doesn't need what little money we make at the Broken P."

"Oh, I don't plan to keep the money for myself." Ruth reached up and stuck in her hairpins before her hair came tumbling down. She took her time, then cupped the brooch and pouch of diamonds in her hands once again. Pressing them to her heart, she said, "I'll use it all for a good cause."

"Charity begins at home." McCain's voice was tough as granite.

"Oh, I'm so glad we agree. You see, I'm going to found a library for the whole town!"

"Daddy's acting funny," Laney said as she crawled into bed.

Ruth wondered why the belt of her dressing gown was so short. She glanced down to find she'd knotted it into a huge mess.

"It's sweet, the way he's hovering over you. It's not my business, and I don't want to pry, but you truly don't have to worry about your future, Ruth. Daddy's right. You belong here with us, and nothing's ever going to change that."

Keeping her head bowed as she untangled the knot, Ruth changed the subject. "Do I need to mix one of the headache powders for you tonight?"

"I'm quite well, thank you." Laney patted the other side of the bed. "Isn't it something, how everything always works out? Why, since you've been staying with me, it left your room vacant for that nice Mr. Farnsworth."

"He is nice, isn't he?" Ruth lifted the kerosene lamp from the washstand and carried it to a small table in the far corner of the bedchamber.

"I'm not overly sleepy. Are you going to read to me?"

"You need your rest, Laney. The doctor said you wouldn't make a complete recovery if we weren't diligent about your sleeping sufficiently." Ruth picked up the portfolio Mr. Farnsworth had given her. "I'm supposed to look this over."

Laney's pretty face scrunched up. "I bet it's so boring, you fall asleep faster than I do."

Ruth laughed as she opened the folder. Grandfather had inherited a small shipping company and invested some of the profits in a Lowell textile mill. When Mama returned home, Grandfather sold his holdings and moved them to St. Louis. No one ever discussed finances, so Ruth hadn't known what a shrewd businessman her grandfather had been.

Learning of the size of her inheritance came as a shock. Now

Ruth got a clear picture as to just how sharp her grandfather had been. Page after page of the portfolio represented the various investments, stocks, and bonds. Though Farnsworth mentioned the collection was well diversified, Ruth marveled at the wide range of companies and products. Two railroads. Western Union. The Overland Mail Company. The I.M. Singer Sewing Machine Company. Otis Safety Elevator. The list went on. A list of how many shares, what their current value was, and how they'd been earning accompanied each listing.

The second section contained certificates to accompany the diamonds. Other than an emerald ring she occasionally wore and a pair of ruby earbobs, Ruth owned no jewels. The prices listed for the diamonds shocked her. She opened the velvet pouch and poured two-dozen ice-like stones into her palm. They glittered in the lamplight. Their value didn't make sense. A man could labor for years and never spend a penny of his wages before he could buy the smallest of the diamonds. Ruth shook her head as she carefully poured them back into the bag and tied it shut.

A knock sounded at the door.

Ruth slipped the pouch into her pocket, then scurried to the door before whoever was there would knock again and disturb Laney. She opened it a crack.

"I wanted to check in on you and Elaine."

"Laney is already asleep, Mr. McCain."

"But you can't sleep? Poor little Ruth. Dear, you don't need to worry your pretty little head over all of these business matters. I feared that Farnsworth overburdened you."

"Not at all. I appreciated his recognizing that I have a sound mind and am eager to use it."

He nodded sagely. "That's good to know. The other good thing is knowing whom you can trust."

"Oh, I agree!" She nodded her head in agreement but didn't meet his eyes. "Well, thank you for checking in on us."

"I could stay for a time and keep you company . . . until you fall asleep," McCain suggested.

Ruth tried hard to look notably shocked. "That would hardly be appropriate, Mr. McCain. We are not related."

"Well, you're practically a daughter to me. Indeed, I think of you that way."

His expression made Ruth most uncomfortable. Josh and Farnsworth's voices drifted up the stairs. Ruth could hear them drawing nearer and raised the volume of her voice as much as she dared. "Good night, Mr. McCain."

McCain hesitated, then seemed to realize it would do him little good to protest. "Good night, Ruth." He turned and said, "Laney's already asleep. Ruth's settling in nicely."

"Ruth?"

She opened the door about six more inches. "Yes, Josh?"

He bid good night to Farnsworth and came to her door. "I suggested to Hilda that she bring up a breakfast tray for you and Laney. It should give you a little more time to get ready to go into town, and I want my sister to have as much sleep as possible."

"How thoughtful! She's still recovering."

"Good idea, son." McCain slapped Josh on the shoulder.

"Thanks, Dad. Good night." Josh didn't move an inch.

Ruth wanted to hug him for being so stalwart.

"It's not seemly for you to be at the door of a young lady's bedchamber," McCain muttered.

Ruth opened her mouth to tell McCain he had no room to cast stones, but Laney's sleepy voice called, "Josh, is that you?"

"Yeah, it's me, Laney Lou."

"Ruth showed me her grandmother's brooch. It made me remember Mama's cameo. Do you know where it is?"

McCain shouldered past Ruth and into the room. "I'm the one you ought to ask. I've been keeping it for you."

Ruth stood in the wide-open doorway, astonished at his nerve.

He'd just faulted his son for standing out in the hall, yet he'd barged straight in!

Josh tugged on her sleeve, and she stepped out of the room. He dipped his head. "Wait until I come to get you in the morning. Otherwise Dad will sneak in and nose through your papers."

Ruth nodded. Next, she slipped her hand into the pocket of her dressing gown, closed her fingers around the velvet pouch, and slowly withdrew it. Pressing it into Josh's hand, she murmured, "For safekeeping."

"I stored the cameo away for you," McCain told Laney. "Your mother received it on her eighteenth birthday, and I always thought you'd want me to give it to you on yours."

"I'm sorry if I spoiled your surprise, Daddy."

"You didn't spoil it, sis." Josh casually slipped his hands into his pants pockets and shrugged. "If anything, I think it will make her appreciate the cameo more now, Dad. She'll anticipate it."

"I think that's enough excitement for Laney," Ruth announced. "She needs to get back to sleep. If you gentlemen will excuse us . . ."

"Of course we will," Josh said. "Come on, Dad. I'll see you girls in the morning."

Josh managed to get his father out of the room, and Ruth immediately shut the door. She rued the fact that the door didn't have a lock. Laney slipped back to sleep, then Ruth scoured the room to find a safe hiding place for her portfolio. Finally, she settled on stuffing it in her pillowslip.

The next morning, Hilda bustled into the room with a breakfast tray. "Don't know what got into Josh. He suddenly thinks you girls are delicate or something. Of all the nonsense in the world, your not being able to gather yourselves together enough to show up at the breakfast table."

"We'll put the extra time to good use. Maybe Laney can help me finally tame my hair into a respectable style."

Setting down the tray, Hilda snorted. "There's not enough time in all eternity for that. Why you think you have to make your hair look like everybody else's beats me. Nothin' wrong with plenty of curl. You don't see ducklings trying to slick down their fluff. Your hair's just like that—yellow down. Only curly."

"Ducklings are adorable," Laney said. "And so are you, Ruth."

"Hans Christian Andersen has a fairy tale about the Ugly Duckling. I always loved that story."

Hilda turned to go. "Anyone who thinks a duckling is ugly just ain't looking from the right angle. That's what I say. Maybe you need to think on that good and hard, Ruth Caldwell."

"Here we go. Ruth, let me help you up." McCain bustled over to her.

"I've got her, Dad." Josh curled his hands about Ruth's slender waist.

"Thank you, Josh." Ruth smiled at him. *Is she glad I'm holding her, or just that it isn't Dad?*

He'd no more than begun to lift her when his father snapped, "What do you think you're doing? Ruth belongs on the seat, next to me."

"Please put me back with Laney, Josh. I couldn't possibly sit up front."

He held Ruth suspended in midair, not at all sorry for the opportunity to show her his strength and protection. *If only I'd spoken about my feelings before she revealed her inheritance. Ruth needs to know I will cherish her and be her shelter and security. Dad's acting like a love-struck swain, and it's downright embarrassing.*

She lightly patted his shoulder. "It's only right that Hilda sit up front."

"Hilda?!" McCain spluttered.

"I'm coming, I'm coming." Hilda stepped out onto the porch and fussed with her new dress.

"You have work to do. You can't go gallivanting to town," McCain snapped.

As he tucked Ruth in beside his sister, Josh injected a casual note to his voice, "I asked Hilda to go."

"And look how charming she is in her new gown!" Laney handed Ruth a parasol.

"Ruth, sugar, you come on up front," his father ordered.

"Dad, you're embarrassing her."

"I couldn't possibly..." Ruth allowed her voice to trail off as she waved her arm over the full skirts surrounding her.

"Age before beauty," Hilda trundled over.

"You're not old," Laney said. "And you are beautiful."

Josh lifted Hilda up, and she settled in. She glanced at his father, then declared, "That scowl would curdle even goat's milk. You sufferin' from indigestion? If you are, you'd best stay home and nibble on a dry biscuit."

"The last thing I need is an old woman telling me what to do." McCain climbed into the buckboard and grabbed the reins.

Farnsworth had already mounted up. Josh unhitched his own mare and swung into the saddle. "Let's go. We have a lot to get done today."

He and Farnsworth rode their horses on either side of the wagon. Laney chattered like a happy little magpie. Farnsworth proved adept at keeping conversation flowing easily, so he and Ruth only needed to put in a well-timed comment or two.

Before getting out of the wagon when they reached town, Ruth slipped Hilda a coin.

"What is this?" McCain demanded.

"I've made extra work for Hilda. It's only fair that I pay her a little for all she's done."

Hilda glanced down at the double eagle and sucked in a loud

breath. "Child, I think you gave me—"

"Far less than you deserve," Ruth cut in. "Please, Hilda, spoil yourself a bit. It would make me so happy if you did."

"That's why you need me to look out for you." McCain shook his finger at Ruth. "You're making foolish choices and will spend yourself into penury with rash decisions."

"Oh my!" Ruth hastily opened her reticule. "Here, Hilda. I want to make sure you have more before I fritter away everything." She took out two more double eagles, pressed them into Hilda's hand, and curled the gaping housekeeper's fingers around the coins. Smiling, Ruth addressed his father, "Thank you for reminding me to keep my priorities straight."

"Miss Elaine," Farnsworth said, "I'd be honored if you'd allow me to help you alight."

"How kind of you," Laney said.

Josh reached upward. "Come here, Ruthie."

As he helped her down, Ruth said, "It's the funniest thing. When your father called me 'Ruthie,' it reminded me of my grandfather. You call me 'Ruthie,' and it's just different somehow."

Hilda cackled but didn't say a word.

Dad jumped down from the wagon and ignored her. Josh turned loose of Ruth and helped Hilda descend. "Ruth's attorney and I are going to escort her to the bank. I'm not sure how long we'll be. If you finish up, go on ahead to the Copper Kettle and we'll meet you there."

"I'll take Ruth." McCain took her hand and threaded it through his arm. "You stay close to me this time, my dear. We can't have you falling as you did the first time you came to town."

Ruth slipped her other hand around Josh's arm. "Isn't this fun? Your daddy's going to drop us off. Oh, I'm not supposed to know, but it's really okay, Mr. McCain. You feel free to toddle along to the saloon. Mrs. Tudbert—she was the headmistress at one of the schools I attended—well, she claimed I could drive all but the heartiest men to drink."

"Me? Drink?" McCain gave her a wounded look.

"Yes, you. Or you do a fair imitation of it," Hilda said. "Either that, or the whiskey in the hutch sure is evaporating quick as greased lightnin'."

"Mercy." Ruth covered her mouth with her gloved hand. Of course the glove was smudged, but Josh grinned at that fact. She might be wealthy as a queen, but she'd end up looking like a happy peasant a good portion of the time. Shoulders slumping, she sighed, "My mouth gets me into difficulty all of the time. I should have thought about what I said, and I didn't."

"No harm done," McCain said.

Ruth went on, "It's just that when you came to Lester's Mercantile the other day to pick us up, you said something about the Nugget. I just assumed . . ." Her eyes widened and she whipped out her fan. Fluttering it at an impossible speed, she gasped, "My. Oh my."

"Laney, you come along with me." Hilda hauled Laney to the store.

"No need to be in a dither." Dad tried to pat Ruth.

Her fan kept fluttering, bumping against his fingertips. Having seen how inept she was with a fan, Josh figured it was just Ruth being clumsy. Dad continued to try to soothe her and received several thwaps before he grabbed the frippery. "See here now, girl. There's nothing wrong with a man wetting his whistle. One or two whiskeys while I talk over business with associates isn't really drinking."

She went pale as dandelion fluff and her hold on Josh's arm tightened. He reached over and slid his other hand over hers. "Ruth?"

"Perhaps it would be best to have Miss Caldwell out of the sun," Farnsworth said.

Ruth extended her other hand, palm upward. Even through the covering of her smudged glove, Josh saw how her hand shook. So did her voice. "Please."

McCain beamed and tucked her hand into the crook of his arm. "I knew you'd see reason." He took a step, but Ruth didn't follow along.

She yanked her hand away from him and half-whispered, "The fan."

McCain pivoted toward her and forced a chuckle. "I'd rather face a man with a bullwhip than you with a fan." He half opened the fan, but his left arm and hand were awkward. His thumb broke a few of the thin ivory spokes, and part of the silk tore. "Wretched little thing. You're better off without it." He flipped it onto the ground.

Immediately Ruth knelt and reached for it.

Josh stooped and swept the broken fan from the ground. He turned. The look on Ruth's face knocked him to his knees. "Here, Ruthie."

Dusty and mangled though it was, Ruth pressed the fan to her bosom.

"All this fuss about a cheap little nothing," Dad groused.

Blinking back tears, Ruth started to rise. Josh popped up and braced her elbow.

His father cleared his throat. "I'll buy you another one."

Folding the fan with near reverence and carefully tucking it into her reticule, Ruth didn't give a response. She squared her shoulders. "Joshua, please take me to the bank."

McCain stepped back, and Josh led her to the boardwalk. He could feel her shaking. "What is it?"

Ruth didn't look at him. Eyes lowered, voice full of pain, she rasped, "It was Mama's fan."

CHAPTER TWENTY

The house felt empty. Even with five of them moving about and Da in the bed, the place seemed too roomy, too quiet. Galen set the pitcher of yesterday's cream from the spring house on the table.

Sean stuck his head over the loft railing. "Ma, can we have flapjacks with raspberry syrup again?"

"Nay, boy-oh. Your father's wanting oatmeal with blackberries."

"No better way to start the day," Da said. He chuckled a little before he coughed. "I take that back. The best way to start the day is openin' my eyes and seeing the fairest woman God ever fashioned."

Ma blushed. "You and your blarney."

"'Tis nice to see you in that new dress," Colin said.

"Me in a store-bought dress is like putting silk on a sow."

"Kelly-mine, you'll always be the queen o' my heart."

Ma laughed like a young girl. "Serve a man his favorite food, and his tongue turns silver."

Dale scrambled down the ladder from the loft and over to the bed. "Let me see!"

"See what?" Colin asked.

"Stick out your tongue, Da. I want to see a silver one. Mine's red. See?" Dale stuck out his tongue.

"Silly boy." Galen ran his fingers through his brother's short-cropped, unruly curls. "'Tis a saying. If a man has a silver tongue, it means he can turn a pretty phrase."

"Can girls have silver tongues?"

"Sure, they can. Why?"

Dale sneezed and started to wipe his nose on his sleeve. Galen handed him a bandana with a stern look. After using the bandana, Dale declared, "Laney has a silver tongue. She has sweet words for everyone."

"Aye, she does." Ma set bowls on the table. "She, Hilda, and Ruth all have hearts o' gold, too. Just look at what they came and did."

Five stacks of jars lined the far wall, partially blocking the window. Each stack was eight high. "I've ne'er seen the likes of that," Da marveled.

"I'll carry most out to the barn. Pick and choose what you want to keep in the house, Ma."

"Your father and I talked it out." Ma motioned everyone to the table. "I'll set aside what our family'll be needing, but you, Galen, can go to town and sell the rest of that to Lester. Stop by the Broken P on the way home and split the money with them."

Shaking his head, Galen sat down and said, "Pony's coming through any day now. I need to be here and have a mount ready, just in case."

Ma rested her hand on Colin's shoulder. "Your brother's more than able to ready the horse for the Pony today. He'll see to that chore whilst you make the jaunt."

Colin stretched to his full height and flashed a proud smile. "Of course I can do that. I've been watching. Pony used to come through about two in the afternoon. I'll have the horse ready by one-thirty."

Galen squinted across the table and pretended to assess his brother. "'Tis a hefty responsibility."

"One I'm up to."

"Lula would be my choice to do the run."

"She's the mustang with the brown coat and white tail," Colin declared. "Sweet tempered, too."

"Aye, you'll do." Galen bobbed his head. "But 'tis a man's job." Colin nearly popped the buttons off his shirt from puffing out his chest, but that was exactly what Galen wanted.

Ma winked at him. If push came to shove, Ma could ready the mare, but Galen knew she wouldn't need to. She'd planted the idea, then stayed out of the exchange so Colin would feel he'd had a man-to-man conversation. *I don't remember, but I bet she and Da did the same thing with me when I was young.*

"Dale and Sean," Ma said as she carried a bowl over to Da, "the both of you best go weed the garden today. Hilda said she'd be coming back sometime soon, and you don't want her to be thinking you shirked your duties."

Da accepted the bowl. "Perhaps, if you boys are good, Galen'll bring back candy from the store."

Sean wrinkled his nose. "God knows if we're good, but how will Galen?"

Colin put his finger to his lips. "That's a secret."

Dale leaned closer and whispered loudly, "Like Ma havin' eyes in the back of her head?"

"Shhh!" Colin hissed while nodding slowly.

After breakfast, Ma directed which jars were to go to town. Galen and Colin loaded the buckboard, and then, as Ma fussed over how to keep the jars from breaking, Galen went back inside. "Da, was there anything you'd like?"

Da reached for Galen's hand.

Cautiously sitting on the edge of the bed so it wouldn't jostle his father, Galen clasped his father's frail hand in his. *There was a time when his hand was so much bigger and tougher than mine. I never thought he'd be anything but strong and capable.*

"There's but one thing I always wanted to buy."

"What's that, Da?"

"I couldn't afford to buy your ma a ring. Nothing would gladden my heart as much as to slip a pretty band o' golden love upon her finger."

Eyes and nose burning from unshed tears, Galen couldn't speak a word. He gently squeezed Da's hand.

"I ask so much of you, son." Da's voice broke. "But God's given me the assurance deep in my heart that He'll stay alongside you and be your fortress when I'm gone and you carry on."

Choked with emotion, Galen cleared his throat twice before he managed to speak. "I'll rely on Him, Da. But I'd take it as a favor if you'd not rush to the pearly gates."

"None of us knows the dear Lord's plan or timing. 'Tis our place to take His lead and obey. The path is oft rocky, but the view is always best when we get where He's taking us."

"Ready, Galen?" Colin yelled.

Galen forced a smile. "For the time being, I guess God's leading me to town." He rose and settled Da's hand on the covers, then pressed a kiss to his gaunt cheek. He murmured softly, "And the view there'll be the finest band of gold you ever saw."

Da's smile stayed with Galen the whole way to town. When he pulled up to the back of Lester's store, he spied three strangers coming up the road from the opposite direction. The sorriest mule he'd ever seen pulled a rickety wagon with sparse belongings. Judging from the way the people all boasted the same white-blond hair and worn-down look, Galen guessed they were father, son, and daughter.

"Feed my sheep." The Bible verse went through his mind. But how could he up and offer charity to complete strangers without offending them?

Lester opened the back door. "I wondered who pulled up. What've you got there?"

"Plenty." Galen smiled. "I have crates of the usual fresh vegetables, but I also have canned tomatoes, green beans, jelly, syrup—"

"Well, well." Lester rubbed his hands together.

"I thought I'd give you first chance before going over to the diner."

"I'll take it all. We'll need to tally it."

The dusty family and flea-bitten mule drew close. *"Feed my sheep."*

Galen waved at them to stop. "I could use a little help unloading this and carrying it into the mercantile. I don't have ready cash, but I could maybe give you a dozen jars."

"Done." The father motioned to his rawboned son to get to work. He and the girl coaxed the mule to turn into the open dirt field that held the wagons of others who had come to town.

Lester slapped Galen on the back. "Smart move. Business is brisk today. I'll give you credit for half of the jars since I'm getting out of the work."

Galen turned and shook hands with the stranger. "Galen O'Sullivan."

"Ishmael Grubb. Glad to meet you." He glanced at the food and admitted, "Gladder to have vittles. Been a while since I et anything other than corn mush."

The girl came over. Her bedraggled dress still showed faint red and blue markings here and there from the BEST flour sacks she'd used to make it. What might have been pretty, moon-colored hair scraped back toward her nape, and a leather thong disciplined it. Her shoulders drooped as if she carried the weight of the world, but she gave her brother a sweet smile.

If I ever had a sister, it would break my heart to see her living hand-to-mouth as this girl must.

She stood on tiptoe to look at the contents of the buckboard. "You want us to tote them jars inside?"

Stunned that she'd ever think to haul such weight, Galen shook his head. "Your brother and I will see to it, miss."

"But Pa sent me to help."

"Ivy's strong," Ishmael said as he hefted a flat of jelly jars.

"Miss Grubb, we'll carry in the jars. You could help by tallying them for us."

"Cain't." She raked her right foot back and forth. "Cain't read nor write. Ishmael, he got three years of book learnin'. He cain keep tally whilst you and me tote the jars."

"He's payin', Ivy. He cain keep tally. You an' me'll—"

"Actually," Galen cut in, "Miss Grubb could do us the favor of asking Lester if he'd like the jars on shelves or just stacked in the back room."

Galen lifted two flats and headed into the store.

Ivy scampered ahead of him. By the time he entered the back-room, he could hear her soft, twangy voice. "'Scuse me, Mr. Lester, but d'ya'll want the canned goods on the shelves or in the back room?"

"I'd like some jelly out right away."

"You got jelly?" someone said.

"Yee haw!" another man hollered.

Galen chuckled as he pushed past the curtain and into the store. He smiled at Ivy. "I think you'd better go out and choose what you'd like for your family before everything disappears out the front door."

"We'll jist take whate'er is left. We ain't choosy."

Three men surrounded Galen and started grabbing pint jars. He craned his head around and peeked at her. "Go on, Miss Grubb. Take first pick."

On his next trip out to get more, Galen stopped Ivy. "Take quart jars. You're feeding three. Pint jars won't fill all of you."

Her mouth dropped wide open.

Galen reached into the crates and pulled out a head of lettuce, a cabbage, and a fistful of carrots. "Take these, too. Traveling as you've been, you probably haven't had anything fresh-picked in a long while."

Ishmael hefted more and said quietly, "Mister, yore pure hickory."

Galen dipped his head in acknowledgment of the compliment, then reached for the tomatoes. He and Ishmael entered the back room, and Lester stood at the curtain. "May as well bring those on in here. I've got half a dozen men champing at the bit to see what else you've got."

With Ishmael's help, it took no time at all to unload the buckboard. Before he went back inside the store to reckon with Lester, Galen grabbed the flour sack with the sandwiches Ma made for him from beneath the buckboard seat. "Here." He laid it atop the goods Ishmael intended to carry to his own wagon.

"No need," Ishmael said.

"Ma figured it'd take me half of forever to unload everything. I plan to fritter away a bit of time and eat over at the diner."

Ivy wound her arms around her ribs. "If you wait a minute, I'll bring back yore poke."

"Poke?"

"Sack." She tilted her chin toward what her brother held. "Hit's a purdy one. Comes from fine flour, not middlins."

Galen remembered when they'd first come to America and his mother bought lower-grade flour. They'd been thankful for it—any food on the table counted as a great blessing after prolonged hunger. Ma had originally made a nightshirt for Galen out of two of the sacks, and Sean now used it. "Don't worry about returning the sack. Just a glance proves the poke ought to belong to you—what with it having that ivy pattern all o'er it."

Her eyes widened in surprise.

"Ain't that the beatenist?" Ishmael chortled. "Sis, yore gonna look right pretty iffen you stitch you a bodice outta it."

"Oh, thankee, mister."

"You're more than welcome. I thank the both of you for your help. God go with you now."

Ishmael and Ivy walked away, but Galen heard Ivy whisper, "He wished us to have God go with us. D'ya thank he's one of them good Christian men who rejoice, like the song goes?"

"Must be."

Galen called to them, "Church is at eight on Sunday. You're welcome to join us!"

"We'll be movin' on," Ishmael said over his shoulder, "but 'twas nice of you to give the invite."

Galen went back into the mercantile. Lester grinned as he tallied up another customer's order. "Word's out on the street that your ma sent in her goods. Mark my words: It won't be two full days before every last jar is gone."

"Ma's out of jars. When will you get more in?"

"Train's due in at two. I ordered some since Josh cleaned out every last one I had."

"Be sure to hold them aside for me."

"We'll make sure he does," John Wall said as he cradled three jelly jars in his arm as if they were fragile babes. "I'm already tickled to have these, but if your ma takes a mind to make orange marmalade, I'd ask you to set aside a whole dozen jars for me."

Lester tucked his pencil behind his ear and hitched up his green canvas apron. "Since Miss Caldwell ordered a couple of camellias, I could have someone drop the jars out at their place at the same time if they don't arrive on today's train."

"Hilda and Ma were talking about making marmalade. May as well go ahead."

Lester beamed. "When the train starts goin' back East, all of the fine fruit from California will be in high demand. That farm of yours is better than a gold mine."

"Hold it just a minute there." John Wall glared at Galen. "Don't get so all-fired busy that your mama stops makin' these treats for us bachelors."

"I'll tell her you said so."

While Lester busily totaled up sales, Galen went to the fine-goods case and stared at the rings. Eight glittered in there. Three of them were men's rings, though. Concentrating on the women's, Galen tried to remember the size of his mother's hand when he'd briefly clasped it before leaving home.

"Shopping for a ring?"

Galen jumped. He glanced over at Lester and realized the line of customers had dissipated. "Da wants me to buy a ring for Ma. One of these is bitty and another ought to go through a bull's nose instead of on a woman's hand."

Lester grinned. He walked over and unlocked the case. "Let's get them out where you can see them better. This one is etched with orange blossoms. Very romantic."

"Too fussy for Ma."

Lester set it back inside the case and pulled out another. "This one is classic. Plain gold, but the sentimental value is enduring."

"Might work. How's about that other one?"

"I saved the best for last." Lester smiled at him. "What do you think?"

Galen took the ring from him and tilted it back and forth. As rings went, it was shiny as could be and about a quarter inch wide. Etched deeply into the front was a cross with a tiny diamond chip in the center. He pushed the ring down onto his little finger. "I guess it's the right size. I'll take it."

"You didn't even ask about the price."

Galen pulled off the ring. "Da wants it. I trust you to be fair."

Puffing out his chest, Lester walked back to the counter. "I kept a tally going of what I sold. While you looked at the rings, I added in what's left. The fresh vegetables are worth two dollars and ten cents. I counted thirty-one flats of jars. Ten were pint-sized, the rest were quart. Jelly goes for twice as much because it's more expensive to make." Lester scribbled on paper, then underlined the last figure. "With the fresh stuff added in, I owe you eighteen dollars and ten cents."

Galen hadn't asked how Ma wanted to split the money; now he'd have to decide. Dividing it four ways would be best. Since his land provided most of the produce, but the Broken P brought the jars, sugar, and such, that seemed fair all around. After deducting the two dollars for the fresh produce, that worked out to an even four dollars apiece for all the women.

"I'll be needing to take home a few pieces of candy for the lads, and you still haven't told me what I owe you for the ring."

"I just filled the jars. I ended up with a handful of sticks that were broken, so they won't sell. You may as well have them."

Galen's eyes narrowed. "So the ring costs that much, eh?"

"The diamond chip in it ups the price. My cost was a dollar eighty. What if I sell it to you at that price, provided you give me a promise to bring all of your mother's canned goods to me instead of offering them to the Copper Kettle?"

"I can't promise there'll be much more. The women from the Broken P came over and helped. The orange marmalade was a special favor—John Wall's been good to drop everything and fix my plow or sharpen my pruners."

"I appreciate your candor, but I'm willing to make the deal anyway."

Galen set the ring on the counter. "Aye, and I'm thanking you on my dear father's behalf." After he stuffed the money in one pocket, carefully tucked the ring in his chest pocket, and picked up the candy, Galen asked, "Have you any mail for the Broken P? I'll be passing by there."

"Oh, everyone's in town. Even Hilda. They've all gone to the diner for lunch."

"Mind if I leave my wagon out back?"

"Nah. As a matter of fact, I have more than just the canning jars coming in on the two o'clock train. Are you interested in driving over to the train and bringing it all back?"

"You know me—I never turn down work." Galen headed toward the door. "For now, I think I'll get a bite to eat."

CHAPTER TWENTY-ONE

J osh, look! Galen's here." Ruth hopped up from the table. Her chair crashed to the floor, and she didn't care a whit.

Josh stood as well. "Galen, come join us."

"Don't mind if I do." Galen strode over and gallantly set Ruth's chair upright and motioned for her to be seated.

She stepped back. "Galen, I'd like you to meet Mr. Daryl Farnsworth. Mr. Farnsworth, Galen O'Sullivan—a very dear neighbor." Farnsworth rose, and they shook hands.

Josh motioned for Galen to take the chair Ruth had occupied and seated her in his own, then dragged over another one and sat on her other side.

Ruth flashed him a smile of gratitude. She couldn't bear to be near his father any longer. Mama's edict not to discuss finances made perfect sense. Ever since McCain realized she possessed a fortune, he'd become an absolute pest—even barged into the bank while she was there today.

"I just came from the mercantile." Galen chuckled. "You ladies could form a business. Just about every jar of jelly has already sold."

"What's this?" McCain frowned. "Ruth and Laney are ladies. They have no need to labor."

"Now, I hope you're not saying Hilda or my mother aren't ladies." Galen's jaw hardened.

"I'm sure Daddy meant no such thing." Laney smiled at Galen. "Not a soul on earth could ever speak a word against your wonderful mama or our dear Hilda. Why, their tender care and fathomless hearts hold our households together."

"Now, wasn't that a nice thing you said." Hilda patted Laney's hand.

"Every last word of it is true." Josh motioned to Myrtle. "Galen's joining us."

"Hello, Galen. What would you like to order?"

Galen whispered, "Who's cooking?"

"Daddy."

"I'll have whate'er his special of the day is."

"Pork chops with dressing."

"Grand. I thank you." Galen turned back to Hilda. "Ma told me to split the money from the canning."

"You will not. We were just being neighborly!"

Ruth chimed in, "If anything, Laney and I ought to be paying an exorbitant fee for the private gourmet cooking lessons."

Galen cleared his throat. "Yes, well, you still put your hand to the task and brought sugar and jars and—"

"Just give the money to me," McCain growled.

"You will not." Josh's voice rumbled like thunder.

Ruth was taken aback momentarily at the way Josh stood up to his father. Josh softened his tone. "I'm sure Dad was jesting. It was a gift. As Hilda said, we were being neighborly. After all the times you've shared fruits, vegetables, and nuts with us, it's the least we could do. If anything, the scale's still out of balance."

Hilda slapped the table. "Now there's the gospel truth. Did you all hear Lester talking about the train? Seems folks are selling land for a line that's supposed to go clear across these United States."

"That's the first I've heard of it," Ruth said. She looked at Josh. "Do you know anything?"

"Dad mentioned it was a possibility."

Farnsworth cleared his throat. "Actually, it's more of a probability. Far more. In fact, the eastern end is already well under way. They project they'll reach Kansas sometime in early July."

McCain's eyes glittered. "It's a sure thing. Best investment going."

Ruth didn't say a word.

"Farnsworth, tell her." McCain looked from her attorney to her and back. "She ought to jump on this while she has the chance."

Her attorney said quite blandly, "Any advice I might give would first require detailed information. If Miss Caldwell is interested, I'm willing to research the matter and assess the benefits and risks involved."

Laney whispered across the table, "Galen, Mr. Farnsworth is Ruth's attorney. He traveled clear to California on her behalf!"

Ruth patted Galen's hand. "I have wonderful news."

"Indeed, she does." McCain agreed heartily.

"Josh and Laney and I decided to start a library!"

McCain blustered, and Ruth couldn't help noticing how Josh and Farnsworth both suddenly had to lift their napkins to muffle coughs.

"Is that so?" Galen turned his chair toward her a little, effectively blocking McCain from being able to glower directly at her. "A library. Imagine! I've ne'er been to one, but I read about it in the newspaper."

"I'm collecting titles of books that folks would like to read and also a list of their favorites."

"Ruth says books are like old friends," Laney said. "You can visit them time and again and enjoy the story anew."

"A library is a fine idea," Farnsworth agreed. "Of my more

recent readings, I thoroughly enjoyed Melville's *Pierre* and *The Encantadas*. He's a very gifted author."

"Those aren't on the list." Ruth started rummaging in the reticule. "I need to write them down before I forget."

"I have paper in my case." Farnsworth pulled out a crisp sheet. "I don't carry ink, however."

"Just as well," McCain grumbled. "Working at the table—"

Pulling a stubby pencil from her reticule, Ruth sang, "I have a pencil."

"We're not working, Daddy," Laney said. "We're planning a charitable deed. I think Ruth is kind to allow us to help her so we can all take pleasure in the final result."

That's twice Laney's been the peacemaker at the table. Bless her heart—God gave her a special gift.

"I hadn't thought of it that way. Ruth, you're quite an extraordinary young lady to consider such an undertaking."

"Thank you, Mr. McCain. Tell me, what books would you like to see the library carry?"

"If you'll pass me the pencil, I'd be happy to keep a list," Farnsworth offered.

"I'd appreciate that. I get so enthusiastic, I forget to write things down, or I write them and later cannot read my own penmanship." Ruth laughed.

"I loved penmanship," Laney said. "It's like drawing row after row of pretty little sketches."

"Would you care to keep the list?" Farnsworth started to set the paper in front of Laney.

Laney shot Ruth a panic-stricken look.

Ruth groaned dramatically. "She'll never keep up. Her handwriting is exquisite, but she puts so much into each word, we'll still be here for supper."

"Who are you kidding?" Josh snorted. "Breakfast tomorrow."

"I'm not that slow!" Laney slipped the sheet of paper back in front of the attorney. "But I'm not going to give them a chance to prove their point. Now, Daddy, you were going to tell us what books you'd like in the library."

All through lunch, the conversation revolved around books. Ruth loved having everyone involved in planning what she needed to acquire. The fact that McCain couldn't very well fawn all over her or snap at others certainly helped.

Approaching the table with the bill, Myrtle asked, "Who gets this?" Josh reached for it.

"It's mine." Farnsworth rose. "I must say, I can't recall ever having a more pleasant luncheon."

Galen separated from them, but Farnsworth accompanied the others outside and helped Laney into the buckboard. Josh popped Hilda onto the seat again, then curled his hands around Ruth's waist. "I'm proud of you," he murmured. "I was about to strangle Dad, and you were every inch a lady."

"I gave consideration to spilling something on him."

Josh laughed as he lifted her. "That's my girl!"

"Oh, wait. I dropped my reticule."

Josh set her back down. He knew full well she'd dropped it on purpose. Though he bent to retrieve it, she stooped down as well.

Ruth whispered, "Could you ask Mr. Farnsworth to stay? I think we may need his expertise."

"Sure thing," he said in a low tone, then raised his voice. "Here you are."

"Thank you. It's so dusty!" She rose and beat at the purse with notable zeal.

"Here. I'll lift you up." Josh situated her in the buckboard.

Farnsworth cleared his throat. "Before I departed, I purchased a few books for leisure reading. They're not fine literature, but they do help pass the time. Would you be averse to adding them to your library? They're mere dime novels."

"Dime novels?" Laney's sun parasol popped open as an exclamation mark to her enthusiasm. "Ruth and I just read one!"

"Well, then." Farnsworth pulled two from his case. "I'm happy to share."

"Thank you!"

Josh mounted up. "How do you like that? Your very first books for the library."

Ruth smiled. "This makes my dream seem so much closer to being real now."

"Miss Caldwell, I have no doubt that the library will be a huge success."

"Hey, Josh!"

Josh turned and waved at Galen, then turned to Ruth. "I'll return to the Broken P a little later. I have something I need to do."

Ruth turned back to her attorney. "Have a safe journey home, Mr. Farnsworth. I can't tell you how much I appreciate the personal effort this task has been."

"I enjoyed the trip. After reading about the prairies and vistas, I wanted to see it all for myself."

"You're such a gallant man," Laney said. "I found traveling to school and back to be nothing but endless misery."

"You are a credit to your firm and to your family." Ruth gave her praise with all sincerity.

"Thank you, Miss Caldwell. We appreciate your business and will strive to continue to prove worthy of the faith you hold in Farnsworth, Tabbard, and Farnsworth. Good day, ladies." His smile faded as he curtly nodded toward Josh and Laney's father. "McCain."

"Now there was a fine young man," Hilda said as he walked his mount toward the livery.

"He loomed like a vulture." McCain set the wagon in motion. "If I hadn't asserted myself, he would have tried to court Ruth just for her money."

So there's nothing about me that a man would find attractive?

"That's not true, Daddy. Why, I thought he was quite attentive to me, too."

"Money matters to men." McCain cleared his throat. "At least to most of 'em. I'm a keen judge of character, and we're well rid of that one."

Lord, I know I'm not supposed to judge, but I'm failing here. Mr. McCain is the most dreadful man I've ever had the misfortune to meet.

"I can hardly wait to read these," Laney said as she held the dime novels.

Ruth stopped praying. She couldn't imagine how someone as pure and kind as Laney could have such a wicked man for her father.

"Ruth, why don't you read the first chapter aloud as we go home? I can take up where you leave off later."

"It'll be too hard to read in the wagon. It jostles."

"You'd look pretty as could be in a well-sprung surrey," McCain said.

"Yes, Laney, you would," Ruth said, purposefully shifting the older man's attention off of herself. "Then again, you'd look just as darling in a wheelbarrow."

Laney giggled. "A wheelbarrow might be fun, depending on who's pushing it."

"Enough of that," McCain said. "You're too young yet to think of courting. When you get to be Ruth's age, that'll be just about right."

"I have no need to marry. I rather think being a spinster might suit me quite well." Ruth twirled her paper parasol. "Why, I could have a house built next to the library and live there with two cats and three canaries."

"If you have cats, the canaries won't live long," Laney teased.

"If you don't marry, you'll regret it," McCain said.

"Yes, Ruth. You'd make such a good mother." Laney clutched the novels. "You're so patient and loving."

"There's nothing so sweet as the praise of a true friend," Ruth said. "But I could care about my friends and neighbors, and I could be patient with the library patrons. I was even thinking that there must be a lot of citizens in Folsom who received only minimal schooling. I could tutor them in reading and mathematics."

"You don't have to work for a living. Why bother?" McCain cast a paternalistic smile at her over his shoulder. "I know you want to do good things for others, Ruth, but you can hire someone and dedicate yourself to a woman's highest calling."

"Having children," Laney promptly added.

"No." McCain shook his head. "There are women who never have children, child. Such a woman graces her husband's home with warmth and happiness. She makes sure all runs smoothly and considers being his companion as complete fulfillment."

Ruth heaved a loud, unladylike sigh. "That sounds just like what all of the headmistresses said. Oh, they added in that a lady could bear her husband's heirs, but the nannies would see to their upbringing. I found that whole concept appalling."

"I wouldn't want my children to have a nanny, either."

"Laney, of course you will. You'll wed a man of fine station and not have to spend sleepless nights with cranky babies or tantruming children." Her father nodded his head. "That's the way it will be."

"Good thing the parson isn't here to overhear this. He'd be sure your father is trying to foretell the future." Hilda's wry tone set Ruth and Laney into laughter.

Ruth reached over and took the books from Laney. "*Arabella's Doom*. That sounds spine-chilling. What's the other one?" She handed it back to Laney.

Laney shot her a panicked look.

"I was brave enough to try to read the first one's title as we bounced along. You can do the other one."

"*The Ban—*" Laney moistened her lips. "*The Bandit Rides Again.*"

McCain snorted. "*The Bandit Rides Again*? Sounds like utter drivel to me."

Hilda shrugged. "You gals read the first one. I'm gonna claim *The Bandit*."

"What a wonderful idea. Laney, we'll start as soon as we get home. Then we can trade with Hilda when we finish it."

"Good idea," Hilda agreed. "May as well read the books as have 'em sitting around, gathering dust until Ruth gets that new library started."

"You seem to have a lot of time to spare," McCain said.

"Organization is the key to success." Laney gently tapped Hilda's side so she'd turn around and accept the book. "That's what they taught me at school, Daddy."

"And so it is with Ruth and her little library. She can organize others to run it. I'm sure she'll want to be free to pursue other interests—perhaps travel or do more painting."

"I didn't particularly enjoy traveling out here," Ruth said. "As for painting—well, Laney and I have a lovely time each morning as we paint. Laney is so very gifted. I think even the fine-art academies in Paris would admit her!"

"I'd miss home too much," Laney said. "When I was away at school, I was horribly homesick. I never want to be far away from the Broken P again."

"You won't mind when you have a husband and new family to love," her father said.

"I'm planning to marry someone who lives nearby. Then I'll have everything!"

McCain snorted. "There's not a single man in the state who's good enough for you!"

"Laney," Ruth added, "you can always live with me and the cats and canaries."

When they reached home, Ruth scrambled out of the buckboard so she wouldn't have to let McCain help her down. Hilda disembarked with a few loud grunts, and Laney didn't seem to mind how her father wrapped his good arm around her waist and sort of wheeled her down to earth.

"Come on, Ruth. Let's go upstairs and start reading!"

"What Ruth needs to read is the investment portfolio the lawyer dropped off. Ruth, honey, you scamper upstairs and bring it down to the parlor. I'll go over it with you."

"No." Shocked by his unmitigated gall, Ruth stared at him.

"Isn't any of your business," Hilda groused.

"Mind your own affairs or you'll be looking elsewhere for work," McCain snapped at the housekeeper.

"I can see I'm not the only one whose tummy is upset by that restaurant food." Laney wiggled between her father and Hilda. "We're all a little out of sorts. I suppose we've grown spoiled by Hilda's fine meals, so nothing else measures up."

"Ruth can bring me the portfolio and then go rest."

Forcing a smile, Ruth shook her head. "Thank you for the offer, but it would be best for me to go on up and rest along with Laney. I'm perfectly able to see to my own matters. Besides, I promised Laney we'd read. I couldn't go back on my word." She grabbed Laney's hand and raced away, knowing she'd waylaid McCain's interference for only a time. He was sure to corner her again . . . and soon.

Chapter Twenty-Two

$\;$

Arranging for Galen to call him away had worked well. Josh stayed in town and spoke with the sheriff and Rick Maltby. They'd had a bookkeeper examine the copies of the books Rick made and he confirmed beyond a shadow of a doubt that Dad had embezzled.

"Since Alan is dead, he cannot press charges. At present, it's a crime against only you, Josh. We can turn a blind eye if you're willing to accept being a wronged party; but if Ruth does inherit as much as one percent of the Broken P, we'll have to press charges against your father."

The whole ride home, Josh struggled with himself. He'd asked Ruth to pursue the claim; if her claim prevailed, he'd set his father up to go to jail. *Lord, I'd forgive him and move on, but now I don't know what to do. I'll stand behind what is right and the woman I love, but that means going against Dad and exposing Laney to the truth. There must be another choice. You have to have a plan I can't see. Open my eyes, Father.*

Dad was pacing on the veranda when Josh rode up. "We need to talk, son."

"Sure, Dad." Josh dismounted and started for the steps.

"Out in the yard." Dad cast a quick glance back at the house as he descended those steps. They went out toward a paddock, and Josh propped a boot up on the lowest rung of the fencing. Dad blustered, "I won't have you stealing money from the accounts."

"What?!"

"You bought goods and gave them away. I could have gotten repayment from O'Sullivan at lunch today, but you stuck your nose in and ruined it."

Josh stayed silent for a minute. He about left a groove in his tongue, biting it to keep from angrily accusing his father of deception. Instead, he quietly said, "Cullen O'Sullivan is dying. The family needs help."

"Your mother died. No one helped us. I made her a promise that I'd take care of the two of you, and I did it on my own."

"Dad, think of the few paltry dollars I spent on those canning supplies as an investment in Laney's safety. It gave me an excuse to keep her far from home when you weren't here to keep watch and safeguard her. I can't very well run the ranch while sitting in the house, and I'm relying on you to scare off anyone who might harm either of the girls."

The muscle in Dad's jaw stopped twitching.

"I still can't fathom why anyone hurt her, Dad. I'm glad you're home. If anything more happens, we might have to send Laney away again."

"We won't have to do that. She'll be fine. I'll see to her." He thumped the center of his chest. "I'll see to both of the girls."

Josh chuckled. "Ruth's going to be harder to keep track of. She has a wild streak in her nature."

"I'll tame her."

"She's not a mustang that you have to break. Ruth has a mind of her own."

McCain scowled. "She just proved that point. I told her to bring down the portfolio her lawyer brought. The girl thanked me, then said she'd handle things on her own. If she hadn't already promised Laney that they'd spend the afternoon reading together, I would have had to get firm. Tomorrow—" His father made a fist and banged in on the top rail of the fence.

"She has plenty to live on for a long while. As for her investments—they're back East. She decided before she came out here to leave them be. I doubt she'll change her mind about that."

"They're going to war, son. She ought to cash out and reinvest here. There's a railroad. The girl could make a tidy profit."

"Her grief is still fresh. It's hard enough on her to have moved such a distance. Give her time. Pressuring her will only make her dig in her heels."

"Some opportunities demand that you invest immediately."

Josh leaned into the fence. "Like what?"

"Things." McCain turned his head and squinted into the distance. "Especially the stage and railroad."

"I know we're running a lean operation here—first years are always tight. But if you have a good prospect, we could look at the books and maybe budget for a wise investment." *Lord, please have him tell me he's already done that. Let this whole thing be innocent.*

Dad shook his head. "But Ruth—she could sell her diamonds. I need to know how many she has and what they're worth. She trusts you."

But she doesn't trust you. Neither do I—and for good cause.

When they'd been in the bank, Josh had seen his father's eyes narrow and face darken when he pulled the velvet pouch of diamonds from his vest pocket at Ruth's request. It stung Dad's pride that she hadn't asked him to safeguard her diamonds.

The bank president had the teller go fetch Folsom's one and only jeweler. He'd arrived with his loupe and gone off to a corner desk to independently verify the certifications Ruth held. To Dad's obvious frustration, neither the jeweler nor the bank president mentioned the number or value of the gems.

"Yes," Dad said in an acid tone, "The girl trusts you."

"I'll be worthy of Ruth's trust."

"Is that to say I won't?"

"I said no such thing. Dad, Ruth may or may not be a partner to us when it comes to the Broken P, but that business is separate from her personal finances. We have no reason to interfere."

"She's interfering! She gave Hilda money. Well, Hilda can just go to Ruth from now on to get her salary."

"I've agreed to let you handle the finances, Dad, even though I'm a grown man and part of this ranch is mine. I can still allow for that, but I won't stand for your putting this on Ruth. Hilda cooks, cleans, and does laundry for you and me and Laney. We're paying her. If Ruth wants to reward her with extra pay—that's Ruth's business." Thoroughly disgusted, Josh said, "I have things to do," and walked away.

Having worn good clothes to town, Josh needed to change into his denim britches. Heading inside the house, he made an effort to shed his anger. *I'm not putting Laney or Hilda in the middle of this. It's bad enough that Ruth is wound up in the whole mess.*

"Ohhh," he heard Laney say as he made it to the top of the landing. "Can you believe how wicked he is?"

"Keep reading!" Ruth urged.

"It's dreadful. He's putting rat poison in Arabella's food!"

"Laney, read! You can't leave me wondering what happens to the poor girl!"

Josh grinned. Dear Ruth—her enthusiasm was contagious. He stood and eavesdropped as Laney continued to read.

" 'Every day, William put more poison in her food. Soon Arabella had no ap-pet-ite. Appetite.' "

"Poor Arabella," Ruth said. "Keep reading!"

" 'What little food Arabella ate rarely stayed down.' "

This story is rather gruesome. Josh leaned against the wall and pictured Ruth and Laney side by side, poring over the pages of that silly dime novel. Ladies never discussed such distasteful realities. Reading such words no doubt shocked them, but his sister cleared her throat and kept reading.

"'Or it went through her far too fast.'" Laney gasped. "Oh my."

Josh's brows rose. He hadn't expected a dime novel to be quite so descriptive. He'd considered the attorney to be a good man, but if this book he'd given the girls grew any more raw, Josh would walk in and take it away.

"Here. It's your page," Laney said.

Ruth's voice took over. "'Sores in her little bow-shaped mouth plagued Arabella.'"

Josh's heart began to pound as he suddenly recalled Alan Caldwell's condition. Alan had suffered from a poor appetite, and what little he ate came back up or went through him far too fast. He'd developed sores in his mouth, too.

Oblivious to his eavesdropping, Ruth read, "'The beautiful porcelain complexion she once delighted in turned sallow.'"

Alan's skin went a sickly shade of yellow. Doc called it jaundice. Thoughts flew through Josh's mind. *There must be several maladies that hold those complaints in common.*

"'Arabella dwindled into near nothingness. She'd never been guilty of vanity, but even a mere glimpse in the mirror told her how pitiful she'd grown. Desolate, she ordered her maid to hang a towel over the mirror.'"

Alan grew impossibly gaunt and weak.

"'William sprinkled the dull gray powder on her food and mixed it with glee. Wiping Arabella's cold, damp brow, he urged, "Another bite, darling." Scarcely could she obey.'"

"What are you waiting for?" Laney half shrieked. "Hurry!"

Alan was cold and clammy.

Ruth's voice continued, but Josh went into his room and changed. *Alan could have turned yellow from all of his years of drinking. But why would that happen almost two years after he'd given up alcohol? And who would have wanted to harm him? They couldn't have—not really. We all ate the same food. Anyone who's been ailing for months on end becomes weak and thin. I'm like a spooked animal that jumps at every sound. It's nothing.*

For the remainder of the day, Josh couldn't shake the feeling that something was wrong. After supper, he went out to the stable to check on the newest foal. Laney and Ruth joined him. "No feeding them treats," he scolded Ruth. "If the mama wants anything, I'll get her some oats."

Ruth's beautiful eyes sparkled. "You may as well get those oats."

"Left to your own devices, you'd probably feed them half of the O'Sullivans' vegetable patch."

Leaning toward him, Ruth said in a loud whisper, "Only the cabbage, so Hilda wouldn't make you-know-what."

"That's a good idea!" Laney brightened up. "Do horses eat cabbage?"

"Absolutely not. If either of you comes anywhere near the horses with cabbage, you'll be permanently banned from the stable."

"Oh, poor baby!" Ruth half skipped to the nearest stall. "Don't let mean old Josh scare you. Josh, shame on you. This poor little pony ran and hid behind his mama when you got mad."

"She's been skittish since the minute her hooves hit the ground. I'm afraid she's going to be high-strung. Pretty little thing, though, isn't she?"

Laney slid up on his other side. "Oh, Josh! Those black splotches make her look as if she's wearing spectacles."

"I hadn't come up with a name yet. Spectacle. Sorta fits, don't you think?"

"I think Laney's very clever," Ruth said. She tugged on his sleeve. "And I think this mama needs oats."

"Okay. The two of you stay on this side of the stall. I'll go get mama a treat." Josh went through the connecting door. Dim as it was, he lit a lantern and set it on the table.

The outside door opened. Toledo stuck his head in. "Oh, it's you, Boss. I saw the light and hoped the villain returned to the scene of the crime."

"Nah. I'm grabbing a scoop of oats as a treat for Prance." He took the grain scoop off the nail on the wall.

"Forgot I used the last of 'em." Toledo drew closer. "I'll refill the bin." He hoisted a new bag of oats into the bin, then yanked a knife from his belt sheath and sliced it open. "Been thinkin'." Toledo slid the knife back into the sheath. "Laney and Ruth's riding skirts match."

"Yes."

"Maybe Ruth was supposed to be the victim."

The grain scoop stopped midair. Josh stared at Toledo.

"Could be I'm wrong. Bears thinkin' on, though."

"It does." Josh measured out a scoop of oats and dumped them into a bucket. A strong nudge of his hip sent the bin back in place. It took two tries before he hooked the scoop back on the wall. When he went back to the other side of the stable, the girls were gone.

"Ruth! Laney!" He struggled to keep the panic from his voice.

Ruth popped up. "Over here, Josh. You won't believe it. They're so cute!"

He wasn't sure whether to whoop for joy that they were all right or growl at them for having moved and scared him out of his wits. "What's so cute?"

"The foal's not the only baby, Josh," Laney said softly. "The calico had a litter. She has six tiny little babies."

Josh strode over and hunkered down. "I don't believe it."

"What?"

"She's ruined your saddle blanket, Ruth."

Ruth laughed. "So what? It's for a good cause. Just the joy of seeing a mama cat all safe and happy with her bitty kittens is more than worth it."

"Ruth loves baby animals," Laney said. "Why, when the latch on the pigsty broke and Ruth fell in, she didn't get the least bit upset with the sow for coming after her. I would have perished from fright, but Ruth tromped back in the house, calm as you please."

"Covered in slop," Ruth tacked on.

"I never heard a word about that."

Ruth folded her arms about her ribs. "I didn't want to announce I'd made another mess. I couldn't very well blame the sow for protecting her piglets. Laney and I nailed the latch back on the sty, so it's all taken care of. Did you get the oats?"

"Yeah. Soon as the mare gets them, I'll walk you girls back to the house."

"There's no need, Josh."

"I insist."

When they reached the house, he stopped Ruth. "I'd like a minute alone with you."

"As you wish." She wandered over to the wicker porch furniture and took a seat.

Josh sat across from her, leaned forward with his forearms on his knees, and said, "Ruth, we take excellent care of the animals here."

"I'm so glad you do. You're most diligent."

"Then you can stop worrying."

Her face mirrored her confusion.

Josh reached over and covered her hand with his. He fought the urge to grin. She had a tiny dot of something red and sticky on the back of her hand—most likely from the cherry she dropped from her pie after supper. He'd seen it roll off the table, and she'd quickly looked about to see if anyone witnessed that faux pas. Very slowly, he winked, and she'd bitten her lower lip to keep from laughing. He hadn't realized the cherry glanced off her when it fell.

"I don't understand, Josh."

"I do, though. Ruth, you love baby animals."

She nodded. Her curls sprang to life with the move.

"You love the mother animals, too. You try to give them treats and make them happy and comfortable."

"They deserve it."

"Honey, you did the same thing for your mother, didn't you?

Babied her, coaxed her to eat by giving her little treats, and—aww, Ruthie."

She pulled her hand away and searched in vain for a hanky. Josh pulled out his bandana and gently wiped her tears. "It's okay to miss her. It's okay to cry, too. Just know this, Ruthie: I've seen how sweet you've been to my sister, and she was a stranger. I'm positive you lavished your mother with loving attention."

"I was such a disappointment," Ruth whispered tearfully.

"You couldn't ever be a disappointment."

Ruth closed her eyes and sucked in a breath. "Mama was beautiful." She practically twisted the bandana into a knot, and her shoulders jerked. "H-h-er hair was sleek and stayed in p-place." Again, her shoulders jerked, but this time a strangled *hic* accompanied the motion. Ruth's eyes opened. Tears glossed them, and her voice cracked with grief, "She handled every *hic* situation *hic* with poise. I wanted to be *hic* like her. But I couldn't."

"Of course you couldn't. God made you to be yourself. He counted the hairs on your head—"

Hic "It would have been easier on Him *hic* if they were all straight!" She crushed the bandana to her mouth. "I always say the wrong thing."

"No, you don't. You speak from the heart. I'd rather hear a harsh truth than a pretty lie any day." He stared into her glossy eyes. *Lord, help her to see herself as you and I do.*

Immediately a verse came to him, and he spoke it aloud. "'Though I speak with the tongues of men and of angels, and have not charity, I am become as sounding brass, or a tinkling cymbal.' Ruth, there's a whole symphony out there—but the players only care about themselves and making impressions on others. Your open-hearted honesty is precious to God. It's precious to me as well. Never apologize for staying true to who God created you to be."

"I'm sure He has a good plan. *Hic.* But I keep messing it up!"

"Philippians says, 'He who began a good work in you will carry it on to completion until the day of Christ Jesus.'"

"It'll take me *hic* at least that long *hic* before I'm not a disaster."

"You don't have to be perfect for God to love you." He paused, then added softly, "I love you just as you are, too."

"I know I've been *hic* a big bother."

"You've been a bigger blessing." He squeezed her hand. "Ruthie, do you get the hiccups when you're especially nervous?"

She nodded.

"Then you can stop it, because there's no reason for you to ever be nervous around me. Now I'm going to pray with you before you run off upstairs."

Hic. She groaned.

He chuckled and bowed his head. "Dear Heavenly Father, I'm lifting Ruth up to you right now. You created her in your image and she holds a special place in your heart. Father, touch her heart and soften the ache of her grief. Grant Ruth the reassurance that her mother cherished her exactly as she was. Show her what your will is for her future and teach her to be more patient with herself. Lord, she's been so patient with Laney. Hold up a mirror to her and let her be equally patient as you continue your work in her life. We praise you and thank you. In Jesus' name, amen."

Ruth lifted her head. Her hairpins slipped free, and her golden hair spilled down. Tears streaked her flushed face, but her lips bowed upward. She'd never looked more beautiful.

"Thank you, Josh. No one has ever done that."

"Get used to it." He smiled and rose. "Good night, Ruthie."

"Good night, Josh."

It wasn't until the door banged shut behind her that Josh realized she'd stopped hiccupping.

He sat in the parlor long after the girls went to bed. Toledo's question kept nagging at him. What if Ruth wasn't as clumsy as she seemed to be? Was it possible Laney's assailant mistook her for Ruth? If that was the case, then Ruth's mishaps might not be accidents. Someone could have planted that burr under her horse's saddle. The outhouse door shouldn't have fallen off the hinges. He'd personally reinforced the latch on the pigsty before the sow had her litter; someone had tampered with it.

"Can't sleep?" Dad asked as he came outside.

"Hadn't bothered to turn in yet. Suppose I ought to."

"Thought I'd sit out here and enjoy a cigar. Hilda is finishing up in the kitchen. I reckon just about the time I'm done with my smoke, I'll end the evening with a wedge of cherry pie."

"You had two tarts this morning and pie after supper. I'll have to send Hilda and the girls over to the O'Sullivans' tomorrow in order to replace everything you've eaten."

"No need. With me here, Laney is safe as can be."

Laney might be, but I'm not sure Ruth is. "Kelly O'Sullivan is teaching the girls how to make a braided rag rug. Since Ruth needs one for her room—"

"She can buy a carpet. A fine Turkish one."

"Dad, Ruth needs to be happy here, or she might take a mind to leave. She has her heart set on having that rug so it'll match Laney's. You know how they've started doing things together and want to be alike—sewing those matching riding skirts, for instance."

Is it my imagination, or did Dad just go pale? Just before we went to help Bayside foal, he said Ruth was a complication. There were a couple of times he went into the other side of the stable. He could have been the one who hit Laney. The way he was so shaken and drank all that whiskey could point toward his feeling guilty.

Rolling the cigar between his hands, Dad said, "I don't want my women working."

Exasperated by his father's possessive manner, Josh said, "Dad, everyone knows the girls don't have to work; they're choosing to be productive instead of idle. Folks will consider that virtuous."

"I'll think on it."

"Good night." Josh went to his room. After reading the Bible, he prayed safety for Ruth and wisdom on how to handle the tangled mess with his father. As he placed his Bible back on the shelf, Alan's old cigarette case caught his eye.

Alan enjoyed smoking—especially in the evening. And though Josh never smoked, Alan had bequeathed the case to him. Alan treasured the silver cigarette case, but Josh never knew why until Alan passed away. Inside the monogrammed case were etched, *To Alan, all my love, Leticia.* Alan never mentioned Leticia, but the letter from Ruth's mother made all of the pieces fall into place. He'd sent her away, but he never stopped loving her.

Josh opened the case. Half a dozen cigarettes rested inside, both ends twisted shut. The paper had yellowed, but the cigarettes brought back memories of Alan sitting in a chair by the window, smoke rising above him as he stared out at the land and listened as Josh read to him from the Scriptures each night before they retired. The last week of his life, Alan suddenly collapsed and went comatose, but Josh still read to him in hopes that he'd find spiritual comfort.

Josh touched one of the cigarettes. The paper crumbled, and finely chopped brown tobacco tumbled free. Mixed with it was another substance: a dull gray powder.

CHAPTER TWENTY-THREE

"Good morning, good morning." McCain entered the dining room and bent to kiss Laney on the cheek. He always did so, and Ruth found it charming. He turned and pressed one on her own cheek, and she let out a gasp.

Hilda set a bowl of scrambled eggs and a platter of ham on the table. "What got into you?"

"I got up on the right side of the bed," McCain announced as he sat down and put his napkin in his lap. "Obviously, you got up on the wrong side."

Hic. Ruth grabbed for her teacup. *If I hurry up and drink, maybe—* HIC!

"Laney, it's Ruth's turn to ask the blessing." Josh's voice sounded too civilized. The gold shards in his eyes glittered. "Maybe you could take over."

Laney immediately obliged. As soon as the prayer ended, McCain turned to Ruth. "My arm is bothering me today. Could I trouble you to serve me?"

"Here, Dad. Take my plate." Josh hastily spooned a huge pile of scrambled eggs onto his own plate and exchanged it for his father's.

Ruth took another gulp of tea.

"Josh tells me you admire Laney's rag rug."

"Mrs. O'Sullivan is teaching us how to make one, Daddy." Laney took a dab of eggs and passed them to Ruth.

"That's charming. Why don't I ride over there today with you so you can show me what you've been doing?"

Thump. The bowl of eggs landed on the table as Ruth let out another loud hiccup. She sprang to her feet. "Please excuse me."

"Ruth—" McCain half rose and reached for her.

She evaded him and raced into the kitchen. As she made her exit, she could hear Josh saying, "Let her go."

Yes, let me go! Ruth practically collided with Hilda. Hilda promptly grabbed her by the arms and whisked her into the pantry.

"Girl," Hilda whispered, "that old man is up to no good."

Hic "I was afraid of that," Ruth said in a miserable tone.

"I got me an idea."

"What?"

"How's about you and me move out?"

"Where to?"

"Your daddy's old place, that's where. After breakfast, I'll show it to you."

Ruth threw her arms around Hilda. "Oh, thank you!"

"Now you go on back in there and pretend everything's okay."

"Ruth?" McCain had come into the kitchen.

Hic! Ruth closed her eyes in horror. *So much for trying to hide or get away from him.*

"I've got her in the pantry," Hilda called out as she reached for a canister. "Once I put a spoonful of sugar on her tongue, she'll be cured of these hiccups."

"We have sugar on the table." McCain stood in the doorway.

"I didn't know *hic* about this cure."

Hilda patted her shoulder. "Don't you worry. If the sugar

doesn't work, I'll have you hang your head over the sink and drink out of the far rim of a china cup."

"Thank you. Please, Mr. McCain, *hic*. Don't let me keep you from your breakfast. I'll feel *hic* dreadful, knowing I spoiled the meal."

"I'll just have her stay with me here in the kitchen." Hilda steered Ruth past him. "I'll pull a chair right beside the stove. Could be that you need to breathe warmer air. I'll still see to it she has a bite to eat. Don't you fret, Mr. McCain."

"I've never in my life fretted."

"Good, then." Hilda turned her back on him and grinned at Ruth. "You, young lady, hold your breath as long as you can."

McCain groused under his breath and went back into the dining room.

Hilda grimaced. "That man's harder to shake than a deadly fever."

"Can we send him to town to get something to treat my hiccups?"

Hilda perked up. "You bet! Let me think ... we've got plenty of sugar here." A sly smile tilted the housekeeper's mouth. "Marmalade. Orange marmalade. He won't go if I ask him, though."

Ruth took a moment to gather up her nerve, then went to the doorway and timed opening the door just before her next hiccup. "Excuse me."

Josh and his father both rose.

Ruth hiccupped again. Raising her hand to her mouth, she said, "I'm so sorry. Nothing's stopping these. Hilda said may—*hic*—be orange marmalade would work."

Josh grimaced. "After going to town yesterday, I'm overloaded today."

Hic. She slumped against the doorjamb and tried her hardest to look pitiful. *Hic*.

"Don't you worry your pretty head, Ruthie. I'll go." McCain quickly shoveled in one last bite, then headed for the door.

An hour later, Ruth, Laney, and Hilda stood on the doorstep of a nearby cottage. "I noticed this place, but I thought it was another bunkhouse or something," Ruth said.

Hilda opened the door. It creaked loudly. "The hinges need oil."

Laney peeked inside. "That's not all this place needs. It's filthy!"

"A little dirt never killed nobody." Hilda trundled on in.

Ruth walked around and nodded. "All cleaned up, this will work beautifully. Hilda, which room would you like?"

"That one on the east side'll be good for me. Early mornin' sun helps me wake up so's I get breakfast on the stove. You take the bigger one."

"Wait a minute!" Laney wheeled around and grabbed Ruth's hand. "You can't move!"

Ruth forced out a laugh. "Why do you think we came out here? Laney, I'll be a stone's throw away from you, and I'll still come to the big house for meals."

"You can't. Why, look!" She swung her arm in a wide arc. "You don't have a stick of furniture in the place."

"You heard Mr. Farnsworth. My things should be arriving any day." Ruth squeezed Laney's hand. "Just think how much fun we'll have decorating the place! I'll expect you to come be my guest every other day."

Laney's lower lip trembled as she repeated, "Every other day?"

"Of course, silly! On the other days, I'll come see you, or we'll go visit the O'Sullivans!"

"I don't think Josh or Daddy are going to approve of this."

Hilda stood akimbo and gave Laney an exasperated look. "Child, if women waited for men to approve everything they did, the world would stop turning."

Ruth sneezed. "The dust is thick as sin in here. I think tomorrow, after church, I'm going to ask Mrs. O'Sullivan if Colin and one of his friends can come douse it ceiling-to-floor with buckets of water. After it dries, they can whitewash the whole place, inside and out."

"Now, that's good thinkin'." Hilda pursed her lips. "I confess, I always fancied yella houses. Think we could get tint for the paint so's the outside looks cheery?"

"Oh, yes!" Laney swept her hand toward the windows. "Imagine sunny yellow or green gingham curtains over there. The place will be bright and welcoming."

Getting Laney's support proved easy; Ruth figured Josh would understand how she needed to get away from his father. She'd need his support trying to convince McCain, though. Supper was going to be a trial.

———◦●◦———

"No. Absolutely not."

"Now, now." McCain set down his coffee cup and cleared his throat. "Josh, there's no cause for you to summarily dismiss Ruth's idea."

Josh glowered across the table at her. "You're staying here. There's no good reason for you to up and move out."

Ruth gave him a maddening smile. "Thank you for your offer. I'll be happy to remain here as long as we're cleaning and preparing my father's cabin."

"She's going to ask Colin to bring a friend over," Laney explained. "They'll wash down everything and do the painting."

Hilda came out of the kitchen with a basket of rolls. "We have it all arranged, you know. Ruth's furnishings are supposed to arrive any day now. She assures me we'll have most everything we need."

Dad turned to Ruth. "I'd be happy to take you to town on Monday. I'm sure there are several little doodads you'll want."

"That's so kind of you."

"You're getting ahead of yourself," Josh snapped. "Everyone seems to be forgetting that somebody out there attacked Laney. It's not safe for Ruth to be on her own."

"She's not on her own. I'll be with her." Hilda propped her hands on her ample hips. "Not a soul will come near us without my approval."

That's easy for her to say; she doesn't know Dad's the biggest danger around here. "I'm against this. You need to reconsider."

"Ruth is a mature young woman. I'm sure she's put sufficient thought behind this decision." Dad smiled at her. "I think you've proven yourself, dear. Josh is just in a bad mood. Has been all day."

"Did you have a bad day, Josh?"

Ruth asked the question with such sincerity, he hated this whole mess even more. "I have a lot on my mind." He stared at her, willing her to understand his concerns. "Making any move right now is ill-considered."

"Probably should have waited to spring this on him until tomorrow night," Dad said to Ruth in a confidential tone. "Josh is always in a better mood on Sundays after he's been at church. Give him a day to let the notion take root. You're a patient woman, Ruth. Understanding, too. By the time that old place is cleaned, painted, and your furniture arrives, my son will accept the wisdom behind your decision."

"Don't count on it," Josh said. The rest of supper, he stewed over Ruth's latest harebrained scheme. Sleep evaded him, and the next morning his hopes that Ruth would change her mind soared when she pulled him off into the parlor after breakfast.

"I thought of something."

"Good. I'll—"

"I didn't tell you what I thought of." Her brow furrowed, but the disgruntled expression he reckoned she aimed for didn't work. With all of those darling little springy curls surrounding her face, she couldn't look very peeved. She leaned closer.

Josh fought the urge to pull her closer still and surprise her with a little kiss. "What did you think of, Ruthie?"

"Tithe. I'll need to sell a couple of those diamonds so I can pay my tithe. Would it be dreadful if I just slip a promissory note into the offering plate? I ought to have thought this out before now. God shouldn't be kept waiting for His share. The only problem is, the left hand isn't supposed to know about the right. If I use a note, then it won't be a secret."

"Ruth, think. An attorney personally traveled across the nation to conduct business with you. You've been to the bank. If an enormous sum of money is tithed to the church, don't you think everyone's going to know you were the one who paid it?"

"I'd hope not!" She looked utterly appalled.

"Like it or not, folks are going to know."

"Well, then, I'll just wait a week or two. Then, when the money is tithed, folks—"

"Will still know it's you."

"You're not much help. You weren't any help last evening, either."

"Don't ask me to agree to your moving out. Of all the notions you've taken, that has to be the most insane one yet."

"Are we ready to go?" Laney singsonged from the stairs.

The fire in Ruth's eyes was at complete odds with her calm, sweet voice, "Of course we are, Laney. Is Hilda ready, too?"

"I was ready an hour ago."

Ruth turned to leave the parlor, but her skirts hit the piano and swung in the opposite direction. Josh couldn't be sure, but he thought that beneath all those yards of fabric, she intentionally kicked the piano before departing.

When they arrived at church, Daryl Farnsworth approached the buckboard. "Good morning, everyone."

"Oh, Mr. Farnsworth!" Laney's voice sounded all bubbly. "You're still in town!"

"Indeed, I am. I decided to prolong my stay a short while. It would be a pity to travel all this way and not look around a bit."

"You simply must come to lunch," Laney said.

"I wouldn't want to be an imposition."

"I'm cookin' gracious plenty," Hilda said as Josh helped her down.

Josh helped Ruth down. She started to wander off, but he snagged her arms and pulled her back. He didn't want her asking Colin O'Sullivan to come do any cleaning and painting.

"Is something amiss?"

"No." Inspiration struck. Josh murmured, "You could ask Farnsworth to be your agent. He could go to Sacramento or San Francisco and sell a few diamonds."

"What a wonderful idea!" She barely took a breath before she tacked on, "Why, I could ask him to purchase some tint for the paint. Hilda wants our new house to be yellow, and Lester doesn't stock such things in his mercantile."

"A new house?" Farnsworth asked as he escorted Laney around the buckboard. "I didn't know you intended to invest in property, Miss Caldwell."

"Oh, it was my father's old house."

"I think we'd be better off thinking about our heavenly Father and getting into His house." Josh offered his arm to Ruth.

Frank Hutton preached. "I'll be speaking from John 14:2: 'In my Father's house are many mansions: if it were not so, I would have told you. I go to prepare a place for you.'"

Josh sat in the pew and resisted the urge to turn to Ruth and give her an I-told-you-so look. *She's sensible enough to realize those words straight from Christ's mouth and read today from the Bible are especially aimed at her situation.* He settled in and appreciated the whole sermon.

Immediately following the sermon, Josh excused himself. He pulled Rick Maltby to the side. "I hate to do business on the Lord's Day, but it's difficult for me to come to town without making up ridiculous excuses. I have Alan Caldwell's cigarette case. Dad used to roll cigarettes for Alan. I'm wondering—and I know this sounds crazy—but I'm wondering if Dad used arsenic in them. Can you have it tested?"

Maltby nodded curtly. "I'll talk with Doc. If he can't do it, he'll know who can. Be careful, Josh. If you're right, your father has resorted to murder once already."

"I know."

After supper that night, Ruth went out onto the back veranda. Josh followed her, thinking it was only fair that he speak to her privately. After all, he didn't want to gloat over the fact that she'd come around to his way of thinking and was going to decide to remain in this house.

"I hoped you'd come outside." She smiled at him.

He motioned toward the wicker furniture. "We can converse out here."

She still wore her Sunday-best dress—a stunningly beautiful pale green dress with darker green bows which held up swags every so often on the skirts. It looked fresh and airy and made her eyes shimmer like emeralds. As soon as she confessed her change of heart, he'd tell her just how beautiful she was.

"Today's sermon seemed particularly apropos, didn't you think?" She folded her hands in her lap as she asked.

"Yes, I thought that exact same thing."

"Good, then. So we're no longer at odds."

He smiled. "The difference of opinions did cause some strain. I'm glad you came around."

"I came around?" She shook her head so savagely, pins popped out and pinged on the wooden planks all around her. "No, Josh. I didn't. You were supposed to. Didn't you listen? The verse said—"

"In my father's house." He glowered at her.

She had the nerve to glare straight back. "In *my* father's house." She patted her bosom so hard, it made a thumping sound as she continued, "are *many* mansions. There's no mistaking the implications. I know beyond a shadow of a doubt that I'm meant to move to the cabin where my father and mother once lived together."

McCain came outside. "Of course you are, Ruth. I don't doubt it one bit. Josh, you're not bullying the girl, are you?"

"Bully her?" He snorted. "I've never met a more obstinate

woman." One look at Ruth's white knuckles told Josh she wasn't going to give an inch. He growled, "I'm going to check on the foals."

━━►◄━━

By Friday Ruth could hardly contain herself. Colin O'Sullivan had rounded up two friends, and the trio came over all week long to sluice out, scrub down, and whitewash the cabin. Farnsworth brought back the yellow tint that now adorned the exterior of her new place.

"You boys have worked wonders!" she exclaimed, watching as they finished the last few strokes of a buttery yellow paint on the walls.

"It's a grand little home," Colin declared. "Built solid as the day is long."

"Thanks to the hard work you young men have done, it's pretty as any bungalow or cottage back East."

Reminding herself of the dress she'd ruined while painting the bedchamber back in the big house, Ruth forced herself to keep a distance from the walls. "The red camellias I planted by the other house are so pretty, I think I ought to special order some for this place, too. Maybe not red. Pink. Yes, pink."

"Ma sure loves the ones you gave to her," Colin said. "She about boxed Dale's ears the other day when he ran full tilt into one of them."

"I'm sure she didn't. Your mama is the most even-tempered woman I've ever met."

"You wouldn't think so, if you saw her. Da gave her a gift—a beautiful gold ring. Every time she looks down, she starts to cryin' again. Galen teased her and said if she'd stand out in the garden and keep looking at her hand, we'd never have to carry a drop of water to irrigate the plot again."

Felipe sauntered up. His chaps made an odd flapping noise as he walked, and his spurs jangled. "Miss Ruth, two big wagons drove up. The driver asked for you."

"Oh, my things! Could you please ask them to drive over here?"

"Best not, miss. Them big freight wagons'll kick up a might amount of dust. It'll stick to the paint."

Ruth thought for a moment. "I know! I'll invite them to lunch. I'll have to ask Hilda first, of course. But by the time the men are done eating, the paint ought to be dry."

Felipe gave her a wry look. "Boss said you had a knack for cookin' up big plans."

Ruth laughed. "He should be glad it's plans I cook up. If he'd ever tasted my cooking, he'd be six feet under by now!"

Hilda obligingly made lunch for everyone, and then the men unloaded the wagons. Memory after memory from home washed over Ruth as each item came into view. Hilda and Laney both had opinions where everything ought to go. Though the men left, the women remained in the cottage and rearranged things to suit their fancy.

"I need to get over and start supper." Hilda stretched her back. "It's a crying shame it's so hot. A hearty stew would have simplified the night. As it is, with Josh in such a dark mood, I'd best cook up one of his favorites."

"I don't know what's gotten into my brother." Laney angled a chair into a corner and stepped back to appreciate the effect.

"He's angry with me." Ruth let out a deep sigh. "In his opinion, I should have stayed over at your house."

"Yes, I heard him mention it once or three hundred times," Laney said blithely.

"It makes no sense. I've caused him enough trouble. You'd think he'd be glad to get rid of me. All of the headmistresses were deliriously happy to send me away."

Laney huffed, "Ruth!"

"It's the truth."

"Well, it's perfectly clear why Josh is different from them. He's a man." Laney suddenly let out a squeal. "That's why!"

"I don't find any comfort in knowing I'm able to vex men just as much as I do women." Ruth held a picture up to the wall and tried to decide where it would look best. She'd been trying to keep herself busy in order to mute the miserable feeling of knowing Josh was put out with her.

Laney pulled the picture from her hands and dumped it on the chair. "Don't you see?"

"See what?"

"Josh loves you!"

CHAPTER TWENTY-FOUR

"What!" Ruth gaped at Laney.

"That's what's wrong. He didn't want you to leave the house because he loves you and wants you beside him. I know it." She pressed her hands to her bosom. "I just know it deep in my heart. How could I have been so blind?"

"Laney, you're imagining something that isn't there. When a man loves a woman, he's gentle and kind."

"Josh is always right there to help you in and out of the buckboard. He's supporting your plan to build the library."

"Those are the actions of a well-mannered man. Believe me, I might not know much about men, but when one calls a woman mule-headed, stubborn, and prickly, you can safely say he's not planning to court her."

"Ruth, what I think you ought to do is talk to Mrs. O'Sullivan. She'd be able to advise you."

"I asked her to send Colin to do the cleaning and painting. Clearly, she knows that I'm moving into my father's cabin. If she considered it an imprudent move, she would have spoken up."

"You're using logic."

319

"Naturally I am. Women can be every bit as logical as men."

Laney's tinkling laughter filled the small room. "Mama always told me the heart has no reason."

"Well, I seriously doubt Josh is being unreasonable because he's suddenly fallen madly in love with me." *If only it were true.* The thought stunned Ruth. *How did that happen? When did I begin to think of him as more than a friend?*

"I'll go ahead and help you fix up this place. It's quite charming, but you won't stay here for long. My brother isn't a patient man. When he decides what he wants, he goes after it. Once it dawns on him that he's upset because he cares for you in that special way, he's going to sweep you off your feet and to the altar."

Resolutely telling herself she wouldn't allow Laney's prediction to lead her down a path of hope, Ruth picked up the picture again. "The only problem with your learning to read, Elaine McCain, is that you've decided life is like a fairy tale."

"There's nothing wrong with that. I'd rather see a happy ending for my brother and my best friend than a dreadful happening like William poisoning poor Arabella."

"Where should I hang this?"

Closing her right eye and tilting her head, Laney announced, "Not there. You need a little table there with a lamp on it so you can read and do needlework."

"I don't have a table." Ruth looked around and puffed air upward to get some stray curls off of her forehead. "Bernadette helped me decide what to ship, and with everything else we chose, you'd think we would have included one or two."

"But the tapestry chairs and fainting couch are beautiful. Originally, I suggested gingham for curtains, but I think you ought to do deep green swags." Laney gazed about, then smiled.

"I can recognize that look in your eyes," Ruth said. "You're scheming."

Hitching one shoulder, Laney said in an oh-so-casual tone, "I was imagining lining your bedroom with oak bookshelves. This place will be a lovely setting for the library when you move back home as Josh's bride."

"That does it. I'm going to order a few medical books so I can be a good friend to you and cure you of your wild notions. Anyone else might overhear you and declare you insane."

"Well, I'm in good company, then." Laney's eyes sparkled with glee. "Plenty of the people I know would worry for your stability if they knew you've worn a sash and participated in a suffragette march. I used to be so worried about what other people thought of me, Ruth. Since you've come, I've learned that I don't want to be anybody but myself."

"I'm sure I had nothing to do with that. Josh is the one who's told me that God made me for His unique purposes and I didn't have to consider myself a misfit just because I don't fit into someone else's mold."

"See? You may be at odds with him over one tiny issue, but the two of you get along fabulously."

"Laney?"

"Yes?"

"Will you please find the hatbox I brought over? It has a package of needles and my brush and comb. I can hang the pictures and get things done instead of wasting time on fanciful notions."

"I'll get out your brush—but only so I can style your hair for supper."

After washing up at the washstand that had once been her mother's, Ruth sat down and let Laney see to her hair. *I used to consider the girls back at the academy horribly vain to primp before seeing their beaux. Yet here I am, getting my hopes up. I can't do that. Lord, help me guard my heart. I'm not sure whether I'm moving out here to get away from Mr. McCain or if I'm trying to run away from the feelings I hold for Joshua.*

"Exquisite!" Laney set down the brush and clapped her hands. "Now let's go to supper."

———————

God bless my little sister, Josh thought as he went out to the barn. Laney prattled about Ruth's new place at dinner and made a point of looking directly at him when she said Ruth needed a small lamp table.

When the hands moved from the bunkhouse half of the stable into the current bunkhouse, a few pieces of furniture had been left behind. Josh remembered a small pedestal-style table that had gotten shoved into a corner and often held odds and ends in the tack room. In a matter of minutes he cleared it off, dusted the piece down, and decided a dab of stain here and there would hide the scuffs. Women liked those frilly doilies, and one would hide any imperfections until he bought Ruth a new table.

She'd gone back to the cabin after supper—not because she'd spend the night there, but because she simply couldn't be still. The late evening sun poured through the open windows and door. He stopped at the door and tried not to laugh.

Ruth stood by the far wall. Holding a needle in place with her comb, she poised the brush. "Now cooperate. Just a little nudge is all I ask of you. Then you'll get your reward. I'll hang a beautiful picture on you."

"Talking to needles?"

"Oh!" Ruth jumped. The needle and comb went one direction as the brush went another. "Josh McCain, you rascal! You nearly scared me out of my mind."

"Honey, you're already out of your mind." The endearment slipped out, and he didn't regret it. Ruth needed to learn how he felt about her.

Busy looking for the needle, Ruth laughed. "You're not the first person to make that accusation."

Disappointed she either didn't realize he'd called her honey or was choosing to ignore it, he walked on in and presented the table. "Where do you want this?"

She sat back on her heels and clapped her hands joyfully. "However did you find one so fast?"

Her reaction pleased him. Judging from her guileless smile, she wasn't playing coy. She simply hadn't realized he'd made an open declaration of his feelings. *In time, she'll come to know.*

"It's perfect! Oh, thank you, Josh!"

"It's not perfect, Ruth. It's old and scarred. I doctored it up, and you can hide the bad spots with a doily or something." He looked around the place. It looked nice. Actually far better than nice.

"Could you please place it in the corner over by the chair?"

"Sure." He did so, then turned. "Ruth, we need to talk."

"Not until I find that needle. It's my last one."

"If you take off your shoes, you're bound to find it."

"I thought you were my friend!"

He nodded toward the settee. Ruth relented and took a seat. She'd reclaimed her brush from the plush Turkish carpet and now spun it round and round just inches above her lap.

"I care for you, Ruth. Deeply." He fought the urge to declare his love for her. A woman deserved to be wooed. He tore his gaze from her and looked out the window to be sure they wouldn't be interrupted. "In retrospect, I can see how you might have gotten upset that I didn't want you to move. It wasn't because I think you're helpless or dumb, Ruth. My reason was painfully simple: I don't trust Dad."

"Neither do I, Josh. I'm sorry. You're grieved over his handling of the finances, and I cannot imagine what a terrible blow that is to you. Nonetheless," the brush in her hand twirled at a much faster pace, "I had to get away from him. He started acting . . . odd. Even Laney remarked on it. I feel much safer now that I'll have some distance from him."

"Oh, Ruth." Josh shook his head. "Your safety is exactly why

I'm so opposed to your being in this place. When you're under the same roof with me, I can protect you. Once you're out here, I cannot keep watch without endangering your reputation."

She gave him a look he couldn't interpret. Her lips bowed upward, but her eyes seemed shadowed. "You'd never compromise me, Joshua. Everyone knows you're an honorable man. Any slurs would be because I have a penchant for finding trouble."

"Don't say that about yourself." He rasped, "You don't find trouble. You find adventure and fun. It's not that you seek to cause problems; it's a matter of your simply being curious and intelligent. That spark is what makes you who you are."

Her lips parted in surprise.

I have to tell her what I know. And though I wish I had the luxury of expressing how I love her, I must wait. "Ruth, listen to me. I'm not sure, but ... I've taken in your father's cigarette case. I'm wondering if—" He fought with himself. He could still back out and say nothing.

But then Ruth wouldn't be safe.

"If?" she prompted him.

"I think my dad might have poisoned your father."

"Oh, Josh ... no." The brush slid off her lap and onto the floor.

Leaning closer, he said, "In retrospect, I wonder if many of your accidents were actually attempts to harm you. You said someone bumped you the first time you went to town."

"That could have been me, being clumsy."

"In your full hoopskirts, it makes no sense that you'd be so close to the edge of the walk that you'd fall. The burr under your mount's saddle, the hinges on the outhouse door, and the latch on the pigsty—Ruth, any of those alone would be an accident. Taken together, they spell out something sinister."

"Why would anyone want to hurt me?"

"The land—the inheritance."

" Josh, I've said I might not claim the land."

"But if you did, the books would prove Dad's been dishonest." He heaved a sigh. "There's another motive, too. All of the talk about the railroad going through the Sierras isn't just talk. Land's being bought, and a portion of the Broken P is right in line. When Dad went to Sacramento the last time, I strongly suspect he signed a deal. He had no right to sign when there's a question as to who owns how much of the spread."

She chewed on her lower lip. "That wasn't right. He should have at least consulted you."

"There's more." *Lord, this is so much to put on her shoulders. The woman I love ought never have to bear such burdens. I can't stay silent, though. If I do, her ignorance could cost her dearly.*

"Please go on."

"When Farnsworth went to Sacramento to sell the diamonds and get the yellow tint—"

"Isn't the yellow a lovely hue?"

"Yes, Ruth. But while he was there, I asked him to make some inquiries. It seems Dad borrowed against the land to build the house. The note is due next month."

"So he probably sold the land to the railroad to make good on the loan."

"He hasn't, though. And the money he's been skimming is far more than the amount owed."

"Let's assume, since you asked me to pursue the claim, that we're partners."

He nodded grimly.

"Then as your partner and Laney's dear friend, I'd be more than happy to settle the loan. It's the least I could do, seeing how you've befriended and sheltered me."

"That's wrong. I won't allow it." He stood up and paced back and forth. "I'm scared to death he's going to try to kill you. He's been lulling you into complacency with praise, but I think he's actually plotting against you."

"You have no proof of that."

"I do. Ruth, Laney was hit when she was wearing the riding skirt that matches yours. No one knew you both made a skirt. The only people who saw you in yours the day before were me, Dad, and Toledo."

Ruth buried her face in her hands. A moment later, she looked up. Eyes shimmering with tears, she said, "Josh, I'm so sorry. Truly I am. If I had just been firm from the start and stood by my conviction that all I really wanted was to hear stories about my father so I could get to know him, I'd never have forced your father into such a state."

"Don't you dare take the blame. Ruth, I don't hold you responsible in the least. Dad bears the blame. So do I. I knew Dad wasn't a Christian, but I still expected him to behave with morals. Someone who refuses to walk with the Lord doesn't live by the same rules."

"When you love someone, you make allowances." Her voice was soft. "Mama always took my side and explained away or laughed off my escapades."

"Ruth, she loved you for who you are." He suddenly offered her a broad smile. "Remember King David in the Bible? He wasn't at all what people expected of a king—at least not in the beginning. He didn't look like a king—he was puny compared to his brothers, and he was nothing more than a shepherd. And what about Mary, Jesus' mother? She was a young girl—nobody famous, just a good person who wanted to do the will of God.

"And that's what I see in you. God leads you on a path that is unique, and you don't just walk on it—you skip with joy. How anyone could fault you for that is beyond me."

She parted her lips but said nothing. Finally, Ruth smiled. "Mama was right to listen to God and send me here. I've missed her terribly, but, several times now, God has given you the words that are a balm to my soul."

"I'm glad you came, Ruth. No matter what happens, I won't

regret your coming to"—he caught himself just before he said
me—"the Broken P."

"Josh, you love your father. You've looked past his faults and
wanted only the best for him. You followed the commandment to
honor your father. Please don't consider anything that's happened
as your fault."

"You've got a forgiving heart, Ruth."

"Those of us who manage to make a lot of mistakes learn to
forgive freely. We know what a blessing it is when others follow the
Lord's example and forgive us."

"Honey, for now my big concern is your safety. Hilda's so
excited about living here with you, I'd hate to ruin it, but you have
to promise me you won't ever eat or drink anything brought here.
Only stuff Hilda serves at the table or whatever the O'Sullivans
have. And I don't ever want you alone."

"I'll keep your concerns in mind, Josh. I'll be careful." She
waited a beat. "I'll continue to wear my knife up my sleeve, and I'll
keep the muff pistol at my bedside. Only you and Laney know I
can't aim worth a hoot."

"You had me calmed down a bit until you mentioned the
pistol."

"My hairbrush is heavy. It would make for a good weapon."

"I noticed you were trying to use it as a hammer again. Why
don't I help you hang that picture?"

"We can't. I don't know where the needle went." She rose.

Josh stooped and retrieved her brush.

"I'll put that away." She went into one of the bedrooms. Ruth
mumbled to herself, then he heard a drawer slide open. "What is
this?"

Ruth drew the envelope out of the drawer and turned it over.
Bernadette's familiar loopy script across the top read, *This came after
you left. Hadley and I thought you might want it.*

Josh called, "Ruth, are you okay? Is everything all right?"

She stared at the shakily written address. *Leticia Caldwell c/o Mr. Hadley* with her old address. In the upper left-hand corner the same handwriting simply read "Broken P."

"Ruth?"

She stumbled toward the doorway and over to Josh. He met her in the middle of the room. Concern creased his handsome, tanned face. "What is it?"

"Someone from the Broken P wrote to my mother." She showed him the envelope.

Josh's hands braced her waist. "Here, honey. You need to sit down."

Because she hadn't wanted to struggle with hoops as she worked on the cottage, Ruth didn't need to tame her skirts. Three rows of petticoats whooshed beneath her as she half-fell back into a chair.

Josh hadn't turned loose of her but knelt just a little off to her left. "Do you need a little water? Smelling salts?"

"I'm a strong woman, Josh. There's only been once in my life when I felt in the least bit swoony." She tore her gaze from his and stared at the battered envelope. "What I just said might be a lie. Maybe I'm not very strong. Josh, I'm scared. What if my father wrote this?"

"I recognize the writing, Ruth." He paused, then added quietly, "Your father addressed the envelope."

"The stories you and Laney have told me about him made me grow to like him. If he wrote something unkind to Mama, I couldn't bear it."

"When I first met your father, he had a severe problem."

She nodded. "Grandfather told me my father was a blackguard."

"I'd never say he was a blackguard. He had a terrible problem with whiskey. Even then, when he'd imbibed quite freely, I never saw him get mean. Part of the deal I made when Dad and I bought into the partnership was that Alan had to cork the bottle. He struggled mightily, Ruth. I wouldn't say otherwise—but your father had given his word, and he adhered to it. From the time he made the promise, he never again took so much as one sip."

"He was honorable, then. That's good to hear. But if he was principled, why would he ever send my mama away?"

"I don't know for certain."

Ruth sucked in as deep a breath as her stays permitted, then let it out. Whether Laney was right about Josh having more than just friendly feelings for her, Ruth didn't know. What she was certain of, though, was that she wanted him to be here now. "Would you remain with me while I read it?"

"Of course I will. Let me move the lamp over here so you can read it more easily." Josh rose, brought the lamp to her side, and put it down on the very table he'd delivered. July evening sun filtered in through the windows, but he still lit the lamp. Ruth wondered if he was trying to give her an opportunity to marshal her wits. As he pulled the other chair close to hers, he said, "I understand this is a private moment. You needn't feel any pressure to share any of the contents with me."

Ruth gathered her resolve and opened the envelope. She unfolded three sheets of paper. After moistening her lips, she read the date aloud.

Josh cleared his throat. "Ruth, your father fell into a coma that very day. These were his very last thoughts and words."

Already nervous, that one last fact tipped her over the edge. She hiccupped.

Josh reached over and tilted her face up to his. "Ruthie, you don't have to read it if you don't want to. We can put the letter aside, or you can burn it. If reading this will upset you, you can simply ask me to make it disappear. I'll honor your wishes."

She shook her head. "No. I have to read this. I really do."

Josh laid one big hand over the letter while his other hand continued to cup her jaw. He bowed his head. "Lord, come join us. Prepare Ruth's heart for whatever is written in this letter and equip us for what lies ahead. We ask this in Jesus' precious name, amen."

"Thank you," she whispered. She took another slow breath and realized her hiccups were gone.

Josh removed his hand and she looked down at the page. "'My dearest Leticia,'" Ruth looked back up at Josh. "He still held feelings for her?"

"Yes, I believe he did. The one possession he treasured was his cigarette case. Until her letter came, saying you were to arrive, I hadn't known Alan's wife's name. From the inscription on the inside of the case, I knew it was from her."

"That cigarette case is the one you asked someone to test to see about poison?"

"Sadly enough, yes. As soon as this whole mess is over, I'll make sure you get it."

"No. I have no need for such a thing. With everything that's gone bad, I want you to have a memento."

"That's mighty sweet of you, Ruth. I'd treasure it, but if you change your mind, I'll understand."

She looked back down. "I don't want to read his words just to myself. Do you mind if I read them aloud?"

"I'm honored that you want to share this with me."

Ruth blinked and promised herself she would make it through the whole letter without crying. She started reading the spidery script.

"My dearest Leticia,
A gentleman came to the Broken P. I ascertained his services had been engaged by a Mr. Hadley to make inquiries about me. A very discreet individual, he would say nothing more about his task. I assumed Mr. Hadley had undertaken this on your behalf.
My wife, you were all a man could ever pray for in a mate. It is to my everlasting shame that I was not the husband you deserved. For selfish reasons, I would have kept you by my side all these years; but I could not. I sent

you away in hopes that you would not bear the brunt of my weakness for the bottle. Very belatedly, I beg your forgiveness.

A young man named Joshua came into my life and with a mixture of impressive kindness and indomitable spiritual strength, he showed me God was far greater than my problem. In giving my heart over to the Lord, I found the strength necessary to eschew my weakness. Unfortunately, by then, it had been so many years since you'd left—a whole lifetime that could not be recaptured. My sins, though forgiven by the Almighty, still carried consequences. I'd lost the only woman I ever loved.

The agent left, and months went by. A man by the name of Hadley sent me a short note. He said it was with your consent. In it, he revealed that you'd borne me a child—a delightful daughter. From the date of the birth he listed, I know beyond a shadow of a doubt that Ruth is ours—yours and mine. For all the grief I put you through, it humbles and gladdens me to know you've said you'd have married me again—knowing the pain I would cause you—just to be gifted with such a loving, enchanting daughter.

Were my health better, I would travel to you. As it is, I pray you might consider coming west to permit me the honor of your presence and the joy of meeting our daughter. All I have is at your disposal.

Yours most humbly and sincerely,
Alan"

Slowly, Ruth folded the papers and tucked them into the envelope. Tears rolled down her cheeks.

"Sweetheart, I'm so sorry you never met him. Alan was a wonderful man. I hope you take heart in what he said, though—that your mother cherished you and spoke so lovingly of you, and your father longed to claim you as his daughter."

Ruth looked at Josh. "Can you believe this? It's a treasure, Josh.

God sent this to me as a gift, proof that my daddy cared."

"Yes, He did. I'm sure, had Alan not fallen into that coma, he would have told us all about you." Josh nodded. "And he would have wanted to provide for your future, Ruth. That letter is more than sufficient proof for your claim."

"I don't care about that, Josh. Truly, I don't. My father credits you with leading him to the Lord. That is priceless. Though God will reward you in heaven, I want to show my appreciation. I want you to have my share of the Broken P."

"Ruth, leading your father to the Lord was a privilege. The thirst that once held him in bondage turned into a thirst for God. He blessed me constantly by sharing his insights and quoting a verse that applied to something we were dealing with.

"All along I've said we needed to settle the will according to what Alan would have wanted. That letter tells me very clearly how he felt. Your generous spirit is incredible, but we ought to respect your father and abide by his wishes."

"Josh, if I sign over my share to you, you'll still command control over the ranch."

"First off, I'd enjoy having you as my partner."

Ruth stared at him. "Are you running a fever? Were you out in the sun too long today?"

Josh chortled. "I'm fine. After being around you, I've learned life is a lot more than saddles and grit. I got so entrenched in making my way through each day, I didn't pause to appreciate what surrounded me. God's used you to open my eyes."

"I've never received a finer compliment. Thank you." She waited a moment, then mused, "Even if I want to make a gift to you, I have to legally pursue my inheritance. If I withdraw the claim, your father will still have equal footing with you."

"That's true."

"Oh, I apologize! I'm so sorry, Josh. I didn't mean—" Ruth groaned.

"You haven't offended me. What are you upset about?"

"I didn't want you to infer that I was saying your father is your equal in any way. When it comes to integrity, intelligence, and character, you stand head and shoulders above him."

The corners of his mouth tightened.

"I haven't been around many men, Josh." She decided to be bold. "Of any of the men I've ever known, none could compare to you when it comes to your sense of ethics or the way you walk with the Lord. At times when I've been upset, you've held me up in prayer and lent me your strength. Please know how deeply I admire you."

Josh stared at her in silence. Ruth wished she could tell what he was thinking. *Then again, maybe I don't.*

"Let me escort you back to the house." He stood, helped her rise, and blew out the lamp.

Tucking the letter up her sleeve, Ruth sought to change the topic. "What do you think of the cabin now?"

"I think Hilda will love living out here."

"I agree," McCain said from the front step.

CHAPTER TWENTY-FIVE

McCain invited himself in. Crossing the threshold, he looked around the dim room. "I would have never imagined this place could look so inviting. You've done a wondrous job, my dear."

"Thank you," Ruth murmured, wondering how long he'd been standing there. *Intent as I was telling Josh how I felt, I didn't pay any attention. I've had the creepy feeling that someone has been following me, watching me. It's McCain.* Josh moved so close to her just then that she could feel the tension singing through his muscles.

McCain drew nearer. His eyes narrowed. "Have you been weeping, Ruth?"

She nodded.

"I understand. Seeing all of these lovely belongings probably made you homesick." He patted her arm.

Ruth wanted to jerk back and rub away his touch.

"My, my. If I'm not mistaken, that chair is a Chippendale. So is the highboy." McCain walked away and stood directly in front of the furniture. "Exquisite work. Flame mahogany and those wonderful cabriole legs." He patted the front of the highboy just as he had patted her arm—a possessive move that made her shiver. As he continued to stare at the piece he said, "You must be relieved that the shipment arrived. Quality like this is unmistakable and worth a small fortune."

He's not interested in my feelings. All he wants to do is assess the value of my belongings. I don't care—as long as he leaves me alone.

Josh looked down at her. "I hope you find comfort in surrounding yourself with familiar things."

"They do hold many memories. Happy memories." She slipped her hand into the crook of Josh's elbow. He understood the real value in her inheritance lay in reminiscences.

Josh covered her hand with his—a simple act that reassured her he would rescue her from his father. Casting a quick glance about the room, he said, "It's getting dark."

McCain wheeled around, returned to Ruth's side, and gave her a chilling smile. "I'll take you back to the house. I'm sure my son has several chores that demand his attention."

She clung tighter to Josh's arm and looked up at him, silently pleading with him to spare her his father's attention.

"Actually, Dad, I wanted to discuss a few things with Ruth." Josh started walking, and she hastened to fall into step alongside him. "You mentioned commissioning church windows."

"Yes! Yes, I did." Relieved that Josh gave her a topic, Ruth gushed, "It will make me so happy to have them. Do you know of an artisan who would take the commission?"

"I remember the St. Rose of Lima Church on 7th and K Street in Sacramento. The stained-glass windows were magnificent. Perhaps you could draft a letter of inquiry to the church."

Ruth came to a stop on the porch as Josh halted and motioned to his father. "Come on, Dad."

"You go on ahead. I'll nose around and see what the girls have done out here."

"No!" Ruth blurted out the word, then regretted it. She didn't want him prying around her house, but it was far preferable than having to be in his presence.

"Why not?"

Ruth couldn't concoct a single answer.

Josh smoothly said, "You know women, Dad. Ruth is probably planning a little housewarming party. You'll ruin her surprise if you snoop."

"Far be it from me to ruffle feathers." McCain exited the cabin, and Josh shut the door. McCain offered Ruth his arm.

"Forgive me." She swept her hand downward. "I'll need one hand free. When I had this dress made, my shoes must have had slightly higher heels." She tucked her hand back into Josh's arm, then filled the other with a fistful of her skirts.

"We can't have you trip again." McCain fell in step beside her. "I've never forgiven myself for not balancing you better that first day we went to town."

"Let's not dwell on that." Ruth turned to Josh. "About the windows . . . I suppose we need to have measurements."

"You're just full of plans, aren't you?" McCain's chuckle sounded forced. "A library and stained-glass windows."

"Mama always said knowledge and beauty are never wasted."

"I'm sure she wasn't thinking about buildings when she said that, my dear; she must have been referring to you."

Ruth could feel the tension in Josh's arm. "Actually, she was referring to a breathtakingly illustrated book. I'll have to share that book with you, Josh. I'm positive I packed it."

"You still have boxes to unpack." His voice held certainty, though he'd not actually seen the other rooms in the cabin.

"My son's roamed about the place?" McCain's voice sounded sharp.

"Of course not!" Ruth gave the older man an outraged look. "I resent the insinuation that I'd ever allow a man such liberties."

"Now, now." McCain flashed her a conciliatory smile. "I wouldn't ever think such a thing of you, my dear."

Ruth scowled at him. "You shouldn't think such a thing of

your son, either. Josh is too much of a gentleman to ever compromise a woman's reputation."

McCain pretended not to have heard her. He raised his hand and waved. "Toledo! I need to talk with you." He stalked off without saying another word.

Josh stared at his father's back. "Ruth, I don't care what you have to do to avoid it. Don't be alone with him."

Josh stopped by the cottage the next afternoon to check in on Ruth. Laney stood by the mantel, arranging several little knickknacks. Skirts spread about her, Ruth sat on the floor, pulling books from a crate.

"Hello, fair maidens," he said by way of greeting.

Laney let out a surprised shriek and dropped a small porcelain figurine. It bounced on the plush Turkish carpet, then landed on the edge of Ruth's skirts. "Josh! You scared me half to death!"

"You look very much alive," he teased. Turning to Ruth, he pulled a bouquet of wildflowers from behind his back. "I thought these would look nice somewhere around here."

Ruth's jaw dropped and she went pale as Laney gasped.

"What's wrong?" Josh strode over to Ruth.

"You didn't leave those other flowers on the doorstep this morning?" Laney asked in a baffled voice.

"What flowers?" Josh scowled. He followed Ruth's gaze and spotted a vase full of blossoms over on the table he'd brought. "I had nothing to do with those."

"Ruth, you have two men giving you flowers!" Laney clasped her hands together at her breast. "This is so exciting!"

"No, it's not exciting." Ruth's voice shook.

Josh stared at her. *Is she upset with me? Does she think I'm trying to court her because she has an inheritance?*

Ruth set aside the book she'd been holding and rose. Even

through the plethora of her petticoats, Josh could tell she nearly stomped each step. She went to the table, picked up the vase, and slipped past Josh at the door. A second later, the flowers sailed through the air and Ruth returned. She forced a smile. "Thank you, Joshua. Your flowers are beautiful. They will look nice in here."

He popped them into the vase and waited until Ruth set the arrangement on the table. "I'm glad you like them."

"I've never seen a lovelier bouquet." Ruth stepped back from the table.

Laney scooted beside her. "Neither have I."

Stepping up to them, Josh said, "You can enjoy them more later. For now, why don't we all spare Hilda from having to track us down for lunch?"

Laney turned sideways and clasped Ruth's hand. "Does Josh know?"

"Know what?" he demanded.

"Daddy," Laney said. "He's been acting oddly. Mostly about Ruth. I think the flowers must have been from him."

"The only flowers I see are the ones Josh brought." Ruth's jaw jutted forward, and the stubborn glint in her eye dared anyone to challenge her.

"I'm glad you like them." He reached up and gently tugged on one of her loose curls. "Though they're not half as pretty as you."

Laney looked from Ruth to him and back again. She squared her shoulders and pasted on a smile. "If we weren't so busy, I'd insist upon our painting the arrangement."

"You have been busy." Josh cleared his throat. "But perhaps after lunch you could make a little time to go visit the O'Sullivans. I'm sure they'd love to see you."

"No." Ruth shook her head. "I need to move everything here. Today."

"Of course you do." Laney flashed Josh a smile. "I'll bet my brother can spare someone to bring your trunks over. In fact, I'm going to invite myself to be your very first guest and spend the night with you."

Ruth looked at him. "We could pay a visit to the O'Sullivans tomorrow."

He nodded. "I'll take you over."

Josh didn't want Ruth away from his protection, and he argued with himself as he personally moved Ruth's trunks to her father's old cabin. *With Hilda and Laney here, Ruth has sufficient protection from Dad. He can't very well make a move when they're at her side. But Ruth is the woman I love. I need to protect her.*

"Josh," Laney whispered to him as Ruth went into her bedchamber to put things away, "I don't understand Daddy's behavior, but he's far too old for Ruth. He doesn't love her like you do."

"You're pretty smart for being so young."

"Nothing would make me happier than to have a sister. When are you going to ask Ruth to marry you?"

"Soon. We have some problems to iron out first."

The problems grew more complicated by supper. Dad had gone to town and came back with a friend. "Boaz Crocker is a cousin to one of the men who's intending to lay a railroad to the east," Dad said by way of introduction.

"Crocker." Josh shook his hand.

Dad smiled at Crocker. "My daughter will be down shortly. She's recently returned from finishing school."

"I'm sure she's a very accomplished young lady."

Josh smiled. "Actually, Laney and Ruth have been over at the cabin all afternoon."

"Yes, I can believe it." Dad nodded. "Elaine is helping Ruth decide on how to decorate her place. She's excellent with all of those domestic details."

Laney and Ruth came through the front door and stopped cold at the sight of a guest. Still in the frocks they'd been wearing all day, they looked rumpled. Ruth's hair had long since escaped their pins and tumbled around her in a wild profusion of curls. Hectic color filled her cheeks, making her look all the more fetching.

"Elaine Louise." Dad's voice held uncommon censure. "We've a guest. Go make yourself presentable."

"She's washed up. That's good enough." Hilda trundled over, wiping her hands on her apron. "Supper's on the table. Waiting on a girl to go fancy up's gonna make everything go cold."

Crocker stepped forward. "I'd be happy to escort you to supper, Miss Elaine."

"No, no. That's Ruth Caldwell." Dad jerked him to the side. "This is my daughter, Laney."

"Miss Elaine." Mr. Crocker gave her a polite nod and offered her his arm.

Josh cut Dad off and walked Ruth to the table. After seating her, he took the chair immediately beside her. "Dad tells me Mr. Crocker's cousin is one of the gentlemen who's considering a railroad to the east."

"It's more than a consideration. The decision was made." Crocker took a sip of coffee, then added, "There are those who will yet need to be convinced of the need, but the railroad is an unstoppable force."

"No one needs to convince me," Dad said. "It's a brilliant concept. Elaine, pass Mr. Crocker the bread."

"Yes, Daddy."

Josh's eyes narrowed. As supper progressed, Dad manipulated the conversation shamelessly. He alternated between promoting the railroad and boasting about Laney's accomplishments.

Mr. Crocker seemed like an affable fellow, but Laney rarely looked up from her plate. When he tried to engage her in conversation, she'd barely devote more than a sentence to an answer. Dad urged Laney to refill Mr. Crocker's cup and to pass him various dishes. Clearly, Dad was trying to play matchmaker, and Laney wanted no part of it.

As Laney's disinterest became apparent, Mr. Crocker turned his attention toward Ruth. "Your name is far more common than mine, yet I've never dined with a Ruth before now." He flashed her a charming smile. "Boaz and Ruth. Imagine that."

Ruth set down her fork. "Yes, my name is quite common. Please excuse me. It must be the excitement of moving, but I'm suddenly fatigued."

"Me too." Laney hopped out of her seat.

"Ruth, please feel free to go ahead and retire." Dad gave her a smile that made Josh grit his teeth. "Laney, you've been working on a charming tune on the piano. Stay downstairs for a while and play for us men."

"Daddy, I promised Ruth I'd spend the night with her."

"Go ahead, Laney," Josh said. "It's important to keep promises."

"Thank you." Relief filled Laney's voice. "We'll just get a few necessities and be off."

Hilda brought out big wedges of cherry pie. Josh wolfed down his slice, but he barely tasted it. When he'd discovered Dad's embezzlement, he'd lost all respect for him. Now Dad was crossing a line Josh never imagined he'd traverse: He was trying to bully Ruth and Laney into marriages they didn't want.

"Well, then," Dad drummed the tabletop, "with the women retiring, we men can enjoy an after-dinner cigar."

"Don't mind if I do." Crocker stood.

When Crocker preceded Dad onto the veranda, Dad growled under his breath at Josh, "You're ruining everything!"

"We're partners." Josh stared him in the eyes. "If you have a plan, you need to run it by me first." He heard the girls coming down the stairs and raised his voice. "Crocker, you'll have to excuse me. I'm going to walk the ladies over to the cabin."

Relief poured through Ruth when Josh entered the kitchen. She'd heard footsteps and worried that McCain was going to appear.

Features taut, Josh strode to her side and swiped the valise Laney had packed. "Let's go."

Laney all but ran to the front door. Ruth and Josh hastened to join her, and Josh murmured under his breath, "We're going to stroll to the cabin. Slow and steady. Got it?"

Laney nodded.

Wanting to calm Laney, Ruth gave Josh a mock look of censure. "We're ladies, Joshua. You don't think we'd ever deign to move in anything other than a sophisticated glide, do you?"

Josh's grin and Laney's tense giggles made her silliness worthwhile. Ruth accepted Josh's arm, and they dawdled all of the way to the cabin. Once there, Ruth promptly invited him in.

Wilting into a chair, Laney said, "I don't know what's gotten into Daddy. He's not himself. He's told me I'm too young to marry, but he's flinging me at that stranger. He's chasing after Ruth, too." She heaved a sigh, then tacked on, "Ruth, you're a wonderful woman, so I don't want you to take this the wrong way; but I think Daddy's just after you for your money."

Josh led Ruth to the settee. As soon as she sat down, he took the place beside her. To her surprise, he reached over and clasped her hand in his. Rough and strong, his fingers closed about hers. "Dad's behavior is erratic," Josh confirmed.

"I'm glad I'm spending the night here."

Ruth said to Josh, "I suggested Laney bring her riding skirt. We'll go over to the O'Sullivan's tomorrow, just as we planned."

"Excellent." Josh flashed her a lopsided grin. "I think it would be nice for you girls to have a private breakfast here tomorrow—to celebrate Ruth's being in her cabin. If it's an early one, I can meet you in the stable and take you over to the O'Sullivans' before I dig into the day's work."

"We'll be ready," Ruth promised, knowing she'd be up with the roosters to avoid McCain.

"We make a good team." Josh squeezed her hand lightly.

Ruth looked at him, willing him to see the trust and gratitude she felt for him. His gaze held hers steadily.

"You two know something. You have a secret." Laney leaned forward. "What is it?"

Josh didn't look away. His hazel eyes radiated warmth. "I haven't kept how I feel about Ruth a secret from you, sis."

The world tilted crazily. Ruth could scarcely believe what he'd said.

"That's not it." Laney hopped up and started pacing. "You two know something. Josh has kept my secret from everyone for years, and he's got that same air about him now—only it's the two of you who trade that confidential look."

"Laney Lou, honey..."

Laney shook her forefinger at Josh. "Don't you talk to me as if I were a little child. I'm not. Since Ruth's come, I've learned a lot— not just about reading, but about myself. It's time you stopped shielding me."

Josh rubbed from the bridge of his nose to his hairline with the heel of his hand. "Galen said much the same thing—that you'd grow up if I let you."

"Galen's right," Laney declared. "And if you discussed this issue with him, you can certainly tell me about it."

Ruth tried to pull her hand away. "I'll leave you two—"

"No, you won't." Josh snatched her hand back. He looked at Laney and said, "Dad's bookkeeping for the ranch is..."

Laney gasped. "Did he make a mistake? Are we poor?"

"No, we're not poor." He heaved a deep breath, "If anything, the ranch is doing far better than I'd been led to believe."

Ruth admired Josh for his tactful choice of words. He'd been more concerned for Laney's feelings than his own hurt and phrased the matter in such a way that the impact wouldn't be so harsh.

Ruth rubbed her left thumb across the back of his hand, hoping he'd sense her support.

Brows knit, Laney said, "Dad's been cheating you? Josh, how dreadful!"

"I hoped you wouldn't have to find out. I know how much you love Dad."

"Yes, I love him—but I love you, too! What he's done is wrong."

"He's not aware that I know yet, Laney, and I don't want him to. Soon he'll be confronted. It'll get ugly; embezzlement is a crime."

"But Daddy's always been so generous."

Josh shook his head. "He's been paying the hands and Hilda all less than we agreed upon."

Sinking into her chair, Laney gulped. "That's why Hilda always says he's so cheap."

"Josh already plans to give Hilda and the hands a raise and their back pay," Ruth said. "When this is all ironed out, your brother is the only one who will bear the cost. His sense of integrity is impressive."

"That's not so." Josh shook his head. "Laney, Ruth is part owner of the Broken P. She's been wronged, too."

Laney's jaw dropped open, then she squeaked, "That's why Daddy's after you. Remember in that newspaper article? It said a wife can't testify against her husband. Daddy wants your money, and he wants to keep you quiet."

"No one," Ruth said in a wry tone, "has ever been able to silence me."

A short while later, Josh said a prayer for them to all have wisdom and solace. As he took his leave, he said, "I'll meet you in the morning at the stable."

After he left, Laney burst into tears. "Don't you dare tell Josh I cried. He'll think I'm a baby if you do. But I'm so mad! Josh works so hard. How could Daddy cheat him?"

"I don't know the reasons why he's done the things he has."

"Well, I don't care what reasons he has. It was wrong. And it's wrong that Daddy is cheating you, too. I'm utterly embarrassed this has happened."

"Laney, I'm not concerned in the least about what it might have cost me. What I care about is how hurt Josh is and you are. For now, Josh asked that we keep this between us. Let's do our very best to pretend everything is okay. He's counting on us."

Drying her tears, Laney nodded. "We'd better start talking about something else so Hilda doesn't suspect anything when she gets here."

Ruth and Laney busied themselves by arranging books on the bookshelf, then turned in for the night. Early the next morning, Hilda woke them. "Josh said you're to meet him at the stable. I brought some tarts and cheese for your breakfast. Best you girls get going. McCain and that guest he's got sat on the veranda, making plans last night. I didn't like the sounds of it, and you're better off keeping far away from them."

Ruth skimmed into her clothes and crammed pins into her hair willy-nilly. Laney managed to get dressed, comb, plait, and neatly coil her hair in the same length of time. As they stepped inside the stable, Ruth said, "I'm looking forward to visiting Mrs. O'Sullivan. I wonder how her husband's faring."

McCain's voice rasped from the nearest stall, "What are you girls doing out here this early?"

CHAPTER TWENTY-SIX

———✦———

Josh had already saddled the horses and led them outside, behind the stable. He'd hoped to catch the girls and ride off without Dad realizing they'd left. The minute he overheard his father's voice, Josh knew this was going to be sticky. He headed around the stable to protect the girls.

"Daddy, you like to scared me half to death," Laney scolded.

"You didn't answer my question, Laney. What are you girls doing out here?"

"The O'Sullivans are expecting us today." Ruth's voice sounded crisp and determined.

"You can't go today. You'll have to arrange for another time. We have a guest."

"Mr. Crocker is your guest, Mr. McCain. I fail to see any reason our presence is required."

"Ruth, you wound me." Dad actually sounded hurt. "Surely you must understand that the woman of the home radiates its welcome."

"Laney already met Mr. Crocker and was his supper companion last night. She's fulfilled her obligation. Now I—"

Dad interrupted, "You need to come for breakfast, too, Ruth. You represent our home as well."

Josh strode up. "Are you girls ready to go?"

"Yes!" came the eager duet.

"They're not going anywhere." Dad's jaw jutted forward. "Breakfast—"

Josh made a dismissive gesture. "I saw Hilda just a few minutes ago. She said the girls already ate."

"They can sip tea. It's the way I intended things to go. Ruth's still supposed to come for meals." He nodded to himself, then smiled at Ruth. "I understood why you chose to relocate. The proper thing was for you to be in the cabin while we courted."

"Courted!" she repeated in a horrified tone.

Ignoring her reaction, Dad continued on. "As you're in mourning for your mother, we'll have a private wedding here in a few weeks."

"We will not!" Ruth glared at him. "I don't know where you came up with this notion, but you can put it away this instant. I'm not marrying you."

"Of course you are."

"Ruth's not interested, Dad."

"Stay out of this, son. It's none of your business."

Josh slid his arm around Ruth's waist. Nestling her close, he looked down into her eyes. His voice softened as he said, "The simple fact of the matter is, I love Ruth, and she's going to be my wife."

She'd been trembling when he drew her close. At his announcement, Josh felt Ruth melt into his side. Her eyes didn't flash with anger; they shone—but was it with gratitude, or love? Tearing his attention from her to his father, he said, "I'm sure you'll enjoy having Ruth as your daughter-in-law."

A tense smile stretched Dad's face. "I reckon any woman would rather have a strong young buck instead of a crippled old goat."

"I'm sure you wish us every happiness." Josh stared at his father.

Dad nodded curtly. "As I've said all along, Ruth is like family. Things can continue on as they always have."

"So let's go, Laney," Ruth said. "We always go visit the O'Sullivans."

"No, no." Dad shook his head and stretched out his hand for Laney. "Mr. Crocker will be coming to the breakfast table any minute now. You hurry on upstairs and put on your pink dress."

"I can't. That dress is ruined. Besides, I don't like Mr. Crocker." Laney shuddered.

"You'll learn to like him." Dad's announcement held great certainty.

Josh wondered why his father had been so quick to scare away any other suitor and enthusiastically embraced Mr. Crocker.

Dad continued. "I promised your mother you'd marry well. He's from a fine family. Rich."

Laney shuffled back a step. "Daddy, I think——"

"Sweetheart, your job is to look pretty. I'll think for you. Mr. Crocker is a good man. You need to come to breakfast in one of your better dresses—this riding skirt won't do. Ruth and Josh will be there, too. We'll all share a nice meal, and you'll come to see how pleasantly things will work out for all of us."

Keeping one arm around Ruth and wrapping the other about Laney's shoulders, Josh led them toward the door as he said, "Dad, you and I will speak later. I'm taking the girls over to the O'Sullivans' now."

Toledo stepped into the wide-open doorway. Scratching his elbow, he said, "Boss, a couple of the hands wanna hit town. You were in Sacramento last payday. We figure to get our pay now."

Josh took advantage of the diversion. He sped the girls around the stable and off to the neighbors'. Ruth barely said a word the whole ride. Josh held her back and let Laney take the lead as they approached Galen's. "Are you all right?"

She nodded. "Are you?"

"I meant every word I said back there. I love you. It wasn't how I pictured proposing."

Her eyes suddenly took on a sparkle. "You still haven't." She kicked her horse and galloped off.

Josh sat in his saddle, threw back his head, and belted out a laugh. He yelled, "This is the last time I let you get away!"

Saturday morning, Ruth accompanied Hilda to the main house. Supper the previous evening had been strained. McCain acted jovial, but something about the watchfulness in his eyes made Ruth's skin crawl. She'd been glad to leave and spend the night in her cabin, but leaving Laney in the big house bothered her. By coming early, she could slip upstairs and come back down with Laney—thereby insulating her from Mr. Crocker.

Hilda plowed into the kitchen and stopped abruptly. Ruth bumped into her.

"Good morning, Hilda." Josh sat at the kitchen table with none other than Mr. Crocker. Both men rose as Josh added, "We were up early, so I put on some coffee."

Hilda sniffed. "Scalded it. You never could brew a decent pot, cowboy."

Mr. Crocker chuckled. "He's one up on me. I wouldn't know how to make a pot at all."

Josh gestured toward a chair. "Ruth, come have a seat. We need to talk for a few minutes."

Shaking her head, she said, "I need to go help Laney."

"You'll be helping her more by staying." Josh pulled out the chair.

Ruth shot him a quizzical look, but accepted the seat.

Mr. Crocker lounged back into his place and said quietly, "I'd appreciate it if you'd let Miss Laney know I'm already interested in another woman. Regardless of what Mr. McCain seems to have planned, I came here strictly on railroad business."

"He showed me a picture of his intended," Josh said.

"I assure you, business was my only goal in coming here. My cousin asked me to come here because a certain Mr. Farnsworth made inquiries in Sacramento. Due to his interest, we looked through the agreements for land acquisition. Mr. McCain put forth that he was the sole owner of the Broken P."

"The man's a skunk." Hilda thumped another pot of coffee onto the stove.

"The railroad's already signed agreements along the proposed route with several people," Josh told Ruth.

Crocker nodded and winced. "Which puts us in a difficult spot. By agreeing to plot a line across a specific portion of the O'Sullivans' land, it means we have to lay track straight through the Broken P."

"The O'Sullivans have already agreed?" Ruth stared at him.

"No, they haven't. They've pledged an agreement if, and only if, the specified route is used. They knew it would be contingent on this ranch's cooperation and refused to sign anything until this got settled."

"You're not gonna stick a bunch of rails straight down Kelly O'Sullivan's garden are you?" Hilda glowered at Mr. Crocker.

"No, ma'am. You have my word that we won't."

"Humpf. Good thing." Hilda started cracking eggs into a bowl.

"I have authority to amend copies of the land purchase agreement," Crocker said.

"But we're not able to sign anything now," Josh said. He cast a quick smile at Ruth that melted her heart. "Until Ruth's inheritance is clarified, the ownership of the Broken P remains questionable."

Crocker nodded. "I understood that to be so. I wanted to ask you to stop by my office in Sacramento on Tuesday, after the judge hears your case."

"Our case is being heard by the circuit judge, week after next," Ruth said.

"I'm afraid not." Crocker's brow furrowed. "The docket showed Mr. McCain requested the change to the capital. Notification was mailed out."

Hilda picked up a fistful of silverware and backed through the door into the dining room.

"Dad's been picking up the mail." Josh's voice sounded gritty. "He obviously planned on our not showing up."

"Well," Ruth said as she reached over and put her hand on Josh's arm, "I always did like to surprise people."

Josh stood and extended his arm across the table. "We'll see you on Tuesday. In the meantime I'd appreciate it if you'd not disclose the fact that we are aware of what my father's done."

Mr. Crocker rose and shook hands. "Agreed."

"You got a minute, McCain?" Hilda's voice came from the dining room. "We need to have a sit-down and talk over the grocery budget. It's stayed the same for years, but prices are goin' up."

Josh jerked his head toward the back. He and Mr. Crocker hastened outside. Ruth snatched the coffee mug from where Josh had been seated and took a quick gulp as Hilda bustled through the door with McCain close behind her.

"What's wrong with you, girl?" McCain's eyes narrowed.

Hilda let out a cackle. "I didn't make the coffee."

"Why are there two cups on the table?"

"You sayin' I'm not allowed to have a cup?" Hilda glowered at him.

Ruth stood and reached for the other mug. "Believe me, Hilda, you don't want to have any of this." Dumping the coffee down the sink, she sighed. "I'm glad we have you, Hilda. Left to our own devices, I'm afraid we'd all starve."

"Yep." Hilda shook her finger at McCain. "That's why you need to allow me more money for the groceries." She turned to Ruth. "Go on up and pull Laney out of bed. That handsome Mr.

Crocker is going to be at the breakfast table. With my good food and coffee, he'll be in a fine mood. It wouldn't hurt her to pay him a little attention."

"Make sure she puts on one of her prettiest dresses," McCain ordered.

Ruth scooted out of the room and headed up the stairs. "Lord, thank you for Hilda!"

Reassured that Mr. Crocker wouldn't fulfill her father's plan to propose, Laney relaxed at breakfast. She even managed to sound disappointed when he announced that he needed to take his leave and travel back to Sacramento.

"I'm sure there are a few things you and Ruth would like from town," McCain mused. "Ruth shipped many fine things, but there are always little items one forgets."

"I can't think of a thing I need. Josh took care of providing a lamp table."

Josh patted her hand. "We ought to go in today, Ruth. I'm sure you'll want to decorate the room we'll be sharing."

"Oh, yes! His room is so dreary. Brown coverlet. Brown curtains." Laney shuddered dramatically. "I declare, it looks like the inside of a cave."

"Actually..." Josh drew out the word. "I've decided what we need to do is go to Sacramento. I need to find you a pretty ring."

"A gown!" Laney beamed. "She needs a bridal gown."

"I somehow got the notion that California didn't make such a fuss over weddings. I pictured a calico dress and a handful of wild flowers."

"No, no, dear." McCain shook his head. "Things must be done correctly. We'll find out who the best seamstress is in Sacramento, then send for her. She can stay here and work on the piece."

"Oh." Ruth frowned. "I rather hoped to be able to travel to Sacramento. It sounds so exciting!"

"If I might suggest," Mr. Crocker said, "the two of you could plan that for your honeymoon. Spend a little time in Sacramento—

maybe stay at the Orleans Hotel and take in a show at the Eagle Theater. I understand the *Chrysopolis* sidewheeler is *the* conveyance for elite bridal parties. You could take it up to San Francisco."

"The *Chrysopolis*?" Josh asked.

Crocker nodded. "I've been on it. Magnificent vessel. Mahogany and red plush appointments, lavish meals. Even a band. First-rate travel."

"Dandy!" McCain slapped the table. "I tell you what—I'm going to Sacramento this week. You kids talk to the parson tomorrow and give me a date. I'll make all the arrangements for your bridal trip."

"Ruth and I can't possibly go to town today now." Laney blotted her mouth. "We need to sit down and make lists."

"Lists?" Ruth felt a sinking feeling. She'd always detested all of the pomp and etiquette.

"Of course. A guest list. A list of what you'll need for your trousseau. Once you decide on a date, we'll determine which flowers will be in bloom. Then, we'll have to confer with Hilda about the menu for the bridal supper."

"See?" McCain nodded toward Crocker. "My Elaine is outstanding with organizing such events."

An hour later, Ruth threw herself across the bed and moaned. "Laney, I hoped you were just concocting a reason why we didn't have to go to town. I didn't want to get wrapped up in all of these!" She waved her hand toward the pile of lists Laney had going.

Laney pouted, "All right. We can stop planning the details for the wedding."

Ruth sat up.

"But we need to decide on what kind of engagement party to throw."

Ruth flopped back down. "Laney, I don't want all of that fuss and bother. I'll end up doing something gauche and embarrassing myself and Josh."

"Nonsense."

Grasping at straws, Ruth propped up on one elbow. "The whole thing has to be subdued. I know I'm not wearing black, but I'm in mourning."

"Well, you're still going to have a magnificent gown. Your mother made you promise not to wear black. Queen Victoria made wearing white wedding gowns very fashionable. We'll commission a white gown."

"I have one already. When Bernadette sent the furniture, she included the rest of my clothes. I haven't worn that gown yet because I just know the first time I put it on, I'll spill something all down the front."

"You'll look beautiful." Laney clasped her hands and looked at the ceiling in rapture. "Ever since I was a little girl, I've pretended I was a bride. Mama cut down her own bridal gown and let me traipse around in it."

"She didn't save it in a cedar chest for you to wear when you married?"

"No. It was from her first marriage. Mama was a widow, and she always said Daddy rescued her from being penniless and alone. Isn't that romantic?"

"You could write a dime novel about it someday."

Laney shook her head. "I couldn't. They're supposed to live happily ever after. Daddy's never been the same since Mama passed on." Gathering up the lists, Laney brightened her voice. "We need to go chose what dress you'll wear to church tomorrow. You'll be the center of attention when everyone hears you're going to be Josh's bride."

In no time at all, gowns covered every available surface back in the cabin. Laney declared she needed to survey them all in order to determine what Ruth needed for a trousseau. Standing amidst the sea of extravagantly full skirts, ruffles, bows, and a rainbow of colors, Ruth declared, "I won't need another stitch for a decade!"

"You do have a wonderful wardrobe." Laney fluffed the short, off-the-shoulder sleeves of a silver-shot pale blue party gown. "You should definitely take this on your honeymoon. I'm surprised that some of these gowns are so . . . practical."

Memories of sewing at Mama's bedside swamped Ruth. She ran her hand down the abundant gathers of a brown-, cream-, and green-striped frock. "Now that I look back, I realize Mama was trying to outfit me for coming west. She chose patterns and fabric, and I'd sit by her and stitch by the hour."

"I envy you." Laney clasped Ruth's hand. "Your mother depended on you in her last days for comfort and companionship. Me? I was so flighty and emotional, Mama's friends kept taking me away."

"Mama sent me away to schools until the very end," Ruth reminded her.

"But you and I were alike—as obedient daughters, we did what our mothers wanted. The difference is, in those last months your mother drew you close and found solace in your presence. You have that gift, Ruth—to make others feel good about themselves. Even with everything going wrong around here, you've been our strength and comfort."

"God's been our strength and comfort," Ruth corrected her gently. She smiled. "You, Josh, and I are sort of like Shadrach, Meshach, and Abednego. We're all standing together in the fiery furnace and the Lord is keeping us safe."

"Well, their clothes didn't get burned." Laney let out a sigh and turned around. "Though if a few of these were singed, it would make it far easier to decide what you ought to wear tomorrow."

"You once said Josh's favorite color is green." Ruth fingered a deep green gown with black braid embellishments.

"That's far too serious-looking. Save that for when the judge hears your case in court. What about this one?" Laney held up a white-dotted pale blue gown.

Ruth wrinkled her nose. "That never fit right." Pressing the sides against Laney, she mused, "I'll bet it suits you perfectly. Try it on!"

"Oh, I *couldn't!*"

"Nonsense." Ruth spun Laney around and started unfastening her buttons. "Laney, you're going to need a dress. There's something I have to tell you. . . ."

CHAPTER TWENTY-SEVEN

———◆———

I've written a bank draft already," Dad said at Sunday afternoon supper. "You can set out in the morning and ought to reach the Ortiz spread by Tuesday evening. The agreement is for your choice of one of three bulls. It'll be good to expand the bloodline here."

Josh nodded to acknowledge his father's comments. The depth of his father's betrayal hit hard. He planned this little buying trip to coincide with the court date he'd secretly scheduled. He'd been masterful at manipulating everything.

"Something's wrong." Dad glanced at how Ruth and Laney were pushing food around on their plates. "They're not eating, and you're gritting your molars so hard, your cheek is twitching."

"You know I don't like discussing business on Sundays, Dad. Besides, the topic you've chosen isn't suited for delicate ears."

"Really, Daddy." Laney set down her fork. "How could you spoil Ruth's engagement luncheon by talking about stinky old bulls?"

"You girls will have to excuse me," Dad said in an oily tone. "I was just trying to make sure everything was set before I leave."

"Where are you going?" Ruth's voice sounded steady. Josh

admired her for the control she showed. Though she couldn't seem to swallow a bite, his sweetheart hadn't done a thing to tip Dad off that they were wise to his plans.

"I'm going to Sacramento, remember?" Dad smiled. "With your head in the clouds over your engagement, I can see how you let that little fact slip your mind. Anyway, the last time I was there, you girls and Hilda went over to the O'Sullivans' and helped do a lot of canning and such. I've told Hilda I want you to all go and do that again. Josh tells me Cullen's faring poorly, and they'll undoubtedly appreciate your help."

Laney folded her hands in her lap. "After church today, Mrs. O'Sullivan invited us to come quilt."

"There. Now wasn't that nice? It proves you're meant to go over there. Son, you'd better write down the name of that ship so I can book your wedding trip."

Ruth reached up her sleeve and pulled out a knotted hanky. Carefully working the knot free, she said, "Laney and I have been discussing the wedding. She tells me the tailor you and Josh use is still in Sacramento. I'd love for Josh to have a new suit. Could you please order one for me?"

Dad accepted the double eagle and nodded. "Of course I will."

Josh noted he didn't say a word about the fact that twenty dollars would easily buy three of the finest suits, a dozen custom-made shirts, and a handful of ties.

"Ruth, dear," Dad said as he pocketed the gleaming coin, "it's not safe for you to have this kind of money just sitting around."

"Oh, I'm not worried about that at all. As you've said, we're all family. No one else has access to my things. Besides, even if they did, they wouldn't know where to look." She looked at Laney, covered her mouth, and giggled.

Laney giggled, too. Her eyes sparkled. "Should we tell them?"

"You've never been able to keep a secret," Dad said to Laney.

"Oh, well." Ruth reached for her teacup. "If you must know, I slipped a few of those pretty coins in the middle of my button jar."

"Ruth," Josh said in a warning tone.

"Oh, there weren't many, Josh." She waved her hand back and forth. "Four or seven or eight. I thought it would be too big of a bother to stop by the bank whenever I wanted to buy something."

"You and I are going to have to work on keeping secrets," Josh said to Ruth. He rose from the table. "Why don't we go for a stroll?"

"That's so romantic," Laney sighed.

Ruth frowned at Laney. "You've had too much excitement for today. Maybe you ought to take a little nap."

"That's a good idea," Josh said. He didn't want Laney alone with Dad. "You still haven't fully recovered from that concussion."

"I was going to have Laney help me pack for my trip," Dad said. "She always tells me I'm atrocious at matching things."

Hilda started clearing away the dishes. "I can toss things into a valise for you. Don't know why you suddenly gotta be fancified. Most often, you pop on over to Sacramento and just buy whatever you need."

"I'm trying to economize," Dad said. "I know the bride's family pays for the wedding, but there might be some added expenses."

"Humpf." Hilda took Laney's plate. "Why don't you scamper over and nap in my bedroom over at the cabin? It's a far sight cooler than yours. Since the window faces east, my chamber gets shady in the afternoon."

"That's a good plan." Dad nodded emphatically.

"I'll tuck her in," Ruth pledged. She was as good as her word. Josh stayed in the main room of the cabin and heard Ruth's voice as she soothed his sister into bed. Odd, how Ruth was the most vibrant, earthy woman he knew, yet she could focus her attention on someone and let them benefit from the calm in the middle of her storm.

She exited Hilda's chamber, shut the door, and took his hand. They set out on a stroll.

"Everything's arranged," Josh told her as they wandered down a grassy path. "We'll take the train tomorrow to Sacramento. Farnsworth will meet us there. He's reserved rooms for us at the Orleans Hotel. He'll use the afternoon to go over the case with us and brief you on what to expect when we go before the judge."

"I have the letter. I carry it everywhere with me."

Josh regretted that she needed to do so, but it showed prudence. Dad couldn't be trusted.

"Thank you for having Mr. Farnsworth do all of this. I'm afraid I would have just burst into court and made a scene."

"Rick Maltby is to get the results on the cigarette case tomorrow. Galen's going to stop by the Broken P just before midday to pick up Hilda and Laney. He'll take them to town, where Maltby will have a carriage. They'll meet us tomorrow evening."

"Laney's doing far better than I thought she would about your father, but I'd like to spare her from being in court. Couldn't we just have her stay at home with Hilda?"

"I've been on my knees about this, Ruth. Laney's caught somewhere between being a child and a woman. Galen's told me she'll never grow up until I let her. Then, there's your experience—you would have rather known the truth about your mother. It's been hard for you to accept, even though her motive was to lovingly shield you, that you weren't given a voice in the decision. I've decided to have Laney in Sacramento, and she can make a determination for herself."

Ruth stopped in a shady spot under a spreading oak. Tears glossed her eyes. "Josh, you said you've been on your knees. God answered your prayer by giving you wisdom."

Josh cupped her cheeks. "Thank you, Ruth. I'll let you in on a little secret." She smiled up at him. "Laney told me you've said you might never get married. Especially since you received your inheritance, I've worried you might think I'm courting your money instead of you."

"You'd never do such a thing."

"I'm glad you know that. But, you see, I'm not about to take a chance on the most precious thing that's ever happened to me. Ruthie, I'm not asking you to marry me. I'm telling you I'll never be whole unless you do. I love you, sweetheart."

"Your sister's very insightful. She once told me a man would have to earn my trust before he'd ever win my love. You've done just that, Josh. My heart is yours. I can't believe you'll really have me, but I'd be happy to be your wife."

He dipped his head and kissed her. As he straightened up, Ruth wore a bemused expression and gently lifted her fingers to touch her lips. "Oh my. Laney might have been wrong. A kiss like that would have won my heart."

Josh chuckled as Ruth blushed. "Honey, don't be embarrassed. Your habit of blurting out your thoughts can be quite flattering." They continued to wander along hand-in-hand, but when they reached the cabin again, Laney sat on the settee, sobbing broken-heartedly.

"What's wrong?" Ruth rushed to Laney's side.

Laney burrowed into Ruth's arms. "Daddy came to check on me. I was just drifting off, and I thought it was so sweet. He gave me a kiss on the cheek and tiptoed out."

"Your father loves you, Laney." Ruth petted Laney's hair. "Never doubt that."

"That's not the problem," Laney wailed. "Yesterday, when you had me try on that blue dress, you said we needed to convince Daddy that we trust him. That way, he wouldn't suspect anything was up."

Ruth nodded. "Telling him about the money in the button jar at lunch went well."

"It went too well!" Laney sucked in a choppy breath and gushed, "I heard Daddy go into your bedchamber, Ruth. After he left, I went into your room and found a tiny button on the floor."

Ruth cuddled Laney closer still. "I'm sorry, honey. I didn't think he'd—"

"He did. Daddy robbed you. We put eight coins in the jar

together. There are only three now."

Josh knelt and gathered Ruth and his sister into his arms. Sorrow mingled with his anger. *Lord, why?*

Laney let out a sigh and pulled back, leaving Josh to cradle Ruth close. Brushing away her tears, Laney said, "In my heart, I still hoped maybe the two of you were mistaken. Now I know better."

So that's why. "It's a bitter truth. But you needed to know, Laney." Josh squeezed Ruth. "We'll make it through this together, with God's help."

Monday morning, Ruth went to the main house with Hilda. As the housekeeper made breakfast, Ruth dipped a pen in the inkwell. "Being around Laney is rubbing off on me. I'm ready to make a list."

Hilda chortled as she opened the oven to take a peek at the coffee cake.

"Well, well! Aren't you cheery today." McCain tromped across the kitchen toward Ruth.

Ruth promptly ducked her head and started scribbling on the paper. "Paraffin. Don't we need more paraffin to seal jars?"

"We need it, that's for sure." Hilda poured a cup of coffee and shoved it at McCain. "So when do you leave?"

"After breakfast." He took a loud slurp of coffee. "Ruthie, is there anything you'd like me to bring back from Sacramento for you?"

"The suit for Josh is all I can think of."

"Did I hear my name?" Josh pushed through the door from the dining room. He promptly inserted himself between Ruth and his father. "Good morning, dearest." Suave as could be, he lifted her hand and pressed a kiss on the back of it.

Ruth still held her pen, and as a result, she ended up with

splotches of ink on her thumb and forefinger.

Josh gave her a warm smile. "Better a blot on your hand than on your soul."

McCain snorted. "That's no way to talk to a woman."

"I think it was charming," Ruth said. "So what are your plans for today, Josh?"

"He's going south to purchase the bull," his father said at once. "In fact, you ought to be leaving now. It'll be a lengthy trip."

"Let the cowboy eat before he leaves." Hilda emphatically cracked an egg on the edge of a sizzling skillet. "There isn't a man alive who doesn't do better with a full belly." She turned and leveled a gaze at Ruth. "Remember that. Men are cranky unless they eat well."

Ruth smiled. "I'm glad you're here, then. Your good cooking will soothe him when my schemes give him fits."

Hilda pulled the fragrant coffee cake out of the oven and flipped three eggs onto a plate. "Okay, cowboy. Wolf this down and hit the road. The sooner you leave, the sooner you'll get back. I'll keep Ruth busy so she doesn't mope too much while you're away."

"Between helping the O'Sullivans, planning the wedding, and figuring out what she needs for the library, our Ruth is going to be fully occupied." McCain nodded to himself. "Everything's working out well."

As soon as Josh finished eating, Ruth popped up. "I'll walk you out to the stable."

Hand in hand, they went toward the stable. Josh looked around and murmured, "I'll be scarce this morning, but I'll be back. Be ready to go."

Ruth bobbed her head. "I've already packed a little valise for myself and another for Laney. They're hiding beneath my bed."

"Did you include your mother's Bible? We need it for the marriage and birth record."

"I left my Bible on the bedside table so I could have devotions this morning. After you leave, I'll go put it in my valise."

Josh tilted her face to his. "Be careful."

"I will. You too."

As Felipe brought out Josh's mount, Josh pressed a soft kiss on her lips. "I'm going to be glad when this is all over."

"Me too."

Felipe cleared his throat. "All set?"

"Yep." Josh swung up into the saddle and winked audaciously at Ruth. "Don't miss me too much. I'll be back sooner than you think."

He rode out of sight, and Ruth went back to her cottage. If she failed to pack the Bible, it would be impossible to prove her identity. Mentally reviewing all of the details of her case, she opened the door and walked inside. Immediately an arm cinched around her waist and another slapped over her mouth.

Toledo rasped, "Stay quiet, and you'll stay alive."

CHAPTER TWENTY-EIGHT

Toledo managed to whisk her away to a ramshackle shed she'd never seen. Ruth fought him every last inch of the way, but his strength proved to be far greater than hers. Finally going limp, Ruth hoped he'd ease his hold. *Then I'll grab the knife from my sleeve.*

"You didn't forget her knife, did you?" McCain's voice came from the farthest corner of the shed.

Ruth's blood ran cold.

Josh's dad sauntered closer. His mouth bowed in an obscene parody of a smile. "I haven't forgotten a single thing about you. Laney thought it was scandalously wondrous that you carry a knife. She relished telling me all about it."

Deftly, Toledo pulled the knife from her sleeve, but he still held her tightly around the middle.

"I don't understand what this is all about."

"Really, Ruth. Don't play dumb this late in the game. You almost got me with that little tale about the coins in your button jar. Then I reconsidered. It was a test." His laugh was nothing more than an ugly bark. "Too bad I only figured it out after I'd helped myself."

"You took a coin?" Ruth moistened her lips. "Well, we're going to be family. If you need it, I don't mind." She glanced back at Toledo, then toward McCain. "I've figured it out. You go to the Nugget and gamble, don't you?" She forced a laugh. "I won't tell anyone about your little indiscretion. Compared to womanizing or getting drunk, I suppose a game of cards is just a mild diversion."

"The only words I want from you are written ones." He pushed her toward a shelf that jutted from the wall. A sheet of paper and the very pen and inkwell she'd used in the kitchen now rested on it. "You're going to write a will."

"No, I'm not."

"Ruthie," he cooed her name as he stroked her cheek once, then slapped her.

She gasped and bit her lip.

"Nothing fancy. Just a few lines. You're going to write that if you die, your dear friend Laney is your sole heir."

Ruth glowered at him.

"Of course, you'll date it from last week, before you and Josh decided to wed. No one will question it. Everyone knows how much you adore my daughter. Everyone does."

"I won't do it." *You'll kill me the instant after I sign my name.*

"Stubborn thing, isn't she?" McCain asked Toledo.

"Just like her old man," Toledo said.

McCain chortled softly. "In the end, he still lost out. You will, too, Ruth. Now cooperate."

"No." She lifted her chin. "Laney is going to come looking for me."

"Not for a good long while. You were just at the stable. I'll go back home and tell Hilda that you've gone ahead to the O'Sullivans'. She and Laney will dally, then head over there. By the time anyone figures you're missing, I'll have an alibi."

Lord, help me.

McCain's fingers dug into her arm, and he forced her closer to the shelf. "Pick up the pen. I'll dictate what you'll write."

Slowly, she lifted the pen, then dropped it and ground it into the earthen floor with the heel of her boot.

McCain raised his hand to strike her.

Toledo roughly jerked her. "Boss, time's short. You've gotta get on the train. I'll do what needs to be done. She won't be able to write if she's hurt."

"True. True." McCain lowered his hand. "First things first. Get her to write, then take care of her."

Resolve rang in the ranch hand's voice. "Taking care of her'll be easy."

McCain nodded. "You'll be rewarded."

"I'm countin' on that."

McCain left, and Ruth strained for a way to extricate herself. Nothing came to mind. *Lord, help me. Please, God, be my salvation.*

Toledo forced her to sit on a small stool. "He's gone." He listened for a moment. "Long gone. Won't be back, either. That train ticket's his alibi."

"You won't have an alibi."

"I won't need one." Toledo hunkered down and looked her in the eyes. "I told him I'd take care of you. I didn't lie."

"I won't write anything. If you harm me, Laney won't get anything."

"Listen to me." Toledo's voice sounded chillingly reasonable.

"You're not going to talk me into anything."

"I've been watching you. Shadowing you."

Ruth shuddered.

"Your father was my friend, Ruth. When he died, I had no place to go, so I stayed on here. You showed up, and I knew right off that you were his daughter."

She stared at Toledo, unsure of what to think.

He smiled. "You look just like Alan Caldwell."

In a dress. Tense as she was, that thought put her over the edge. Her laughter sounded hysterical.

"I couldn't hurt you ... never in a million years. In my time here, I've seen plenty and kept my mouth shut. McCain manages to fool most folks into thinking he's a good man. I know better. Times he didn't know I was watching, I could see the hate in his eyes when he looked at you. You can't stay here anymore. It's not safe."

"You'll let me go?"

"I'll take you to Galen O'Sullivan. He's trustworthy. He'll help you get away." He handed back her knife. "Let's go."

Still shaken, Ruth managed to activate the spring. The knife jabbed her as she tried to slide it up her sleeve.

Toledo pulled off the bandana he wore around his neck. "Here." He bound up the small cut, tucked the knife up her sleeve and grinned. "Your daddy would be proud of you."

"My father would be proud of you, too."

"Reckon no one ever gave me finer praise than that. Let's go."

"Just one last thing—could we keep this a secret? I don't want Josh and Laney to know their father tried to hurt me."

"Can't agree to that. Your man has to be able to protect you. You can't keep this from him."

"Then we won't let Laney find out."

Toledo returned to the barn for horses and then took her to the O'Sullivans' through the woods. When they reached the stable, Ruth could hear the low hum of male conversation. "Josh? Is that you?"

He came outside. "What are you doing here?"

"I was going to ask you the same thing!"

Toledo lowered her into Josh's arms. "Your dad thought he'd talked me into getting rid of her. If he sees her, he'll do something rash."

Josh held her tight. "I'll take care of everything."

⟨●⟩

The next morning, Josh helped Ruth, his sister, and Hilda out of the carriage at the Sacramento courthouse. Rick Maltby, Mr.

Farnsworth, and the Folsom sheriff joined them.

Farnsworth murmured, "One of my father's friends from back home moved out here and is a judge. He's graciously offered to let us wait in his chamber until our case is heard."

Maltby waited until they were in the judge's chambers before he revealed, "Additional charges have been added to the case. The judge can ask for a plea, but they won't go to trial today."

Josh nodded. Embezzlement. Murder. The very nature of the crimes in which his father participated left him aching to the depths of his soul.

The door opened, and the Folsom sheriff said, "Mr. McCain just entered the courtroom. We need to go in now."

Maltby offered Laney his arm, and Farnsworth gallantly escorted Hilda. Josh took the lead with Ruth by his side. When they entered the courtroom, Dad turned and saw them. He jolted to his feet, then sank back into the chair as all color bled from his face.

Dad had hired a slick attorney. He started the case out by casting aspersions on Leticia Caldwell's character and stated, "Alan Caldwell stated in his will he'd fathered no children. A man would know such a thing. Leticia Caldwell abandoned her husband and ran back East. Who knows what alliances she made with any number of men? Clearly, Ruth Caldwell cannot lay claim to a single speck of the Broken P inasmuch as not a single drop of Alan's blood flows in her veins."

Ruth yanked her mother's fan from her sleeve. The thing was a tattered mess because of what McCain had done to it, but she opened it with great dignity and fanned herself in Ruth-fashion. Josh didn't stop her from smacking herself with it. If she found comfort in holding the fan, he'd let her beat herself black-and-blue.

Rick Maltby called Mr. Farnsworth to the stand. Mr. Farnsworth gave Leticia Caldwell's character a glowing endorsement. He certified the entries of marriage and Ruth's birth in Leticia's Bible as being in Leticia's own hand.

Next, he called Hilda to the stand. Hilda swore, "The day Mr. Caldwell went into a coma, I found a letter in his room. I reckoned since it was all addressed and sealed, I owed it to him to mail it."

"Was this that envelope?" Rick handed her it to her.

She bobbed her head. "Yup. I know for sure it's the same one 'cuz I set it in the kitchen for a spell while I was cookin' and I splashed on it. Gravy. Chicken gravy. I wiped it off careful as I could, but the mark looked to me like a pear."

"I object!" Dad's attorney rose. "The contents of the envelope could have been replaced with whatever Miss Caldwell chose to insert."

"I anticipated that objection," Rick Maltby stated.

Dad snorted rudely. "If you'd anticipated much of anything, you would have written a better will. Your incompetence is at the heart of this whole mess."

Maltby ignored Dad. He produced the will with Alan Caldwell's signature at the bottom. "Your honor, as you can see, the penmanship on the letter and the formation of the signatures are identical. *Leticia* is on both the envelope and in the salutation. Alan Caldwell had a very unusual way of scribing a capital L."

"The girl is rich. She could have paid someone to forge that," Dad growled.

"Your honor, I object to the plaintiff's producing this so-called letter here in court rather than having made it available for inspection beforehand," McCain's attorney said.

"Josh McCain, Jr. was aware of the letter," Maltby said smoothly. He paused, then stated, "Your Honor, I object to the fact that this case was suddenly changed to this venue instead of the circuit court, scheduled for an earlier date, and no notice was given to me or to Miss Caldwell."

"That's not possible." The judge scowled. "Letters had to be sent out."

"Yes, but McCain, Sr. has been going to town to pick up all of the mail." Maltby spread his hands wide. "If the letters were sent but never received, it poses the question as to what happened to them."

"Hmm." The judge frowned. "Well, I'm satisfied by the evidence that Alan Caldwell wrote this letter. My bailiff will read the contents into the record."

After the letter was read, the judge declared, "Miss Caldwell's birth took place six months after her mother departed from California. According to his own hand, Alan Caldwell sent her away—she was not running away to hide an indiscretion. He freely accepts Ruth as his own daughter. Indeed, since no divorce was sought, any child born while the marriage stood is attributed automatically to the husband. Caldwell writes all he owns is at his family's disposal, thereby indicating he would wish to provide for Ruth. It is my decision that as Mr. Caldwell owned fifty percent of the Broken P, his share's rightful heir is Ruth Caldwell."

He pounded his gavel, then stared at McCain, who was spluttering in rage. "Mr. Joshua McCain, Sr., I have received charges of both embezzlement and murder of Alan Caldwell filed against you. How do you plead?"

Dad rose and turned on Josh. "Embezzlement?"

"I brought both sets of books Mr. McCain, Sr. has been keeping for the Broken P, Your Honor," Maltby said.

Ignoring the attorney and the judge, Dad nearly spat, "You have the nerve to think I've cheated you out of anything?" His attorney tried to shush him, but Dad shoved him away. A nasty bark of a laugh escaped him as he locked eyes with Josh. "You should be grateful to me. Grateful. I reared you as my own. That's right. You're not my son. My brother married your mother first. When he died, I—" He pounded his chest, "I married her even though she was carrying his child. When you were born, your mother insisted upon giving you my name. All of these years, I've provided for you.

"I promised Anna Marie on her deathbed that I'd see to it Laney married well, and I meant every word of my vow. Laney's my daughter, my only child. Every last dollar I have scraped together is going to make sure she gets everything she needs so she will find a wealthy man who can provide for her every whim. You can't fault me for being a good father."

Stunned by his revelation, Josh stared at the man he'd always thought was his father. Shaking his head in disbelief, he said, "I love Laney. I'd gladly make any sacrifice to be sure she had anything she ever needed. There was never any reason for you to resort to dishonesty."

"That's not true! You just sided with Ruth against me. That takes half of the money from the railroad away from your sister. Half! Do you realize how much that land is worth?"

"Alan Caldwell's life?" Farnsworth asked smoothly.

"Oh, you're not going to pin that on me." His father—or was it his uncle?—held up his hands. "No one can prove I did a thing to that old coot."

The Folsom sheriff produced the cigarette case and the doctor's report. "This case and the remaining cigarettes contain arsenic."

Dad planted his hand on the table. "Josh could have done that. He had as much to gain as I did."

"But Josh never rolled cigarettes for Alan. You did, Daddy," Laney said.

"Yeah, and Alan took sick during the time Josh was gone on the trail," Hilda shouted. "Nobody else ever set foot in the house."

The judge said, "If Joshua, Jr. wasn't present, then that leaves either McCain, Sr., the housekeeper, or the daughter, Elaine, as the suspects. Do any of the men present have a pouch of tobacco and papers?"

Dad's attorney objected to the whole proceeding.

Dad promptly told him to shut up and leave.

Hilda was given the tobacco and a cigarette paper. She made a sour face as she took a big pinch of tobacco and placed it on the paper. After patting it across the length and most of the breadth of paper with the pad of her forefinger, she rolled it up. "Sorta like makin' bitty little cinnamon sticky buns or a jelly roll," she declared.

The judge accepted her effort and set it to one side. "Miss McCain, you're next."

"No!" Dad shook his head emphatically. "My daughter's not going to touch tobacco. It's beneath her. I won't allow it."

The judge looked at Hilda's cigarette. "Mr. McCain, clearly the housekeeper didn't know how to fashion a cigarette. Though entertaining, her technique left much to be desired. The result was inconsistent with the cigarettes given as evidence. That means the only suspects are you and your daughter."

Dad glowered at the judge. "Don't you dare even suggest my little girl would ever do such a thing. She's special. She's beautiful, and she's going to have a wonderful life. I promised her mother, and I've done everything I could to fulfill that vow.

"That old man was supposed to drink himself to death, but he got religion and stopped drinking. My plan was still working, but he got that letter from his wife about their having a daughter. I shut him up and burned that letter. No one was supposed to ever know. Then *she* came." Dad pointed at Ruth.

"Daddy," Laney said in a small, tight voice, "all of those accidents—"

"I never meant to hurt you, sugar. I thought it was Ruth in the stable. I didn't know you had matching skirts. You know I'd never hurt you. Everything I've done, I've done for you. There's a bank account for you. With half of the money from the railroad deal, I was going to make you a wealthy young woman who'd attract just the right man."

"How could you, Daddy? How could you?" Laney burst into tears, and Josh wrapped his arms around her.

The judge peered over the bench. "Mr. Joshua McCain, Sr., you were asked to plead in the cases of embezzlement and murder. Am I to take your admissions here as guilty pleas?"

"Laney, sugar..." McCain shoved past his attorney and tried to reach his daughter.

Laney cringed and burrowed closer. Josh tightened his hold on her.

"This is all your fault!" McCain shouted at Ruth. "You weren't supposed to come. You ruined it all!" He drew a small pistol from his pocket.

Josh stepped forward and shoved his sister behind him so Ruth and Laney would be shielded. "No!"

"Drop it!" the bailiff ordered.

Dad cocked the tiny pistol.

Bang!

Dad's face twisted into an obscene smile, then he fell. Josh kicked the pistol from his hand and knelt at his side. The bailiff rushed over, the tip of his gun still smoking.

"Monument." McCain struggled for another breath. "Life insurance."

Josh took hold of the only father he'd ever known. For all the pain and regret of the past, Josh didn't want to see him die without making peace with God. "There's still time, Dad. Give your heart to the Lord."

The dying man gave a strange laugh. "Don't ... need God."

Laney sobbed and clung to Ruth. Josh glanced up only long enough to see the utter despair on his sister's face. "Please. God will forgive you if you ask Him to."

"No." The sneer on McCain's face changed to desperation. "Insurance ... money for ... Laney. Papers ... in my desk."

"She'll be taken care of," Josh promised.

McCain gave the barest of nods and closed his eyes as one last shallow breath gurgled out of him.

Other than Laney's weeping, the trip home was utterly silent. Once they reached the Broken P, Ruth tucked Laney into bed and stayed with her until she fell into an exhausted sleep. Coming down the stairs, she saw Josh in the parlor and joined him there.

"Josh?"

He turned around. "Ruth, I'm sorry for all he did."

"You have no reason to apologize. He was wicked. I hold him responsible for his choices—you didn't have anything to do with them."

"But I should have seen past the façade and realized something was terribly wrong."

She shook her head. "Josh, I didn't sense anything was amiss. Your father was so charming, he had us all fooled. His love for Laney wasn't wrong—it just led him to start compromising his values until he no longer had any values whatsoever."

Josh turned to face the mantel. Gripping it, he bowed his head. "Dad did love Laney. He had to know by drawing that pistol on you, he'd be shot. He loved her so much, he was willing to die just to make sure she got more money."

Ruth slipped up beside him and wrapped her arms around his waist. "I have no doubt that he also loved you, Josh. You wouldn't have grown up to be the wonderful man you are if you hadn't had a good example to follow. When he made a deathbed promise to your mother, he let the grief twist him. It turned a man into a monster. Even then, his last act—misbegotten as it was—was to provide more for Laney."

"What he did . . ." Josh shook his head. "There's no excuse."

"No, there isn't." Ruth let out a sigh. "But we have the Lord to give us comfort and consolation in our grief. He didn't. Satan took that foothold and used every opportunity for evil."

Josh turned and cupped her shoulders. "Ruth, after the attempts on your life and learning how your father died, I'll understand if you don't want to marry me."

"Well, I don't understand at all." She poked him in the chest.

"You already told me you love me. You're not getting off that easy. I'm going to marry you if I have to hire every cowboy in California to truss you up and drag you to the altar."

Four days later, Ruth nearly paced a path in the parlor carpet. Josh lounged against the open doorway and grinned as he listened to her hiccup loudly. "Sweetheart?"

She jumped and wheeled around to face him. *Hic.* "What?"

Josh approached her slowly. Her shoulders convulsed again with another hiccup. "What are you nervous about?"

"Who says I'm *hic* nervous? Laney's done everything on her lists."

Josh nodded. "She could have been a general in an army. Between her organization, Hilda and Mrs. O'Sullivan's help, and the new parson itching to perform his first wedding, it's amazing we weren't already hitched two days ago."

Ruth tried to smile, but another hiccup wracked her.

Josh drew her into his arms and whispered into her mussed-up curls, "Ruthie, you can stop being nervous. Nothing's going to stop me from marrying you. I'm going to be waiting at the altar at noon tomorrow. You could show up covered in mud and mess up every line in the vows, and I'd still claim you as mine."

"Knowing me, *hic* that's exactly what'll happen. Mrs. Cambridge at the *hic* Lawrence School for Refined *hic* Young Ladies used to say it would be a *hic* miracle to see me stay clean for more than five minutes."

Josh pulled back and looked at her for a moment. "Just how many schools did you get sent home from?"

She laughed and hiccupped at the same time, resulting in a strange croaking sound. "More *hic* than you want to know about. I'll probably always be a mess."

He gave her a quick but sound kiss. "Then I'll love you all the more."

"What if *hic* I—"

"Shhh." Rubbing her stiff shoulders, he soothed, "Remember how you told Laney her reading didn't have to be letter perfect for the two of you to still enjoy a story?" As Ruth hesitantly nodded, he went on, "You don't have to be letter perfect for me to love you, either. Don't you understand that I'd rather have your imagination and compassion in our home than a prim and proper woman with ice in her veins?"

"Are you sure?"

"Positive." He smiled as he realized she'd stopped hiccupping.

———

The next day, Josh did as he'd promised. Standing at the altar, he faced his bride as the new "Wedding March" was played on the piano. Galen escorted Ruth down the aisle. Somewhere in transit from home to the church, she'd managed to step on her skirts and part of the hem sagged. Her veil hung the slightest bit askew— most likely because her hairpins had slipped. When she placed her hand in his, Josh spotted a smudge on her glove.

Leaning close, he said with all his heart, "You've never looked more beautiful."

Ruth's smile could have lit a cathedral.

CROSSINGS®
THE BOOK CLUB FOR TODAY'S CHRISTIAN FAMILY

A Letter to Our Readers

Dear Reader:
In order that we might better contribute to your reading enjoyment, we would appreciate your taking a few minutes to respond to the following questions. When completed, please return to the following:

Andrea Doering, Editor-in-Chief
Crossings Book Club
401 Franklin Avenue, Garden City, NY 11530
You can post your review online! Go to www.crossings.com and rate this book.

Title _____ Author _____

1 Did you enjoy reading this book?

❑ Very much. I would like to see more books by this author!

❑ I really liked_____

❑ Moderately. I would have enjoyed it more if_____

2 What influenced your decision to purchase this book? Check all that apply.

   ❑ Cover
   ❑ Title
   ❑ Publicity
   ❑ Catalog description
   ❑ Friends
   ❑ Enjoyed other books by this author
   ❑ Other _____

3 Please check your age range:

   ❑ Under 18   ❑ 18-24
   ❑ 25-34   ❑ 35-45
   ❑ 46-55   ❑ Over 55

4 How many hours per week do you read? _____

5 How would you rate this book, on a scale from 1 (poor) to 5 (superior)?
_____

Name_____

Occupation_____

Address_____

City_____ State_____ Zip_____

Bestselling Author
TRACIE PETERSON
EMBARKS *on a* NEW SERIES

Leah Barringer's life in the rugged Alaskan Territory
changes unexpectedly when the man her heart can't forget
returns after ten long years. But unbeknownst to her,
Jayce is a wanted man. Can the past be made right...
and can she surrender her heart again?

Summer of the Midnight Sun by Tracie Peterson
ALASKAN QUEST #1

⬥BETHANYHOUSE